2

Somewhere Along the Way

Somewhere Along the Way

JODI THOMAS

BERKLEY BOOKS, NEW YORK

THE BERKLEY PUBLISHING GROUP
Published by the Penguin Group
Penguin Group (USA) Inc.
375 Hudson Street, New York, New York 10014, USA
Penguin Group (Canada), 90 Eglinton Avenue East, Suite 700, Toronto, Ontario M4P 2Y3, Canada
(a division of Pearson Penguin Canada Inc.)
Penguin Books Ltd., 80 Strand, London WC2R 0RL, England
Penguin Group Ireland, 25 St. Stephen's Green, Dublin 2, Ireland (a division of Penguin Books Ltd.)
Penguin Group (Australia), 250 Camberwell Road, Camberwell, Victoria 3124, Australia
(a division of Pearson Australia Group Pty. Ltd.)
Penguin Books India Pvt. Ltd., 11 Community Centre, Panchsheel Park, New Delhi—110 017, India
Penguin Group (NZ), 67 Apollo Drive, Rosedale, North Shore 0632, New Zealand
(a division of Pearson New Zealand Ltd.)
Penguin Books (South Africa) (Pty.) Ltd., 24 Sturdee Avenue, Rosebank, Johannesburg 2196,
South Africa

Penguin Books Ltd., Registered Offices: 80 Strand, London WC2R 0RL, England

This is a work of fiction. Names, characters, places, and incidents either are the product of the author's imagination or are used fictitiously, and any resemblance to actual persons, living or dead, business establishments, events, or locales is entirely coincidental. The publisher does not have any control over and does not assume any responsibility for author or third-party websites or their content.

SOMEWHERE ALONG THE WAY

A Berkley Book / published by arrangement with the author

ISBN: 978-1-61664-928-9

BERKLEY®
Berkley Books are published by The Berkley Publishing Group,
a division of Penguin Group (USA) Inc.,
375 Hudson Street, New York, New York 10014.
BERKLEY® is a registered trademark of Penguin Group (USA) Inc.
The "B" design is a trademark of Penguin Group (USA) Inc.

PRINTED IN THE UNITED STATES OF AMERICA

Harmony, Texas, was founded where two streams crossed on the prairie. One running south, the other east. Water had long ago dried, but the jagged ravine still scarred Harmony's core like an X marking the center of town . . . the heart of Harmony.

Prologue

STELLA MCNABB CREDITED HER WILD DREAMS TO HER Gypsy blood.

Her husband of forty-two years felt the dreams were more related to the Mexican food she ate for dinner, but humored her for the sake of peace.

After enjoying the three-enchilada Tuesday night special at Mexican Plaza, Bob McNabb settled into his favorite chair and Stella went to bed.

About the time he got interested in the ten o'clock movie on the Western Legends channel, he heard Stella yelling. Bob climbed out of his recliner, turned on the hallway light, and walked to her bedside. He'd given up rushing in '87.

He wasn't surprised to find her pale as the moon outside and sweating.

"Oh, Bob, I've had another premonition."

When he didn't react, she shouted, guessing he'd already

turned off his hearing aid. "I had a terrible dream and this time I know I was looking flat-out into the future."

"What's your dream, darling? Maybe I can help you interpret it."

Stella calmed a bit and smiled, happy to oblige. "It started with a shadow moving through the streets down in the old part of Harmony. A darkness seemed to creep along that creek bed where the mud's curled up like dead skin."

Bob patted her hand. Stella's dreams had become far more descriptive since she'd taken that creative writing class at the senior citizens' center.

She took a deep breath and continued, "Then, silently, it began to spread like clouds full of poison gas and anyone in its path crumbled. The gas, barely visible, spread out and moved through the town."

Bob nodded, even tugged on his chin, as she continued, but inside, he was thinking he should have taken her to the fish fry at the Methodist church tonight. It looked like he'd never get back to his movie.

Chapter 1

JANUARY 9, 2008
BLUE MOON DINER

REAGAN TRUMAN GRIPPED THE GREASY DINER PHONE SO hard her knuckles whitened. "You'd better be sick, Edith. . . . really sick. When you asked me to cover your shift, you didn't mention intrigue. I thought all I'd be doing was making a few Cokes and maybe pushing the pie."

After listening to more of the waitress's instructions, Reagan added, "I didn't know this was part of your job. I thought I could do my homework unless someone came in."

Reagan heard Edith coughing on the other end and gave in. "Oh, all right, I'll do it."

She hung up and stared out at the empty diner. *Nine o'clock, Wednesday night*, she thought. No one else was coming in, not this late, not with the fog. She might as well go home. Even the owner, grumpy old Cass, had left her to lock up. All Reagan had to do was wipe off the counters, put the frozen dough in the refrigerator, and turn off the lights.

"And," she frowned at the phone, "pack takeout for the local serial killer."

She crossed to the kitchen hoping someone would come in to delay her mission, but the bell over the door hadn't sounded in a half hour. She made two ham sandwiches and spooned up a quart of chili while reminding herself that Harmony was a safe town. Nothing bad ever happened here. Walking across the gully out back was no different than walking around her uncle's orchard. Trees are trees.

After placing the food in a brown bag, Reagan tossed in crackers and a plastic spoon. Hesitating, she considered whether murderers needed napkins. On impulse, she added a bag of Cass's homemade oatmeal raisin cookies. Maybe she'd sweeten him up just enough so that Gabriel Leary wouldn't slit her throat tonight.

"This is ridiculous," she muttered as she headed toward the back. "Why can't the weirdo come in the front door like everyone else?" The kids at school told stories about driving along Timber Line Road and seeing Gabriel walking over his rocky land, stabbing at the dirt like he was practicing killing.

At five feet three, Reagan figured he wouldn't need much practice to murder her. She wasn't really worried about herself. She'd danced near death several times while growing up, moving from foster home to foster home in neighborhoods where even rats fought to survive, but she didn't want to die and leave the old man who'd taken her in as family. Uncle Jeremiah Truman needed her. Even tonight, he'd be waiting up for her until he knew she was home safe.

Reagan tried to keep her grab on the takeout bag from tightening. As soon as she delivered it, she could lock up and head home.

She shoved open the back door and stepped into the cold night. "I'm tougher than I look," she whispered to herself.

Halfway to the Dumpster she decided this alley would be perfect for a crime scene. Dark, freezing night, dumb seventeen-year-old girl walking out alone. Nutcase hiding somewhere in the shadows waiting for his supper. All she needed was a vampire and she'd be starring in a hit.

As she reached the edge of the dull backdoor light, she thought she heard movement to her left. Fighting down a scream, she told herself it was only one of the alley cats looking for scraps. Problem was, *herself* didn't seem to be listening. Focusing on the trees across the dry gully, she measured her steps, testing solid ground before rushing across the scar in the earth to the scattering of old cottonwoods beyond.

Once there, she froze, unwilling to step where shadows crossed. A rustling whispered in the trees as her eyes adjusted to the night.

A man stood up slowly from where he'd been huddling out of the wind. Tall, bone lean, and dressed in black.

Reagan gulped down panic. "I brought your takeout meal."

He took one step toward her and reached for the bag. "Thanks." His whisper seemed to circle in the wind, more shy than menacing.

She didn't miss the holes in the fingers of his gloves or the patch on his sleeve.

Reaching into his pocket with his free hand, he pulled out two wrinkled dollar bills.

"No," Reagan said. "That's all right." She turned away.

"I can pay," he answered. "I always pay."

She looked back, planning to say that payment wasn't necessary, and then she saw his eyes. Pale blue eyes, almost the color of frozen water, glared down at her. Reagan had known times when money was tight and charity hard to take. She wouldn't hurt his pride.

Leaning forward, as if her feet had taken root, she took the two dollars. "Thanks for your business, mister," she muttered.

He straightened, and nodded slightly. "Name's Gabe Leary."

"I'm . . ." She wasn't sure she wanted to be on a first-name basis with this guy.

"Reagan," he filled in the blank.

"Yeah, Reagan," she answered, thinking that on the scale of strange, this one was off the charts. "Reagan Truman."

"I know. Edith told me about you. You're Jeremiah's niece. Tell the old man thanks for me, would you?"

"For what?" For the third time in almost two years someone had thanked her uncle.

Gabe remained still, watching her with no warmth in his eyes. "He'll know, just tell him."

The light over the back door flickered in a sudden gust of wind. Reagan glanced back at the diner, wondering if she could outrun this guy. They seemed to have exhausted all conversation. He was probably thinking it was time for the killing to begin.

When she looked back, Gabe Leary had vanished into the trees along with his takeout meal.

A few flakes of snow brushed against her face, and she ran back inside. If she hurried, she could lock up and drive the few miles to her uncle's place on Lone Oak Road before any precipitation made the roads slippery.

Fifteen minutes later, she drove up to the farmhouse that had been her only real home. When she'd first arrived the place looked like the spook house in a Disney movie, but now with paint and some work, it seemed grand to her.

"I'm back," she said to the dog as she jumped out of her pickup before the engine stopped rattling. Swinging her backpack, she climbed the steps and opened the always-unlocked front door. The ghosts of her almost-ancestors greeted her from their faded photos along the walls.

Reagan had learned all their names and sometimes called good night to each one as if she lived with a house filled with family.

Reagan moved down the hallway to the back of the house, where a wide, warm kitchen welcomed her. They'd knocked a wall out and almost doubled the space. Now, the kitchen was on one side, a table in the center, and couches and chairs on the solid north wall with a TV that no one watched. Reagan had seen a picture of a country kitchen in a magazine and talked her uncle into making the addition. There were many rooms in the old house, but this was where they cooked and ate and talked. The room where they lived.

Uncle Jeremiah sat at the table, his coffee cup beside a stack of week-old papers. She grinned at him; he frowned at her. She'd come to consider any reaction from him an endearment. He might be in his eighties, but she thought of him as somewhere between preschool and kindergarten in his communication skills.

"Home late for a Wednesday," he grumbled, and went back to his week-old newspapers.

"I took the last three hours of Edith's shift at the diner. She claimed to be feeling sick, but I thought I saw a bruise on her face." Reagan sat her book bag down and grabbed two plates and the last of the pie she'd made Monday. "I'm getting too old for you to worry about. I'll be eighteen soon, you know."

"I can count," he protested, "and I'll stop worrying about you when you're thirty and carry a gun." He stopped frowning when she set the pie down and cut the last big slice into two small pieces. "Didn't they feed you at that roach café they call a diner?"

Reagan laughed. "No. I'm not sure I could get down one of their pies. They come frozen from the freezer. Once I get out of school in May, I'm thinking I could make pies to sell as a full-time job."

"It'll take us all summer to work the orchard, and in the fall you'll go off to college. I don't figure that leaves much time for starting a small business."

She opened her mouth to argue, then decided to eat the pie. She'd made up every excuse she could think of to claim she couldn't go away to school next year. How could she leave him? Arthritis was slowly twisting his bones, and he couldn't see well enough to find his glasses in the morning. Dear God, she loved this old man, who'd claimed her as his kin when no one else would. She couldn't—wouldn't—leave him.

He carefully divided his slice of pie into quarters and ate the crust part first.

"I met that man who lives up on Timber Line Road tonight. Leary was his last name."

As always, Uncle Jeremiah didn't seem interested in talking while he ate, and he was never much concerned with other people.

"You know him?" she pried.

"Not well," he answered as he chewed. "Not even sure I'd recognize Gabriel Leary if I saw him in town. Talked to him when he came home from a hospital in San Antonio, but couldn't see much of him for the bandages. The man looked like a mummy."

"You know about him? How come he's up there all alone?"

"I fixed an engine for his pa back about five years ago. He said he needed it to go get his boy fast, so I worked all night. Everyone knew his only child left ten years before when he wasn't even out of high school. Sheriff came by looking for him. Said he ran off, but I always figured Gabe Leary just left. I'm guessing he must have been in bad shape if he asked for help from his old man. Old Leary was a hard man and about as worthless as his land."

"How was Gabriel hurt?"

"Didn't ask."

"What kind of hospital was it?"

"Didn't ask." Jeremiah swallowed the last bite. "Just fixed the car."

"That's it?"

Jeremiah thought a minute as if he didn't understand the question. "Old man died in town at the doctor's office the winter Gabriel came home. They say he was sitting in a crowded waiting room and by the time they called his name, he no longer needed the doctor. Don't know that anyone, including his son, mourned him."

Reagan tried again. "Want to tell me why Gabriel said to thank you tonight?"

Jeremiah lowered his gaze, as he always did when he was considering a lie. "Nope," he said as he collected the dishes and moved to the sink.

Reagan knew she'd get no more information out of him. Maybe one day he'd tell her, but not tonight. She stood, lifted her backpack, and met him at the bottom of the stairs. Without a word, she kissed his cheek and headed up to her room.

She heard his "Come on, boy" to the dog as he shuffled down the hallway to his bedroom at the back of the house. Her uncle held as fiercely to his secrets as he did his land. She knew without a doubt that he'd never told anyone in town that she wasn't really his niece. To him, she was his kin. She'd gone from being a runaway to being the next generation of Trumans a week after she'd hitchhiked into town. She'd stepped from having no roots to being the future of one of the three families who'd founded the town.

It was too heavy to think about, she decided, but then thinking about school and Noah didn't give her much peace either. Noah McAllen was her best friend, and he'd been acting strange lately. Why couldn't everything stay just like it was? Why did the world keep changing on her?

Plopping onto her bed, Reagan pulled out her cell and punched speed dial for her best friend. "Noah, you awake?"

"I am now, Rea," he mumbled.

She laughed. "It's not that late."

"I know, but my dad had me up at five moving cattle before school. He seems to think a storm's coming in."

Reagan tugged off her shoes and settled in for her nightly talk with Noah. They'd dated occasionally until they both decided they were meant to be friends. She wasn't ready for a boyfriend, and he was too focused on rodeo to have time to date.

Only lately, he wasn't as open as he'd always been, and she didn't know how to ask what was wrong. Half the time he acted like he was mad at her, and she couldn't think of anything she'd done.They talked of school and homework, but he didn't mention the date he'd had with Jennifer and she didn't tell him about Gabriel Leary. When she said good night, Reagan wished she hadn't called.

Maybe it was the fog, but all the world seemed lonely tonight.

Chapter 2

TIMBER LINE ROAD

THE CHILI WOULD BE COLD BY THE TIME GABE WALKED the three miles home. He knew the back path well and had no problem moving through the shadows black as spilled oil across the land. He'd walked them all his life. First to school because he didn't want to ride the school bus, then as therapy when he came home from the army wounded in both body and soul. And now he made the walk because it was Wednesday and he didn't want to eat his own cooking.

He favored his left leg and knew he should have brought his cane, but he hated using it. The stick reminded him of a life he'd given up. One explosion, one glance in the wrong direction, and the world he'd known, the one he'd built on another man's name, had vanished.

Holding on to a bare branch, he climbed out of the dry

gully at the edge of town and began crossing open fields. Memories walked beside him tonight. He'd just turned seventeen when his father beat him for the last time for not completing all his endless chores. He'd packed a change of clothes, a dozen of his favorite comic books, and seventy-three dollars, then walked all night.

It was noon by the time he'd traveled the more than thirty miles to Bailee and caught a bus to Amarillo. From there, he tried a dozen businesses downtown before a sweet lady gave him a job at a little breakfast/lunch place called the Hickory Inn a block from the train tracks. Minimum wage and a meal on his break. She agreed to pay him in cash if he'd show up sober every morning at five and promise to stay for the lunch run. He figured out he could shower at a shelter a few blocks away and hang around there until late afternoon. Then, Gabe learned the hard way that it paid to be off the streets before dark. A storage shed behind the little café became his home for a year until he turned eighteen.

Gabe shivered remembering that cold shed. Sometimes it would take him a half hour to warm up enough to move at normal speed. He'd spent that year planning. The number one thing on his list was never to return to Harmony, but he had.

He crossed Timber Line Road and saw his father's old house in the distance. It had been a Sears Kit home, shipped by train a hundred or so years ago. It was small, with only one story; the wind had beaten on it over the years until it blended into the landscape. This weather had a way of doing that to everything around. Sometimes Gabriel thought his whole world was the color of the dirt that constantly blew.

Part of him hated being back, even with his father long dead. Part of him knew this might be the only place left on the planet for him to hide.

A few minutes later when he entered the house, he

checked the alarm system. Most folks driving by might think the old barn and house were abandoned. They'd never guess it had a hundred-thousand-dollar security system he'd installed himself.

Gabe pulled off the Glock strapped to his good leg and left it on a shelf by the door. The years in the army had taught him well. Never be unprepared.

He walked through the rooms stripped of all furniture except work tables and long desks loaded down with classic comic books and his own drawings. A living room or dining room would have been worthless to him. Gabe needed workspace and the basics. Nothing more.

A stray dog, who'd taken up residence with him a few years back, wandered in from the hallway, looking bothered that Gabe had awakened him. He was German shepherd tall, but greyhound thin and the color of wet sand.

"Some guard dog you are, Pirate," Gabe said as he scratched the mutt's head. "With only one eye you'd only see half a burglar anyway."

Pirate followed him to the kitchen, his nose bumping into the sack of food with every other step Gabe took.

Gabe ignored the dog. Pirate had been hungry since the day he arrived with ribs poking through his chest. Someone had probably dropped him out on the road, thinking it kinder to let a car kill him than to have him put to sleep. Only Pirate was a survivor.

Sitting down, Gabe pulled the meal from the bag, remembering how he'd been walking the midnight streets of Harmony one night a few years ago, staying in the shadows, when Edith Franklin, from the Blue Moon, spotted him. She'd been a few years older than him in school, but she recognized him and stepped out into the cold.

"Gabriel!" she'd shouted in a voice a mother would use to call her children inside. "Come in for some coffee before you freeze. I've got a pot I'm about to toss."

He'd circled around to the back door of the Blue Moon

and sat in the diner's kitchen drinking coffee as she cleaned. They didn't talk much, not like old friends. He guessed neither had any memories of the past dozen years that they wanted to share. Life hadn't treated her any better than it had him. He had a wide scar across his chest, a thin one along his jawline, and another that ran almost the length of his leg. Judging from her sad eyes, he'd guess her scars were more on the inside. She couldn't be more than thirty-four, but she looked fifty.

So this is what happens to shy, gentle girls who marry at sixteen to get away from home, he thought.

She'd packed him a takeout dinner that night without asking him what he liked and charged him two dollars.

He'd been returning every Wednesday since for whatever she packed in the bag. Sometimes, if it was cold outside, she'd invite him in for coffee, but most of the time she just thanked him for the business and told him to take care of himself.

Guessing from the premature age lines on her face and her tired eyes, Edith had her full quota of sorrow. She didn't need any of his. So, he'd thank her for the meal and vanish back into the night.

Until tonight, the pattern had never changed. He usually circled through the old part of town, feeling strangely at home there because nothing had changed since he'd been a kid. On warm nights, he'd stand by the storm drain outside the sheriff's office and listen to people talk. Between dispatchers yelling and deputies passing time with stories and news, Gabe knew pretty much everything going on in town. On cool nights he liked to lift himself silently up in the old tree on the square and pick up conversations as folks passed. Legend was the town's founder, Harmon Ely, planted the tree hoping his grandchildren would play beneath it. But his wife and children never came west and when Harmon died, he left all his land to the three men who worked for him. The McAllens, the Mathesons, and the Trumans either owned or had sold off all the property for miles around. They weren't rich, but rooted. Gabe thought that might be more important.

The three families were also the town's longest-running soap opera.

From what Gabe could tell, nothing much had changed in Harmony over the ten years he was gone. The three families still pretty much ran the town. Alexandra McAllen was sheriff, Hank Matheson was fire chief, and a half dozen of each family served on the town council. Only the Trumans hadn't populated. As far as he knew, the girl he saw tonight would be the last Truman soon.

Gabe pulled out a bag of cookies from the takeout she'd given him and smiled. "Thanks, Reagan," he said aloud, and wondered what the little redhead must have thought of him. *That I'm crazy*, he decided. Why not? Half the time Gabe thought he was nuts. When he'd come home five years ago he'd sworn he'd leave as soon as he could walk, and then his dad died and he decided to stay until he was ready to face the world again. Two tours of duty had left him craving solitude.

But the time to step back into life never seemed right, and thanks to the Internet he could order anything he needed and have it delivered. In the solitude of his farm, he'd found a way to make a living and no one around would ever know. The drawings he'd done as a child and his love for comic books had morphed into a career in graphic novels. He could step into his imaginary world and be whoever he wanted, without scars and fears.

"Someday, I'll get back to the world," he promised himself as he ate his supper. Chili, a ham sandwich, and cookies, plus he'd actually talked to someone tonight. For the first time in a long time, life was almost normal.

While he ate, he thought of Reagan. She was small, but probably grown as tall as she'd ever be. Her hair reminded him of the color of rust and seemed to bounce around her face. He'd watched her earlier from the side window of the diner. She had to stand on her toes and stretch to reach the shelf where all the paper goods were stacked.

She was brave too. Walked right out and handed him his meal. Now and then someone saw him moving about the town or across his fields. Most acted like they didn't see him. A few darted away as if afraid. But Reagan Truman, despite her small frame, had shown Truman blood and stood her ground.

Gabe stopped eating and left his supper on the table. He needed to do something about the Truman girl, and the sooner he got started, the sooner he'd be headed back to town.

He'd barely made it out the kitchen door before Pirate raised his head table high and lived up to his name by finishing off the takeout.

Chapter 3

Liz Matheson carried the last box from the moving truck into her first office and paid the two muscle men who'd unloaded the furniture. Nobody in Harmony thought she'd finish her law degree, but she'd fooled them all. A month short of thirty, she would hang her shingle tomorrow and wait for her first client. Her life was a string of false starts and broken dreams, but this time she'd get somewhere.

As she opened a box, she heard footsteps clanking up the metal stairs of her run-down office building facing the town square. A moment later someone pounded on her open door frame.

Liz watched her big brother step into her space without waiting to be invited. Hank Matheson was the only one in the family who always seemed to do everything right.

Since he'd turned twenty-five, he'd run the ranch and the family of women like he had been appointed godfather. Tall, handsome, and always serious, he made her feel not only younger and smaller, but somehow dumber.

"Hi, Hank. Come on in." She frowned as he looked around at the mess. "Oh, sorry, you're already in." Her brother constantly bugged her. He was perfect. Honest, responsible, caring, wise. Liz felt like she'd been forced to take what was left on the character chart. Flighty, unpredictable, absentminded, self-centered.

He hesitated, as if expecting the walls of her office to fall in like stacked dominoes, then smiled at her as if she were a child playing house. "Looks nice," he said obviously lying.

Liz fought back anger. Her office was a run-down, neglected little place over a dry cleaners and bookstore. It was anything but nice. But then, her family always encouraged her, even though they never believed in her. "It's a mess and you know it. I'm guessing it will take me a week to get everything in order."

"Mom and Claire offered to come help paint." Hank held his Stetson like a shield before him as he slowly maneuvered around a pair of wicker chairs with tiny chips of paint hanging on for dear life. "They could do wonders for this place."

"No thanks." Asking two artists to paint walls would evoke more drama than Liz could handle right now. She'd graduated from law school, broken up with the professor she'd been sleeping with, and moved out of her mother's home for good this time, all within a month. The last thing she needed was conflict. Her older sister and her mother hadn't agreed on anything since her older sister, Claire, moved back in at the ranch house three years ago with tiny little Saralynn in tow. Her sister and mother needed each other, loved each other, and conversations through Post-it notes seemed enough for them both.

Hank shrugged, as if he hadn't expected her to take any help. He crossed to the wall of windows and looked out over the town square. "Nice view, at least. I can see the roof of the fire station from here and part of the roof of the Blue Moon at the wall of the diner. It almost looks like the moon is rising over the buildings between us," he said more to himself than her, and then with a fluid movement of a man in great shape, he turned and met her gaze. "You didn't say where you got an apartment, Liz. Mom asked me at breakfast."

"I know," she answered. "I need a little space alone to think. When I get all settled in, I'll call and invite everyone over." In this size town he could probably drive around and check every apartment complex if he wanted to, but Hank was too honest to spy.

Just my luck, Liz almost said aloud. Only one perfect man born this generation and he happened to be her big brother. It was hard for any guy she dated to measure up to him.

"You need any money?" he asked, as she knew he would.

"Nope." She hesitated, then lied again. "I'm set." She'd taken enough from him. It was time she made a little on her own. "I'll call if I need anything," she promised as she walked him down the hallway to the outside door.

Liz watched, with the door open, until he got halfway down, feeling change covering her like rain. *Good-bye, big brother*, she almost yelled, knowing that she was cutting strings even if he wasn't aware.

Hank looked back. "Maybe we could go to lunch sometime? I'm usually in town on Tuesday." By the time he'd offered, he was at the bottom and in front of a dry cleaners and a used bookstore that rented the first floor of her building.

"It's a date." She waved as he shoved back his midnight hair and planted his Stetson solid before facing the wind. She almost felt sorry for the guy. He ran a ranch, served as chief of the volunteer fire department, and tried to make the women in his life happy. With an out-of-touch mother who spent her days designing pots, two divorced sisters, two great-aunts, and a niece living at the ranch, Hank's job wasn't easy. Liz moving out gave him one less female to worry about. Maybe he'd have time to finally marry the woman he'd loved all his life.

Turning back to the mess of cheap furniture and office supplies, Liz almost wished she'd given in and let everyone help her.

"No," she said as she pushed the first box aside. "I have to do something for myself. I have to be good at something besides going to school." She might not be ready to move to New York or Chicago and be a big-time lawyer, but she could stand on her own two feet for once right here in Harmony.

By late afternoon Liz had managed to get all the furniture in place. The office had two rooms. One small front reception area and one large square office with north windows running from floor to ceiling.

"North windows," Liz could almost hear her mother saying, "they're the best. Unchanging light. Artist light."

Liz only hoped they might prove to be lawyer light as well. She'd like to make a go of something for once. It would be nice to live without change for a while.

She crammed the wicker chairs, small table, semicircle desk, and two plastic plants into the reception area, leaving only a huge desk, six file cabinets she'd picked up at a salvage store, and a long blue couch to fill up the big office. Nothing matched. She'd seen room arrangements at Goodwill that made more sense.

The south wall of the office had a tiny white sink, a small kitchen area for making coffee, complete with a black microwave and a green mini refrigerator.

The ladies' room was down the hallway, near the back

door that went to a small parking lot. She shared the second floor with three other offices. All of which looked empty.

As she began unpacking a box that had been in storage for the three years since her divorce, she fought back tears. The day she'd left her husband, Eddie, had started with them yelling as she tossed dishes into a few boxes. She hadn't planned where she'd go, she'd just wanted out, so the odd assortment of cups and plates she now unpacked were just the first things within reach.

In the end, Eddie had helped her load her car, as he'd always helped her. The last time she saw him, she'd been pulling away from the condo he'd bought because he thought she wanted it. Tears were running down his cheeks, but he hadn't said he loved her. He'd only told her that she'd be back. He'd yelled that she was going to miss him and his money and all their things. If he'd just said he loved her, or needed her, she might have turned around.

Liz tossed a pot under the sink, realizing no one had ever needed her. She was the extra, the accessory everyone liked having around, but didn't see as vital. She'd been just one of the "things" Eddie had collected on his way up the corporate ladder.

Grabbing her bag, she headed for the gym she'd joined yesterday. Once there, she stormed right past the exercise equipment and went to the dressing rooms. After fifteen minutes in the hot tub, she took a shower, washed her short hair, combed the curls with her fingers, and left. No one seemed to notice her coming or going. Somehow she'd slipped into that age, or that size, that was gym invisible. In a month she wouldn't be twentysomething, she'd be thirtysomething, and that was only a few steps away from dead, she figured.

Shadows were long when she got back to her office. If anyone noticed her car parked in the back lot, they'd think she was working late. Not that anyone would notice.

A person would have to be walking in the old dried-up stream to pass within sight of the lot. She'd noticed the bookstore owner parked in front of his shop, probably to show people he was open, and the dry cleaners closed at three. It appeared the parking lot was all hers.

She pulled the dusty curtains closed before she turned on the lamp atop her desk. Nine o'clock, time for bed, she decided. With no TV and no one to talk to, it seemed her only option.

Pulling pillows and a blanket from her empty file drawers, she made her bed on the couch, tugged off her tennis shoes, and climbed in.

"Perfect." She giggled to herself. She couldn't afford an apartment, but this place, with its large storage room for her clothes, could double as both office and apartment. She'd have to work with the ladies' room, but being able to shower at the gym would solve most of her problems.

Liz snuggled in, smiling. She was alone for the first time. She'd moved from home to the dorm, from the dorm to marriage, from marriage back home. It was time.

She wasn't just an extra in this game of life, she was a lawyer. People would need her, need her help, ask her advice. Before her family found out she was homeless, she'd have clients and be able to afford a place. Maybe she'd buy a house. There were a few in the historical district a block away that only needed a makeover. Big old homes like Winter's Inn that had been turned into a bed-and-breakfast by the past three owners and little bungalow homes in between that would be more her style.

The desk lamp flickered a warm glow on the brown carpet, the yellowed-white walls, and the army-green curtains. "Definitely a house, painted in sunset colors." She whispered her dream. "With a swing on the front porch and flowers everywhere."

The wind howled outside and the curtain billowed slightly, letting in cold air. Liz wrapped the blanket tighter, figuring out why old Mr. Kaufman had insisted that the place rented "as is." Apparently, paint wasn't all it needed. North windows didn't seem so perfect anymore.

By six the next morning when the heating system clicked on for the day, Liz wore two pairs of socks and her coat beneath her blanket. She climbed out of her couch/bed, grabbed her makeup, and ran to the ladies' room. Thirty minutes later, she was dressed, all evidence of her bed had vanished back into the file cabinet, and she had coffee brewing.

At eight, when she placed her new sign in the window, she was ready to welcome clients. At ten, when someone knocked on her office door, she was asleep with her head on her desk.

Liz jumped up and frantically looked for her shoes. She found only one, so after a few moments of panic, she limped through the reception area to the door.

A potbellied postman raised his eyebrow as he looked her up and down, but didn't comment on her missing shoe. "Name's Jerry. You're new on my route." He never stopped chewing his gum as he talked.

"Yes." Liz didn't feel the need to tell the postman her name. It was on the door and probably on every piece of mail in his hand.

He handed her the stack of letters. "I've been holding these for you since you signed the lease." He glanced around her to the small front office with its tiny desk and plastic plants. "If you leave a box by the door, I'll drop any mail off there and won't have to bother you if the receptionist isn't here."

"Okay," she said aware that he was trying to see into the next office. A receptionist was so far down on her list of things she could afford, she hadn't even thought of hiring one.

"Thank you." She crossed her arms, waiting for him to leave. Jerry the mailman was nosy, and in a small town where everyone talked about the Mathesons, she didn't need nosy. "Anything else?"

He looked down at his pack. "Yeah, would you hold G. L. Smith's mail so I can quit dragging it up here every day? He's across the hall from you." Jerry frowned at the door. "Up until last week I could open his door and toss his mail in, but about the time you rented, someone locked his door."

"Maybe G. L. did?" Liz took her neighbor's mail and tossed it on one of the wicker chairs. Paint chips flicked off and dusted the carpet like dandruff.

Jerry shook his head. "He hasn't in years. Don't see why he would now. I'm betting Mr. Kaufman locked it. He keeps a key to all the offices just in case there's a water leak or something."

"When will Mr. Smith be in?"

"Don't know. Never met the guy. He gets UPS and Fed Ex deliveries too. The lady in the laundry told me she signs for them and brings them up to the office. She said she did it just to be nice, but every time she climbs up with mail, she finds a few dollars dropped in her mail slot." Jerry raised his bushy eyebrow again. "You don't think he's dead in there, do you?"

"No," Liz answered. "We'd smell him by now."

Jerry nodded.

Liz grabbed the door frame. "Thanks," she said, closing the door before he could ask any more questions. G. L. Smith had as much right to his privacy as she did. It made sense that Kaufman had a key, but she didn't like the idea. Tonight she'd be shoving a chair against the door.

She tossed her mail, which looked like mostly bills and "Welcome New Neighbor" notices, on her desk and microwaved the last cup of her morning coffee.

Before she remembered to look for her shoe, she heard the front door open again. Limping to the front, Liz was surprised to see Edith from the diner a block over. All the locals knew her and loved her. Edith had been waiting tables at Cass's Blue Moon Diner since she was in high school. She was sweet and kind; her only flaw had been in her choice of husband. If Harmony ever had a citywide cleanup day, he'd be part of the trash they took out.

"Morning, Edith." Liz's smile was honest this time. "May I help you?"

"I brought you a few of Cass's blueberry scones for your first day at work. Hank was by this morning and told me you were setting up an office. Now that's exciting, girl." The woman, still in her apron, handed Liz a plate covered with a napkin. "I bet your mother is real proud of you."

"Thanks." Liz doubted her mother had noticed, but that wasn't Edith's problem. She motioned with her head toward a chair in front of her desk. "Got time to stay a spell?" Edith always looked tired, and Liz realized she'd never seen the woman sitting down.

"No. I got to get back before the lunch run starts. I was just wondering if you charge for hypothetical questions about the law."

"No. Ask away. If I can pass the bar, I should be able to come up with an answer." Liz was already guessing the question would be something about declaring tips on income tax forms, which wasn't her specialty, but she'd do her best.

"And what I say in here, is that like something you say in confession with a priest? It can never be told?"

"That's right." Liz smiled, happy that Edith trusted her.

Edith looked down at the mud-colored carpet. "I was just wondering, if a woman killed her husband accidentally, would she go to jail?"

Liz took the shock of her question without flinching. For the first time she noticed that the dark circles under the waitress's eyes were bruises. "If it was an accident or self-defense, she would not go to jail." She set the scones down and took Edith's hand. "Are you okay, Edith? Is there something I could do?"

Edith shook her head so hard her whole body seemed to vibrate. "No. I'm fine. I was just asking for a friend."

Liz suddenly felt very old. "Well, tell your friend that there are other ways out. If she wants to, she could come talk to me. I wouldn't charge her for a visit."

Edith wiped her hands on her apron. "I'll tell her. I got to be going. Cass will run off the folks if he's there alone."

Liz welcomed the change. "He is a bear of a man. I've never heard him talk except to yell."

Edith smiled. "Yeah, but that don't bother me. Underneath, he's a good man. Never known him to cheat anyone or turn down any drifter who can't afford a meal."

Liz's opinion of the man lifted slightly, especially because if she didn't get paying business she might be one of those drifters dropping in for a free meal. It would beat going home to a thousand questions and her sister's I-told-you-so attitude.

Chapter 4

REAGAN COVERED FOR EDITH AT THE DINER AGAIN. THIS time Edith said she had to drive to Amarillo to see a doctor about her cold. This time Reagan didn't even try to act like she believed the waitress.

The weather held an icy stillness over the air, hesitating between winter storms. By eight o'clock, Reagan was surprised at how many people had wandered in. Most only wanted coffee, stayed an hour, and left a quarter tip. Noah dropped by to keep her company, but she was busy enough that they talked little. When she finally had time to sit down, he was into his homework and only wanted to ask her questions about algebra.

Edith's husband came by a half hour before closing. He

said he was looking for his wife, claimed he'd forgotten about her trip to the doctor. Lloyd Franklin was somewhere in middle age. Reagan marked him as one of those loser types who might have been good looking in his teens but settled into overweight, dumb, and sloppy. He winked at her as if he thought he was doing her a favor by talking to her, then left. Reagan noticed he walked across the street to the bar.

She sat back down across from Noah and continued checking his homework. Unlike her, he had his future all planned out. He wanted to travel the rodeo circuit for ten years or so, then settle down on his land and raise horses and cattle. For Noah, algebra didn't seem a necessary skill, but he had to keep his grades up to go to college, and he only wanted college so he could ride with the team at Texas Tech. Reagan often thought God must have tattooed *Rodeo* on Noah's brain before he set it in place.

About the time Reagan decided to tell Noah the details of seeing Gabriel Leary last week, Noah packed up his books and hurried out. From the window she watched him pull out his cell once he was off the steps, and she couldn't help but wonder who was calling him. A year ago, even six months ago, he would have told her. She would have talked to him about Gabe, but now the world's slowest earthquake seemed to be separating the earth between them, and the gap was too wide to jump by the time they noticed it.

She went back to refilling coffee for mostly old men who were busy solving every problem with the government.

When she passed the pass-through, she yelled to Cass, "Thanks for putting in the step. Makes it a lot easier for me to reach all the paper goods."

He looked up from the sink. "I didn't put it in. Edith must have."

Reagan glanced down at the step that swung down from being flat against the wall. She could flip it up or down with the toe of her shoe and, when up, it was completely out of the way. When down, it added five inches to her height.

Cass moved closer to the pass-through. "You think you can lock up? Ain't nobody else coming in and, if I leave now, I can watch my show."

"I can lock up." Reagan almost giggled, wondering if Cass's favorite program was *Project Runway* or gator wrestling.

He grabbed his coat. "Don't forget to wash the coffee-pots and wipe down—"

"I know. I won't forget." As he passed her, she added, "What about takeout?"

"We don't do takeout after five," Cass answered, and was gone.

Reagan watched him go, realizing he didn't know anything about the Wednesday night delivery.

The last two old men left a little before nine. Reagan went to the kitchen and packed up a meatloaf sandwich, stew, and two cinnamon muffins. This place had more mysteries than one of those CSI shows. Evidently Cass and Edith had a communication problem. No wonder new waitresses only stayed a few weeks.

She walked out into the stillness of a night that froze her breath. The lean figure of a man stood just at the edge of the back light. He must trust her, for he'd crossed out of the trees. It dawned on her that maybe Leary had been as afraid of her as she'd been of him last week. Suddenly, he wasn't nearly as frightening.

"Evening, Gabe," she said, seeing his whiskered face. "Nice night for takeout."

He stammered just a bit before he answered, "Evening."

"If you're walking, I could give you a ride home." She noticed his cheeks were red from the cold already, and it was a long way back to his place.

"No thanks, I've seen you drive."

She laughed. She did like to drive fast, and more than once she'd called Noah to come pull her out of a ditch.

"Do you drive?" she asked, guessing that if he'd walked tonight, he might live out on his place without a car.

"Yeah," he answered. "Doesn't everyone?" He took the bag from her. "But mostly, I like to walk. There was a time I thought I'd never walk again." He fished in his pocket and pulled out two bills. "Thanks for the supper."

"You're welcome." She stood, watching him move down the gully and across to the trees all dead with winter, and wondered if a part of this man wasn't dead too. She knew without asking that he'd just talked to her more than he'd talked to anyone in a long time.

Gabriel Leary no longer frightened her. Reagan just felt sorry for him. He wasn't crazy or a madman running loose, he was simply alone and she knew how that felt. Once in a group home she'd gone a month before one person talked to her. The house mother had a habit of just pushing kids along and pointing as if she were herding cattle. That winter she'd turned twelve and cried so much a lifetime of tears spilled out.

When she walked back into the diner, a woman huddled in the middle booth, her suitcase by her side.

Reagan filled a glass of water and moved to her table. "What can I get you?"

A thin wrinkled face looked up at her. "Just water and an order of fries."

"With chili or cheese?" Reagan smiled, remembering a few years ago when she'd been asked the same question by Edith. "This late at night there's no extra charge for chili or cheese."

The woman nodded and straightened as she warmed. "Then I'll have both, if you don't mind."

"Just get in town?" Reagan asked, guessing the woman to be in her sixties. Not old, but worn down like some people get about that age.

The woman nodded and turned her face toward the window, telling Reagan she didn't want to talk.

When Reagan delivered the food, she said, "I put the chili in a bowl with cheese on top. That's how Edith, the usual waitress, gave it to me when I first got here."

The woman smiled, pulled off her gloves, and slowly began to eat.

Reagan moved to the counter and started cleaning as she kept an eye on her one customer. There was something about this town, she decided, that made her feel . . . that made her care. People here wore their hearts on their sleeves. If the woman had a suitcase, she must have come in on the late bus. Since no one met her, she'd have to walk a ways in the cold to find a hotel.

When she refilled the woman's water, she said, "We'll be closing soon. I could give you a ride somewhere if you like. Not much of anywhere is out of my way in this town."

"Thanks. The bus driver said he thought there was a hotel about four blocks over near the cemetery. I could walk, but I won't turn down a ride on a night like this."

Reagan collected her empty dishes and turned off the lights. The woman was waiting by her pickup when she locked up. They didn't talk on the drive to the hotel, but when Reagan pulled into the hotel lot, she said, "If you're planning to stay, I think the diner might need a waitress, at least part time."

"Thanks, but I'm not looking for work." The woman stepped out. "Good night, dear."

Reagan watched her go into the tiny office of the rundown hotel. The lady would have no trouble getting a room; only one car was parked in the lot. Reagan couldn't help wondering what the woman's story might be. Her clothes looked well made but wrinkled from days of wear.

"I got to stop covering for Edith," she said aloud. Every time she did, she found another character. People, their lives and dreams, were starting to fascinate her. When she first came, she would have walked right past everyone on the street without caring, but now, Reagan wanted to reach out and help.

On her way home she drove around the old downtown square. In a window on the second floor of one of the buildings was a sign that read ELIZABETH MATHESON, ATTORNEY AT LAW. She circled again and read the smaller print. CIVIL LITIGATION PRACTICE—WHEN YOU NEED SOMEONE ON YOUR SIDE.

Reagan stared at the sign for several minutes. Maybe she should go to college. If she became a lawyer, she could help people. She could take classes online or drive over to Bailee's community college for night classes, and then she could still watch over Uncle Jeremiah.

She shoved the pickup into reverse and swung back on the road heading home. What a crazy dream. She was barely passing English. You probably had to be able to spell to be a lawyer. Plus, nobody liked lawyers. She'd already spent enough of her life with no one caring about her.

As she drove along Lone Oak Road in the dark, Reagan tried to think of another dream she might follow, but none came to mind. Wishing for something was new to her. She hadn't even thought a town like Harmony existed until she met Miss Beverly one day while cleaning rooms at a nursing home. Miss Beverly told her all about Harmony, and Reagan's first wish ever was to be from such a place. She'd never been from anywhere. When she finally hitchhiked into Harmony, she felt like she'd found home.

Her cell rang as she turned down the dirt road to the house.

"Rea." Noah sounded excited.

"What's up, Preacher?" She smiled, thinking of how announcers always called him Preacher when he rode bulls because every time he climbed on more than a thousand pounds of meanness, Noah McAllen got religion.

"I had to tell you all the news, Rea. I feel like I'm going

to explode if I don't tell someone. Dad says he'll take me to the finals at Oklahoma City next month. Not a high school rodeo, but the big time. He thinks I may be ready soon to go pro."

"That's great," Reagan lied, wishing she could be happy for him, but every time she watched him ride, she remembered the night in the hospital after a bull had tried to stomp him to death.

"And another thing." He lowered his voice as if hesitating. "Stephanie Summer agreed to go to the prom with me. She must have had a dozen other offers and she picked me. Can you believe that?"

"Terrific." Reagan fought back tears. She'd told him she didn't want to date. She'd even coached him on how to ask girls out and what to say, but deep down she'd hoped he wouldn't go out with anyone. She wanted them to be best friends forever, but she guessed for a guy of eighteen, forever's not as long as she hoped it might be.

"You all right with it, Rea?"

"Sure," she answered.

"You planning on going? I've heard lots of kids say they're going without dates."

"Sure." She pulled to a stop. "I wouldn't miss seeing you try to dance with Stephanie Summer."

He said good night as she walked into the house. Reagan made it to the kitchen and held it together while she said good night to her uncle and climbed the stairs. Alone in her bedroom, she fought back a scream. Not because she wanted to go to the prom with Noah, but because she didn't want him to go with anyone else.

When her muscles finally relaxed, she hiccupped a laugh, wondering if they let crazy people be lawyers. How could she give others advice if she couldn't even understand herself?

Chapter 5

JANUARY 17, 2008
HARMONY FIRE STATION

HANK MATHESON FINISHED UP HIS PAPERWORK AT THE fire station and glared at the clock. He still had an hour to wait until Alex McAllen could leave work. The need to see her ate at his gut. He'd loved her for as long as he could remember. They'd been engaged for almost two years and he couldn't get her to decide on where to eat, much less a date to marry. She ran the county sheriff's office with great proficiency. He had no doubt she loved him, wanted him, needed him.

Why didn't she want to be married to him? Hank asked himself for the thousandth time.

All he had to do was walk out of the fire station and cross the street to the county sheriff's office. Since her Jeep was in her parking spot, she'd be in her office. He could just ask her flat out. Alex liked directness.

Only, Hank wasn't sure his heart could take the answer. If she said no . . . if she said good-bye . . . He was a logical man—part of his job was to plan for emergencies—but he had no backup plan if Alex said good-bye. So, they played a game. He didn't push, and she never planned.

He walked to the window and stared out at the traffic that moved down the street between them. If he went to her now, people would talk and they'd both had enough of being the topic of conversations in town. He'd even heard that Buffalo's Bar had a pot going on whether they'd ever get married.

Leaning against the window frame, Hank tried to think of something to kill the time. He could call his little sister and see how she was doing, but Liz had made it plain she wanted the family to leave her alone. He was proud of her for stepping out on her own, but that didn't keep the big brother in him from wondering how she was doing. She was the youngest and they'd all babied her. He'd seen her practically go into cardiac arrest over a broken fingernail or no ice cream left in the freezer. How could she possibly handle living alone?

His little sister reminded him of a girl he'd dated in college ten years ago. Priscilla Prescote. She'd been so needy, she could have had her own box to check on the United Way form. If Liz was growing up, maybe Priscilla had too.

Hank laughed, remembering how Priscilla had talked him into getting engaged, not because she loved him and wanted to spend the rest of her life with him, but because she thought it would be fun to tell everyone. Now all these years later he was engaged again and still seemingly no closer to getting married.

Hank thought about driving home, but this was his day in town and every woman at the ranch, including his six-year-old niece, would want to know what was wrong. *That's my problem*, Hank decided, *I'm too predictable. I come to town Tuesdays and Thursdays. Take Saralynn to breakfast and then to school, work at the office, then take Alex to dinner.* The rest of the days of the week he worked on his ranch and didn't see Alex until he stopped by her place after dark.

Last week he drove into town to surprise her for lunch. The moment she looked up and saw him, she said, "It must be Wednesday." He realized for the past four Wednesdays he'd surprised her.

He grabbed his coat and headed out with no real mission in mind. If anyone needed him, he had his cell strapped to his belt. Otherwise, Hank Matheson planned to do something different for a change. When even his spontaneity was getting predictable, he figured he was moving from predictable to boring.

He backed out into the street before his cell went off.

"Matheson here," he answered as he pulled to the curb.

"Hank, it's Tyler Wright. I got a problem out here at the cemetery and I don't know who else to call."

"A fire?" Hank found that hard to believe. Two years ago they'd had enough grass fires to last a lifetime, and he and Tyler had had their hands full. Somehow, the heat of that spring had shown him the solid steel in this man he knew he could always depend on.

Tyler Wright was over forty, his good friend, and the town's funeral director. Hank suspected he hadn't told a joke in this lifetime.

"No, no fire." Tyler sounded frustrated. "Just a woman. She's sitting on one of the benches and when I walked over, she didn't even act like she noticed me standing in front of her." He lowered his voice. "I don't know what to do. She's not doing anything illegal or acting crazy, she's just sitting."

"Is she ill?" Hank threw the truck into drive and headed the few blocks to the cemetery.

"No, I don't think so." Tyler's normally calm voice sounded nervous. "If she stays out here much longer, she'll be sick. Between the drizzle and the sun setting, it's got to be close to freezing. I told her she'd have to leave, but I don't think she even heard me and I can't drag her out."

"You ever see her before?"

"No. She was just sitting out there when I came by this morning to check the location of a grave, and when I circled back a few minutes ago, she was still there. I don't think she's moved from that bench all day."

Hank swung into the front gate of the beautiful old cemetery. The headstones beneath barren branches made the air seem ten degrees colder. He parked next to Tyler's funeral-black Cadillac and walked toward the woman sitting in the oldest section of the graves where huge elms stood guard, the shadows of their bare limbs crossing the dead grass like spiderweb lace.

Tyler met him a few feet before he reached the bench. The plump funeral director never wanted to hurt anyone's feelings, but as always he seemed to sense heartache. Hank saw the worry in his friend's face.

Hank knelt in front of the woman. She was gray headed, thin, and wrapped in a tailored wool coat. "Hello." Hank extended his hand. "I'm Hank Matheson. If you're looking for a grave, we could help you find it. Most of my ancestors are scattered around this place, and Mr. Wright's family started this cemetery."

She stared straight ahead as if she hadn't heard him.

"Do you need any help?" Hank asked.

"It's getting late." Tyler stood beside Hank, looking anxious. "You don't want to be here in a few hours. This rain will turn to sleet."

Still no answer from the woman.

Hank placed his hand on her gloved fingers laced together. "Are you all right?" When she just stared ahead, he looked at the stones around the bench and picked the name carved on most of them. "Can we help you, Mrs. Biggs?"

Slowly she turned her head. "No one's called me that in years."

She stared at the grave in front of her with the name BRICE ANDREW BIGGS carved on its small stone. Birth 1968. Died 1998. Hank figured the dates were off to be her husband, but it could have been her son. He looked around at several other Biggs graves and saw a few with birth years in the forties. One of them could have been her husband.

Hank smiled. "Would you like me to call you something else?"

"No. I think I'd like to be called Mrs. Biggs again."

Tyler moved forward. "I've got hot cocoa in my car. Would you like a cup, Mrs. Biggs?"

She nodded, and he hurried off to his Cadillac.

Hank sat down on the bench close enough to touch her side lightly, hoping to offer some warmth. He put his arm on the back bar, wanting to cut some of the wind blowing her hair. They didn't talk. He wasn't even sure she noticed him so close.

Tyler brought the thermos and two mugs and sat on the other side of her. He poured her a cup, offered Hank one, and then, using the lid, he poured himself some. They sat in silence for a long while, drinking the cocoa and watching the sun lower.

Hank wondered what people passing by thought, but he didn't much care. He and Tyler just didn't want Mrs. Biggs, or whoever she was, to be alone. He'd watched Tyler and his father before around the grieving. Since Tyler was from generations of funeral directors, you'd think he'd know just what to say, but the thing Hank noticed most was that Tyler didn't say anything at all. He was just there when needed.

Hank glanced over at his friend. Tyler had never been popular in school, never dated much, never played a sport. He hadn't gone off to the big city to make a fortune or become famous, but Hank realized he respected this quiet man more than just about anyone. Tyler Wright had never harmed anyone, and in this world that was a gift. If Alex did ever set a date, Hank decided he'd ask Tyler to stand up as his best man.

Finally, Mrs. Biggs handed her cup back to Tyler. "Thank you. That was lovely."

"You're welcome. It's about time for me to lock the cemetery up for the night. If you like, I could drive you home."

"Can I come back tomorrow?"

"Of course."

Hank stood and offered his hand to help her up, then tucked her fingers at his elbow as he walked her across the grass to where his truck and Tyler's car waited.

Tyler hurried ahead and started his car, then climbed back out to lock the gate. Hank waited for him outside after Mrs. Biggs was seated and the heater turned up. "Any idea who she is?" he asked with his back to the woman in the front seat.

"No. Far as I know, all the Biggses are dead. We haven't dug a grave there in ten years or more. No one has ever left flowers."

"Well"—Hank shrugged—"she doesn't want to talk and I don't think she's crazy or ill, so what do we do?"

"I'll bring more cocoa for tomorrow," Tyler said simply.

"I can probably find a blanket and an umbrella. If she wants to sit out here, we might as well try to make her comfortable." Hank climbed into his truck. It was past five; Alex would be waiting for him.

As he drove to the county offices, he wondered what it would be like to be the last in a family. Since the Mathesons settled here over a hundred years ago, they'd been procreating. He had more cousins than he could count. Alex and her family, the McAllens, were the same way. There wasn't a business in town that didn't have at least one McAllen or Matheson working at it. Alex didn't have to go out looking for crime; she had relatives calling it in. When he and Alex finally did marry, they'd have to have the wedding at the biggest church in town just to hold the family.

Hank realized he didn't have to ask Mrs. Biggs if she had any relatives left. If she had, she wouldn't have been sitting in the cemetery.

Chapter 6

Tyler Wright closed his office door and flipped on his computer. Every night he logged the day. A routine he never broke. Only he didn't keep the logs, he mailed them to an e-mail address that hadn't answered a message in two years.

Dear Kate,

Today the wind seemed to blow in winter on frosted breath. I met a woman in her sixties who is probably the last of her family. She asked me if she could come sit in the cemetery every day. I don't think she has anything else to do.

*When we were talking, Kate, I never got around to
asking if you had family. I hope you do.*
Good night. Sleep well,
Ty

By now, he knew she wouldn't answer him, but as long
as the messages didn't come back, he figured there was
hope. In a time when all the world had secrets, Tyler had
no affairs, no addictions he kept quiet, no strange obses-
sions. He simply wrote a woman each night to tell her he
was still waiting.

Chapter 7

AS THE DAYS PASSED, MAIL FOR G. L. SMITH BEGAN TO collect on Liz Matheson's wicker chair. Jerry the mailman stopped trying the door after a few days and just plopped Smith's letters down before he yelled, "No mail for you again today, Miss Matheson."

He'd listen for a while, then leave if she didn't answer. He always had time to talk, so Liz developed a habit of always looking busy.

Late Friday afternoon Liz decided that was now her job . . . looking busy. She'd been open a week and the only people who came in, besides the mailman, were curious folks with usually hypothetical questions. The bookstore owner downstairs wanted to know if killing a barking dog was a crime. When she said yes, he frowned, took back the 20-percent-off coupon he'd laid on her desk, and left. Two high school kids dropped by to ask her if she'd ever represented a serial killer. When she said no, they picked up their skateboards and ran out.

So, Liz was left with what she did best, looking busy. Tonight she was busy watching the sunset behind the trees of the old homes and wishing she had somewhere to go. It was Friday night. When she'd been in college she'd had dates lined up on the weekends. Those were the days. She smiled as she tossed her pen toward the invisible receptionist's desk.

A shadow moved in the hallway, making Liz jerk back. She hadn't heard anyone come up the rickety stairs. The floor just beyond her office creaked, and she became very much aware of how alone she was.

"Who's there?" she shouted, looking around for a weapon.

A tall man, covered in winter work clothes, stood before her. Between his hooded coat and his beard, all she could see were his eyes. Winter blue, she thought. Cold as blue-gray steel.

Killer eyes, she decided.

Before she could scream, he looked down at several yellow squares of paper in his hands. "Sorry to interrupt you, miss, but I'm glad you're still here. These things taped to my door say you've got my mail."

Liz tried to slow her heart down to under a thousand beats a minute. "Oh, you're G. L. Smith." She stood and moved closer.

He didn't answer her question. "Kaufman must have locked my door. I leave it unlocked for deliveries, but now and then he drops by and locks the place up."

"Aren't you afraid someone will steal your mail?"

He glanced at the stack of boxes and papers on her wicker chair. "No one ever has, until now."

"Oh, I'm sorry. Please, take it."

He loaded up an armful and crossed the hall. While he unlocked his door, she picked up a stack and followed. Liz wasn't sure what she expected to be in Mr. Smith's office, but one box marked *Mail* wasn't it. The office looked to be the same size as hers, but he had nothing. No desk, file cabinets. Not even a worthless wicker chair.

"You just move in?" she asked as she passed him her load.

"No," he answered, tossing the mail into the box before crossing back for his remaining deliveries.

"You remodeling?" Maybe he'd moved everything out so he could paint.

"No."

"I get it. You're a minimalist. I knew a girl in college who was one. She only owned one pair of shoes, can you imagine that? One pair and they were SAS's. Now that just goes against nature, if you ask me."

He finally looked at her. "I don't even know what you're talking about, lady."

"Oh, I'm sorry. We haven't really met. I'm Elizabeth Matheson. I just rented the office across the hall. I'm a lawyer. What kind of work are you in?"

He frowned, or at least she thought he did. It was hard to tell with all that brown hair covering his face. "Look, lady, I just want my mail. I didn't mean to bother you."

Liz considered herself an excellent communicator. She got along with everyone in her dorm and sorority house and even in the one job she had before coming home. Therefore something was majorly wrong with this guy. Maybe he had some kind of conversation disability.

She straightened, up for the challenge. "Oh, I'm sorry."

"You've already said that, twice." He watched her like she was a windup toy he was waiting to run down. "Thanks again."

He closed the door in her face.

She fought the urge to stomp her foot. "There was no

again to your thanks." She nodded as if she'd scored the last point and walked back to her office.

The next morning, a trash bag of empty boxes and padded mailing envelopes sat in the hallway. Liz couldn't resist trying the door. It was unlocked and empty except for the cardboard box that had *Mail* scratched on it with a pencil.

As the days passed, Mr. Smith became her project. She checked his office every morning. Mail piled up in the box and a large delivery came overnighted, but he didn't return to pick anything up.

She asked the lady in the dry cleaners about Mr. Smith, but the woman just shrugged, saying she'd never seen him, but she liked him. Nice and quiet. The bookstore owner, a man who read even as he rang up customers, had nothing to add. However, he did give Liz a half-off coupon to have her palm read any Thursday night or Saturday morning. "We got some wannabe writers who meet in the store, and one of them can read your palm better than I've ever seen."

"You seen a lot?" she asked, trying to be friendly.

The old man raised an eyebrow and went back to his book.

Liz shrugged and walked up the stairs. Reading palms in this town wouldn't be hard. Everyone pretty much knew everyone's life story. She knew what folks said about her. *Smart when it comes to school but no sense at much else. Left a man for no good reason.* Liz even heard a woman whisper once when she thought Liz wasn't listening, "Someone said she left her husband because there was no passion in the marriage. A woman who's holding out for that is destined to sleep in a cold bed."

Liz reached the top of the stairs and turned to look out at the winter gray of town. She'd sleep alone for the rest of her life if she had to. She wouldn't settle—or worse, she wouldn't stop dreaming that somewhere in this world caring mattered . . . *she* mattered.

She walked inside and stared at the second-floor office across from her.

Mr. Smith, the invisible man, had rented the office for years and never met anyone but her. She didn't know if she should consider herself lucky or cursed. Maybe she'd consult the palm reader.

Liz tried to stay busy, but only one client came in all day. A woman who wanted to adopt her sister's seventh child. It seemed she couldn't get pregnant and her sister managed to get in that condition every time she was let out of the house. Liz thought the group meeting might be touchy, but when the sisters showed up, six other children in tow, it appeared to be the perfect answer for them both. Even the husband of the childless sister agreed. The husband of the mother of seven hadn't been seen in two pregnancies. Apparently his presence wasn't needed for her to procreate.

Liz drew up the papers with the help of one of her textbooks and filed the proper forms at the courthouse.

Then she went back to her office and thought about Mr. Smith. Short of putting flypaper down, she couldn't think of how to catch him checking his mail again. The man must move silently down the hallway. He looked to be about her age, but she didn't remember anyone like him in school, and she knew most of the names of boys two grades above and below her.

He didn't seem an outsider either. She thought of going through his mail trying to pick up a clue to what he did, but even she knew that was illegal. Somehow having her first trial case be herself didn't sound too appealing.

Frustrated, she crossed the hall, opened his office door, and pushed the lock button. Now, eventually, she'd see him again.

Three days later Liz finished her nightly shower at the gym and drove back to her office. She'd signed on for a month's free membership and, after almost two weeks, no one had noticed she was using it as her bathroom and never exercising. If she didn't have enough income for an apartment next month, she could buy a six-month club membership and survive.

Everything was working out as planned. She'd managed to live on almost nothing the second week, thanks to the family checking on her. Hank took her to lunch twice; her mother, Joyce Matheson, insisted she have dinner out one night with the aunts; and her sister, Claire, dropped by with homemade bread. Plus, she'd made a hundred fifty dollars drawing up a will for a young couple.

The guy reminded her of her ex-husband, Eddie. The couple didn't have much of anything, but he'd read that all married people need a will, so he was checking it off his to-do list.

Liz used to swear that number fourteen on Eddie's list was *Make love to wife once a week.* If she suggested twice in seven days, he'd look at her like she was oversexed. If it had been seven days, nothing put him off his clock. Once she'd had the flu and he'd complained that she wasn't participating, so she shared her flu.

The wind whipped Liz's still damp blond curls as she darted from her car and ran up the back stairs. Once inside her office, she pulled the bag from the hardware store out of her storage closet and looked at what the clerk claimed was "all she'd need" to caulk the windows. Liz forgot to mention that she'd be making the repairs by only the streetlight because she couldn't very well let anyone see what she was doing. If anyone noticed her making repairs, they'd ask why she didn't go home to her apartment after the heating unit went off in Kaufman's building at ten.

After unwrapping everything, Liz slipped into black leggings and a black T-shirt she used to sleep in during her years at the dorm. The thought crossed her mind that she might need to smear coal on her face and wear a black cape to be impossible to see, but if someone did spot her she'd be shot as a burglar. Sleeping in her office was far more complicated than she'd thought it would be, but it was time to get the job done so she could sleep without a draft.

Just as she wished she'd asked for more directions from the clerk, someone knocked on her door.

Liz panicked. She darted around for a moment, then forced a deep breath out and headed for the door, her caulking gun behind her back. As she walked through the reception area she told herself it was probably just the young couple dropping by with one more question. They'd been adding little points to the will for two days. Yesterday, they'd willed their dog to a cousin.

As she touched the knob, logic reminded her that it was after nine. Both doors to the outside were locked. Mr. Kaufman was probably checking on her, making sure she wasn't using too much electricity or something. The man at the bookstore said the landlord liked to drop in on his holdings at odd hours.

She thought about it for a few seconds, then opened the door.

Mr. Smith stood in the hallway dressed as before, like the Harmony Mugger in all black and looking none too happy. He'd be perfect to work for the Unwelcome New Neighbor group if there were one.

"My door was locked again," he said, glancing toward his mail.

Liz almost said, *I'm sorry*, but reconsidered. "No problem. Your mail is safe." She pointed with the caulking gun.

He raised an eyebrow. "Planning a raid or remodeling?"

Liz measured her attire and realized she was dressed as the mugger's twin. The truth seemed her only defense. "I'm tired of the draft from my crummy windows. I thought I could do it myself and save money. Of course, I had to pick night so none of my potential clients would think I can't afford to pay someone. . . ."

"I get the picture." He stopped her rambling confession. "You know how to do this?"

"Not a clue."

He dropped the mail back in the chair, shrugged out of his coat, and took the gun. "How about I give it a shot? This could be a real mess if you've never done it before."

"So *you've* done it before?" She raised an eyebrow as she noticed the muscles along his arms as he rolled up his sleeves. The town mugger worked out.

"Are you kidding?" he said, moving to the window. "Duct tape and caulk are all that hold my house up."

Liz had no idea what to say. She just watched as he crossed her office and pulled the curtains wide. He had the lean body of a runner and, beneath all that hair and beard, might be passable. Too bad his attitude was so unfriendly. He had *raised by wolves* written all over him.

Mr. Smith looked back at her, and she was glad she couldn't read his face. He was probably considering turning her in as a nutcase to be studied. Those blue eyes seemed to take in every detail.

Realizing they could be seen from the street, she snapped off the desk light.

"Got a flashlight?" he whispered, as if they were smugglers. "The streetlight isn't bright enough for this kind of work."

"On my key chain," she answered, and pulled it out of her purse.

When she moved to his side and pointed the light at the corner of the frame, he asked her to move closer. She took a step.

"Closer," he said, again and again, until she was brushing his arm and the tiny beam of light lit where he needed to work. He'd grabbed all the supplies from the desk and seemed to know what he was doing.

They progressed along the windowsill, with him guiding the caulking and her holding the light just over his shoulder. After a few awkward bumps, she calmed down to the nearness of him. If she didn't stay close, he didn't have enough light to work. It was as simple as that.

Liz wasn't sure what she'd expected him to smell like—dirt maybe, or campfires and cigarettes, but he didn't smell that way at all. He was more soap and leather blended with a hint of the outdoors. Not bad, she decided, not bad at all. She even liked the brush of his flannel shirt against her arm.

She watched his hands smoothing out the caulking with long, strong fingers. The kind of fingers that would play a piano, or be an artist, but the scars left no doubt that the work he'd done with his hands was hard.

She tried to think of something to say, but for once, nothing came to mind. When she didn't follow him closely enough, he'd cover her hand and point the flashlight where it was needed. Each time, his hand rested over hers a few seconds longer than it had the time before.

Liz had dated a lot of guys, been friends with a few, worked well with several, but she'd never felt quite the way she did tonight. She knew nothing about this man. He could be married with ten kids out on the farm, or have sworn off all females for life. He could be a good guy or dumb as a rock. The only thing she knew for sure was he was not her type. She liked men in expensive suits. Men who carried briefcases, not tattered backpacks.

Rolling her eyes, she thought of one other thing she knew for sure about this man. She was attracted to him. Probably some kind of basic animal attraction left over in memory cells from cave-dwelling ancestors, because it certainly wasn't logical.

He tugged her hand. "Pay attention, Elizabeth. We're almost finished."

"My hand is getting tired," she complained, then added, "Mr. Smith."

"You want to stay warm in here? Stop complaining." He worked a few inches and added, "Gabriel, not Mr. Smith."

"Do people call you Gabe?"

"People don't usually call me, but it doesn't matter. Now, if you'll keep quiet we can get this done."

She huffed out a breath. This man didn't even know her and he was bossing her around. She thought of slugging his arm, but he was helping her, and after all, he did have a gun, though she doubted anyone had ever been caulked to death.

Slowly less and less cold air came in. The room would now grow slowly colder when the heat was turned off. She should be able to sleep the night without freezing.

Finally, he straightened and wiped his hands on a paper towel. It had taken an hour, but the job was finished. She clicked off her flashlight while he closed the curtains, smothering the streetlight's glow and leaving only a thin sliver of light coming from the hallway.

"You should be able to sleep a little warmer."

She started to correct him, but decided not to lie. "Thanks, Gabe."

"You're welcome, Elizabeth."

"Everyone calls me Liz." She moved toward the hallway and knew he followed. "How can I repay you?" He had to know she didn't have any money or she wouldn't have tried to do the job herself. "Maybe dinner at an inexpensive place?"

"Forget it." He bent, picked up his mail, and shoved it into the old backpack he'd left by the door. "Tell Kaufman, if you see him, to stop locking my office."

Without thinking, she leaned close and kissed the small spot on his cheek that wasn't covered with whiskers. "Thank you," she whispered.

He straightened slightly and kissed her back, a touch of his lips on hers, no more.

All reason told her to back away, but reason had never ruled her. Liz moved closer, brushing her body against his, wanting the kiss to continue. She knew when a man wanted her, and she knew how to respond.

Gabe granted her wish. Without moving, he took the gentle press of her against him and his kiss continued.

She raised her arms to his shoulders and let them rest there, not holding but moving closer so that she felt him breathing. Either one could have stepped an inch away and broken the spell.

Slowly, his kiss turned hungry. His arm circled her waist and pulled her to him; her cry of surprise was lost in his open mouth. In all her life from dating to marriage, she'd never been kissed like he kissed her. He wasn't playing or testing borders. He was telling her how he felt. This one kiss consumed her, and her entire body warmed with need.

Then, like the blink of blackness after a lightning strike, he shoved away from her so fast he pushed her into the wicker chair.

"I'm sorry," he mumbled. "I shouldn't have . . ."

He was gone without finishing the sentence. Liz sat in the chair, listening to his footsteps run down the hallway and out the back door. Slowly, her heart slowed to normal.

After a long while, she stood and locked the door to her office, then automatically shoved the chair beneath the knob. If she could, she would rewind the last hour of her life and try to figure out what had happened.

Secretly, she'd always considered herself a pretty shallow person. Dating guys for their cars in high school, for their brains in college. But this . . . was different. Gabe hadn't even asked her out. He didn't look like he had anything to offer, and even if he did, he wasn't offering it anyway.

He'd turned her down. She was ready and willing in his arms, and he'd run like she was a new strain of plague.

Liz sat down at her desk and held her head in her hands. She'd been rejected. No not rejected, almost tossed away.

No man, not once in her almost thirty years of life, had broken up with her. But Gabriel had before they even had a first date.

Liz's world no longer had a center.

GABRIEL MADE IT HOME IN HALF THE TIME HE USUALLY took, his left leg throbbing from the effort. He unlocked his door, checked the system, and slammed his gun on the shelf along with his mail.

"Damn!" His one word rattled around the room, echoing off the walls.

Tugging off his shirt, he headed for the shower. But even when the hot water poured over his head, he couldn't shake the feeling that he'd just broken one of his big rules. Rules that had kept him alive. Rules that had kept him safe through years of travel with the army. Men like him were sometimes called "smokies." They had no roots, no family, no home ports. They floated from one assignment to another without leaving any print of where they'd been.

Never get involved! Never!

He grabbed a towel, drying off as he walked down the hallway to the one windowless room in the house . . . his bedroom. By the time he'd pulled on a pair of sweats, he'd convinced himself that he hadn't really stepped over the line. One kiss probably meant nothing to her. She still didn't know him. Hell, she thought his name was Smith.

Gabe smiled. Half the time *he* didn't know what his name was. He'd been Leary until he ran away. In those months before he was eighteen, he'd told everyone his name was Smith just in case the law tried to make him go back home. The army made him step back into Gabe Leary's shoes when he enlisted, but he'd traded last names with another Gabriel in basic training. He'd gone by Wiseman for almost ten years, but once he came back home to recover, the Gabe Leary shoes were waiting for him. He used Smith on all correspondence related to his work. He'd even rented the office to keep the two separate.

Moving to the main room of his home, he flipped on the light and sat down at one of the three drafting tables. He pulled a piece of drafting paper down and drew an outline of Elizabeth's face, chin up, big bright eyes, pouty mouth, and light yellow hair that curled around her face like sunshine.

All in all, he knew it would be her mouth that would probably haunt his dreams tonight.

Chapter 8

FRIDAY
JANUARY 25, 2008
WINTER'S INN BED-AND-BREAKFAST

MARTHA Q PATTERSON HAD BEEN CONSIDERED THE TOWN slut for so long she'd learned to embrace the title. When she was in her teens she'd take any dare. In her twenties and thirties, folks claimed she married half the eligible men in town and slept with the other half.

Which wasn't true, Martha liked to remind everyone. Two of her husbands were from Bailee and one from Oklahoma City. But in the twenty years she considered her "marrying phase," she did marry seven times, if she counted Bobby Earl Patterson twice, him being both her second and seventh.

The part about sleeping with other men was a flat-out lie. Martha had her morals. She believed in marrying first.

In her forties Bobby Earl got cancer, and she stayed with him for ten years as lover, friend, and finally nurse. She didn't consider him the great love of her life, but he considered her his, and sometimes that's enough to stay with a man.

He died when she was fifty-one, leaving her the business she'd kept running all through his illness and an old house on North Street that his grandparents had built. Martha sold the tire and lube business and remodeled the old house into a bed-and-breakfast that she called Winter's Inn because Bobby Earl's favorite time of year was winter.

She averaged three or four paying guests a month, but that seemed to be enough to keep the lights on.

Martha Q was now fifty-three—the prime of her life, she decided—and she had no mission. No real job. No cause. It had been her experience in life that when she had nothing to do, trouble usually walked in to keep her busy. She didn't need to go to work. Another man was the last thing she was looking for. She'd given up on the cause of losing weight ten times, and children were much admired as long as they belonged to someone else. Though she'd accepted a wide variety of sperm donations, none had provided her with a child, which she told everyone was to her liking.

In the drab cold of a January morning, Martha sat among her antiques and tried to think of one reason to get dressed. She didn't have a booking at the B&B until next month, and the Red Hats, who had lunch in her parlor, weren't scheduled today.

She downed the last of her cold coffee and looked through the paper, then mumbled to herself.

Her big tabby cat lifted his head and stared at her.

"I'm not talking to you, fat cat." Martha wasn't really that crazy about cats, but someone had told her every bed-and-breakfast should have one. After living with the tabby, Mr. Dolittle, for two months, she decided the cat was the reincarnation of her third husband. He ate at all hours and peed on the bathroom rug. He also had the habit of sleeping with his eyes partly open, which gave her the creeps.

She flipped the page and saw a small notice about Elizabeth Matheson opening a law office. Martha smiled, deciding she'd pay a visit. It had been her experience in life that it never hurts to know a lawyer. Maybe she'd even invite Elizabeth to lunch. She'd never been one to seek out women as friends, but a woman lawyer would be different.

Martha stood. "Well, Mr. Dolittle," she said to the cat. "I'd better get out the trowel and smear on some makeup. I've got a visit to pay."

The fat cat looked like he couldn't care less. He turned his head to the bird feeder just beyond the window that Martha had put there just to torture him and she had a feeling they both knew it.

Chapter 9

HARMONY FIRE DEPARTMENT

HANK CAME TO TOWN FRIDAY MORNING, SOMETHING HE rarely did. He liked to work at the ranch and considered his workweek from Friday through Monday. Then, Tuesday or Thursday, he'd put in his time at the fire station and Wednesday he spent the day at home keeping the books. Hank almost never took a day off, and when he was forced into it by Thanksgiving or Christmas, he usually spent his time wandering about the house wishing he were outside taking care of business.

But this rainy Friday in January, he had to get away from the ranch. He couldn't point to what was bothering him. Maybe the fact that Alex had canceled their usual Thursday night dinner, claiming she had too much paperwork to catch up on. Maybe the realization that his sister Liz hadn't come home for almost a month, and she'd missed lunch with him at the diner. Maybe his mood was brought on by watching Mrs. Biggs go to the cemetery every day, rain or shine. She was living among the dead as if nothing on the other side of the cemetery fence interested her.

He felt lousy, not physically, but emotionally. He liked order. Everything should make sense. Nothing had changed in his world, but it was shifting and he didn't like it or know how to stop it.

At nine o'clock, he ran through the rain and into the county offices. Alex was walking from the break room with probably her third cup of coffee when he caught up with her.

"What brings you in, stranger?" She smiled, that warm, knowing smile a woman gives a man when she thinks she knows him completely.

He didn't answer. He just walked into her office, waited for her to follow, closed the door, and tossed his wet hat on the nearest chair. Then he carefully took her cup from her, pushed her against the wall, and kissed her as if he were starving for the taste of only her.

When he let her go, he swore and said, "Marry me, damn it. I don't like waking up without you."

She brushed rain from her clothes. "Good morning to you too."

"You're not answering me. Alexandra, I've loved you for longer than I can remember. We've been engaged two years now and we're no closer to marriage. I don't like sneaking over to your place in the middle of the night. I want to go to bed every night with you and wake up with you every morning."

Alex walked around her desk, putting some space between them. "You make it sound so exciting. Tell me one thing, Hank, if we married, where would we live? In my two-room cabin, or at your place with your mother, aunts, and sister?"

"We could get a place in town. We're both here as many hours as we're anywhere."

She shook her head. "Neither of us would survive in town."

"We could live at your cabin." He grinned. "It borders my land. I could walk to work."

"It's too small. Can't we just be happy the way we are?"

Hank gave in, like he always did. She loved him, and that should be enough for now. All the women in his house needed him, depended on him. His mother and sister Claire were so into their art they'd forget to pay the electric bill, and his two old aunts only thought of gardening in the summer and quilting in winter. They worried as much about characters on soap operas as they did people. His six-year-old niece was the only one in the house with any brains. By the time she turned ten she'd be running the place.

He picked up his hat and took a step toward the door. "If I have to, Alex, I'll build us a house on the line between your land and mine. I'm going to grow old with you by my side."

"That sounds like a plan. I'll see you tonight." She smiled. "I'll have a hot supper ready."

He nodded. "Grilled cheese sandwiches and tomato soup?" One of the few things she could cook, but when they'd decided always to stay in on Friday nights, the menu hadn't been one of the considerations.

"I'll have the fire going."

He winked at her double meaning and opened the door. "You got time to have lunch with Liz and me?"

"No, not today, I've got too many problems to solve. We've already had two break-ins reported this morning. Strange, both did damage, shattering glass and kicking in doors to get in, but nothing seems to be missing."

"Have any suspects?" he said, thinking about how much he liked just watching her move.

"Maybe a gang of boys I've been watching. No proof, just a feeling. I caught them shooting at squirrels a few weeks ago. Only thing they seem to be able to hit were windowpanes." Alex crossed to the window and looked out. "Odd, the break-ins don't make sense. Why would anyone risk getting arrested for nothing?"

"The victims have anything in common?"

"Yeah." She smiled. "Get this, they were both named Smith."

He stepped closer. "How many Smiths we have in town?"

"I already checked. Eight families with homes, two singles in apartments, and three with businesses."

The dispatcher yelled. Someone wanted to speak to the sheriff.

"I got to get to work." Her eyes said far more than her words.

"Tonight," he whispered, and turned away. If he looked at her much longer, they both would have forgotten all about work.

Her place was so small, half the time when they tried to make breakfast in her closet of a kitchen they ended up making love instead. Loving her was as easy as breathing, but getting her to marry him seemed more like trying to plow with a spoon.

Hank climbed into his truck and decided to drive by the cemetery. Surely, Mrs. Biggs wouldn't be out there in weather like this. For once the wind wasn't blowing, but icy rain fell straight down, making the town look like a melting painting of small-town America.

A few minutes later he was surprised to find that Tyler Wright had put up one of the funeral tents over her bench, and Mrs. Biggs was there, waiting as she had been all week.

He climbed out and ran to the bench. "Mind if I sit a spell with you?"

"No," she said, but her smile was as sad as always.

He knew she wouldn't talk much. Wouldn't answer any personal questions. She wanted to just be there in silence, her slender form as unbending as the iron fences surrounding some of the graves.

Sitting down next to her, he watched the rain dripping off the tent, curtaining them from the world. He had a hundred things he needed to do, but right now nothing seemed more important than being here on this bench. He held no illusion that he was keeping her company. Mrs. Biggs would still be very much alone even if half the town turned out to huddle under the Wright Funeral Home tent.

Tyler came by with Stella McNabb, who acted as one of the hosts at the funeral home on family viewing nights. While Hank and Tyler moved to the back of the tent, Stella, in her sweet way, talked Mrs. Biggs into coming back to the funeral home with her. They'd all tried to take her to lunch without success, but when Stella said she needed help with a family meal after this rainy-day funeral, Mrs. Biggs agreed to leave for a few hours.

Hank helped Tyler walk the ladies to the Cadillac. After climbing into his truck, he called his sister Liz to try to book another lunch date.

Her line was busy.

He decided to just drop by. They'd been close as children, even though Claire had been between them in age. Liz liked to follow him around and ask questions about everything she saw. She'd always been smart, in a dingy kind of way. She could make the dean's honor roll, but she couldn't remember to put gas in her car. She could make him laugh, and she could make him furious.

The past month Hank wasn't sure how she was doing. He had a feeling she was trying to prove something to herself and he wished her well, but as her big brother he still felt the need to keep an eye on her.

Chapter 10

OFFICE ON THE SQUARE

LIZ LEANED AGAINST HER LONG WINDOWS AND WATCHED Mrs. Patterson try to open her umbrella as she climbed out of her '98 Lincoln. No other woman in town had her name used more with "I'll tell you what she should do" than Martha Q Patterson.

For as long as Liz could remember, she'd heard people giving Martha Q advice—not to her face, of course, but behind her back. Years ago most women hated the flaming redhead, and most men watched her because though she wasn't a beauty, she was one of those rare women who drew men as if by smell.

About the time age turned Martha Q's hair more brown than red, the hate that folks felt toward her also dulled. Maybe partly because she lived with Bobby Earl and took care of him, but slowly the women of Harmony accepted her back home with the same kind of tired shrug with which they might have accepted a bothersome creak in the flooring. They didn't include her in their circle of friends or invite her to anything that didn't involve a donation at the door, but they no longer talked in death-threat tones when her name was brought up.

Liz grinned as Martha Q started up the steps to her office. Liz had secretly always loved the woman. Martha Q had lived her life by her own rules and standards. Even today she wore rhinestone-red cowboy boots and a hat to match with her olive-green jogging suit. Liz remembered stories of Martha Q climbing the water tower and flashing the town when she'd been sixteen and only a B cup. She'd done it again at twenty with double Ds. She'd gotten engaged so many times years ago that folks said she should have her own column on the social page every Sunday. She'd married her third husband because he'd told her he was dying. After six months, with him looking no sicker, she shot him to hurry the process along. He'd gotten so mad, he'd dialed 911 before he started beating her with the phone. When the police arrived, they arrested him and forgot to list the bullet wound in the report.

Giggling, Liz waited with her office door open. Martha Q had to be coming to see her. The morning was certainly no longer dull.

The woman hurried in, a powder puff cloud of perfume and bling. "Hope I'm not bothering you, miss, but I'm here to see Elizabeth Matheson, the lawyer." She dropped the dripping umbrella on the wicker chair, took off the red cowboy hat, and shook her head. The damp, sprayed hair didn't move.

"I'm Liz Matheson." Liz circled her desk fighting down a laugh. The lady looked like she was wearing a helmet.

Martha Q wrinkled up one eyebrow. A painted-on shadow

of the brow wiggled just above like an echo. "You sure you're old enough to be a lawyer? You don't look a minute past ponytails and braces."

Liz tried to stand taller. "I promise." She pointed at the diploma on the wall. "I got proof."

Martha nodded. "All right then, Miss Elizabeth Matheson. You got time to see me?"

Liz didn't want to look too hungry. "I had my morning court appointment postponed." She'd been practicing "sounding busy" during her "looking busy" afternoons. "Luckily, I can work you in, Mrs. Patterson."

Martha Q moved to the chair in front of Liz's desk. "You know who I am?"

"I do." Liz took her seat. "Now, Mrs. Patterson, how may I help you?"

Martha fiddled with her scarf for a moment before she began. Her pink scarf clashed with her green-studded jogging jacket, which clashed with her boots, which clashed with a canary-yellow purse that looked almost big enough to hold a small car. The woman was a nightmare's rainbow twin.

Liz offered her coffee. As she fetched it, Martha Q patted her face dry and caught her breath.

When Liz sat back in her chair, Martha Q began, "First, Miss Matheson, we just might become friends and, with that possibility in mind, I suggest two things. One, that you allow me to take you to lunch, and two, that you call me Martha Q."

"I'd love to," Liz agreed. "Call me Liz."

Settling into the chair like a nesting hen, Martha Q said, "Well, now that that is taken care of, we can do our business before we eat. I'd like to know how much you'd charge for me to have you on retainer."

"Are you in some kind of legal trouble?"

Martha Q shook her head. "No, not right now, but legal trouble is like lint to my way of thinking. I have a way of attracting both. I'd just like to know that I could call you if I had a question about something and you'd always answer the phone."

"I'd answer without the retainer," Liz said honestly.

"But"—Martha frowned—"if you was on retainer and something bad came along, you'd be bound not only to answer, but to stick by me."

Liz saw it then. No more than a flicker in the light, but there. Martha Q Patterson was alone, totally alone, maybe for the first time in her life. She probably wouldn't even admit it to herself, but she needed to know someone would be there.

Having no idea what to bill, she guessed. "I charge three hundred a month retainer. If something legal comes up, I'll represent you and bill my hourly rate, but no matter what, when you call, I'll answer. And"—Liz smiled—"I don't charge for any discussions over lunch as long as you pick up the check."

Martha relaxed. "Fair enough. I like to eat out once a week. Is that agreeable with you?"

Liz grinned. "I can work you in, but I warn you, I'm not a light eater."

Martha barked a laugh. "Good for you. I don't believe in taking small bites of nothing in this life. Now, to the first question. Where do we have lunch?"

They were still discussing possibilities as Liz locked up the office, and they walked down the stairs ignoring the mist of rain that remained in the air. Nothing but a direct downpour would have affected Martha Q's hair, and Liz's short curls only got curlier.

Martha Q seemed to know all the places in town, but Liz could never remember seeing the woman eating at any of them.

Liz wasn't surprised to see her brother climbing out of his pickup when they reached the parking area in front of the bookstore.

"Morning, ladies," he said, removing his hat.

Liz introduced him to her new client even though she guessed Martha Q already knew who Hank was. To her brother's credit, he was as polite to Martha Q as he would have been to anyone. He was a man who judged people on what he saw, not what he heard.

Martha Q, on the other hand, was herself. "You're one fine-looking man, Hank Matheson. If I was twenty years younger, you'd be using that fire hose at the station to cool off after I got through with you."

Her brother had always been comfortable around women, and he didn't disappoint Liz now.

"Mrs. Patterson, if you were twenty years younger and looked my way, I don't know if my heart could take the blow."

Martha Q laughed. "How is it you're not married? The women in this town go blind?"

Liz saw the indecision in his glance, but Hank's honest way won out. "I've been wondering that myself lately. I've been chasing the same woman for a long time, and I can't tell if I'm any closer to catching her."

"Maybe if you stopped chasing, she'd turn around and come to you."

Hank nodded, but Liz knew he wouldn't change. She invited him to join them, but he declined. Liz climbed into Martha Q's boat of a car and spent the afternoon having lunch, touring the B&B, and driving up and down Harmony's main streets.

When Martha Q dropped her off, the sun had already touched the horizon and Liz had learned things about the people of Harmony that were not in any of the history books. She went up to her office, put three one-hundred-dollar bills in the only locked drawer of her desk, and relaxed. Thanks to Martha Q, Liz had just had her most profitable day.

By the time Liz finished her shower, half the town was

probably talking about her afternoon with Martha Q. Not that they'd think it anything unusual. After all, lawyers were supposed to have lunch with all types of people.

When she returned to her office after her nightly shower, she tried to find something clean to wear. She'd been sleeping in the sweatshirts or jogging suits she went back and forth to the gym in for two weeks. She'd also carefully dressed up every day for work in case someone came in. She'd reached the point where she had more clothes in the laundry bags than on hangers.

Slipping into her oldest jeans and a T-shirt, she decided tonight had to be laundry night. She'd wait until she knew the bookstore was closed and then sneak down the back stairs and drive over to one of the apartment complex laundry rooms. With luck, she could be back in two hours.

On her third load down the stairs, she spotted a dark figure standing by her open trunk. For a moment adrenaline exploded across her muscles, and then she recognized Gabe's lean form.

He didn't offer to help her. He just watched as she lugged a trash bag full of clothes down the stairs.

Liz had no idea how to start a conversation with the man. Talking wasn't in his top hundred list of things to do, she guessed, but he'd ended the last conversation by running out on her, so she figured it was his turn to start.

He waited until she stuffed the last bag in her tiny trunk. "I thought you might be carrying down a dismembered body," he said casually as he crossed his arms over his chest.

"No, just laundry." She didn't look at him. "I usually take out the bodies on Monday nights. Fridays it's always dirty clothes."

"I know, I checked," he said.

Glaring at his dark shadow, she fired, "You looked at my laundry?"

"I had to make sure." He seemed to think his actions made perfect sense. "People are often not what they seem."

"Right," she said, still stuffing her bags inside.

"You have any idea whose blue Mustang that is?" He pointed at a car parked on the side street halfway between the front and the back of the building. "Could be a stalker. That parking spot allows whoever's in the car to see both stairwells. You should really park out front, Elizabeth. It's safer."

Liz slammed the trunk. "This conversation is over, Mr. Smith. Stop trying to frighten me."

He grabbed her arm to stop her retreat, then let go an instant later as if realizing his mistake. "I didn't mean to. I came to say I'm sorry about what happened the other night. I . . ."

Liz waited several seconds before she realized he wasn't going to continue. "Let me make it easy on you, Gabe. Let's try a multiple-choice question. *A.* You're sorry you kissed me. *B.* You are sorry you stopped. *C.* You're involved with someone else and figured your wife and kids wouldn't approve. And of course, *D.* We should just be friends." She moved away. "Oh, wait, we're not friends in the first place, so forget *D.*"

He followed her, standing just behind her as she opened her car door. "*B,*" he said as she backed into him trying to open her door. "I'm sorry I stopped."

She turned to face him. "Let me get this straight. You don't want to be friends. You don't want to talk or hang out. You just want to drop by now and then and kiss me."

He was so close she could feel his breath. "That's about it," he said as he shoved her door closed and backed her against her car. "You interested, Elizabeth?"

"You're nuts," she answered.

He moved away. "Yeah, you're right, but I've lived alone for so long, one kiss a week is all I can handle right now, and you're about the most kissable woman I've ever met."

He turned and walked into the shadows close to the building. "I had to give it a shot. No hard feelings."

Liz had to hurry to catch his arm before he started up the stairs. "How about a bargain?" she whispered. "One kiss. One answered question." She wasn't ready to admit that she wanted the kiss, but she knew she wanted to know more about this man. In her world she usually figured out the males within a matter of minutes, sometimes seconds, but this man was different. He wasn't playing her, or flirting. He wasn't even trying to be friendly. He was simply attracted to her.

He didn't move, but she could feel his eyes watching her even in the dark. "What question?"

She said the first thing that came to mind. "Where'd you get that limp?"

"Roadside bomb," he said slowly, as if he'd never told anyone.

"When?"

"That's two questions," he answered as he lifted his hand and slid it around the back of her neck.

Liz felt his warmth just before his lips brushed her cheek and moved slowly over to her lips. For a moment, he hesitated as if finding his way to what he wanted, and then he buckled her knees with the most delicious kiss she'd ever felt. When all thought gave way to feelings, he gently shoved her down on the third step of the stairs and left her.

By the time her mind returned, she realized he was gone. In a world where people went to bed after a kiss like that, he'd walked away. In a strange way she felt rejected and cherished at the same time.

When her body finally cooled, she walked upstairs, completely forgetting about her laundry. She flipped on her computer and began listing all the facts she knew about Gabriel, aka G. L. Smith. He had an office. He could do home repairs. He was paranoid.

With the skill of a professional student, she began to research. She found nothing. Gabriel L. Smith seemed to be the only person in America living completely off the grid.

A hundred G. L. Smiths. One a broadcaster in Oregon, one a writer of comics, one a singer in New York. Even a few Gabriel Smiths, but none who lived around here.

She added one more thing she knew about Gabriel L. Smith. He was a liar.

Chapter 11

SATURDAY
JANUARY 26, 2008
HARMONY RODEO ARENA

REAGAN TRUMAN STOOD AT THE EDGE OF THE BLEACHERS so no one would notice her as the bull riding started. Noah "Preacher" McAllen was riding tonight. Maybe his last ride before he went to the big time. She wanted to see him. She needed to know he was all right.

Pushing her hands deep into her jean jacket, she wished she hadn't argued with Noah at school yesterday. They'd both said things they didn't mean. He'd been her only friend for a long time after she'd moved in with Uncle Jeremiah. He'd been the one who wouldn't stay mad no matter how she tried to shake him off. He'd been the first boy she'd ever really kissed.

And now, she thought, he'd be her first heartbreak. He

wanted to be more than friends, and Reagan didn't think she could allow anyone that close. During the two years she'd been in Harmony, she'd done a great deal of healing, but the scars were still there, just below the surface, reminding her, warning her, that people are not always what they seem.

"You waiting for Preacher to ride?" a voice said from somewhere in the shadows behind her.

Reagan didn't turn around. She didn't need to. "Yeah, what you doing here, Brandon?"

Brandon Biggs was eighteen, but no less a thug than when she'd met him a while back with his younger brother, Border. The smell of cigarettes must be baked into his clothes. His hair needed to be washed and cut. Everything about him reminded her of a big, shaggy dog left outside to face the weather year round.

He pulled a pack of cigarettes out of his pocket but didn't light up. "I drove over to see what the worthless bums in Harmony are doing tonight. Bailee's so dead on Saturday night there must be a line for who gets the job of rolling up the streets."

Reagan guessed Brandon liked talking to her because she was one of the few high school kids not afraid of him. He'd tried to pull the tough-guy routine on her once and it hadn't worked. Reagan had lived in places where boys like Brandon were minor league.

They watched the first bull rider fall off his bull before he could clear the chute. She turned her attention back to Brandon. "I heard you dropped out of school."

He laughed. "My stepdad told me I'd learned everything I needed to know. He kicked me out two months ago. Said waiting any longer wouldn't change anything, I'd still be dumber than dirt and eating up his food."

Reagan looked at him, trying to read his face in the shadows. "What'd your mother say?"

"She was too drunk to say anything." Brandon straightened. "I'm better off without either of them. She's all the real kin I have besides my little brother. She's not much to want to hang on to, and Border runs off every chance he gets. Half the time she's telling folks she wished her two boys had never been born. Since I'm gone, he's probably staying with some of my relatives on my mother's side. None of them are worth much, but any place is better than with my stepdad without me to run interference for him."

"If he's like you, he's tough. He'll be fine." They watched the next rider. He didn't make the eight seconds.

In the silence between riders, Brandon lit his cigarette, then hid the light in the curl of his hand. "I got a chance at a job working construction. We'll be just north of Harmony working. I'll start on flags, but they said if I show up regular and sober I could be running a machine by the time I'm nineteen. Then the real money would come in. Twelve, maybe fifteen bucks an hour."

She was glad to change the subject. "Great. That's good money. If you get the job, drop by after work sometime at the Blue Moon. I apparently am working there every Wednesday night. I didn't apply for the job, it kind of got passed to me, but since I'm there, I'll buy you a slice of pie to celebrate."

She saw him nod in the dark. "I'll do that. You still with Preacher?"

"I'm not *with* anyone. I never plan to be."

He seemed nervous, like a ball of dynamite looking for somewhere to explode. "I got to go," he said as he ground out his cigarette in the mud.

"Keep in touch, Brandon, and stay out of trouble."

"You too." He laughed. "Be seeing you."

Reagan nodded, then turned her back on Brandon Biggs. It was time for Noah to ride. As always, she held her breath counting out the seconds in her mind. He was good, very good. His father's coaching not only helped him ride like a pro, it also taught him how to be safer, if anyone could ever be safe in this sport of bull riding.

Noah McAllen's father had been the best in his day. Folks talked about those days when he rode as if he were a legend. Some said riding was in Preacher's blood, but Reagan knew they were wrong. It was in his heart. Noah McAllen loved the rodeo like he'd never love anything else in his life.

She yelled along with everyone in the stands as he made the ride and jumped off. He waved his hat in the air, and she thought she saw him nod once toward his father sitting on one of the empty chute fences, and then Preacher moved to a blond girl at the corner of the corral.

Reagan didn't see the girl's face. She didn't need to. Who she was didn't matter to Reagan. She crossed the lined shadows behind the bleachers and walked to her old pickup. Her uncle would be waiting up for her.

Chapter 12

TUESDAY
JANUARY 29, 2008
WINTER'S INN BED-AND-BREAKFAST

MARTHA Q SLIPPED INTO HER WASHER-FADED BLACK PANT-suit, blue running shoes she'd never run in, and Bobby Earl's hunting hat with ears. In a few hours it would be dawn, and she had work to do.

Though she'd never tried, she had a real desire to help people, and today was as good as any to start.

She giggled as she lifted an old briefcase that had belonged to husband number five. She'd taken it when she'd left him because she had to have something to keep her makeup in. She'd married number five because she thought he was a businessman, dressing in suits and always carrying the case. But, after six months of wild sex, she'd finally gotten bored enough to ask questions and found out he sold used car parts harvested off stolen cars. Not exactly the banker she thought he might be. So she'd emptied the Playboys and candy bars out of the case and put it to better use.

Tonight, the black case was the perfect size for her self-printed posters.

She slipped out the back door and slid into the ravine that zigzagged across the old downtown like a scar. No one except a few locals knew the dried-up creek. It wasn't exactly a tourist destination. She saw only two advantages. One, the creek was lined with huge old trees that offered shade for many backyards and rear parking lots. And, two, it was a shortcut for anyone mindful of the root stumps and loose dirt.

When she'd been married to Bobby Earl, the first time, he'd always say he was going over to the old house to visit his eighty-year-old aunt. Then, he'd go out the back door, across the dry creek, and have a lunchtime quickie with a widow a block down. The third time he came home with a sprained ankle, Martha Q followed him.

Bobby Earl begged and cried, but she divorced him. Later, when she'd married him again while he was dying, he admitted to her that he'd never really been attracted to the widow; he only loved the thrill of sneaking off. Martha Q doubled his sleeping pills and took two days to decide that he was lying and to forgive him all over again.

Now, walking in the creek bed, she decided maybe he was right. It was exciting to be in the center of town and have no one know.

Martha Q moved from telephone pole to community bulletin board putting up her special signs and giggling.

She loved making mischief more than chocolate, she decided.

It was almost dawn when the last poster was stapled to the board in front of the library. Martha Q retraced her steps, stuffed the briefcase in the trash, and hurried back into the house. No one may have seen her, but she'd watched enough crime shows to know to make all the evidence disappear.

An hour later she was sitting at the Blue Moon Diner having her third cup of coffee at a back table when Hank Matheson walked in.

He helped his niece with her crutches and walked to hang up his hat on the rack by the door when he was mobbed.

Martha Q giggled into her cup as every woman in the place hurried to kiss him. Some shyly on the cheek, some boldly on the lips. Hank seemed too shocked to react.

Tyler Wright came in and stood between Hank and the women long enough for Hank to take a seat, but that didn't stop the women from leaning over to kiss him as they passed his table.

Martha wasn't close enough to hear what was being said, but from Hank's face it was obvious he hadn't seen a poster yet. Tyler Wright, the funeral director, couldn't seem to stop laughing.

The sheriff stormed in a minute later and plopped one of the flyers down in front of the much-kissed Hank. Martha Q didn't have to hear a word; she could tell from Alexandra McAllen's face who the love of Hank's life was, and that lover wasn't happy. Jealousy fired her eyes so hot Martha Q thought it could easily burn the toast in the entire diner. Maybe Alex would get the hint and marry that handsome man.

"You want more coffee?" Edith asked as she passed by with a pot in each hand.

"No, thanks," Martha Q said. "Have any idea what's going on?"

"Not much. Someone said there are signs all over town saying this is National Kiss Your Fireman Day. No one seems to have ever heard of it before, but that don't stop the women of this town from doing their duty. I got Willie Davis in the kitchen. He's been a fireman for a few years, but he's afraid to come out. He said he got mobbed when he went out this morning to post the flag at the station and he's in danger of being overkissed."

Martha Q smiled and collected her belongings, left a ten-dollar tip, and walked out of the diner without even glancing at Hank.

She stopped to admire one of her signs outside the grocery store after stocking up on her weekly intake of chocolate and diet meals. When she pulled into the drive at the bed-and-breakfast, Tyler Wright was waiting for her.

"Am I dead?" she asked, thinking of all the times the kind middle-aged man had helped her bury first her parents, then three of her husbands.

He smiled, that polite smile that hinted he might have heard the question a few thousand times before. "No, Miss Martha Q, you look very much alive to me."

"Well, if I'm not dead, you must have come to call, and I'd better tell you, Tyler Wright, I'm too old for you and even if I was willing to take a chance on you, I wouldn't. You see, I kind of like being a widow. It's easier to spell than *divorcée* and I don't have to share the bathroom or the remote with anyone."

His grin was real. "I'm here to ask a favor. I'd never come to call, Miss Martha, 'cause you and I both know I'd never have a chance."

She took the compliment with a nod and said, "Name your favor. I'll help any way I can."

An hour later Stella McNabb brought a rail-thin woman to Martha's door. Tyler had told Martha all about Mrs. Biggs. When she'd helped out in the small kitchen at the funeral home, she'd been unbelievable. Stella had brought a roast for the six family members who were supposed to attend the funeral. When they counted close to thirty at the funeral, Stella fretted and Mrs. Biggs went to work. She cut up the roast, threw in vegetables, and made the best stew even Stella McNabb, a retired homemaking teacher, had ever tasted. While the family went to the graveside service, Mrs. Biggs made cornbread and chocolate pies. Tyler and Stella decided right then that the woman would be perfect to work at Winter's Inn Bed-and-Breakfast.

Martha Q lived by a grab-bag set of rules for life, some legal, some not, but one she always favored was never to take advantage of a man or woman while they were down. She wouldn't do so now.

"Mrs. Biggs," she began. "I'm honored that you'd consider staying with me."

The woman, maybe ten years older than her, offered a hand that seemed only bone and skin. "Mr. Wright tells me you're in need of a cook for the breakfast part of this bed-and-breakfast."

"I am," Martha Q lied. "When the crowd hits this place I know I couldn't do it all. I have two girls who come in to clean once a week, but there's still a hundred things to do. If you'll do the breakfast cooking every morning, I'll provide you the bed part and we'll call it even."

Mrs. Biggs nodded once. "Sounds more than fair."

"Good. I'll get you settled in, then show you the kitchen. You can start tomorrow practicing on recipes until the crowd comes." Martha walked her through to the room nearest the kitchen. "I'm looking for something special folks will remember having for breakfast. Something that will bring them back to Winter's Inn."

Mrs. Biggs set her suitcase down on a stand in a cozy room with a small seating area tucked away inside a big bay window.

The fat cat looked up at the two ladies as if they were trying to sublet his room.

"Hope you don't mind a cat. I call him Mr. Dolittle, but I should have named him Mr. Do-nothing. He thinks he owns the place."

Mrs. Biggs's smile didn't reach her sad eyes. "We'll get along fine as long as he stays off the kitchen counters."

Martha Q laughed. "He wouldn't make the effort to jump that high. Mr. Dolittle doesn't even chase mice, much less that varmint out back that keeps getting into my trash. I don't know what it is, but it's big and I'm about to declare war."

When Mrs. Biggs told her the dog pound had cages for trapping animals, Martha Q took it on as a mission. While two girls cleaned the house, a yard man kept the lawn clear of leaves, and Mrs. Biggs took over the kitchen, Martha Q tried to stay out of trouble.

Martha Q had believed all her life that trouble found large-busted women easier than it did the A and B cups of the world. She'd been a B cup by the eighth grade. By the tenth grade she'd discovered boys and learned quickly what they liked.

Now with nothing to do at home, she feared trouble couldn't be far away. If she'd been a few years older, she might have tried the senior citizens' center. She had a feeling she could be engaged by dark in a place like that. If she were ten years younger, she'd head straight for Buffalo's Bar. Afternoon drinkers were always talky, often lonely, and either rich or unemployed. But the last time she'd wandered into a bar, some kid wanted to buy her a drink because she reminded him of his mother. Martha Q slapped him and walked out, deciding her drinking days were over.

Martha Q drove out to the pound and picked up the biggest cage they had, then drove the town square looking for trouble.

All she found was a sign in the used bookstore saying, SPECIAL ON PALM READINGS TODAY . . . TWO HANDS FOR THE PRICE OF ONE.

Martha Q drove past and circled back home. She asked the yard man to unload the cage. He was one of those disagreeable men who always looked like he was about to break into a swearing contest with God.

As always, when she told him what to do, he complained and said it wasn't part of his job. Then she'd say maybe he didn't want to get paid and he'd give her one of his *Drop dead, lady* looks and do the job.

Martha Q knew a great many people who disliked her, a few who hated her, but Lloyd Franklin, the yard man, was the only one who looked like he might be willing to murder her for a tip.

She'd fire him, but then she'd have to go to the trouble of finding another, who would hate her in no time and she'd be right back where she was now. So, she watched Lloyd carry the cage to the backyard, put it next to the tool and garden shed, and walk away without even glancing back.

Climbing the stairs, she decided to take a nap. Worrying about the yard man killing her had worn her out.

How much trouble could she get into by staying an extra hour in bed? She giggled, refusing to answer her own question. Husband number four hadn't liked her habit of napping at all. He complained once too often about supper being late, and she gave up napping and him at the same time.

The third morning Mrs. Biggs made what Martha Q had been searching for . . . the perfect breakfast. Walnut-apple pancakes layered with a thin caramel middle that recreated heaven with the first bite. Perfection was served next to fresh bananas and strawberries brushed with cinnamon honey.

Martha Q was so pleased she invited Tyler Wright and her lawyer to breakfast the next morning, and they agreed she'd found heaven on a plate. The next day Tyler invited his friend Hank Matheson and he brought along his love, Sheriff Alexandra McAllen. When Liz found out her brother was having breakfast at the Winter's Inn, she asked if she could come too, and the table was suddenly full.

Martha Q had never had so many friends at her meal. She fussed over them all while Mrs. Biggs insisted on staying in the kitchen so she could be cleaned up and ready to go to the cemetery by nine.

A week later bookings began to come in. State inspectors that Alex had recommended staying at the B&B. A visiting fireman from Oklahoma giving a program for the fire department. Relatives staying over after a funeral for the reading of the will.

Between guests, Mrs. Biggs continued trying new dishes, and Martha Q soon found even her jogging suits were growing tighter. She decided to walk after she checked the trap every morning, but the street would never do. Too many people would see her without her makeup.

So Martha Q had the yard man build her steps down into the dried-up creek bed behind her house. She could walk there, out of the wind and alone.

While she walked, she thought of how good it felt to help people and decided she was getting so good at it, she should teach a class.

Chapter 13

THURSDAY
JANUARY 31, 2008
WRIGHT FUNERAL HOME

The sun decided to come out here today. Hope it did wherever you are. I remember two years ago when we used to e-mail over our dinner every night that you said you liked sunny days.

Since that spring and all the grass fires, folks in town figured out how much I like old maps. I'm not sure how the word got out, but now every time someone finds an old map in their attic, they bring it to me. I thank them all, but most are worthless. A few are very interesting. I got one the other day that was hand drawn in the time before there were many settlers here. It was drawn on the back of a receipt for a hundred head of sheep to be delivered to an early ranch. Some of the ranchers would be surprised to learn that sheep were here long before cattle.

Oh, I almost forgot, Martha Q, the widow who runs Winter's Inn caught a little border collie in a trap today. She couldn't stand the thought of turning it in at the animal shelter, so she asked me to find it a home. The dog is half starved, but I think must have been someone's special pet once upon a time. She's really quite polite. She's sleeping on a throw in the corner of my study right now. I'll find her a home tomorrow.

Well, my Kate, I've probably bored you enough for tonight. I wish I could write exciting letters, but truth is I'm just a regular man who spends most of his time working.

Tomorrow it'll be February. The time when we have our worst weather some years. I planted a magnolia out at the cemetery just because you said you loved them. It's sheltered from the wind and wrapped for winter, but I don't know if it'll be alive come spring. Hope so. As it grows I'll think of you.

Until tomorrow,
Ty

TYLER CLICKED SEND AND WONDERED IF HE SHOULD TRY to find Major Katherine Cummings. He knew she worked for the government and she traveled all over. She'd even come to Harmony during the grass fires.

If he asked Alex, she could probably find Kate. He could hire a private eye or check into one of those websites that claims to be able to find anyone.

But he wanted *her* to contact *him*. She'd been the one to walk away. She was the one who never showed up where they'd agreed to meet if either stopped e-mailing. He remembered what she'd written one night, because they hadn't exchanged names or locations. She'd said that if anything happened and they lost contact, both of them should go where they'd met one stormy night. Quartz Mountain Lodge. The first Monday of the month. She'd even added, *Order me a glass of wine because I'll be there.*

Monday he'd make the drive to southwest Oklahoma one more time and wait again.

He couldn't search her down. He wanted her to come back . . . to him.

Chapter 14

Gabe stood between the storm drain and the window of the county sheriff's offices. The moonless night made him invisible in the shadows of the building. He listened, picking up information as always. Only tonight, for the first time he wasn't collecting information for a story he might write . . . this time it was personal.

Three homes and one apartment had been broken into this week. All four were occupied by Smiths. What he'd dreaded for five years seemed to be happening. Someone was looking for him, and they weren't wasting time being discreet about the hunt. They were breaking in fast, tracking mud through the place, and leaving without taking anything.

He took little comfort that whoever was searching didn't know his real name. If his office somehow was on their list, they'd find nothing to connect G. L. Smith to Gabe Leary and the farm. Gabe had been very careful never to mix his pen name with his real life. He didn't even bring envelopes home with the Smith address on them, and he paid for the office in cash.

Reason made him take a deep breath. Maybe he was wrong. Even if someone was searching for him under his pen name, the odds were they knew of no connection between him and the sergeant named Gabriel Wiseman who walked away from an army hospital one night five years ago and disappeared. They couldn't have tracked him. No one in the army knew his real name was Leary, or that he'd called his dad to come pick him up that night. Once he got home, he'd picked Smith to use on all business deals simply because it was so common. He'd had three names in his life . . . three lives . . . and he'd kept them all separate.

Five years ago flashed in his thoughts. He'd been near death when he'd heard two men talking beside his bed.

One said, "Any chance Wiseman will recover?"

"He might." The other's voice had the hint of a New York accent. "A nurse at the desk said if he makes it through the next few days, he'll have a chance. She also said the guy has no family. Lucky for us, he came from a long line of generals who go all the way back to dying in the Revolutionary War and he's the last of the clan. They said the only name he listed to be notified of his death was Uncle Sam."

"Good, that'll make it easier. Less questions. No visitors. No one asking for an autopsy. But I say we wait a couple of days. No sense silencing him if nature will do our job for us."

"I guess you're right," the New Yorker said. "We come back in three days, late at night. You distract the nurse with questions and I'll slip in and make sure Sergeant Wiseman takes his last breath. There's only one way to make sure he tells no one about what he saw a moment before that bomb went off."

"What if he didn't see anything?"

"We can't take that chance. Plain and simple. The last Wiseman has to die, one way or the other."

Gabe's mind had been so fuzzy from the drugs he could barely think. It took him two days to focus enough to use the phone by his bed. He'd asked the nurse the date so often she'd thought he was out of his head, but every time his mind had cleared, he'd been counting down the hours and planning.

He remembered being surprised when his dad took the collect call. Then even more surprised when his father agreed to drive for hours down to San Antonio to pick him up.

The old man never asked a single question when he followed Gabe's instructions into the back of the hospital; he just listened to Gabe's directions, wheeled his son to the car, and drove home.

Gabe was so tired by the time they got to the farm he barely noticed the ramp Jeremiah Truman had built on the porch or the braces he'd hammered to the bed so he could pull himself up. All Gabe remembered was swearing beneath his breath that he was home, then closing his eyes and realizing he was safe.

In the following weeks, what tortured Gabe more than the recovery without painkillers to take the edge off was the fact that two men planned to kill him and he didn't know why. He'd seen nothing before the bomb went off.

That night, leaving the hospital, he abandoned the name Gabe Wiseman and stepped back into the life he'd left ten years before. In Harmony he was Gabe Leary, but when he recovered enough to work as a graphic novelist, he took on the name G. L. Smith. He never had the feeling that he was somehow more than one person. Mostly, he felt he was no one inside, and the names were of little more importance than the clothes he wore. Leary had been a frightened kid, Wiseman a soldier, and Smith a writer. None reflected him.

Logic told him there was no way the two angels of death could find him as Smith or Leary. The only record of Smith was a lease on an office where he picked up his mail, and he used the drop-off office only for mail related to his work.

He moved from shadow to shadow, working his way to the far side of the town square. The bookstore lights were still on. A hand-lettered sign read: Special Friday Night Coffee and Readings. The dry cleaners shop was dark and closed up tight.

Circling, he noticed Elizabeth's car and took the back stairs.

Her office light shone beneath her door. He tapped.

It seemed to take her a while, but she finally opened the door.

He stepped inside. "Don't open your office door after hours. It's not safe."

"Okay," she replied evenly, though he swore he saw anger spark in her eyes. "Step out and knock and I'll take your advice."

He couldn't hide the smile. "All right. I'll amend that comment. Don't open the door to anyone but me."

"But how will I know it's you?"

He looked at the door. "I'll put a peephole in tomorrow, and a bolt if you like."

She relaxed. "I'd like that very much. I have this worry that Mr. Kaufman will just unlock the door and come in one night. If he caught me sleeping here, he'd probably charge me double."

Gabe looked in at the papers on her desk. "I didn't mean to interrupt you working. I just wanted to tell you to watch out. I'm worried that my office might be broken into."

"I thought of that too when Alex told me about the Smith break-ins around town. The sheriff's department can't see any logic to it. The thieves don't even take anything of value. They seem to be looking for something, but whatever it is, they're not finding it."

Gabe followed her into her office and took the chair across the desk from her. "You've heard the details."

Elizabeth smiled. "Everyone's heard. This is Harmony, the only town that will never need a local radio station." She stared at him. "But I wouldn't worry, Mr. Smith. No one will have to knock your door down. It's unlocked and there is nothing to steal except a box."

She was speaking calmly, too calmly. Something was wrong.

"What else have you heard?"

"Nothing," she answered. "It's what I know, Mr. Smith."

"Stop calling me Mr. Smith."

"Why, because that is not your name?" She smiled, but he wasn't sure he liked her smile any better than he did the know-it-all attitude.

Standing, she circled the desk. "I've done some searching. You rented this place about four years ago. Pay in cash a year in advance. There is no G. L. Smith living in this county and never has been. No car registration. No library card. No voter signed in on the county books."

As she moved toward him, he saw the lawyer in her, but he had no intention of playing the witness on the stand. He simply watched her.

She paced half the room, pointed at him, then paced the other half. "You're lying, Mr. Smith, admit it."

He smiled slowly. "Is that your question for the night, Elizabeth?"

She blinked and would have stepped back, but he caught the hand that was pointing at him and pulled her toward him.

"I'm lying. My name's not Mr. Smith. It's just a name I use for a mail drop." Before she could ask another question, he pulled her onto his knee and closed his mouth over hers.

For a moment she was stiff in his arms almost as if she were trying to decide whether to fight and make him let her go, or surrender. He loosened his grip, silently telling her he wouldn't hold her if she wanted to leave.

The slight gesture seemed to be all she needed to make up her mind. She circled her arms about his neck and kissed him back.

Gabe had known a few girls over the years. Most he dated casually until they asked one too many questions or wanted more than he could give. He'd slept with a few one-night stands, but the next morning always made him feel more empty than if he'd never met them. But Elizabeth was different. He doubted he'd ever get tired of the taste of her, the feel of her.

When he walked away from her, he had a feeling he'd ache for her forever. Nothing had ever felt so right.

She made a little sound of pleasure as he ended the kiss and moved to her throat for one more taste of her skin. Her skin was cream as he slid his tongue over her delicate collarbone, then lightly bit down at the side of her throat.

He swore he heard her purr as his hand brushed along her rib cage a moment before he pulled away.

"I have to go," he whispered an inch away from her throat. He wasn't touching her, but he knew she could feel his warm breath against her damp skin. "I'll be back tomorrow night to install the peephole and the bolt."

Like a pouty child, she climbed off his lap and went to the door. "I wasn't finished," she said.

"I know." He smiled, knowing she'd probably gotten everything she wanted, when she wanted it, since she was born. "Tomorrow night we'll start with the kiss and save the question for last."

"Maybe." She crossed her arms. "If I open the door. I don't like being lied to."

"I didn't lie to you, Elizabeth. I just didn't correct you when you called me Mr. Smith." He met her gaze. "I'm not very good at talking about myself."

She smiled. "No kidding, but I see things when I look in your eyes sometimes."

He raised an eyebrow.

Laughing, she added, "I don't know how to explain it. I think I see an honesty about you that frightens and intrigues me."

Pulling her against him, he kissed her again, deep and long. This time his arms held her close and his hands were bolder, feeling the curves of her. He wanted to tell her that this wasn't just a game they played, but he guessed she knew it even if they both realized it was too early to say the words.

When he finally pulled away he whispered, "I owe you a question. Now, lock the door behind me."

He stepped through and closed the door before she could answer, then waited until he heard the click of the lock before he headed down the back stairs.

Chapter 15

WEDNESDAY, 8:30 P.M.
FEBRUARY 6, 2008
BLUE MOON DINER

REAGAN STARED OUT AT THE EMPTY DINER. WHEN THE place was busy, packed with people eating and talking, she didn't notice how shabby the booths were or how the walls had faded to gray with no one to remember what color they'd once been.

"It's my birthday," she whispered to the vacant diner. "And no one knows."

Last year she hadn't mentioned it to Uncle Jeremiah. He'd done so much by giving her a home she couldn't just say, *Hey, it's my birthday, how about a gift?* Reagan could never remember really celebrating the day she was born. Her mother probably gave her away that day, and No

Name, her father on the birth certificate, was undoubtedly relieved he didn't have to pay child support.

Speaking of her birth certificate, she'd carried it with her from foster home to foster home and now she couldn't find it. After she moved in with Uncle Jeremiah, she'd no longer felt the need to look at it every so often to make sure she was alive. With him, she had a family, even if it was only one member.

"His old house is full of junk," she mumbled as she wiped the cabinet. Jeremiah saved everything. He'd probably put her folder, with all her papers, on a stack of mail. He wouldn't throw it away; he never threw anything away. At least she'd gotten him to put his bonds in a safe-deposit box. It was just a guess, but she figured if the house ever burned, he'd have enough to rebuild.

Until then, she'd make little changes. He complained, but he never said no to any of them.

Her phone sounded, making her jump. "Hello." She caught it on the second ring.

"When you coming home, girl?"

Reagan grinned. Her uncle rarely used the house phone she'd made him install, and he never bothered with *hello* or *good-bye*. "Ten minutes, tops. I just have to do one more thing, then I'm locking up."

"You drive careful. The radio says the roads are getting slick."

"I will."

He hung up without another word.

She picked up the takeout meal and headed to the back door. It was a little early, but she wanted to go home. No one but Gabriel would be stopping by on a night like this.

At the back door, she didn't see him, so she grabbed a flashlight in her free hand and walked across the back lot. Thinking more about it being her eighteenth birthday than about the cold, she trudged over frozen weeds to the trees that wound along the old creek bed. This part of town, where old houses and businesses curved along the memory of streams, always seemed odd. People and traffic moved on the streetlight side, unaware that just behind the buildings a wilderness waited.

A huge cottonwood branch swayed, crackling and showering tiny pieces of ice down on her.

Reagan jumped out of the way. Her left foot touched solid ground, but her right slid into the gully that had eroded its way between two trees.

Screaming, she tumbled backward.

The wind carried her cry through the frozen branches. More ice tinkled to the ground, muffling the sounds as she rolled over the hard earth until she finally landed among roots rigid as rocks.

Reagan lay still for a moment, feeling the cold, the uneven ground digging into her back, warm blood washing across her face. She tried to move, but all the world spun in protest. "Help me," she whispered. "Someone help me."

One arm was wedged behind her back. Her sweater must have caught on something because it pulled against her throat, choking away most of her air passage. One leg felt as if she'd skinned her knee and to her horror, she couldn't feel the other knee at all.

"Help," she whispered again. "Help."

When there was no answer, Reagan closed her eyes and drifted away from the pain.

Chapter 16

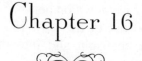

ALEX MCALLEN WORKED LATE IN HER OFFICE MOST Wednesdays, but tonight the rain turning to ice against her windows kept her nerves on edge.

The middle of the week was usually slow, and she could get to the paperwork that she never seemed to finish. Her being sheriff was more a calling than a job. If law enforcement had old-time revivals, she'd walked the aisle and given her life over to the badge. Some would say she decided on the career the night her brother, a highway patrolman, had been killed, but the job was already in her blood. His death only directed her to come home and run for sheriff.

Leaning back in her chair, she thought of Warren and how he'd been murdered while making a routine stop. No big gunfight, no war, just one shot, late one night on a lonely road and he was gone. She'd read over his files a hundred times, but couldn't find a way to solve the most important case in her life. Somewhere his killer was still out there, and Alex hoped she'd be lucky enough to face him one day. When she did, she prayed she wouldn't hesitate.

The killer had left two clues. Sometimes, she searched cases all across the country that fit the MO. But it had been five years . . . five long years. What were the chances he'd leave the same footprint at a crime scene, or that he smoked the same brand of cigarettes. The pack might not have been dropped by the man who shot Warren, or it might have been tossed from a passing car a day or two before the night her life changed forever with Warren's death.

"Sheriff?" The night dispatcher drew her out of her thoughts.

"Yes, Jess, what's up?"

Jess wouldn't overreact to alien attacks, but for once, he did look worried. "We got a call from Jeremiah Truman out on Lone Oak Road. He said his niece should have been home a half hour ago." Jess hesitated. "The old guy threatened to come down and beat me to a pulp if we didn't get out there and find her."

"He's near ninety," Alex said, already pulling on her coat. "But if we don't locate her, I'd be worried if I were you. Did you get hold of Phil? He should be out that direction with radar tonight."

"He's working a fender bender, but he said he'll be driving the road from their place to the Blue Moon, where she was when Truman talked to her. She's just a kid. She probably stopped off on her way home at some friend's house. I tried to tell the old guy not to worry, but he hung up on me."

Alex nodded, letting Jess know that he'd done right, but that didn't stop her from fighting down panic. She knew Reagan. She wasn't the type to stop off somewhere. The girl was as protective of the old man as he was of her. "I'll start at the diner and work my way toward Truman. Tell Phil to keep his eyes open for tracks. The Truman girl tends to drive fast, and her old pickup could be broken down or might have slid off the road somewhere. Tell him to work his way toward me as soon as he can."

She shoved her Colt in its holster and snapped the guard. "Call Hank too. He lives on the next ranch. Ask him to go over to Truman's place. If she's hurt, I don't want the old man driving anywhere on these icy roads."

"Got it," Jess said as he headed back to his desk. She thought she heard him add, "Who is this kid, the town princess or something?"

Pretty close, Alex thought as she ran out of the office. For more than a hundred years, three families had run this little spot on the map. A hundred years of three families working together, arguing, helping each other. Reagan was the last of the Truman line, and in this place that pretty nearly made her the town princess even if no one had ever thought about it.

Alex's cruiser was covered in ice. She should have parked it under the carport when she returned from lunch. For a second, she thought of taking her Jeep, but the ice would be thicker on it than on the city's car.

She swore at the time she wasted cleaning the windshield and waiting for the heater to warm. By the time she climbed in and backed out, she couldn't feel the tips of her fingers thanks to the cold, but she couldn't afford the time it would take her to run back inside for gloves.

Five minutes later, she pulled up in front of the diner and saw Truman's old pickup, which the girl usually drove, parked to the side, out of the storm.

Alex hit her radio. "Jess," she said when he answered. "Tell Phil to meet me at the diner. The girl's still here."

"He's on his way. Just talked to him. Called in to say Lone Oak Road was clear."

Call it instinct or maybe it was just knowing the patterns of the folks in her town, but something didn't feel right. If trouble had a smell, it was in the air as Alex jumped out of her car without turning off the engine and ran for the diner entrance.

The door was unlocked. The lights still on. Alex moved inside very slowly, taking in every detail around her. Halfway through the café, she spotted a backpack on the counter near the phone.

"Reagan?" she said trying to keep her voice calm. "Reagan, are you in here?"

No answer.

She reached the swinging door to the kitchen and pushed it open with one hand while the other rested on the butt of her weapon.

The kitchen was bright and looked clean and shut down for the night, but almost as cold as the outside.

Alex let out a breath and stepped farther in, passing a workstation in the center of the area. Pots and spatulas were lined up in wait for the morning breakfast run.

Cold air blew in from an open back door. Alex tensed at the sight of mud and blood streaking from the door to . . .

For a second, Alex didn't see the whole scene, but only pieces that didn't make sense. An old work coat tossed on the floor. White towels stained in blood scattered like Kleenex across the tile. A girl's snow boot lying on its side, muddy and abandoned. Blood pooling around her head just as it had around Alex's brother's on a back road five years ago.

She forced the past aside and stared.

Then she saw it all. A man, bearded and spotted in blood, leaning over Reagan. Her red hair flying around her face covered in blood. Her body lifeless on worn tile.

Alex reacted. "Freeze!" she ordered as she pulled her gun and held it before her with both hands. "Step away from her."

The man raised his head. He looked slightly familiar, like someone she'd once known, but his eyes were hard, icy blue. Killer eyes, she thought.

"Step away from her or I'll fire," she said as she heard someone enter behind her.

"Then shoot," he barked. "Because I'm not letting go."

Her cold finger tightened on the trigger as her eyes saw the palm of his dirty hand pressed against a towel at Reagan's temple. She couldn't tell if the man was helping or hurting the girl.

"Phil!" Alex yelled.

"Yes, Sheriff." The door swung. "I'm here."

Alex kept her gun pointed at the stranger beside Reagan. "Call in an ambulance." She tried to think of what to do as the deputy made the call. If this stranger was holding a pressure point, keeping blood from flowing, she couldn't ask him to step away. If she moved closer and he'd done this to the girl, he might try to overpower her.

He looked little better than homeless, but young and maybe strong enough to fight her for the gun. If he won, they could all be dead in seconds. She knew the drill was to ask if he had a weapon but he didn't look like he'd hand over his ID and a gun right now even if he had one.

"What happened here?" She barked the question.

"I don't know." The stranger didn't look up. He didn't look afraid either, which frightened Alex even more than if he had a weapon. "I found her like this down in the creek bed."

"Who are you and what are you doing here?"

"I'm no one. Just get the ambulance here."

Alex took a step closer but didn't lower her gun. "Did you drag her in here?"

"I tried to carry her, but my leg wouldn't take the weight," he said, only half listening to Alex. "I think her leg's broke. She's lost a lot of blood."

Alex heard the medics banging their way through the front door and Phil yelling at them to hurry. She kept her gun on the stranger as they moved around her toward Reagan.

The stranger slowly stood and let them take over. Without even glancing in Alex's direction, he headed toward the back door.

"Wait," she shouted. "You need to come with us and answer a few questions."

He didn't stop. Just kept walking as if he had no fear of death.

The medics lifted Reagan onto the stretcher and started moving out. Phil rushed ahead, holding the door.

"Stop!" Alex yelled at the stranger almost to the back door. "Stop or I'll shoot."

He hesitated as if debating whether he cared if he lived or died, then faced her, his cold eyes showing just how much he wanted to run. He raised his hands, more in frustration than defeat.

"Tell me what happened here."

"I already told you. I don't know," he answered.

"Got any ID on you?"

"No," he said still staring at her.

Alex pulled the cuffs from her belt. "Then like it or not, you're coming with us until we get this straightened out."

Phil was back. He stepped behind the guy and cuffed him. "Is he under arrest, Sheriff? Should I read him his rights?"

"Not yet. Just hold him until I can see how badly Reagan is hurt."

Phil pulled the lean man a few feet, and Alex noticed the limp. He hadn't been lying about his leg.

"If you hurt this girl . . ."

"I didn't." He almost spit the words.

She waved Phil on. To the stranger's back, she added, "I'll have questions for you later."

He glanced back, telling her he didn't plan to offer any answers.

She locked the back door, then turned out the lights and locked the front. If this was a crime scene, and it sure did look like one, it would be safe enough for a few hours. Her first concern was Reagan Truman.

She hit speed dial to Hank.

"Evening, darling," he answered on the first ring. "I'm at Truman's place."

Alex gripped the phone tighter, wishing Hank were with her. "Can you drive him over to the hospital?"

"Sure." His voice cracked with concern. "What's wrong?"

"I'm not sure." Alex said the only thing she could think of. "She may have a broken leg. We'll know more when the doctor sees her."

"We're on our way."

Alex's hand shook as she closed the phone.

Chapter 17

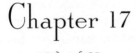

WEDNESDAY NIGHT
FEBRUARY 6, 2008
MATHESON RANCH

LIZ MATHESON FINALLY BROKE DOWN AND WENT TO DIN-
ner at the family ranch. When she drove up, she caught herself wishing for the thousandth time that the place looked
like an antebellum home out of the Old South and not the
rambling southwest look of an old mission.

The main body of the house was two stories, with
room enough in the roof line for an attic where her sister
painted. Her great-aunts' suite of rooms shot off to the left,
surrounded by gardens now gray and bony with winter.
Hank's quarters had been built over the three-car garage.
He also claimed the huge office downstairs in the main
house. It had an outside entrance complete with porch so
any of the hands could ride in and visit with Hank without

ringing the main doorbell. Her mother's studio—built in
the old mission style, charming as a painting—sat a dozen
yards away from the house. Mom had been a potter all
Liz's life. Some said she was the best in the Southwest, but
her mother rarely talked about her work. Her pots might be
perfect, but her children always needed advice.

Liz frowned as she pulled to the end of the circle drive
out front. Frankenstein must have been the architect of
this place. No one but company used the front drive. The
family never opened the front door except to put a wreath
up at Christmas. Maybe her family would get the hint and
not ask when she planned to come to her senses and move
back in if she stepped into the house through the company
entrance.

Her mother, Joyce, had gone all out for dinner. Her
aunts actually made two Jell-O dishes, and her six-year-old
niece claimed to have baked cookies. They dined in true
southern style, late.

Hank joined them for the first course, then got a call
on his cell and excused himself. He was often called out
to put out a kitchen fire or cover one of the other volunteer
firemen's shifts at the station. The women in the house long
ago gave up asking him questions, but Liz felt his absence
the minute the door closed.

Hank was the only one in the Matheson clan who didn't
try to mother her constantly. Maybe it was because he had
so many women to worry about.

Claire, her older sister, came down from her studio in
the attic, filled her plate after everyone had finished the
main course, and entertained them with all her plans of a
gallery opening in Dallas. Her paintings were catching on,
it seemed, and making loads of money, or would be any
day, Claire said more than once.

Liz didn't miss the fact that she never mentioned moving out. Claire wouldn't. If she took her daughter, Saralynn,
somewhere else, she'd have to have almost round-the-clock

babysitters. As it was, the whole family pitched in to make sure Saralynn got to school and to the doctor, and to therapy. Rarely, when Joyce had to go to Dallas on pottery business, she hired a young nurse to babysit Saralynn. All the other Mathesons could have taken care of her fine, but Joyce overprotected her only grandchild while she encouraged her oldest daughter to push harder with her art.

Claire claimed she had an artist's soul and everyone knows souls don't wear wristwatches. All the others seemed to agree, because no one, not even their mother, asked Claire to keep up with a time schedule.

During a break in Claire's stories of success, the aunts cleared the table and Liz leaned near Saralynn and whispered, "How you doing, kid?"

The little girl smiled. "Fine."

Liz winked at her. A few years ago they'd had to evacuate the ranch because of a grass fire. Claire had run past Liz in the hallway and told her to take Saralynn in her car, because she needed all the van room for paintings. Saralynn hadn't shown back up in the garage, so Liz thought she'd caught a ride with one of the others. The little four-year-old on crutches had been left alone. Luckily, the fire didn't reach the house, but they all blamed Liz.

Everyone except Saralynn. She'd even held Liz's hand while everyone else in the family took turns yelling at her.

Liz leaned near the frail little angel again. "I love you, kid."

"I love you too," Saralynn whispered. "I miss you reading to me."

"How about I read to you tonight before I go back to town?"

Liz's mother heard the last bit. "There's no need for you to go back to town on a night like this. You might as well sleep in your own room."

Liz felt an imaginary fishhook catch in her skin at her mother's attempt to reel her in.

"You're not dating anyone, are you? No one's waiting up for you?" Claire asked with a giggle. "I know it's been three years since the divorce, but if you're like me even the thought of going out with someone gives me the shakes. Of course, I'm a divorced woman with a child . . . not exactly the top of the dating pool, but I still can't think of one man in Harmony that would be worth putting on makeup for, much less spending hours on a date trying to talk to." She glanced at the corner of the room and when she looked back, Liz knew another painting had come into her mind. The prized piece of artwork would probably be called *Man Killed by Clock* or something like that. All Claire's paintings were of dead men.

Saralynn tugged on Liz's sleeve. "What pool?"

Liz looked confused, then answered, "It's not a real pool. It's like the gene pool. It's just something people say."

"What's a gene pool?"

Liz was saved from answering by her Aunt Pat, who stepped in from the kitchen. "Elizabeth," she said with eyebrows raised. "Some man from the county lockup is calling for you."

Liz jumped up, almost knocking her chair over. Surely Martha Q hadn't already gotten herself arrested and in need of a lawyer. Since she was Liz's only client, it had to be the round little legend of a woman. Who else would call?

"I'll take it in the living room," she said. Liz walked across the hall, picked up the phone, and waited for the click from the kitchen before speaking.

"Elizabeth Matheson," she said in her most professional voice.

"I need your help."

He hadn't said his name; he hadn't needed to. She'd know Gabriel's voice anywhere.

"Where are you?"

"County sheriff's office," he said. "They're about to take

me up to a holding cell. Ask for Gabe Leary, Elizabeth, not Smith, and get here as fast as you can."

She'd already figured out that Smith probably wasn't his real name. "What did you do?"

"Nothing," he answered. "But they think I may have killed someone."

Liz told herself she was a lawyer. Whether he did or didn't commit the crime, he had a right to counsel. Only she wasn't sure she could go through with it if he had. She wasn't sure which bothered her most: that he might be lying, or that if he was, she'd kissed a murderer.

She gripped the phone for a minute, trying to think.

"Elizabeth," he whispered again. "Are you still there? I'm no good around people. I seem to be causing more trouble for myself than helping." He was quiet as if listening to her breathe, and then he added, "I need you."

She straightened. "I'll be right there."

She hung up and walked back into the dining room, where everyone was having dessert. "I have to go. I'm needed over at the jail."

"A client," Claire said. "Oh, how exciting. Little sister has a real client."

Liz grabbed her coat and purse. As she walked out the door, she yelled back, "No. A date."

Chapter 18

WEDNESDAY, 10:00 P.M.
FEBRUARY 6, 2008
HARMONY HOSPITAL

ALEX RUSHED TOWARD HANK STANDING BY THE EMERGENCY waiting room's long black windows. Adrenaline was still pumping through her blood. When she'd walked in and seen that man leaning over Reagan's body, she'd almost fired.

As she knew he would, Hank hugged her tight before he said a word.

"Where's the old man?" she whispered against his cheek, loving the feel of him.

"He's in the restroom throwing up, I think." Hank pulled away, but his arm remained around her waist with his thumb tucked into her service belt. "He's already taking it hard, and we don't know anything. If she's hurt bad, I'm not sure the old guy's heart can survive it."

"The doctor's with her now. We should know something soon." Alex held tightly to her man. For once, even in a public place, she didn't care who was watching. She needed to lean on him, draw strength from him.

"What happened? Did she slip on the ice?"

Alex shook her head. "We don't know. I have to talk to her as soon as she wakes. I have no idea what happened." Alex couldn't lie to her Hank. "She may have been attacked. When I got to her, there was a man standing over her. I don't know if he was helping or hurting her."

Before he could ask questions, she hurried on. "I don't know anything else. Nothing."

"What's your gut feeling?" Hank asked.

"That he was helping her," she admitted. "But he was in one big hurry to get away, which makes me wonder."

As always, Hank seemed to read her thoughts. "Then we tell the old man that she may have fallen. Once he sees her, knows she's all right, then he can take the possibility of her being attacked."

"I agree."

She looked up and saw Old Man Truman moving slowly toward her. He was trying his best to walk tall and straight as a soldier, but age had twisted his body and stiffened joints that no longer allowed movement. His eyes were puffy and gray as fog. They seemed to have a hundred years of sadness floating in their depths. He seemed a man who had cared for very few people in his life and feared he might lose the last one now.

"Where is she?" he said when he reached them. "I told her to be careful, that it was icy. . . ." He trailed off, realizing it no longer mattered what he'd told her.

"The doctor's with her. The medic told me it looked like she had a break just below the right knee and a cut on her forehead." Alex silently said she was sorry for lying. The cut was a gash and the break probably in more than one place.

Truman raised his head. "She's strong. A broken leg and a cut won't slow her down much." He nodded as if convincing himself. "We Trumans can take our hits and survive."

"There's nothing to do now but wait." Alex took his arm, and they moved to the waiting area.

Hank offered them both coffee. While he went to get it, Alex sat beside Truman. She couldn't help but wonder if the man had ever cared about anyone the way he cared about this niece who showed up on his doorstep two years ago. His parents had died young, his sister never spoke to him, he never married or had children. Reagan seemed to be all his family rolled into one person.

They sat waiting, drinking coffee, and listening to the ticking of a clock on the wall. No one wanted to talk.

Finally, the doctor came in and went straight to Truman. The old man stood to take the news.

"She's going to be fine." The doctor rushed on. "The cut on her head took eleven stitches. It'll leave a scar just at the hairline. We're waiting for the X-rays and the swelling to go down before setting the leg, and I'd like to run several tests to make sure there was no internal damage." He smiled at the old man. "She took quite a fall."

Alex echoed, "A fall?"

The doctor looked at her for the first time. "She's awake, but groggy from the painkillers. She told me she walked out back to deliver a takeout meal and accidentally tumbled down into the ravine. She said a man named Gabriel Leary found her." The doctor looked back at the old man. "If he hadn't, she could have bled to death."

"I want to see my niece." The old man was already moving to the door. No one stopped him. "After I do, I want to talk to Gabriel Leary, if I can find him, and tell him any debt he thinks he owes me was paid tonight."

Alex hurried beside Truman. "I know where he is. I'll take you there as soon as you check on Reagan." She knew the old man probably wasn't listening, but she added anyway, "I've got an apology to make also."

Jeremiah didn't slow, but he said, "That boy don't like talking to people."

"You're telling me," Alex added.

Chapter 19

WEDNESDAY, 10:45 P.M.
FEBRUARY 6, 2008
COUNTY SHERIFF'S OFFICE

GABE LEARY PACED THE HOLDING CELL THAT SMELLED LIKE old vomit, his leg aching with each step. He hated the weakness the bomb had left behind. From the time he'd joined the army, the day he'd turned eighteen, he'd thought of himself as a machine and kept that machine in top shape. He'd been a runner, loving long distances where he felt like he could run away from his past forever.

Tonight he hadn't even been strong enough to lift a girl and carry her inside. He'd lifted her, even made it up a few crumbling steps out of the creek bed, but his leg wouldn't take the load. In the end he'd pulled off his coat and made a sleigh for her. It hadn't worked well. The ground was bumpy and rough, tousling her and ripping the coat, but it had worked. He'd gotten her inside still breathing so he could see where she was injured.

Gabe moved to the cell window. It was barred and the thick glass layered with what looked like chicken wire. He couldn't see out, but in his mind, he could still see the blood. Blood rolling down her face from a wound. Blood darkening her jeans almost black from what had to be a compound fracture of her leg. Blood dripping from scrapes and cuts on her back where she'd encountered branches and rocks on her way down the incline to the bottom of the creek bed.

He rested his forehead against the cold glass. Somehow this was his fault. If he hadn't been so afraid of seeing people, she could have handed him the meal at the front door. If he'd walked over early like he usually did, she wouldn't have gone looking for him. If he'd been stronger, he could have moved her inside faster.

Closing his eyes, he remembered the night he'd been hurt. There'd been no warning earlier in the day. No hint of trouble. His team was on a routine guard assignment for a group of senators he'd never heard of. Their names weren't really important, only their safety. Just starting his third tour of duty, he thought he had his job down, nothing would surprise him. Only he'd been wrong.

One of the senators wanted to stop to take a picture. Gabriel said no. He had his orders. But the guy must have talked the driver of the car into stopping, so the entire patrol pulled to the side in a part of the city where he'd have preferred to speed through.

Gabe and two of his men got out, fully armed and on full alert. After that, everything happened at once. Gunfire from a roof above them. Men scrambling back to the vehicles. He remembered blocking the senator with his body as he lifted his weapon to return fire. Then a bomb exploded, and all he remembered was black pain.

Hours later he thought he must have awakened briefly as men loaded him on a plane.

"Easy, soldier," a medic yelled above the noise. "We're transferring you back to the States. You're stable, but we're going to keep you under for the trip."

"My men?" Gabe remembered whispering.

"I think they're all dead, pal. I heard you were the only one alive when help got there. Lucky, I guess."

Gabe fought back a scream. Max, Nathan, Jack, all gone. "Lucky, I guess," he whispered, thinking of how he'd been with most of them since the first day of special training. They'd grown from boys to men together. They'd molded into warriors together.

A week later he'd been in San Antonio when he heard two men plotting to kill him, the only survivor of the raid. The men standing in the shadows of his room somehow thought he'd seen or heard something he shouldn't have. If Gabe could have cleared the fog in his brain, he would have told them they were wrong.

The door to his cell clicked, drawing him back from the hell he now called his past.

Turning, he was surprised to see Elizabeth Matheson step in. She had on a pink ski jacket lined in white fake fur and looked far more like a Playboy bunny than a lawyer. Instead of a briefcase, she carried a purse big enough to hold a file folder and an entire desk set.

"Don't look so surprised to see me," she snapped. "I *am* your lawyer. You called me, remember?"

"I didn't think you'd come," he answered. "And even if you did, I didn't think they'd let you in here." He glanced around.

Elizabeth did the same. "Of course I'd come. That's what lawyers do. I've seen it in the movies."

"You don't know?"

"You're my first case." She set her purse down on the

steel table. "Don't look so strange; someone has to be my first case. You just happen to be the lucky one."

"Great." He looked back at the window. It had been raining bad luck most of his life, and it looked like the clouds wouldn't pass anytime soon.

She didn't seem to notice he'd stepped out of the conversation even if he was still in the room. She walked around the cell telling him how bad it smelled and how they really needed to paint the place and how if she were him she wouldn't sit on anything in the room. When she circled around to him and complained that he could play the Mud Man in a horror flick, she finally got his attention.

"Aren't you supposed to ask me questions or something? Don't you want to know what happened tonight?"

Elizabeth shrugged. "I already know what happened. My brother called me from the hospital to tell me Reagan explained everything. It appears, Gabriel *Leary*, you're a hero."

"I learned a long time ago that there are no heroes, only survivors."

"The doc said you may have saved Reagan's life. He said if the gash on her forehead had gone untreated five more minutes, she might have died. If she'd been out in the cold much longer, wet and bleeding, she might have frozen to death. Like it or not, you saved her life."

"If I'm such a hero, why don't they let me out of here?"

"My brother said they're heading over now so Alex can apologize for almost blowing you away." She raised her hand and pulled a dirt clod from his hair, then made a face and tossed it in the corner. "What did you do, roll in the creek?"

"Something like that." Gabe frowned and pushed her hand away when she reached for another clod. "I don't want to talk to them. I just want out of here. You're my lawyer, get me out. Even a bunny should be able to do that for an innocent man." He fluffed the fake fur of her hood, still tucked around her face.

She crossed her arms just below her breasts and looked pouty . . . absolutely nothing like a lawyer should look. "I'm not a rabbit or a genie from a bottle. There's paperwork to fill out . . . probably . . . and who knows what else."

"Who knows?" he snapped. "Shouldn't you know?"

"Stop yelling at me," she yelled. "I'll figure this out." She moved to the door. "Jess." She tapped. "Can you take my client somewhere to clean up and cool off? If he gets any harder to talk to, I may have to clobber him with my purse."

Jess opened the unlocked door. "He can go anywhere he wants as long as he doesn't leave the building. Sheriff said she wanted a few words with him. They should have been here by now. I guess the blizzard slowed them down a bit."

"Blizzard?" Gabe asked.

"Yeah, it's coming down like crazy. You folks might want to stay here tonight. We got lots of empty cells."

"No thanks," Gabe and Elizabeth said at once.

Gabe pushed past them both and moved down the hallway to a restroom. He washed some of the blood off his hands and neck where Reagan had rested her head against his chest, but he could still smell it. A few hours ago, he'd walked over thinking he'd beat the snow back home, but now he was stranded without his coat, and his supper was probably spilled somewhere along the creek bed.

A few hours ago he'd only been thinking of walking through the cold and getting a meal. He'd worked hard all day and needed the fresh air to clear his mind and his thoughts of Elizabeth. He'd even noticed he'd penciled her image on one of the layouts for a graphic novel he was working on.

Gabe told himself he'd only see her once a week. One time, one kiss if she'd allow it. That was all he could hope for. But deep down he knew he'd circle by the office every time he walked into town. Not to check his mail, but to see if her lights were on. He liked to stand in the shadows of the courthouse and watch her turn off the lights in her office. Even with her drapes closed, he could see a few tiny pinpoints of light from her nightlight. He knew she was in there, sleeping. He knew she was safe.

Most nights it was enough just to know she was there.

Gabe ran his fingers through his hair, shaking away dried mud. He stared at himself in the restroom mirror. Little of the soldier he'd been five years ago looked back at him now. He'd loved being Gabe Wiseman. He'd traded names with the real Wiseman one night in boot camp. Wiseman was sneaking out, planning to get high. The guy was so messed up on drugs, he had trouble remembering he was in the army. The two Gabriels looked so much alike people were always getting them mixed up, so Wiseman thought it would be fun to wear Leary's uniform on his outings just in case he was caught. He'd said simply, "I'm from a long line of dead heroes. If I got busted, it'd make the papers, but with you, Leary, no one would care."

Gabe hadn't liked the idea, but Wiseman offered the use of his car as a bribe and swore he'd never be caught. At eighteen, the car seemed worth the risk.

Only Wiseman didn't get busted. He got dead three nights before they were to graduate and ship out. The next morning when the drill sergeant woke Gabe up, he kept calling him Private Wiseman. Gabe buried his past in the coffin with his uniform and picked up his new name along with the advantages that came with it. He'd been young and dreamed of being a hero. Switching names gave him the chance.

Doors began to open for him. He was now the son, the grandson, the great-grandson of warriors, not like Gabe Leary, the son of a worthless, lazy drunk who farmed just enough to pay the bills and buy more booze.

So Gabe kept the name and his mouth closed. No one

noticed. The day after he buried his friend, he climbed on a plane and flew to one of the best training camps in the country, a program Wiseman's name had gotten him into. The only thing in his pack from his past were a dozen comic books and a sketchpad. At the time he thought he'd said good-bye to the name Leary forever, but one bomb blew him all the way back home.

Gabe squared his shoulders. Because of what had happened tonight, he was about to have to talk to people. People who would judge him as a Leary. They'd know nothing of the soldier he'd been, the hero. In this small town, he'd never be anything but the son of a drunk.

He walked out of the restroom and down the hallway to a large room full of desks.

Elizabeth handed him a cup of coffee. "Jess says we can wait in Alex's office. By the way, how'd you know where to find me?"

"Jess told me I might want to call my lawyer. When I said I didn't have your number on me, he told me you were out at the ranch. Apparently, he'd already called there looking for Hank and had a visit with one of the aunts."

She laughed. "That's a small town for you. How'd you stay out of the loop for so long?"

He hesitated. He'd spent five years avoiding the people of Harmony. Dreading how they'd treat him. "Just lucky, I guess," he lied. "Do we have to wait? I'd just as soon go."

Elizabeth seemed to understand. "It's all right. I'm here with you."

"As my lawyer?"

"As your friend." She hesitated, then added, "But that doesn't mean I'm not going to charge you for the consultation before they released you."

"What consultation? The only advice I remember was on redecorating the holding cell."

"I know," she admitted. "But I thought about your problem all the way into town. That should count. I'll bill you fifty dollars for the half hour I spent scraping off my car and getting here."

Gabe glared at her. "Lucky you didn't stop to change clothes or I'd owe double."

He followed her into the sheriff's office and sat down at a round table by a long row of windows. Gabe could see snow coming down hard. "I walked in tonight," he said more to himself than her. "Know of a place where I can rent a room tonight and maybe get a meal? Someplace quiet with a shower and a bed. I don't like being around people."

"I figured that out already. I'm surprised you didn't take off out the back door a few minutes ago."

"I thought about it," he admitted.

"Why didn't you?"

"No coat. Snowing. You." Smiling, he added, "Not necessarily in that order."

She pulled out her cell and dialed a number. "You got money?" she asked as she waited.

"I got money," he answered.

She looked away. Someone on the other end must have picked up. "Martha Q," she said into the phone. "Can you put someone up for the night? It's an emergency."

She listened for a minute and then added, "I'll bring him over in a while. I'm glad I didn't wake you."

As he watched Elizabeth click her phone closed, the silence of the room ended. Three people hurried into the office—Alexandra McAllen, the sheriff he'd heard a hundred times from his place outside her window and met once with a gun between them; Hank Matheson, Harmony's fire chief; and an old man who had to be Jeremiah Truman.

Gabe stood and managed a nod at their greeting. First the old man thanked him for saving Reagan and gave a report about how she was doing. "She's all I got in this world, son." Jeremiah's voice cracked slightly. "If you ever need anything . . . anything, I'm in your debt."

Gabe wished he could have told the old guy that if it

hadn't been for him fixing his father's junker of a car five years ago so his father could get him out of the hospital, Gabe would be dead.

Jeremiah took his hand, not shaking, just gripping it. When they stared at one another, Gabe thought he saw the image of a warrior in the old guy's eyes and wondered if Jeremiah saw it in his.

Then Hank insisted on taking the old guy home and the moment was gone. Jeremiah shuffled out as Hank said good-bye to Gabe, kissed Alex on the cheek, and nodded for Liz to follow him out.

Suddenly, Gabe was alone with the sheriff.

"Please, Mr. Leary," she began. "Sit down. I'd like to go over the details just for the report. It won't take a minute."

He followed orders.

"Just tell me in your own words what happened."

"I always go by for a takeout meal from the diner on Wednesdays," he began. "I like to walk over even when it's cold. Reagan must have thought she'd meet me at the trees near the old creek."

"Has she done that before?"

"Yes."

"Go on, Mr. Leary."

"I like to follow the creek bed into town. It's off the streets and I run into fewer people."

"You don't like people?" she asked.

"It's not that," he lied. "I just like being alone. I was about to climb up the incline to the back lot of the Blue Moon when I spotted her lying real still. For a second, I thought she was dead, but when I lifted her head, I felt the warm blood. I couldn't carry her with my bad leg, so I dragged her atop my coat into the café. I'd just started emergency aid when you came in."

He met her stare. Guessing what she was going to ask him.

"How'd you know I wouldn't shoot you?"

"I saw it. Nervous people fire by accident, but your hand was steady. I saw your eyes. You don't have what it takes, Sheriff, to kill an unarmed man."

She leaned forward. "You were armed. Jess found the gun strapped to your leg."

Gabe nodded. "But you didn't know that, and I never would have drawn on you." He knew he remembered enough of his training that he could have disarmed her, or shot her before she could fire, but those days were long past.

"Then why do you wear a gun, Mr. Leary, if you wouldn't have drawn it?"

He looked away, thinking of how to answer the question. He hated lying, but he wasn't sure she'd understand the truth. "It feels right. I feel complete knowing it's there." He turned to meet her gaze. "I need to be prepared. Maybe nothing will ever happen in my lifetime, but if it does, I need to believe I'm ready."

"And if you draw your gun?" she asked.

"I'll fire if I have to."

He saw the flicker of understanding in her eyes. Something terrible had happened in her life. Something violent. Maybe she needed to always be prepared, just like him.

She finally leaned back. "Is the gun registered?"

"No."

She didn't look surprised. "I suppose if I asked you to it would . . ."

"Fall in the lake," they both said at once.

Alex smiled, knowing that trying to get all Texans to register all their guns was like trying to catch fleas with a bass fishing net. "Carry it on your land, but leave it at home when you come to town."

He didn't bother to nod, guessing they both knew he wouldn't follow her order.

She offered her hand. "I was wrong. I'm sorry I yelled at you, Mr. Leary. You saved a girl's life by acting as fast as you did. Thank you."

"No thanks necessary." He took her hand. "She's my friend."

Alex's grip was strong. "I hope you'll count me among your friends after tonight."

He finally smiled. "I'll do that."

Without another word, he walked out of the office and found Elizabeth waiting in her tiny little sports car.

Gabe leaned against her door when she rolled down the window. "I'm not sure I wouldn't be safer walking."

"Get in," she said. "It's only a few blocks. How many light poles can I hit between here and there?"

Gabe circled the car and climbed in, favoring his bad leg as he crammed it into the car. She took off before he closed the door, sliding from one side of the street to the other.

Giggling, she said, "I've never gone down to lockup and gotten a client out before. I feel like a real lawyer."

"You didn't get me out. I didn't do anything. They just released me."

She stuck her tongue out at him. "I'm the best lawyer. Don't forget, you used your one call to phone me tonight."

Gabe laughed. "You're the only lawyer I know. Hell, now your mom's house is the only number I know."

Liz slid into the driveway of the Winter's Inn Bed-and-Breakfast.

Gabe leaned low to stare up at the old two-story mansion. "You've got to be kidding. You booked me a room here?"

She ignored him as she cut the engine, climbed from the car, and headed toward the porch. He had no choice but to follow.

Ten minutes later, he'd stripped off his muddy clothes and stepped into a hot shower, ignoring the funny little bottles lined up along every surface in the bathroom and the hand towels twisted to resemble monkeys hanging from the racks. The shower felt great. He hadn't realized how bone cold he'd been. He washed his hair and beard, then stood letting the steamy downpour ease his leg pain for a while before turning off the water. He took a deep breath and slid the shower door open in a now-foggy room.

Martha Q stood at the door, her arms loaded down with clothes.

Gabe grabbed a towel and wrapped it around him. He wasn't shy, and from the way she looked at him, she wasn't embarrassed about interrupting either.

"I brought you some clothes. You should find something that will fit. I liked my husbands in all different sizes, kept me from getting them mixed up." She giggled. "There's pajamas on your bed if you sleep in them."

"I don't," he said as he took the clothes from her. "You always walk in on your guests?"

"I didn't figure you'd mind. You didn't lock the door."

"I'll remember that," he said as he watched her waddle out.

"When you're decent," she yelled, "I've got sandwiches in the kitchen for you and Liz."

"I'll be right down." He closed the door, locked it, and dried off, still smiling at the woman. He might not be modest, but she was certainly bold. He picked out a white T-shirt and a pair of well-worn jeans that almost fit him. The crazy lady had thought of socks, but forgot underwear. She'd guessed his size well, but after all, the old girl had taken a full look at him. He wasn't sure Elizabeth would have recommended the place if she knew how nuts Martha Q was.

When he walked into the kitchen a few minutes later, Elizabeth looked up at him and blushed. "Martha Q told me she saw your scar." Liz giggled. "Along with everything else. She said you're one fine-looking man."

"Where *is* the old witch?" he mumbled.

"Gone to bed, but she left us food." She moved away from the table to reveal a feast of sweets, sandwiches, and fruit.

Gabe headed straight to Liz and pulled her against him.

"I'm hungry for the taste of something else first, if you've no objection." His lips brushed hers lightly, waiting for an invitation. "Think you could forget I'm your client long enough to kiss me?" The tip of his tongue slid along her upper lip.

She made a little squeal of surprise before leaning into him. He tasted strawberries on her tongue and pulled away. "Food," he whispered, "then more of you."

They sat at the tiny kitchen table and began to eat. Their chairs were turned at an angle to each other, and he didn't miss the way their legs brushed as they filled their plates.

He'd take a bite of something, then offer her one. She concentrated on the bowl of strawberries, dipping each in powdered sugar before eating. She'd start to offer him a bite, then pull it away just before he tasted it and pop the treat into her mouth. The third time she did it, he cupped the back of her head and pulled her to him, kissing her as he tasted the fruit.

When he finished, she had powdered sugar outlining her lips.

"You're the best-tasting lawyer I've ever had," he teased.

"You tasted a lot, have you?" She giggled.

"No, they're not usually on the menu." He dipped a strawberry and fed it to her.

The night seemed enchanted. For once, she said she didn't want to talk, she just wanted to unwind from a dinner at her mother's she called an inquisition. Gabe felt like he'd already done more talking in one night than he usually did in a month. Memories threatened to haunt him, and the only cure seemed to be staying close to Elizabeth tonight.

They were in a strange house in a storm that seemed to block all the world out. They cleaned up the kitchen, refilled their wineglasses, and moved around the downstairs looking at all the treasures Martha Q had collected over her life.

Finally, they ended up on the couch in what Martha Q

called the parlor. Gabe lit a fire in the old stone fireplace, and Elizabeth curled up next to him so they could share a quilt. She said the fire reminded her of Christmases at her family's ranch where she grew up.

He listened, only needing to ask a question now and then to keep her talking. She told him of her childhood and her brother and sister. She told him of a life that sounded like a fairy tale compared to his childhood only a few miles away. Except for her father dying, Elizabeth Matheson sounded like a child who got everything she wanted. Hell, Gabe thought, she even got a pony. She had a mother who was a real artist and an older brother and sister to watch over her and enough of her own money by the time she got out of high school to buy a sports car.

He had trouble picturing her life, but it was nice to listen. Finally, she slowed and nestled closer for warmth. He wrapped his arm around her and watched her fall asleep, thinking how could something so beautiful be so close to him.

Watching out the window, he thought he saw a blue Mustang rolling slowly down the icy street, but with the falling snow, he couldn't be sure. Any car out tonight would be in the gutter in no time.

Instinct, bred in years of training, told him seeing the Mustang once parked by Liz's office was nothing, but twice might mean someone was watching him. Gabe pushed the idea aside. No one was watching him. He was simply being paranoid.

In the still night air, he heard the whisper of the clock in the tower on the town square chime the hour. No one noticed the clock during the day, but at night it seemed a lonely sound drifting in the air, stealing silence.

Wrapped in one another and a few handmade quilts, he listened to their breath keep time and finally fell asleep.

For tonight . . . for this one night . . . he wasn't alone.

Chapter 20

THURSDAY, 9:00 P.M.
FEBRUARY 7, 2008
HARMONY HOSPITAL

REAGAN HEARD THE DOOR CREAK OPEN AND WAITED FOR one of the nurses to start bothering her. In the twenty-four hours she'd been in the hospital, she swore she'd been mothered a hundred times. Some checked on her head wound; others looked at the top of her leg, now in a cast; other nurses took her temperature and blood pressure; and a few just wanted her blood, as if she hadn't lost enough.

When they came in, they always seemed to want to talk, not noticing that she'd been trying to sleep. "How do you feel? Are you dizzy? Sick at your stomach? Hungry?" When they finished with the questions, they usually became weathermen. "It's really snowing. Worst blizzard we've had in years."

Every time they woke her and left, Reagan reached for her cell phone and called her uncle. She could almost see him sitting in the kitchen waiting for his hourly call. She'd tell him everything was fine and he didn't need to try to come and see her. Then Jeremiah would give her a weather report and hang up.

Reagan opened one eye. The door had sounded some-one's coming, but no one had touched or poked her.

It took her a few seconds to make him out in the shadows of the room. Tall, thin, and dressed for Alaska in winter. Only his smiling brown eyes gave him away.

"Hi, Preacher," she whispered. "What are you doing here?"

Noah moved closer, tugging off his ski hat and gloves. His hair flew in every direction. If possible, the ski hat had done more damage than the cowboy hat he usually wore. "I heard about you from my sister. Sheriffs know everything, but they're bossy. She made me swear I wouldn't try to get my pickup out on these roads before she told me you were in the hospital. I guess she knew I'd be headed this way."

Reagan smiled. "So how'd you get here?"

"I caught a ride on the truck plowing the streets. He said it didn't matter which way he went, snow would cover what he'd done in a half hour, anyway." Noah unzipped his jacket. "They called off school today and probably tomorrow."

"Sorry to hear," she lied. Most days she just survived school until she could go home. Everyone else her age tried to think of where they could go, but for Reagan, home always seemed the right place. She liked baking in the kitchen and rummaging through rooms in the old house. She even liked doing her homework on an old table Jeremiah had said was brought to Harmony in a covered wagon. As near as she could tell, no Truman had tossed anything in three generations.

Noah sat down on the edge of her bed. "Broke your leg, did you?"

"No," she answered. "They just don't want me dancing around with this head wound so they wrapped up my leg."

Noah laughed. "Pretty dumb question, I guess. How about telling me what you were doing out back of the diner in an ice storm after dark?"

"You sound like a cop." She frowned.

"Maybe I will be someday. Who knows, it's in my blood. My brother being a highway patrolman and now my sister the sheriff. Maybe, after I'm all broken up in the rodeo, I'll apply to the Texas Rangers."

"You'd really want that?"

He shook his head. "Nope. I think I want to make the big money and come right back here to ranch. I'll move out on the land, redo the old house so more than rats can live in it, and just watch my horses run."

"You'll never get rich that way."

"I know, but it sounds like every day would be an adventure."

"I wish I had a plan." She stared out at the snowy night. "I want to stay here, but my uncle insists on college. I'm hoping he'll compromise and let me take classes online. I have this fear that if I ever leave here I might not be able to find my way back."

Noah leaned forward and rested his head on the pillow next to her. "Rea, you got to consider the possibility that you don't have enough brains left for college. You probably lost what little you had in the gully last night."

She raised her arm to hit him, but the IV tubes got in the way.

They both laughed. Deep down, no matter what happened or how different their lives turned out, they both knew that they were friends. Real friends. Deep-down, blood-brother kind of friends.

He brushed his hand over hers. "If either of us ever

does go away and get lost, we should promise each other that we'll come after whichever one is lost and bring them back. I have this feeling that sometimes people leave and get into big cities and forget they're lost. The bright lights trick them or something."

Reagan wanted to laugh, but deep down she decided that he might be right.

He settled beside her, lifting his arm as she cuddled against his shoulder. "They'll kick me out of here soon, Rea, but I'll stay with you as long as they'll let me. When I was hurt once, you stayed near me and I'd like to return the favor."

She closed her eyes. "Fair enough."

Like she knew he would, he talked about his dreams. Noah McAllen was different from any eighteen-year-old in town. He had his life all planned out, and Reagan envied him.

Smiling, she listened. They hadn't just talked in a long time. Lately, when she called him he seemed to have a list of things to tell her, but nothing he just wanted to talk about.

She was almost asleep when the duty nurse came in to tell him he'd have to go. Reagan remained still, hoping the nurse would let him stay a minute more, but Noah pulled away.

When he was gone and the room silent once more, she felt the cold all the way to the bone even though reason told her the room temperature hadn't changed.

For a strange reason, she felt something was ending. She wanted to call him back and make him promise they'd always be friends, forever and ever and ever.

Chapter 21

FRIDAY
FEBRUARY 8, 2008
COUNTY SHERIFF'S OFFICE

SHERIFF ALEX MCALLEN PULLED ON THE SNOW BOOTS that she kept in the supply closet at the office and bundled up against the cold. Though almost daylight, the snow was still coming down. If she planned to do any investigating, she'd better walk the streambed before it got any deeper. Any hope of a clue was probably long gone by this time.

With radio, cell phone, and broom in hand, she went out the back door of the sheriff's office. Though she could have driven to the diner, she knew if she followed the creek's path it would be shorter.

She walked across the back parking lot and the alley to the cottonwoods that marked the edge where the creek had once crossed through Harmony. Grabbing a branch, she lowered herself down the steep six-foot incline and began tromping along the uneven ground.

She watched carefully for anything out of order, but all she saw were a few animal tracks. A few dogs, a cat, and a raccoon had all left footprints in the white powder.

Snow circled around her, whispering of danger. Alex told herself she was in the center of town, within fifty feet of businesses and roads. This wasn't some unknown land-scape, this was Harmony. But it had been years since she'd explored the creeks. A few times in her life, when rain pounded hard and fast, the creeks had risen a few feet, but never to where they'd been when the town was founded.

Alex took big steps, feeling the bite of cold on her cheeks. She glanced up through bony branches. Buildings she knew well looked foreign and distorted from the back.

Twenty steps later, she saw the corner of the diner, painted dark blue. The snow swirled, making her feel like she was in the middle of a snow globe. A blue moon had once been painted on the back wall. Now faded and weathered, only the moon's smile shone clearly in the falling snow.

Lifting her broom, she began to sweep away at the pow-der as she took slow steps forward. Five feet. Ten. Twenty, before she brushed away a few inches of snow and found what she was looking for.

The remains of what had been Gabriel Leary's takeout supper. An animal had probably ripped open the paper bag. The sandwich was mostly crumbs, but the paper cup of soup hadn't been touched. It still had a plastic spoon taped to the top.

Alex knelt and opened the soup, now frozen. She had told herself she believed Reagan and Gabe's story, but a part of her had to be sure. She didn't know Leary. If he had been doing something bad, he might have threatened Reagan. It was her job not only to check the stories, but to check the facts.

Looking up, she saw the break in the trees where he

must have carried her out of the gully. The snow covered any tracks, but she moved over the ground, piecing every detail into place.

Gabe was a hero. He'd saved the girl's life, but something didn't fit. He was hiding something. She'd stake her career on it. When he'd looked up at her pointing a gun at him, it wasn't that he hadn't panicked. He hadn't cared. She had the feeling he'd faced down a gun before, maybe many times. He seemed a man who didn't care if he lived or died. No one gets that way without reasons.

Alex reached for her cell phone and punched Hank's number.

"Harmony Fire Station," he answered.

"You didn't go home last night?" she said without identifying herself.

"Is this an official question?" He lowered his voice. "Let me rephrase that. Is this the sheriff or my future wife calling?"

"Either way, I have a gun," she answered, laughing. "So, always tell me the truth. Did you sleep at the station?"

"Yes, and you slept at the office," he answered. "If I'd have known that, I'd have been tempted to cross the street."

"Don't try to sweet-talk me, just answer a few questions, Chief Matheson." She fought down a giggle. "You have any idea what your sister did with her client last night?"

"Nope. I never ask Liz what she does with any man. I'm probably not old enough to hear the answer. Now, my other sister, if and when she ever gets a date, I'll be looking for body parts around the house. Claire doesn't just hate men, she spends most of her waking hours trying to figure out how to torture them on canvas."

"So, Claire's still painting murdered men."

"No, not just murdered, mutilated. Last week she shipped one off to Dallas called *Holidays, Just Hanging Out with the Boys*. It was a bar scene with men strung like Christmas lights along with the garland."

"I'm glad she found a direction."

Hank groaned. "I guess I am too. Every painting seems to draw double the price of the last one. I just wish she painted bluebonnets or cats or anything except dead men. It creeps me out sometimes."

They both laughed before Hank added, "Funny you should ask where Gabe is. You're the second call about him this morning. Some man, sounding all business, called about a half hour ago and said he had to talk to Leary. He claimed he'd already tried the sheriff's office and every hotel in town. Maybe Leary has more friends than we think."

"Or enemies."

Chapter 22

FRIDAY MORNING
FEBRUARY 8, 2008
WINTER'S INN BED-AND-BREAKFAST

GABE WOKE TO THE SOUND OF SOMEONE CRYING SOFTLY. He stretched, remembering how Liz had clambered away from him just before dawn. She'd mumbled something about finding a real bed, and she hadn't invited him to come along.

He rarely felt the cold, or the heat after years of taking whatever assignment the army had open no matter where it sent him, but he felt the chill of being alone when she left. Elizabeth Matheson was self-centered, chatty, and out of his league, but she certainly felt good under the covers.

He stood, thinking of what he would have done if she had issued an invitation to climb the stairs. He was far too screwed up to get involved right now, but it would have been tempting. Most of the night, while she slept, he watched her in the light of a dying fire, amazed that something so beautiful would allow him to hold her.

The few times in his life that he'd slept with a woman, it had been more a case of some lonely woman picking him up than him making the first move. Most of the time he'd been on leave somewhere, and the kind of woman who invited a soldier home wasn't usually looking for more than a one-night stand.

He folded the blanket and heard the sound of crying once more. Moving through the still house, he followed the sound of a woman gulping down sobs as if trying to muffle her sadness from the world.

When he opened the kitchen door, he saw her. A thin shadow of a woman several years older than Martha Q. She sat up straight in one of the two kitchen chairs, fighting back each sob that seemed to rattle forth from deep inside her.

"Are you all right?" he asked softly so he wouldn't frighten her.

She looked up at him, pulling her sorrow around her like a shawl. "I'm fine. You must be our new guest, Mr. Leary." She moved with grace to her feet as she pushed a tear from her cheek. "I'm Mrs. Biggs, the breakfast cook. Would you like some coffee? It's a little early for breakfast. We usually serve at nine in the dining room, but I start the coffee as soon as I get up."

Gabe wanted to know what made this woman so sad, but he wouldn't pry. "I'd love some coffee, Mrs. Biggs. Black and strong."

She almost smiled. "Black and strong it is, then."

"What is that wonderful smell?" he asked as he took the chair she hadn't been sitting in.

"Pull-apart cinnamon bread baked with apple and pear slices." Mrs. Biggs opened the oven and used one corner of her apron to pull a pan out. An aroma from heaven filled the warm kitchen.

Gabe winked at her. "Any chance that comes as the appetizer to breakfast? I missed dinner last night."

"Of course it does. Only way to eat it if you ask me." She flipped the loaf onto a plate and served it with butter on the side. "I've always had the thought that everyone should eat whatever they love most when they wake up. Starts the day off brighter, and on this snowy day, we could use a little sunshine."

He settled at the kitchen table, drinking his coffee and munching on the best-tasting breakfast bread he'd ever tried, while Mrs. Biggs went about pulling eggs and sausage out of the refrigerator. They didn't talk much; neither felt the need to. She'd ask if he wanted more each time she passed him and watched the slices of bread vanish one by one from his plate.

"I may eat all of this," he finally said. "What will you feed everyone else?"

She smiled. "You're it, I'm afraid. When Martha Q stays up after ten she never makes it down before noon, and your girl passed through here about the time I was getting started to tell me she planned to sleep through breakfast."

"She's not my girl," he said. "She's my lawyer, or was for about ten minutes last night."

This time Mrs. Biggs did smile. "You could have fooled me."

When he didn't comment, she added, "How do you like your eggs?"

"A half dozen, over easy," he answered. "Burn the sausage and those hash browns you're making."

She nodded and turned back to the stove. Gabe stood, leaned against the sink, and watched the snow outside. This was the worst storm he could remember in years. Or, maybe it was just the first he'd noticed. On bitter cold days he didn't pay much attention to the weather; he just worked. Sometimes, when he was creating a story, he'd be lost in it for days, barely remembering to eat much less look out the window.

He usually drove over to Bailee and bought his groceries once a month, and if the trip had to be delayed a few days, he still had plenty of stock. Once in a while he had to turn on his computer just to see what day it was.

He sometimes thought he lived more by seasons than by months. He loved building a fire in the winter and drinking his soup out of the same mug he'd used for his morning coffee. In the spring and fall, long walks gave him a kind of peace, and in the summer, he liked lying out in the warm grass on hot nights just listening to the sounds around him.

As he stared out at the snow, he thought of the things he hated about living out on the farm. The silent, black night that left him waking sometimes and not knowing where he was. The fear that he'd die and have no one find him until his bones were chalk. The days that would pass without him hearing a single voice other than his own.

But there were things he loved too. He loved putting the stories he'd told himself since childhood on paper. He loved living with the few memories of his mother. Sometimes he wasn't sure if he remembered her, or if he'd created her just to balance out his childhood a bit. He loved feeling safe, even though he never let his guard down completely.

Mrs. Biggs handed him his platter, then filled her own plate, and they sat down at the little table together as if they'd done so every morning for years. "I thought I'd keep you company if you're eating in here. Guests usually eat in the dining room." She pointed with her head to the door behind her. "When we have guests, of course. Most mornings I've been here it's just me and Martha Q."

"I would go in there," he said as he poured ketchup on the eggs, "but since I don't have any shoes, I thought I'd better stay in here if you've no objections."

She nodded and lifted her fork. "I'd be proud to have breakfast with you, Mr. Leary. Shoes or no shoes."

"And I you," he answered, thinking that once in a great while you meet someone who somehow seems to fit in your world.

"Maybe when I finish I'll talk my lawyer into taking me shopping. I haven't bought clothes from anyplace but mail order for years."

"You could go to the mall."

Gabe laughed. "A few stores, a Penney's mail-order place and fast food doesn't qualify as a mall."

"You don't need clothes for work?"

He shook his head. "I work at home. I draw, and sometimes write graphic novels."

She looked up, her eyes round in surprise. "You write dirty books?"

He laughed. "Graphic novels are like longer comic books. Trust me, they're sold in stores. They don't arrive wrapped in brown paper." He'd never told anyone what he did. He wasn't sure why he told Mrs. Biggs, other than it just felt right.

The one egg and toast she was eating seemed so little compared to what filled his plate. He cut off a slice of the breakfast bread. He'd already eaten a half loaf. Putting the slice on her plate, he said, "I saved you a piece."

"I don't usually eat sweets," she protested.

"Me either. I don't know how to cook them and what you buy in the grocery store tastes like cardboard."

She laughed. "You're right."

He attacked his food. Between bites, he asked, "Where'd you learn to cook like this, Mrs. Biggs?"

"My second husband owned a bakery. He was a strong man who worked ten-hour days, six days a week, until the day he died last month. It was midmorning and he was lifting a wedding cake we were already late delivering. He yelled for me to go start the van, and then he stopped, set the cake on the counter, and fell over. His last words to me in the ambulance were to make sure one of the employees delivered that cake. He said, 'We can't afford to lose business.'"

"That why you were crying?" Gabe was sorry he'd asked once the words were out of his mouth. It wasn't his way to pry. "Losing a husband must be hard."

"No." She sat her fork down. "I do miss his company. We were together for almost twenty years, but would you think it terrible if I said I never loved him? We just worked together, occupied the same quarters at night, but I'm not sure we were ever close enough to even call one another friend."

Gabe could feel her loss. Not of her husband, but of what might have been and never was.

"Did you two ever have children?" Gabe thought maybe that was the reason they married if it wasn't for love. Twenty years ago she would have been in her early forties and maybe still in her childbearing years.

"No, not together. He was eight years older than me. Fifty-four when we married. He had two sons that I didn't meet until after his funeral. They inherited everything. He'd never changed his will to include me, you see. A lawyer said I could have fought the will and won a share, but the bakery, or our apartment above it, had never felt like mine. I packed the same suitcase I arrived carrying and walked away from that life without a backward glance or a memory worth taking."

They sat for a while, watching the snow. Gabe finished his meal and poured them both more coffee. He had the feeling that Mrs. Biggs and he were very much alike. Sometimes the only time a quiet person talks is around another quiet person.

Finally, she spoke, more to herself than to him. "I was crying earlier because I wanted to go to the cemetery today. I wanted to sit by my son who died ten years ago and I didn't even know."

"I'm sorry," Gabe said for lack of anything else to say.

"Until last month I thought he was still alive. When his father died, my only son blamed me for not insisting his dad go to the hospital. He swore he'd never take my call if I tried to contact him. He was grown, and turning on me was maybe the only way he could handle his dad's death. Brice grew up to be as stubborn as his father. Only my son didn't have the gentleness in him that took the edge off my husband."

She blew her nose on her paper napkin. "When I left the bakery I thought I'd stop by just to see Brice, but I couldn't find a number for him. I called a policeman who always came in for blueberry cake donuts at the bakery and told him my problem. He did some checking and found out my son had died over ten years ago in a bar fight. The obituary listed no next of kin, so he never married or had children. I didn't know if I was sad or happy about that. I don't like to think that he was all alone. So, I thought I'd still come and set with him awhile. I like to remember how he was as a little kid, not the cold young man who promised he'd never speak to me."

Gabe looked out the window, thinking Brice Biggs must have been a real bum to toss away a mother like this. His own mother had died before he was five, and Gabe often swore his father blamed him for her death instead of the cancer.

Looking over at Mrs. Biggs, he knew what she was thinking. "Not much chance of leaving this house today."

"I know," she whispered. "I left Harmony just after my first husband died, running away from the heartache of losing him and having my only child turn his back on me at the same time. But the pain never left me, not all those twenty years of working and living with a man who always talked about his sons, but never once asked about my boy.

"Finally, I decided I'd come back home and do what I'd wanted to do for twenty years. I wanted to talk to my boy, but he was resting beside his father. I plan to spend the rest of my days grieving and when I die, I want to be buried next to them."

Gabe patted her hand. "Sounds like a plan," he said, thinking the last thing he wanted was to be buried in the Leary plot.

They heard the front door open and close, and both knew their time together had ended. With a single nod, they agreed to a pact of silence. They sat, listening to someone in the hallway. When the sheriff appeared a few minutes later, neither of them looked surprised.

Mrs. Biggs stood and offered Alex coffee. Gabe thought about trying to disappear, but he had a feeling the sheriff was here to see him and there was no getting around her. The sheriff was a pretty lady, tall and built like a runner, but she had a hardness about her that told him the only way to deal with her was straight on.

"You drive here?" he asked.

"No," she said as she cradled the hot coffee mug with both hands. "I walked over along the creek bed. It wasn't all that far, first to the diner and then another dozen houses to here."

"Cold, though," he said as if he were just finishing his coffee and not waiting for her to get to the point.

"I found your takeout meal. The one Reagan must have dropped when she fell."

Gabe watched her. "You're still not convinced I wasn't attacking the girl. You figure maybe I knocked her in the head out by the creek bed and dragged her back in the diner to finish her off, or maybe I was planning to rape her and didn't fancy doing it out in the cold."

Alex shook her head. "No. I know you and she had to be telling the truth, but something doesn't fit."

"About last night?"

"No, about you." She stared at him as if waiting for him to blink. "How could you be living three miles from town and I don't know you? Edith knew you. Reagan and her uncle knew you. Even Liz Matheson knew you, but somehow you were not on my radar." She leaned closer, still staring, and added, "It seems to me you might make a habit of being invisible to the law, and people who do that are usually hiding."

When he still didn't answer, she continued, "Something about you doesn't make sense. How'd you know what to do to keep Reagan alive? Why do you carry a gun? Who are you, Gabriel Leary?"

"I'm nobody," he answered. "Just someone who likes to live alone and not bother people. As soon as this storm blows over, I'll go back home and you can forget you know me. Everything will be back to normal."

She frowned. "Mind if I ask you a few questions?"

"Mind if I don't bother to answer?" he countered. "If you want to interrogate me, read me my rights and I'll go wake up my lawyer."

Alex felt the hair on the back of her neck stand on end. Most people in this town would tell you their life story fifteen minutes after you met them, but this man had something to hide. She'd bet her badge on it. Problem was, he was a hero, not a suspect. She had no right to push, and she had a feeling she'd have to push hard to learn anything he didn't want her to know.

She tried another door. "Someone told me when I asked where you were that I was the second person who wanted to know this morning. Dispatch said a call came in from Oklahoma City looking for you. When I checked, I learned some man had called all over town trying to locate you."

Gabe raised an eyebrow. She finally had his attention.

"You wouldn't have any idea who that man was, would you? We traced the call to a phone booth just outside of town. You happen to have relatives, Mr. Leary? Someone who panicked when you didn't call in or answer a phone? Someone who took the time to check the hotels in town?"

"No idea," he answered. "Didn't he give a name? What time did he call?"

She smiled. "You want any answers, maybe you should wake up your lawyer."

Liz stumbled in wearing one of Martha Q's dead husband's shirts and a pair of men's socks that went up past her knees. "Coffee," she mumbled like a dying man. "Coffee."

Leary grinned. "My lawyer."

Mrs. Biggs poured her a cup. Gabe offered his knee for her to sit on, and the sheriff stared.

Liz downed a long gulp before forcing her eyes open enough to notice anyone else in the room. "Morning, Alex," she said simply, as if sitting on a client's knee while wearing nothing but a shirt was totally normal. "You come alone, or is my brother with you?"

"Morning, Liz. I'm alone. I don't think your brother even knows where you are." Alex turned her gaze to Gabe, leaving no doubt that she'd just added one more question to her list that he hadn't answered.

Mrs. Biggs offered both women breakfast. Both declined.

"I was just leaving." Alex stood and looked at her future sister-in-law. "You want me to send your brother over in a truck to get you out of here?"

"No," Liz answered as if there were nothing unusual. "I think I'll wait here until the snow stops."

Alex backed her way out, with Mrs. Biggs going ahead to hold the door for her. Gabe could hear them talking in the hallway as Elizabeth leaned against his shoulder like a cuddling child wanting to go back to sleep.

When Gabe heard the front door close, he lifted her off his knee and sat her on the chair beside him. "You made quite a scene." He smiled.

She shrugged. "If Alex tells my brother, which she probably will, he'll think business as usual. It won't be the first time I've shocked him. Besides, you're not a client, you're my friend. You don't need a lawyer, remember."

Gabe glanced to make sure Mrs. Biggs hadn't returned through one of the three swinging doors circling the kitchen before saying, "You get caught without your clothes on quite often?"

"It seems that way," she answered. "But not really. I was wild in high school and most of college, and then I married and settled down. When I divorced, I tried to fly solo, but there was always someone around to keep me company. But I haven't slept with anyone for almost two months, so that about makes me revirginized, doesn't it?"

Gabe grinned at her logic.

"How long for you?" she asked.

"Is that a question?"

She smiled. "Yes, and be honest."

"Almost six years."

"Since what . . . you were married . . . involved?"

"Since I slept with a woman."

"You're kidding." Her eyes widened. "How long were you two together? Six years is a long time to get over one woman."

"We were together one night. If you count from the time the bar closed until I boarded a plane at oh six hundred the next morning." He almost laughed at the shock on her face. "And before you ask, I don't remember her name."

"But . . ."

Before she could think of another question, he pulled her up and through the door into the curtained darkness of the huge dining room. "The way I figure it, you're three questions ahead of my kisses."

He lowered his mouth over hers. Like he knew she would, she melted into his arms, pulling his head down as she stood on her toes. There was nothing shy about Elizabeth or about what she liked, and she liked kissing him.

When they finally came up for air, he whispered, "One."

She broke into a run up the back stairs.

He caught her outside her door and kissed her again.

"Two," he said as she opened her door, pulling him with her.

He lifted her off the ground to meet his mouth as he whispered, "Three."

She held on tight as if she thought she could rock the foundation of his world with one long, wet kiss.

And she almost did. Another minute of this paradise and he'd have trouble remembering his own name.

When she tugged him toward the bed, he stepped back with a sudden jerk and left them both surprised.

"Sorry, baby," he said. "There's nothing I'd like more than to spend the day in bed, but I've got to get home."

"But it's snowing out there." She stomped her foot like a child. "You couldn't get a snowplow down Timber Line Road right now." Her hand drifted over his chest. "Stay a while. We could use a little time to get to know each other."

He loved it when she pouted. Elizabeth had no idea how cute she looked. It took every ounce of sanity and survival instinct he had to back away from her. "I'll borrow some heavy clothes and walk home."

Before she could argue, he almost ran from the room.

Halfway down the stairs he heard her yell, "Drop dead, Gabe Leary."

He smiled, glad she was mad at him and not worried about him. Right now he had enough worry for both of them. The sheriff said someone had called about him. Since no one knew he was alive, the call could mean only one thing.

The men who wanted him dead were still looking for Gabriel Wiseman, and somehow they'd linked him with Gabe Leary. The safest thing he could do for Elizabeth and everyone else in town was to stay away.

If trouble came for him, Gabe could fight it on his own terms. He'd be ready.

Ten minutes later he was out of the inn and heading for the creek bed with so many layers on he felt like a walking snowman. Before he took the incline, he found a branch to use as a walking stick. With it, his leg was strong enough to move fast. Once he reached the edge of town, he used the fence post to center the road and made quick time.

The wind was bitter, but he kept moving. He wouldn't be safe until he got on his land, inside his house. He watched for signs, but as far as he could tell, no car or person had cut the snow. The farther he walked away from the town, the safer he felt. Whoever was looking for him would be looking in town, not outside. If they knew about his place, he would have seen the signs.

An hour later, when he finally opened his door, he took a deep breath. For a moment last night and this morning he'd forgotten that the only way for him to stay alive was for him to stay away from everyone.

Following his usual routine, he checked the locks. Scanned the security system for any breaks in the perimeter. When he was satisfied all was secure, he changed into his own clothes, but he still couldn't shake the feeling something was wrong.

Finally, he flipped on his computer and began to scan the newspapers. If the sheriff was telling the truth and not just playing mind games with him, then someone in the area was looking for him.

Ten minutes later, he found a clue. On the fourth page of the *Oklahoma Daily* was a small article about a man saving a girl's life in the middle of the first winter storm of the season. There, in print, was his name. Gabriel Leary. The last sentence read, *Harmony, Texas, has a hero.*

He sat back in his chair, trying to decide exactly what to do. Maybe it was just a coincidence that someone called from Oklahoma City the same day he made the news? Maybe not?

What action should he follow? *Run* came to mind first.

Run as far and as fast as he could. He had enough money to disappear for a few years, maybe even buy another identity. Only problem was, anything bought could be traced. He might be able to make Gabe Leary disappear, but what about G. L. Smith and the career he'd spent years building?

The publishers might think it a little strange after almost five years if he wrote and asked them to start sending advances and royalties to someone else.

Maybe he was panicking. Maybe the caller from Oklahoma City had been a reporter and just wanted to check on him. The paper made him out to be a hero, like he'd done something superhuman pulling Reagan to safety and doing first aid. Heroes always have more friends than they know. Some guy in Oklahoma City probably just wanted to talk to him.

Gabe tromped down to the basement, where he'd built his own private gym. He began to work out, thinking that if he hadn't been so paranoid, he could be sleeping with Elizabeth right now at crazy Martha Q's bed-and-breakfast.

He looked over at Pirate staring at him. "Shut up," Gabe said. "I don't want to hear what a fool I am."

The dog's ears dropped and he turned his head sideways as if to get a better view of his idiot master.

Chapter 23

FRIDAY MIDMORNING
FEBRUARY 8, 2008
HARMONY TOWN SQUARE

ALEX WALKED BACK TO HER OFFICE IN THE TRAIL OF ONE of the snowplows. Nothing moved on the streets. The town could have been abandoned.

She felt like a fool. She hadn't planned to stop at Winter's Inn, but she'd noticed Liz's sports car, half covered in snow, parked at the end of Martha Q's long drive, and she guessed Liz might have taken Gabe there to stay. It made sense. The two women knew each other, and Gabe Leary would probably want somewhere quiet. Martha's was about as quiet as he could get. The woman didn't even keep the B&B sign up half the time.

Alex swore. She'd only gone in to talk to Gabe, maybe

have a cup of coffee and get to know this newest hero of Harmony. But, he wasn't an easy man to talk to. If Liz hadn't interrupted, they probably would be yelling at each other about now.

He had a right to his privacy, but this was her town. She needed to know who lived here. A man with a military bearing about him, who walks the back streets at night, was someone to watch. A man who carried a weapon, polished and well-oiled for battle, wasn't the bum he appeared to be in his old clothes and worn boots. A man who knew how to save Reagan's life couldn't be ignored.

Something the doctor had said kept running through her mind. He commented that if Gabe had taken the time to call 911 instead of applying pressure to the head wound and putting a tourniquet at the top of her leg to slow the bleeding, she might not have lived. She'd been close to death and Gabe had not only recognized it, he'd done what had to be done to keep Reagan alive.

Not one man in a hundred would know where to apply pressure to two wounds or have the skill to do it fast enough to save a life.

When she reached the other side of the square, Alex thought of stopping off at the fire station, but she wasn't sure she could see Hank right now without telling him what was going on over at the Inn. Hank worried about his little sister as if she were seventeen and not nearly thirty. When he wasn't worried, he was usually mad at her for doing something foolish.

Any way she looked at it, Alex thought what she'd seen this morning fell into one category or another. Right now Hank probably had all he could handle at the fire station. He didn't need to be worrying about Liz.

Alex turned toward her office. With this weather they'd be getting calls all day.

She had barely made it inside and pulled off her

coat when Jess was at her side, his headphone cord dangling.

"We got a strange call a few minutes ago, Sheriff," he started. "Domestic violence, I guess you'd call it."

"Give me the details."

"A woman just called in to say she'd accidentally knocked her husband out and needed someone to come over and see if he was dead."

"Did you ask her if she needed an ambulance?"

Jess frowned. "That's where it gets strange. She said if he wasn't dead he'd be furious that she'd called an ambulance, and if he was, it was too late anyway."

"She leave a name?"

"No." He shook his head. "But the caller ID said the call came from Lloyd and Edith Franklin's home."

"Edith from the diner?"

Jess frowned. "I've met her husband a few times. He's not a man you'd want to cross. My brother was in school with the guy and used to laugh that Lloyd knew sign language."

Alex waited, knowing Jess would get around to the facts eventually.

"You know"—Jess moved his fingers, then doubled them up into a fist—"he talks with his hands. I heard someone say a few years ago that the guy wanted to go pro in wrestling, but he had a head injury that gave him a stupidism."

"You mean astigmatism?"

"Whatever. The strange thing is how could Edith, a woman who makes a broom handle look fat, knock out Lloyd? He's a head taller and double her weight."

"Try to call her back." Alex reached for her coat. Her feet hadn't even had a chance to get warm and it looked like she was heading out again.

While Jess tried to get Edith on the phone, Alex called Hank and filled him in. If Edith didn't want an ambulance,

Hank would be the next best thing. He knew how to handle most medical emergencies, and his huge pickup would make it out to the trailer park at the edge of town. She might have drafted a deputy to come along, but they were all out working weather-related accidents.

"No answer!" Jess yelled, and Alex was out the door.

Hank met her at his Dodge, and they climbed into the cab still warm from the run he'd made a half hour ago.

"Busy day?" she asked.

"I feel like I've already put in a day's work and it's not near lunch yet. How about you?"

"I took a few minutes off and had coffee over at Martha Q's house." Alex didn't want to admit to more.

He stopped at a light and leaned over to kiss her cold cheek. "I love you, you know."

"I know." She smiled. "Otherwise why would you go on this call with me? Lloyd Franklin is huge, and Jess said he almost went pro wrestler."

Hank winked at her. "I'm not worried. I got the big bad sheriff with me."

Alex wished she felt as confident as he did. In truth, she wasn't too worried about Lloyd. If he came to and came up swinging, she'd taken men down before, and Hank could hold his own in a fight. What worried Alex more than confronting Lloyd was what he might do to Edith after they left.

Once, about a year back, she'd seen bruises on Edith's arms, but when Alex asked about them, Edith made up excuses. Unless she saw the violence or had Edith file charges, there wasn't much she could do.

"This one's it," Hank said as he pulled up to a single-wide trailer parked under hundred-year-old trees. "I took Edith home one night when her car wouldn't start and I remember it. Told her to have her husband trim away some of those branches before they fall. You'd think since he does lawn work on the side, he'd have all the tools he'd need in that junker of a van parked under the shed." Hank leaned forward so he could see the tops of the trees. "Doesn't look like he did."

They climbed out of the truck and walked through six inches of snow to the door.

Edith met them before either could knock.

"Morning," she said. "What brings you folks out this morning?"

Alex saw the worry in the woman's eyes. She could almost smell the fear. "We're checking on folks," Alex lied. "Making sure everyone's got heat."

A big man shoved Edith away from the door. "We got heat." He held the door with one hand, making sure Alex and Hank couldn't see into the house.

Hank stepped closer. "I'm Hank Matheson."

"I know who you are."

Hank tried again. "I was wondering if you could check on your neighbors and make sure they're all right."

"Most of them wouldn't open the door if they saw me on their porch, and I'm not feeling like getting out in the cold again. I got under the house to make sure all the pipes were wrapped and the blasted trapdoor almost took my head off." He dabbed at the side of his scalp with a stained tea towel.

"You want me to take a look at it? I've got a first-aid kit in the truck."

"No. I've had worse. You folks best be on your way before you freeze out there." Lloyd pulled the door closed.

Hank and Alex had no choice but to back away. When they were in the truck, Alex whispered as if Lloyd might hear, "That man's no good. I'll bet he's beating Edith. I don't like leaving her here with him."

Hank started the engine. "And she's the one trying to kill him. I'd be willing to bet that trapdoor didn't just fall. Maybe you should arrest them both. They could share a cell."

Alex leaned close to him, wishing they both didn't have

on heavy coats so she could feel his warmth. She loved curling up to him in the early mornings. When she'd snuggle close, he'd circle her with one arm and pull her against him, and for a while she'd feel like all was right with the world.

He must have been thinking the same thing because he kissed the top of her head and whispered, "How about I call Martha Q at the inn and book us a room for the night. Then we wouldn't have to fight the ice all the way home and we could wake up tomorrow to a hot breakfast."

Alex shook her head, remembering who was already snuggled up at the inn. "Everyone in town would know."

He laughed. "You think everyone in town doesn't already know?"

Chapter 24

MARTHA Q WOKE UP TO ANOTHER MORNING OF SNOW falling outside her window. Not the big heavy kind from yesterday, but the light snow, barely more than white dust in the wind. She pulled the covers up and sighed. Cold mornings always made her long for a man to keep her warm.

With that thought, her eyes flew open and her feet hit the floor. The last thing she needed in her life was another man; coffee would do just fine. "After seven marriages, there has to be a time to call it quits."

Evidently, she couldn't even keep one in the inn. Gabe Leary had paid for two days and left before she got up yesterday. If Elizabeth hadn't agreed to stay another night,

Martha Q would have had to refund money. Something she never wanted to do.

Pulling on her robe as she climbed down the back stairs, Martha Q tried to plan her day. She would have gone nuts yesterday if the little lawyer hadn't been there to keep her company. Mrs. Biggs liked to stay in her room, but Elizabeth played cards and talked and even watched a movie with her, popcorn and all.

She opened the door to the kitchen and found the girl, dressed in her pink ski outfit, reading a magazine as she ate her breakfast. Mrs. Biggs was nowhere in sight.

"Morning," Elizabeth said. "I'll be heading out in an hour. Looks like the worst of the storm is over."

Martha Q raised her hands as if shooing flies. "No, no, dear. It'd be too much trouble for you to dig that car out. Stay another day. We're running a three-nights-for-two special."

"Since when?" Liz asked raising an eyebrow.

"Since I just thought of it," Martha Q testified. "We'll make supper and invite a few folks over."

"Who?' Liz asked.

"I don't know. I haven't been around much lately," Martha Q complained. In truth she had no one in town she really called friend. "How about you invite that good-looking man of yours? He left yesterday before I had a chance to say good-bye."

"He's not mine. I'm just his lawyer." Liz shrugged. "Besides, he lives outside of town and I don't think he has a phone. I even called the sheriff's office and they said he hadn't listed one. Anyone coming to eat today will have to be close enough to walk over. My guess is, after making the three-mile walk back to his place yesterday, he won't be interested in doing it again."

"You like that man, scarred as he is."

"I didn't see his scar, you did," Liz argued. "Remember,

you saw *all* his scar. And, yes, I do like him, but it's just a physical thing. I don't even know him, really."

"Don't play down the importance of physical attraction. I married because of lust all seven times. Trouble is, lust cools when you can't pay the bills, so always check the bank account before you fall too far in love."

Liz laughed. "I'll remember that." She picked up her cup and took it to the sink. "Now, Miss Martha Q, you plan the menu and I'll think of people within walking distance that we can invite."

The doorbell rang. Both women jumped.

Martha Q frowned. "Now who could that be coming to call before I even get my makeup on?"

"Only one way to find out." Liz held the swing door open.

They were halfway to the front door when Mrs. Biggs stepped out of the parlor. "That's Mr. Wright for me," she said. "He said if the roads were clear enough, he'd come get me in the funeral home's four-wheeler."

Martha Q shook her head. "It's awful cold to be sitting by a grave."

Mrs. Biggs nodded. "He told me he'd pull the van up close so I could stay inside while he checks on things at the cemetery." She opened the door.

Tyler looked bundled up and ready to climb Denali in winter. "Morning," he said to both women as he offered his arm to Mrs. Biggs. "Now don't you two worry about her. She'll be fine while I go off with my groundskeeper to check on the damage this storm's done to our old elms."

Mrs. Biggs wrapped her scarf around her head and took his arm.

Tyler waved as he took baby steps across the porch. "I'll have her back by noon."

Martha Q gripped her robe at the throat and closed the door. When she turned back to Liz, she said, "You got that man's cell number?"

"I could make a call and get it."

"Good. Invite that undertaker to dinner. He's always been nice to me, and I like to watch a man who loves to eat. If he was ten years older, I might consider him for number eight."

Liz laughed. "Somehow I can't see shy Tyler Wright with you . . . or me. He's too . . ."

"Nice." Martha Q finished her sentence. "You may be almost thirty and I'm—" She hesitated too long before adding, "almost fifty." The lie was so apparent they both laughed before Martha Q continued, "But you and I, girl, we have one thing in common. We like our men a little rough around the edges. Tyler is the type of man who would always fold his napkin. Polish his shoes. Pull out your chair."

"Wear pajamas. Return your calls," Liz added to the list. "And of course ask if tonight would be a convenient time to make love."

Martha hooted a laugh. "Whereas our kind of men, the ones who make our blood warm, are the kind who already have our clothes off before they remember to turn off the light and close the door."

Liz hated to admit it, but the old girl was right. The wild ones, the bad boys, the outlaws had always been her type, even when reason convinced her to play it safe. "So, if I'd like Gabriel Leary to be my man, what do I have to do? Give me a little advice."

Martha Q smiled as if she'd been waiting for someone to ask for years. "I heard a movie star get asked that same question. What does a woman have to do to let you know she's interested in you? The star said simply, 'Show up.'"

"So, when this snow clears, I should just drive out to his farm and knock on the door?" Liz somehow didn't think it would be that easy.

Martha Q nodded. "That's it." Grabbing a slip of paper, she added, "Now you get to calling people and I'll go see what we can cook for dinner. I've got half a beef in the freezer, so it shouldn't be too much trouble, and with this snow, no one will have plans even if it is Saturday night."

"It's Saturday?" Liz had been so busy, she hadn't given it much thought.

"You got plans?"

"No, but I almost forgot. It's Saturday, February ninth. It's my thirtieth birthday."

Martha didn't miss a beat. "No it's not, dear, it's your second twenty-ninth and this dinner just turned into a party." She was halfway upstairs before she shouted down, "Call some people while I get dressed. We've no time to waste."

Liz crawled onto the window seat in the dining room. First she called her brother, who could easily walk over from the fire station, and told him to bring Alex, his fiancée. Then she got Tyler's cell number from Hank and called him. Tyler seemed delighted, and Liz couldn't help but wonder if the man ever got invited to anything but funeral meals.

Then she froze. Elizabeth knew almost everyone in town, but she couldn't think of another person to invite. Her mother, sister, and aunts wouldn't want to leave the ranch. The few friends she'd kept up with since high school had families, and somehow she doubted Martha Q would welcome toddlers wandering around.

A strange ache gripped her chest as she realized the only person she wished was with her was Gabriel, and she didn't really know him. Martha Q was wrong about one thing. Liz had thrown herself at him more than once, and he'd always walked away. Even if he did kiss like double heaven covered in chocolate, he still ran. Maybe he thought she'd be turned off by the scar that Martha said ran from his hip to his calf. Maybe he was worried about his limp. She'd mentioned it the second time she'd seen him, and she'd known without asking that the leg gave him pain when he moved, but she'd also touched his body when they'd hugged. He was made of pure muscle.

Liz closed her eyes and remembered how he'd felt pressed against her. They might not have much to say to each other, but everything about him, from his height to the way he smelled, made her want to draw closer.

She opened her eyes and looked out in the direction of the old Leary place. Buildings and trees blocked her view, but Liz still whispered a promise. "I'm coming," she said. "Like it or not, I'm coming for you, Gabe Leary."

She had no idea if they'd last one night or a lifetime, but she'd bet the time they spent together would be time she'd remember down to the seconds for the rest of her life.

Chapter 25

SATURDAY NIGHT
FEBRUARY 9, 2008
WRIGHT FUNERAL HOME

Sorry I'm so late in writing tonight, Kate. I went to din-
ner at Winter's Inn with friends. This bed-and-break-
fast wasn't here when you visited Harmony two years
ago during the grass fires. I wish I'd known you were
here. I could have given you a tour of my town. I have a
feeling most people drive through Harmony and won-
der why anyone would want to live here. They don't see
it like I do. They don't see the beauty of it.

When I think about how we started e-mailing, I wish
I'd been honest from the first with you about where I
lived and who I was. People don't do that on the Inter-
net. It's not safe, but I waited too long to tell you. If

*you'd known I was in Harmony, you could have called
when you came.*

*I guess there are no "start-overs" in life. If I could
wish just one, though, I'd wish it with you.*

*Tonight we celebrated Liz Matheson turning thirty.
She thinks she's getting old, but she seems so young to
me. I remember when I was thirty, I thought everything
was a possibility. Now in my forties I find myself now
and then afraid to dream. I don't want to spend my life
dreaming.*

*The snowstorm's over, but the snow will hang around
for a while. Speaking of things hanging around, remember the border collie I told you about? Well, she's still
living with me. When the days are warmer, I'm sure I'll
find her a home. She's a smart pup. She's learned to use
the kitchen elevator. Goes up and down. If I'm upstairs
or in my study, she wants to be right with me. Folks don't
seem to mind. When they come in my study, they often
stop to pet her before we plan.*

*I miss talking to you, Kate. If you ever find the time,
let me know you're out there and doing okay.*

*I'm still driving over to Quartz Mountain and
ordering you a glass of wine on the first Monday of the
month. Don't think of me as sad if you ever read this.
Think of me as remembering all the times we e-mailed
over dinner. Good memories, even if they don't grow
over the years, are still good memories. I feel like if I
gave up on them, I'd be giving up on you and I'm not
ready to do that yet.*

Until tomorrow,
Ty

Tyler clicked Send and leaned back in his chair.
He'd had more to drink than his usual one glass of wine
tonight. Maybe that's why he wrote more from the heart

than usual, but what did it matter? No one was on the other end anyway.

"Come on, Little Lady," he said to the border collie. "It's time we go upstairs."

Chapter 26

February 11, 2008
Harmony Hospital

Uncle Jeremiah paced Reagan's hospital room, mumbling, "The doc says you can go home tomorrow, but I don't know. I've had a bed delivered and set up in the front room, the room you think is yours anyway. It's got all those windows, so it may not be warm enough. I worry about that. I should stop by the hardware store and pick up one of those little heaters. The nurse here called a home nursing company and they said they'd send someone out every morning to see to you, and I can do the cooking. I know what you like. If you stay here another day or two you'll be nothing but bones. I never saw so many colors of Jell-O in my life."

"Uncle." Reagan tried to stop him. "Uncle!"

He turned. "What is it, kid? You in pain? I can get that nurse in here."

"No." She smiled at him. "I'm fine. I don't need to be pampered. We Trumans are tough, remember. I can get out of bed all by myself and go to the bathroom. I don't need a babysitter every morning." She'd already talked him down to a half day, so she doubted she could cut the home nurse much more. The bed he'd ordered would come in handy for a few weeks until she felt like she could manage the stairs.

"Well, I've already paid her for a month, so she's coming." Jeremiah could be as stubborn as she was.

"All right, then." She made a show of giving in.

He smiled, obviously loving winning. "The snow's off the roads, so I'll be in first thing tomorrow morning to get you."

"I'll be ready," she answered. "I can't wait to get home."

He nodded his understanding and leaned forward so she could kiss him on the cheek. "Good night, kid," he said.

"Good night." She watched him go. He'd been a bear every day at the hospital. He thought the buzzer worthless. When she needed something or it was time for her medicine, he simply went out in the hallway and yelled until one of the nurses came running. More than one nurse had told Reagan that he was the orneriest man they'd ever had in the hospital as visitor or patient.

Reagan just smiled. That was her uncle, and she loved him. Once she made the staff understand that he was simply worried about her because she was all he had, they changed their attitudes.

The chime sounded in the hallway, announcing that visiting hours were over. Reagan dimmed the lights and closed her eyes, picturing the view from the front window at home. Tomorrow she'd be there.

She was busy planning what she would cook as soon as she could get around on one crutch when the door opened and closed.

Reagan rose on her elbows and stared at the shadow. She made out the shape of a tall man, too wide to be Noah. "Who's there?"

The visitor stepped closer. "I just heard you were in the hospital."

Reagan relaxed, recognizing the voice. "Brandon Biggs, you scared me."

"I'm sorry." He moved to almost within reach. "I just wanted to stop by and make sure you're all right."

"I broke my leg and took a hard hit on the head, but I'm on the mend." She couldn't believe he came all the way from Bailee to Harmony to see her. They weren't even friends, really, but he might not see it that way. Her being one of the few people who liked him well enough to talk to him might count as being a friend in his book. "I'll be going home to recover tomorrow. Doctor says if I do all right, I can go back to school on crutches next week."

"Good," he said. "I got that job with the highway department. Been working two weeks already. I'm waiting for that slice of pie you said you'd buy me to celebrate."

Reagan smiled, barely remembering the offer. Then she realized she might be the only person Brandon Biggs had to celebrate with. As far as she knew, he had no family to go home to, or friends. "I remember, and we will celebrate. I'm proud of you, Bran. I'll just bet you're going to show that old man of yours."

Brandon laughed. "I am for a fact. If I show up and stay sober, I could be making more than he does in five years. I might just go home and kick his ass."

Reagan shook her head. "Forget that. He's not worth your time."

"You're right." He patted her hand awkwardly. "You get better. When I'm around you, I see things clearer. Some people are levelers for others, like that tool with a bubble floating in it. You're that for me, Rea. Without you I'd be a bubble off balance."

Reagan laughed, then groaned in pain because she forgot that if she moved she'd start hurting all over.

Brandon seemed pleased with himself for making her happy.

"You got a place to stay?" she asked, knowing what it was like not to have one.

"Yeah, a guy I work with guessed I was sleeping in the junk heap of a car I drive. He offered me the extra room at his place. His wife left him about a year ago, and he hadn't cleaned up since. She must have not been much of a housekeeper either, because it's like digging through layers of the earth around the place. He said if I'd clean up, he'd let me have the room free until I got my first paycheck, and then he's only charging me a hundred a month, plus I have to buy all the food. Only, he don't eat much, he mostly drinks his meals. But he's not a mean drunk like my stepfather. He just passes out."

Reagan smiled, guessing that was more than Brandon had talked to anyone in weeks. "Can you cook?"

He shrugged. "I can open cans."

"Good enough."

He backed away. "I guess you need your sleep. I'd better get out of here."

"Wait." She raised her hand.

He moved closer and took it. "What's the matter, Rea, you hurting somewhere?"

"No," she said, wondering if she was about to make a mistake, then rushing forward. "Do you know where I live?"

"Sure, down Lone Oak Road. That old Truman place has been there since the dawn of time."

"Sunday." She pushed forward before she changed her mind. "Come to dinner at six."

"I don't . . ."

"I owe you a pie. If you want to collect, you'll have to come."

He shrugged. "All right, if you're sure your uncle won't shoot me on sight."

"I'm not making any promises, but if you make it to the porch without any bullet holes in you, he'll probably let you sit down to dinner. Don't expect him to be happy about it. I think Uncle Jeremiah was born depressed, and it's been a downhill battle ever since. I'll invite a few other people so you won't be the only target, fair enough?"

"Fair enough. I'll come." Brandon backed out of the room.

He bumped into Noah McAllen at the door.

Reagan almost giggled as the two boys, tall enough to be men, glared at each other.

"Hello, Preacher," Brandon said. "Spilled any more brains over the rodeo dirt lately?"

Noah wasn't so friendly. "What are you doing here, Bran?"

"Visiting a sick friend." Brandon puffed up like a toad.

Noah glanced into the room.

Reagan nodded, backing up Brandon's story.

"Well," Noah said. "Since you're leaving, I guess it's my turn."

Before either could move, a nurse appeared from nowhere. "Visiting hours are over, gentlemen. You both need to clear the hallway." When Noah opened his mouth to argue that he'd just arrived, she added, "Now."

He had no choice but to stand in the hallway and wave good-bye to Reagan.

As the door closed, she heard Brandon call back, "I'll hold the elevator for you."

Reagan puffed up her pillow and relaxed, wishing she could roll over on her stomach to sleep, but the cast was far too uncomfortable in that position.

"Home," she whispered. Tomorrow she'd be home.

In a week she'd be back in school, at least for a half day, and in six weeks she'd be out of the cast and back to normal. Funny, she looked forward to going back to her Wednesday night job at the diner.

Of course, it wouldn't be the same. She'd probably have to fight to keep from hugging Gabriel Leary's neck when he picked up his takeout. He was her own private angel, she thought.

And Brandon would probably become a regular in the diner the night she worked. When no one else was in the place, she'd sit and talk to him. In a strange way, they *were* friends. Most of the time she didn't like him—he smelled of cigarettes and cussed worse than a *Deadwood* character—but he seemed to need a friend, and that was about as good a reason to be his friend.

Chapter 27

WEDNESDAY MORNING
FEBRUARY 13, 2008
LEARY FARM

GABRIEL ROSE AT DAWN AND DRANK HIS COFFEE, WATCH-ing the sun fight to brighten a gray, foggy day. His mood was no better than the weather. He'd planned to go into town before now, but each day he seemed to find one more reason to stay away. He told himself he wasn't afraid to face Elizabeth. He'd never been afraid of anything much after he'd run away from home, but somehow that short little blonde had him stalling.

Just sitting in the cold kitchen, his hands seemed to warm thinking about the way her curly hair felt. Like her, it seemed to circle his fingers, pulling him closer. His attraction for her was perfect; he'd never met a more touchable woman. What he couldn't understand was her attraction to him. He guessed he was two, maybe three years older than her; he had a high school education along with several specialist courses in the army, none of which would translate to civilian life; and at his best, before the bomb, he'd never thought of himself as good looking. Now, with the scars and the nightmares, he'd put himself near the bottom on the guys-you'd-want-your-sister-to-date list.

Elizabeth, on the other hand, was a lawyer, which made her about twice as educated as him. She was drop-dead beautiful, even in her caulking outfit when she'd first kissed him. She came from a good family, the best he figured; they loved her, protected her, spoiled her, and occasionally drove her crazy, she claimed.

Gabe glanced through the kitchen doorway at one of his drafting tables, pushed near the window for good light. He could draw. Not paint, just draw. That didn't exactly put him in the same league with Elizabeth's sister and mother. Over the years he'd read articles about her mother's pots selling worldwide, and her sister's dark paintings were showing in places like Dallas and New York. They were real artists. With his pencils he saw himself as more of a craftsman. Claire Matheson's paintings sold in galleries; his work sold at the comic book stands for a dollar.

He'd been drawing all his life. When he was about ten he started tracing the characters in comics and rewriting their stories on his own. His school notebooks were full of, first, cartoon heroes and superpowered avengers he'd read about, then with his own characters, molding and changing with each drawing.

In the army, on long rides or when bored at remote camps, he often drew underworld warriors fighting crime or a band of superpowered soldiers who fought evil all over the world. During the months of recovery, writing the stories and laying out the plot in panels that would fit together into a graphic novel kept him busy. The fantasy kept him sane.

Thanks to the Internet, he'd taken a few courses, developed a voice and style that were unique, and, most important, found talented people to collaborate with. There'd been a dark grittiness to his first series about seasoned warriors fighting evil from an underworld, but some of the horror of war faded when he started his second series about postwar specialists who returned home as crime fighters, all scarred, all gifted.

Pirate pulled him out of his thoughts. The dog loved his morning run. He liked to shoot out the door, barking and running until Gabe whistled. Then Pirate would stop, take care of business, and run back. When Gabe walked out with him, the dog stayed at his side as if on guard.

Gabe walked through the house, shut off the alarm system, and opened the front door. "Take off, boy," he commanded.

Pirate darted out into the crisp air so thick with fog it swallowed him after twenty yards.

Gabe laughed, listening to the dog bark as he ran.

Once he'd forgotten to turn off the security system. By the time Pirate made his run, the panel on the far wall of what had once been a living area was lit up like Christmas. Gabe had spent weeks placing sensors around his home when he finally was able to walk. The security system and two guns within reach of his bed were the only things that made it possible for him to sleep at night.

Gabe listened as the dog's bark came from farther away. He wished he could run like that. Before the bomb he used to love to run in the rain, feeling almost like he was crossing into another dimension. Now, when he tried to run, it was more a straight-legged hop across the ground, one that had caused him to tumble more times than he could count before finally giving in to the idea that he'd never run again.

He whistled and knew Pirate had turned back. In a few minutes he'd hit the porch wet, exhausted, and probably muddy. He reached for an old towel he kept on a hook

beside the door. He'd learned the hard way that it was easier to clean Pirate up on the porch than to clean the floor
inside.

The last spot of snow a few feet from the door caught
his eye as he waited. For a second, he stared at it, thinking it might be some kind of freak of nature, and then he
recognized the sign pressed into the snow and his heart felt
like it might pound out of his chest.

In the dirty snow, an arm's length away, someone had
drawn a smiley face. A circle head, a smiling curve for a
mouth, and two spent shells for eyes pushed into the snow
until, at first glance, one might think they were gold buttons.

He grabbed the empty shells, cold as ice to the touch.
M16s, the same kind they'd always used on assignment.
A secret code. Only a handful of men had ever known of
it, and most, if not all except him, were dead. The smiling face was a joke. The marking was sometimes left at
a spot that had been cleared but that no one believed was
truly safe. If Gabe had to translate the friendly face with
bullet eyes, he'd say it said, *Come on in, friend, the bullets
are waiting.* Only this time it marked the snow next to his
home and not the sand in another land.

Pirate bounded past him, shaking Gabe into action.
He dropped the unused towel, closed the door, locked it,
turned on the alarm system, and rushed to an extra bedroom he rarely entered.

Once there, he stripped down to his underwear and
opened a trunk neatly packed with what he'd need: a warrior's uniform almost exactly like he'd worn as a soldier.
Only this one was put together, one piece at a time, from
Internet orders. He dressed with practiced speed, not needing the light, checking each weapon to make sure it was
ready for use.

Four minutes later, he stepped back into the living space
fully armed and dressed in battle gear.

Whoever had left the sign in the snow wanted Gabe to know that he was out there, walking on his land, getting close enough to the house to look in the windows, easily within firing range. He also wanted Gabe to understand that he knew the truth about Gabe's past. Whoever was out there knew Gabe would know what the sign meant and also figured that Gabe would be ready when he came to call.

The only question Gabe had: Was the stranger a friend, leaving a message of greeting from the past, or an enemy dropping the gauntlet before the battle began?

Logic told him that with his bad leg, he'd have little chance standing on equal ground outside, but inside he had the advantage.

He pulled a chair to the middle of the house so that he could see both the front and back door as well as most of the windows that were not boarded up. Then he shut off the security system, opened the front door, and sat down in the chair, his rifle resting at his side.

Gabe guessed that he wouldn't hear anyone coming. If whoever was out there had already gotten so close without being detected, he could do so again.

Pirate sensed something was wrong. He sat at attention next to Gabe's chair. "Easy, boy," Gabe whispered. "We won't have to wait long."

When the dog suddenly turned his head toward the back door, Gabe lifted the rifle, swung around, and took aim in one swift movement.

A shadow of a man, framed by the watery sunlight, froze.

Gabe held his finger a hair away from firing. The man before him was tall, broad shouldered, and dressed in the layers of a hunter.

The shadow slowly lifted his hands. "I'm not armed," he said almost calmly. "Sergeant Wiseman, don't fire. It's Lieutenant Denver Sims." He hesitated, as if forcing a breath out. "Or I was in another lifetime."

It took Gabe a moment to place the name. Denver had been in their unit on his first tour of duty. He'd been hit in the shoulder by a sniper, but Gabe had heard he returned to duty. He remembered being happy when, a few weeks before the bombing, he'd heard Denver was scheduled to be assigned near his company. They might not work together, but they'd be stationed at the same post. If they'd had more time, they might have been friends. Not best friends. Neither had any. They might have been each other's only friend.

"I'm not Wiseman," Gabe said without lowering the weapon. Five years ago Sims had been a good man, a good soldier, but in five years a lot can change. "You've got the wrong man."

"I know. You're not Wiseman or Smith either, but I do have the right man." Sims laughed. His face might still be in shadow, but Gabe recognized the laugh. They'd always laughed at the same things, things no one else thought were funny.

"Look, Gabriel whoever-you-are," Sims almost shouted. "Shoot me or invite me in. I'm half dead from waiting out in the cold without coffee for days for you to open the door."

Gabe lowered the rifle and stood. "I almost didn't recognize your voice without the swear words." He used to kid Denver that he thought *damn* could fit as any part of speech.

"I know. I cleaned up my act." Denver took one step into the house but didn't lower his hands. "My wife said she'd leave me if I didn't. Damn waste of time. I thought she was putting in a request and come to find out she already had her bags packed and was simply listing complaints."

"Sorry to hear that," Gabe said, watching Denver move closer, both still unsure of the other.

"It was for the best. She was too good for me." Denver opened his jacket, showing that he carried no weapons.

"In fact, that's the only thing we ever agreed on. We both thought it, and she said it daily."

Gabe smiled, guessing both of them needed time before getting down to why Sims was here. "If you'll leave those muddy boots on the porch and close the door, I'm offering a cup of coffee."

Denver knelt and unlaced his boots. "Any chance the coffee could come with a side of breakfast? I've been washing down energy bars with water for so long I swear I'll start mooing if I have any more ground fiber with barley."

Gabe wanted to ask why, but he knew there would be time for that later. They needed to size one another up. Look for the truth and honesty they'd both shared once before they sorted today's truth from lie.

He set the rifle by the sink and made breakfast, still fully armed, while Denver circled around the big open living/dining area like he thought Gabe's home was a museum and he'd paid admission.

"So this is what a big-time writer's studio looks like. I can see it all, the pieces that fit together. I feel like I'm in the delivery room where novels are born." Denver moved to pages of script taped to a wall. "This must be the script." He looked down at the graph paper on the table. "These must be the thumbnails, your first sketches of how the story will be laid out. I've read about how it works. It all seems so complicated."

Gabe stopped beating a half dozen eggs and watched Denver sorting through a rough idea he was working on for a story. "You know a lot about my work. Thinking of taking it up?"

"No. I just did my research." Denver looked up, his smile as easy as ever. "I remember you used to doodle on paper when all the other guys were writing letters home." He lifted a metal T-square from a drafting table cluttered with pencils, erasers, and half-finished sketches.

Gabe set the bowl down and slowly lowered his hand toward the weapon strapped to his waist.

Denver didn't miss the action. "Easy," he said as he set the T-square down on a light box. "I wasn't choosing a weapon. I'm here as your friend, Gabriel, nothing more. Whatever you went through must have been bad if you're so jumpy. I respect that."

Gabe nodded. They understood one another. He finished cooking breakfast, and they sat down across the table from each other. Halfway through the meal, Gabe picked easy ground to start on. "How'd you know I wrote graphic novels?"

Denver finished chewing and said as he raised his coffee cup, "I was in a bookstore in L.A. looking for something to read for a long flight I had to make. I passed by the comic books and thought of you and how you used to read the damn things like they were real books. Then, just by luck, I saw one of yours. Something about the cover looked familiar. You know, like sometimes you see a face and swear you've seen it before but can't place it."

When Gabe didn't answer, he continued. "I bought the book. Hell, before that day I didn't even know that comic books came in novel form. As I read it, I couldn't shake the feeling that someone was pulling from my memories. Your characters might have been superheroes fighting monsters from the underworld, but they were using strategies I'd learned. I figured whoever wrote the stories had to have been in Special Forces, but when I Googled G. L. Smith, he was a ghost."

Gabe pushed his plate aside. "So, you decided to find out who I was? Awful lot of effort for a man who doesn't even read comics."

Denver shook his head. "I think in my gut, I knew from the first it was you." He looked straight at Gabe with all guards down. "You're the closest friend I ever had. It's always bothered me that you just disappeared. Five years ago, when I heard you were wounded, I tried to contact you. No one seemed to know where you were. The hospital said you just vanished. The nurse I finally talked to at Brooke Army Medical Center acted like alien abductions weren't all that uncommon in San Antonio.

"So, I had a puzzle. G. L. Smith didn't exist, and Gabriel Wiseman walked away into nowhere one night five years ago." He spread his hands and grinned. "And I'm sitting around with a half million dollars' worth of training on how to find people who want to stay lost and nothing to do but look."

Denver stood and refilled his coffee. For a man his size, six feet four and over two hundred pounds, he moved silent as a cat. "I'm an air marshal now, flying back and forth across the U.S. like a lone Canada goose. I flirt with stewardesses most days, sleep with whoever I find at the hotel bars when I can, and read. And"—he grinned—"look for the one guy who I ever thought of as a friend. The guy who apparently would shoot me if I made one wrong move. Maybe we weren't as close as I remembered."

"Hand me your wallet," Gabe ordered.

Denver hesitated, then passed it across the table.

When Gabe flipped it open he saw the marshal badge. After flipping through credit cards, he asked, "No pictures of kids?"

"No. Old habits die hard. After a dozen years in the army I still haven't learned to develop ties. If you kill me and bury me in that mud hole you call farmland, the only person who'll miss me will be a ticket agent at American in Dallas. I promised I'd come to her retirement party next month."

Gabe let down his guard an inch. In a strange way it was good to know that he wasn't the only one who had trouble falling into the circle-of-friends-and-family story. "What weapons you got on your body right now?"

Denver smiled. "A knife in my boot on the porch and a Glock strapped to my calf. And before you ask, no you can't have it. You might not trust me, Gabriel, but for all I know, you've gone full-blown nutcase since we last saw each other. A few weapons between us will keep everything polite. Fair enough?"

"Fair enough," Gabe answered, thinking he wouldn't surrender all his weapons either, even to a friend.

Someone pounded on his front door before he could ask any more questions.

"Yours?" Gabe looked at Denver.

Denver shook his head. "I came alone."

The pounding came again, along with a female shouting, "Gabe, are you in there? It's freezing out here. Open the door."

Denver smiled, not able to hide his surprise. "Your girl?"

"No." Gabe moved to the door. "My lawyer."

Opening the door, he swore she must have catapulted herself into his arms. He took a step back as he caught her.

He hadn't had a visitor in five years and now it seemed he needed a traffic light on his door.

Elizabeth kissed his cheek with cold lips and then backed away, pulling off her gloves and hat. She was dressed totally in purple from her stocking cap to her boots, and, of course, she was in the middle of a sentence before he realized she was talking.

"I didn't know if my car would make it down that dirt road of yours. Gabe, you need to get that paved or at least graveled. I probably should have waited another day, but I was worried about you. Martha Q thought you were surely dead halfway between here and town. Mrs. Biggs said if you were alive you were probably starving out here, so she sent food. Martha Q made me promise to call. . . ."

Elizabeth stopped, frozen in midsentence by the big man standing on the other side of the room. He looked like some kind of mountain man with a week's worth of black beard and hair that hadn't been washed or combed in days. Even in stocking feet, he was tall, and she swore mud was caked to every part of him, including his eyebrows.

When she turned back to Gabe, he knew the second she became aware of what he was wearing.

"What is this, some kind of Halloween party? You guys are a little late, or way too early, and I doubt one person will give either of you candy."

Gabe had no idea what to say. He wasn't good at explaining anything, and he had no idea how to explain this.

Denver, on the other hand, just started talking as if there were some scenario that would make sense to the purple bunny at their door.

"Hello, miss. Gabe tells me you're his lawyer. I have to say I didn't know lawyers came as beautiful as you or I'd be out committing crimes." He moved forward.

Elizabeth backed up until she bumped into Gabe, then looked at him like she blamed him somehow for letting this chatty creature into the house.

Denver kept talking. "I've been out deer hunting, so I must look frightening, but I promise I'm harmless. Didn't even kill anything on the hunt this year. I thought I'd stop off and see my old army buddy before I head back to Dallas, but my car broke down a few miles back. I hiked in to see if Gabe would give me a hand." He smiled. "I figured, looking like I do, no one would give me a lift."

For once Elizabeth was speechless. She looked Gabe up and down. Dressed as the town mugger, he knew he was frightening. Dressed as a commando, he watched her eyes go wide with terror. He had no doubt she was probably considering having the farm quarantined due to an outbreak of rampant insanity.

Denver saved him again. "Don't let Gabe scare you, darling. I just made him a bet he couldn't fit into his old uniform and so he proved he could. I swear, I haven't seen the man in five years and he hasn't gained a pound."

Gabe unbuckled his heavy belt and set it on one of the tables. "Other than worrying about me being dead, Elizabeth, what brought you out?" If he'd left the security system on, he would have known when she turned off the main road and onto his land. He pulled off the camouflage shirt and faced her in a black turtleneck.

She didn't look any less frightened.

Finally, she seemed to see him more than the uniform. When he saw her relax, he winked at her, and that seemed to be all it took for her to move close. Gabe decided it was time for them all to start over. "Elizabeth, I'd like you to meet Denver Sims. He may look a little frightening, but he's a federal air marshal and a friend from years ago."

Denver was smart enough not to push his luck and offer his hand. "Nice to meet you," he said. "Can I help you carry some of that food in?"

"I hope you're hungry." She looked up at Gabe.

"We're starving," Denver answered. "It's been far too long since we had breakfast. Did you say someone baked something? I haven't had anything homemade in years. I spend most of my days eating breakfast out of a vending machine, then lunch and dinner on a plane."

Both men followed her out and carried in two pies, a cake, and a half dozen loaves of bread. Gabe made more coffee and listened as they talked. Years without having anyone in his house made the two of them seem like a crowd.

After they finished sampling everything Mrs. Biggs had sent, Elizabeth walked around the big room looking at his work, but it was Denver doing the explaining.

Gabe wouldn't have known where to start.

Two hours later, when Gabe finally walked Liz to her car, he put his arm around her shoulder, realizing how few times in his life he'd done such a simple thing. "I'm glad you came," he said.

"Me too." Her arm circled his waist. "Would you have invited me?"

"Probably not. I've never invited anyone."

"What about Denver?"

Gabe shook his head. "I haven't had anyone but the mailman stop here since my dad died over four years ago except for old Jeremiah Truman, and I didn't invite him in. He's a funny old guy. He acts like he doesn't like a soul on the planet, but he worried about me like I was kin when I was still laid up."

"That's good." She stopped at her car door and turned to face him.

Gabe smiled. "I think he'd consider it a curse when his caring side shows."

She was so close he could smell her hair and feel her warm breath against his collar. "I'm glad you came," he whispered against her ear.

The need to hold her washed over him like a flood. Lifting her up, he pressed her against her car and molded his body along hers to hold her in place as his mouth lowered to her lips.

His sudden passion surprised her, but she didn't protest. In fact, she remained perfectly still, her mouth slightly open, her hands at her side.

Gabe might not understand women, but even he knew something was wrong. He pulled far enough away to look down at her, but his body could still feel her chest rising and falling against him.

"Too much. Too fast," he whispered, already hating himself for ruining what they might have had between them.

She shook her head, then buried it against his shirt. "He's watching," she managed.

Gabe looked up to see Denver leaning against the front door frame, smiling like a fool. Lifting his hand over

Elizabeth's ear, he shouted, "I'm going to kill you after she leaves."

"Sorry to interrupt," Denver said, not looking sorry at all. "I just wanted to ask if she had a sister."

Elizabeth turned her face up to Gabe. He could feel her giggling against him and knew she was thinking the same thing he was. Everyone for a hundred miles around knew of Claire's hatred of men.

Gabe cupped her ear again as if he were keeping her from hearing his shout. "On second thought, Denver, I'm going to let you live. There's someone I'd like you to meet."

"You'll come over tomorrow night?" Elizabeth whispered. "My mom's making chicken enchiladas. It'll just be family."

"Yes." He liked the way she smiled. "And I'll bring him." Gabe pointed with his head.

"Clean him up first," she said loudly.

"Did you hear that, Denver, we've been invited to supper, if you'll take a bath and shave."

Denver hooted. "Mind if I use your shower? I need to get started right away to get the layers off in time."

Gabe waved him away with one hand and pulled Elizabeth closer with the other. "Everything all right, now?"

She looked over his shoulder to make sure Denver was gone, then nodded.

"Mind if I kiss you?" He wanted to make sure he'd be welcomed if he got closer.

She answered by standing on her tiptoes and brushing her lips over his.

Chapter 28

My fourth funeral for the new year.

TYLER WRIGHT WAS WRITING HIS DAILY E-MAIL. HE WROTE every night just like he used to write to his friend Kate. She hadn't answered an e-mail in two years, but he still wrote.

He leaned back, thinking he was probably the greatest fool ever born. A lonely bachelor in his forties who sent an e-mail to a woman he'd seen only a few times. They'd shared a dinner once at an out-of-the-way lodge on a night too icy to drive. They'd agreed that if the e-mails ever stopped, they would both go the first Monday of the months following for three months and wait for the other.

He'd been going on the first Monday to Quartz Mountain Lodge for two years. She never came.

I'm still missing you, he wrote. He'd told himself he wasn't going to write those words again, but he just wanted her to know. *Not much has happened here. Remember Reagan Truman? I told you about her getting hurt. She's out of the hospital and on the mend.*

Stella McNabb poked her head into Tyler's office. "The Hendersons are gone, Mr. Wright. Mrs. Biggs was a lot of help tonight. You want to drive her home while I finish up? I hate keeping her out too late when she might have someone besides Martha Q to cook for in the morning."

"Sure. Glad to," Tyler said, a moment before he clicked Send. He could have thought about it for a while, but no one was reading his e-mails anyway. "I'll get my hat and be right there."

He rushed around the desk and grabbed his hat and coat. "Come on, Little Lady, let's go take Mrs. Biggs back to the inn."

The border collie stood and shook, as if fluffing her coat for the trip.

Mrs. Biggs was waiting for them when they reached the reception area. Since the mystery lady had showed up at his cemetery, Tyler had somehow become responsible for her.

When he had her tucked into the car, he said, "Thanks for helping out tonight. The Hendersons are a big family and sometimes get a little rowdy when they have a night visitation. Stella can usually handle them, after corralling high school kids for forty years, but I'd hate to think what they'd do if the food ran out."

Mrs. Biggs laughed. "You know, they're sweet people. I went to school with a few of them before I moved away. We used to play a game when they weren't around. Someone would say Hendersons and we'd all try to name them in order as fast as we could. With all the names starting with *H*, it wasn't easy."

Tyler smiled. "It probably didn't help that Mrs. Henderson got mixed up and named two of them Henry."

"Henry the first and Henry the second. I'd forgotten that."

"They're both dead. The oldest Henry of cancer about ten years ago and the younger one in a car wreck in Houston. I made the long drive to bring him home."

They were silent for a minute before Mrs. Biggs said, "You're a good man, Mr. Wright."

"I try," Tyler said, thinking of one person on the end of an e-mail connection who must not think so. "A few years ago we had someone setting grass fires around Harmony and the federal people Alex brought in thought it was me. I even got arrested." He shook his head. "It wasn't my finest hour."

"I'm glad it was cleared up, Mr. Wright, or I'd have to bake you a cake with a file in it."

They both laughed, but remembering the day his Kate saw him in handcuffs made him sad. It had been the last time he'd seen her wonderful hazel eyes.

Tyler waited until Mrs. Biggs made it inside, then turned on the radio as Little Lady jumped into the front seat. They both drove home listening to the mellow sounds of jazz.

Chapter 29

❦

GABE WASN'T SURE WHAT HE EXPECTED A FAMILY NIGHT supper at the Mathesons' to be like, but a table for ten wasn't it. The fire chief, Elizabeth's brother, was there with his wife-to-be, the sheriff. Two little old ladies who told him to call them Aunt Pat and Aunt Fat were there. They looked so much alike he knew he'd never keep their names straight. A frail little girl on crutches smiled up at him when she answered the door and kept staring at him as he was introduced to the others. Elizabeth's mother, Joyce, was nice, but had that now-what-are-you-two-guys-doing-here look about her as she showed them into a large living room decorated in leather.

Elizabeth was nowhere in sight, and minutes after

meeting everyone, Gabe had run out of anything to say. He'd gone into town and bought a new pair of jeans and a white sweater, so he assumed he looked presentable enough. He'd even made a trip to the barber shop and gotten a shave. Denver had followed along, buying tan slacks and a turtleneck, but skipping the shave and haircut in favor of fast food next door. He looked more like a young Hemingway than an air marshal.

Denver and Alex started talking shop, leaving everyone else, including Hank, out of the conversation. The aunts and the mother vanished back into the kitchen, leaving Gabe sitting next to the kid on a long couch.

"How'd you get that scar?" Saralynn, about six, asked.

Gabe looked at her. No one had ever asked him that. As soon as the wound on his face had healed, he'd grown the beard. He regretted shaving. "I was in the army."

The kid looked at him as if she could see all the way to his soul. He'd never been around kids and couldn't help wondering if they all seemed so creepy. "Where'd you get those crutches?" he asked, hoping she'd get mad or bored and move away.

"In the army," she answered without blinking.

"Oh yeah, what branch?"

"The willow branch." She giggled. "I was a hero. I got a purple heart to prove it, but you can't see it 'cause it's still inside of me."

He smiled, realizing the kid was playing with him. "That's a good branch. They go into the windy fights, don't they?"

She nodded. "We carry laser guns." She raised her crutch like it was a rifle. "We can shoot the bad guys and freeze them solid in a second. When they thaw, they never do bad things again . . . and hair never grows on their face for as long as they live."

"You know a lot about laser guns," Gabe said, fascinated by her imagination.

"I go with my great-aunts to a place where they zap the chin hair off people. But the doctors have no idea what a great weapon they have."

Gabe, who spent most of his days in fantasy, had no trouble stepping into her world. "What are we going to do if hairless invaders try to steal our lasers?"

"We'll have to fight them off with huge rubber bands because everyone knows bullets don't kill hairless invaders. They slip right over their heads."

"Of course," he answered. "Unless they're sunburned, of course."

Saralynn nodded once. "Of course, but very few people know about that." She studied him a few seconds and then asked, "Can I touch your scar?"

He leaned closer and she placed her thin hand on the side of his face, where a scar almost as wide as her little finger ran from the corner of his ear along his jawline to almost his chin.

"Does it still hurt?"

"No," he said. "A scar just becomes part of you, like a memory, but it doesn't hurt."

"Good," she said. "The doctor says if I have surgery on my legs, I'll have scars. I'm glad they won't hurt."

He saw it in her eyes. Saralynn had lived her whole life with pain. He felt weak for complaining about the few months he'd suffered. "When it's over," he said, "the scars will let everyone know you're a hero."

"Like you," she said, pulling her hand away. "You saved Reagan Truman's life. I heard Alex and Uncle Hank talking about it."

Before he could say more to this angel on crutches, he heard laughter and turned to see the Matheson sisters step into the room. Elizabeth's sister was a complete opposite of her. Where Liz was petite with curly hair and had an excitement for everything in life, Claire was tall, slender, and remote. She glanced around the room with big brown eyes and seemed to be silently chanting that nothing and no one interested her.

Elizabeth rushed over to Gabe. "You shaved." She smiled. "Now I can see your face." She put her hand on the side of his face, touching his scar as Saralynn had. "It's a great face."

He watched closely, but she didn't blink at the scar. He wasn't sure she even saw it. Funny, he'd worried about how people would react to it for years, and the first two he'd met hadn't turned away at all.

"Everyone," Elizabeth yelled over the talking, "have you all met Gabe and his friend Denver?"

"No," Claire said, standing right in front of Gabe so that he would have had to push her aside to stand. Her jeans and spotted white shirt told everyone that she hadn't bothered to dress for dinner and that coming down to meet them was interrupting her work. "I don't believe I've met your client. Gabriel, is it? The inmate."

Gabe was at a disadvantage with her towering above him, and he had a feeling Claire knew it. He nodded once as Elizabeth made the introductions. She ended with, "He's not an inmate, Claire, he wasn't even booked."

Claire's smile blinked so fast across her lips, Gabe wasn't sure he'd seen it. "I'm glad to see they let you out of jail in time for dinner," she said, glanced at Alex, and added, "Sheriff, are you sure he didn't try to murder that poor girl and only played the savior after you arrived?"

Alex looked embarrassed by the question, and Hank opened his mouth to stop his sister from continuing, but it was Gabe who spoke first.

"If I were a murderer, we'd have a great deal in common. I understand you murder men on canvas for money. Kind of like a hired killer." Gabe swore he saw her claws come out. Beneath the beauty was an angry woman he wished he could get at least a room's length away from.

"Dinner's ready." Joyce Matheson called her guests and children to the dining room.

Claire glared at Gabe but turned quickly, as though she'd messed up the introductions completely.

Before she could think of something else to say to Gabe, Denver stepped between them. His height towered above everyone, even Claire. "Nobody introduced me." Denver offered his hands to her, unaware of the claws. "I'm Gabriel's friend, but don't hold that against me. I'll help you kill him if you're set on the idea. He must be nuts to think a sweet woman like you would even think of murdering anyone. You're Claire Matheson; I've heard of your work."

Claire blinked and looked at Denver as if he had the brains of a sopapilla. "You know my work?"

"No, but I'd sure like to. I read an article about you on the airplane the other day. I would have guessed you would have been older to be so well known." He stared for a moment, then lowered his voice. "There's something about tall brown-eyed women that always stops my heart. I apologize for staring."

Gabe thought Claire looked like she was getting another idea for one of her paintings. Denver didn't seem to notice; he just picked up her hand, put it in the crook of his arm, and asked her to show him in to dinner.

Elizabeth laughed at Gabe's side. "Hope she doesn't kill him before dessert. They make an interesting couple, don't you think? In fact, if he were wearing armor I'd say they were the perfect couple."

Gabe started to offer his arm to Liz, then had a better idea. He leaned down toward Saralynn. "I got a limp, sweetheart," he whispered to the little girl. "But if you'll trust me, I think I can manage to carry you into dinner."

She raised her arms and he lifted her feather-light body. Liz showed him the way into the wide dining room that probably had a hundred years' worth of Mathesons sitting around the table. Tonight everything was done up in red and black, with smells of onion and peppers drifting in the air. Bowls of beans, flour tortillas, and Spanish rice were already on the table. As they took their seats, the two sweet old aunts brought in platters of chili-covered burritos and creamy chicken enchiladas. Huge baskets of hollow sopapillas and corn bread packed the table as everyone began filling their plates while they passed food.

Somewhere in the bedlam wine bottles circled the table, and Hank made a toast to winter ending and an early spring. Gabe thought he might have mentioned that it was Valentine's Day, but with this group it might not be the right holiday to celebrate. Better to play it safe and talk about the weather.

With females outnumbering the males seven to three, Gabe wasn't surprised he said little. Elizabeth must have told her brother what he did for a living because Hank asked a few questions about his work. Gabe returned the favor by asking how the fire department in town was doing. Neither cared enough about the other's work, but to keep the conversation going they both had satisfied their conversation requirements.

Denver, on the other hand, was used to meeting strangers and talked to everyone at the table. He was one of those gifted people who acted like he was truly interested in whatever anyone had to say. When asked about his work, he kept everyone laughing about funny things that he'd witnessed on planes. By the time dessert was served, everyone was begging him to drop by if he was ever out this way again.

Gabe watched, guessing some of Denver was an act. A man who meets new people every day would have time to polish his art. He was almost like an actor on stage going over lines he said at every performance. The only crack, Gabe noticed, was his fascination with Claire. She never directed a word she said to him, but he listened to everything she said, and several times Gabe noticed Denver watching her.

When the old aunts started talking about their quilts,

Denver told them he was dying to see a frame hanging from a ceiling. As soon as dinner was over, they took him off down the long hallway to their quarters where a quilting frame had been set up in their sitting room so they could watch their soaps while they quilted.

Claire waited for Saralynn to say good night to everyone and then helped her daughter off to bed. Elizabeth's mother vanished in the kitchen, leaving Gabe and Elizabeth on one side of the table and Hank and Alex on the other. Alex reminded him of some of the women he'd served with in the army: strong, efficient, and all business. Only tonight, with Hank's hand on her arm gently stroking, Gabe saw another side of the sheriff. She was a woman cherished, but he wasn't sure she knew it yet.

"I'm glad you came to dinner." Hank sounded honest. "It was nice to meet you." The way he said the last words made it sound like he didn't plan to see Gabe often.

That was Gabe's feeling exactly about everyone in the room except Elizabeth. He'd never really thought about it before, but the perfect girlfriend would be a woman who was raised in an orphanage . . . no relatives and had amnesia . . . no friends or ex-boyfriends. Gabe almost laughed aloud at his own joke. He doubted Elizabeth would think it as funny as he did.

Alex leaned against Hank's shoulder and asked if he'd see her home, which Gabe thought strange because he'd noticed both their cars in the drive. Hank nodded and smiled just for Alex.

Gabe stood, shook hands, and mumbled something as they said good-bye. When he sat back down, he noticed Liz playing with the pie she hadn't eaten. He couldn't think of anything to say, so he just watched her. He liked watching her.

"Sorry about my sister," she finally said. "We probably should have warned Denver about her."

Gabe smiled, thinking the ex-lieutenant could take care

of himself, but saying, "At least we know he's safe with the two aunts."

She looked up at him. "You surprise me, Gabriel Leary. The more I learn about you, the more different you seem from anyone I've ever met. My brother likes you too."

"Hank? You could have fooled me."

"No, he likes you. Hank measures everyone by how they react to Saralynn. Trust me, when you carried her in to dinner, you won him over."

"How about Claire? Does she like me too?"

Elizabeth grinned. "She hates you, but don't take it personal. She only mildly liked her husband. I think she dreamed of a wedding when she was a kid and the groom was just an accessory like the cake, and preacher, and flowers. After she married, he didn't measure up to what she wanted, so she tried having a kid. That didn't help make her world perfect, so she told him she wanted a divorce. He got mad and through court battles managed to make her hate all men. When she said good-bye to him, he said good-bye to them both."

"She loves Saralynn. She may be obsessed with her work, but when she looks at her daughter I noticed her hard eyes softened."

Liz agreed. "Of course, now, but at first while they were going through the divorce and Saralynn was in and out of hospitals, I'm not so sure. Her husband thought she went way overboard as a crusader to make sure Saralynn got the best of everything: doctors, treatments, new medicine. I think when they couldn't *fix* her, Claire took it hard. She thought it was somehow her fault."

Liz turned her chair toward him and put her bare feet up on his leg. "But don't worry about Claire. I think Mom likes you, and she's the only one who gets the vote around here. If she likes you, she'll be asking me when you'll be back to dinner."

He didn't care one way or the other if they liked him,

but he liked seeing her smile. He also liked being here tonight, seeing all the action at a family dinner. They had all watched him tonight, not because of who he was or what he was but because Liz had brought him home. "I'll come whenever you invite me."

He put his hand over her small foot. "Those shoes hurt?" he asked, trying to think of something to talk about besides how much he liked touching her.

She glanced at the high heels beside her chair. "All shoes that look good hurt," she said. "Want to go in and watch TV? It may take hours for Denver to get away from the aunts."

"Sure," he said, hoping she didn't ask him what he liked. He hadn't watched anything but the news in years.

They settled onto the couch in the big living room and she flipped through channels. Gabe just watched her.

When she found an old movie, she cuddled up against him and pulled one of the multicolored throws over them both. Gabe took a deep breath and relaxed. He loved the feel of her so close.

He could so get used to seeing her like this.

Chapter 30

THURSDAY, 9:30 P.M.
FEBRUARY 14, 2008
MATHESON RANCH

DENVER HEARD THE MUFFLED SOUNDS OF A TV AS HE left the aunts' wing and moved down a long dark hallway to the main house. Paintings, many he guessed were originals, crowded the walls. There were also tall shelves packed with books and tables loaded with pots. Just the kind of home he'd expect an artist to grow up in.

He'd had fun tonight. The dinner reminded him of his home in Wyoming. Big meals, big family, lots of laughter, and a little fighting. Only in his family there were always kids. By the time his mother had her last child—him—his two oldest sisters were both into their second pregnancies, and no one except him ever thought of leaving home. The ranch headquarters was starting to look like a little village. His grandfather had built two cottages for his kids when they married. When babies started coming, he'd just clear a spot and build a bigger place for them. Now his grandfather lived in one of the cottages, and the main house had a dining room that would feed twenty-four and did every Sunday.

Denver was in college before he spent a night alone in a room. He grew up on bunk beds, slept on a single bunk in college, and went back to bunks in the army. Now, when he crashed in a hotel every night, he still woke during the night trying to hang his arms off both sides of a king-sized bed.

Halfway down the hallway he sensed someone. Years of trusting his instincts had kept him alive, making him slow now, allowing his eyes time to adjust.

Five feet away, he smelled her. Not a perfume, but more the hint of oil paints blending with her shampoo and the light lavender scent of a hand lotion she'd left on his palm when they'd touched.

"Claire," he said simply, and waited for her to move away from the shadows of bookshelves.

She stood in his path, tall and still, her head high, her arms at her sides. He could hear her breathing, and it reminded him of a strong animal frightened for the first time.

"Claire," he said more gently as he stepped closer.

She didn't move, or speak. She just stood staring at him with those big brown eyes he felt like he might drown in if he ventured too close.

When they were inches apart, he wrapped his arm around her waist and pulled her hard against him. He could see her wonderful eyes in the hint of light and knew that she'd been waiting for him.

Without a word, he cupped the back of her head and pulled her mouth to his.

The kiss was fast and hungry, unlike any kiss he'd ever given a woman. Or taken, he thought. She was perfectly still against him, making no move to step away.

He pushed her back into the shadows, pressed her against the wall with the length of his body, and ordered against her lips, "Open your mouth, Claire. Kiss me back."

She did, timid at first, then more boldly.

She remained stiff in his arms, but he didn't stop. He'd watched her all evening and wished for a moment alone with her. Now that he had it, Denver didn't plan to waste it. He moved his hands over her boldly as he bruised her lips with his hunger. The need to touch her fired like a cannon in his brain, blasting out all other thought. She felt every bit as good as he prayed she would.

He spread his hand over the layer of cotton covering her small breast and she jerked, but still didn't step away. He moved his palm over her again and again, more a man taming a wild animal than a lover. He could see her mental struggle not to react, but her body wouldn't move away. In her eyes, he saw it all. She hated the simple fact that she wanted him.

He straightened away from her, then slowly raised his hand once more and gently cupped her breast again. "If you don't want this," he whispered, lightly stroking her, "then you'd better say something."

She waited but didn't say a word.

He lowered his hands to her waist, then spread his fingers over her body to her shoulders.

She didn't move, but he felt her swaying to his touch.

Turning her to face the wall, he moved his fingers down her back, dying for the need to touch her. She sighed as his hands pressed over her hips.

"Turn around," he whispered into her hair.

She did as he asked.

"Close your eyes, darling," he said before pushing her gently against the wall and kissing her again.

When he pulled away, he waited.

She breathed hard, glared at him, and waited for him to kiss her again.

He did. Each time bolder, hotter. Each time expecting her to struggle and pull away. Each time surprised when she remained silent and waited for more.

Slowly, she melted against him and his kiss turned tender. She hated all men, and he knew she would have cut a gentle man to shreds before he could have ever gotten so close to her. It had been so long since he'd felt anything, but now the need for her burned inside him and he had a feeling the same was true for her. He'd known the moment he'd seen her that he'd hold her like this.

Without backing away, he moved his mouth to her ear. "Now, put your arms around me, darling. That's right." He moved his fingers along her rib cage, gently stroking her sides. "Now, arch your back away from the wall." She did. "That's it, baby, press against me."

He kissed her again, deep and long, with her body so close against him he could feel her heart pounding. The need to touch her skin became as important to him as breathing air, but the last ounce of reason in his brain thought of what might happen if the aunts or her mother stepped into the hallway. This was not the time for making love.

Stepping an inch away, he pressed his cheek against hers. "We can't do this here. Meet me, Claire."

"Where?" she whispered, out of breath.

"Anywhere," he answered just before he lowered his mouth against her throat. "Anywhere," he mumbled. "Any time."

She moaned softly and pulled his mouth back to hers. Her kiss was filled with need, but he tasted regret. They both knew nothing more could happen.

He kissed her again the way he'd longed to kiss a woman all his life. Denver felt he'd been searching for perfection in a kiss, and he'd finally found it with a woman who hadn't said one nice thing to him since they'd met.

"Meet me," he whispered as she pressed her hand on his heart and pushed him away.

"I can't," she answered with a cry, and moved away.

He reached for her, but she was gone. He raised his arms and pushed against the wall as he let out a whispered oath. The first woman he'd wanted in forever had just turned him down. He took the knowledge of it like a blow to the gut.

It took him a few minutes to get a grip on what had happened. This wasn't a hotel, but her home, and she wasn't someone he could pick up, she was a respected artist and mother. He'd been swimming in waters without rules or values or restraints for so long, he had no idea how to stay afloat here.

He walked back to the living room and found Gabe and Liz sitting in a corner of the couch wrapped in one another and sound asleep. Grabbing the remote, he began to flip channels without being aware of anything that was on.

He'd done it all wrong, Denver decided. Grabbing a woman in a dark hallway wasn't the way to start. He was thirty-five, totally alone, and bored. If he hadn't figured out relationships by now, there was probably no hope for him. Maybe he should take his mother's advice and go home to marry one of the list of girls his relatives had picked for him. Then he could live in the big family house and raise horses, pigs, and kids.

Denver looked at Gabriel. He couldn't even talk to people and he'd managed to find a woman who seemed to think he was worth inviting home to meet the family.

Denver swore and decided to wake Gabe up and demand, if they'd ever been even passing friends, that Gabe shoot him and put him out of his misery.

Chapter 31

Thursday, 10:00 p.m.
February 14, 2008
Timber Line Road

"I think I'm in love with Liz's sister," Denver said simply, as if it were a disease he'd contracted. "I've got all the symptoms, and I've been running a fever since the second I saw those brown eyes."

"Get real. The woman didn't even look in your direction at dinner. If you get within ten feet of her, she'll have her future sister-in-law arrest you."

Denver closed his eyes as if in thought. "No, I think she's crazy about me. Only problem I see is I'm going to have to stay with you for a while to get close to her."

"I don't have a guest room," Gabe said flatly.

"I'll sleep on the floor. After the ground it was fine last night."

"Don't you have to go back to your job?"

"I took a few weeks off. Besides, we've still got to go down the road a piece and pull my Mustang out of the mud."

"It wouldn't be blue, would it?"

"How'd you know?"

Gabe frowned. "Lucky guess. How long have you been stalking me?"

Denver shrugged. "Awhile. About the time it started snowing. On my days off I'd catch a flight to Dallas and drive up. I figured out Wiseman was G. L. Smith fairly quickly, and then I thought you were pretending to be Leary. That twist caught me off guard. If I hadn't seen you picking up your mail one night, I don't think I would have ever put it together."

Gabe pulled onto the muddy road to his place. "I should have pulled the trigger when I first saw you in the doorway. I can't believe you managed to find me. Maybe I should start packing. If you found me, anyone could. You couldn't have full brain capacity and think that Claire Matheson likes you."

Denver straightened in the seat. "How many guys did you show your sketching to in the army?"

"No one but you, and I wouldn't have shown you except you kept asking."

"How many people know you're G. L. Smith in town?"

"Until yesterday, one. Now the news is spreading." Gabe smiled. "Only, no one knows any connection between Gabe Wiseman and me but you."

"You're safe." Denver laughed. "Everyone here knows you as Leary, and most couldn't care less that you draw comics. I'm guessing, in the world of art, graphic novelists are right up there between sign painters and graffitists."

"Thanks. Where do you put artists who paint dead men?"

"At the top, of course." He grinned. "Or maybe right under me."

Gabe glared at him, considering opening the car door and tossing him out in the mud. Finally, he settled for saying, "It bothers me that *you* figured it out."

"I wouldn't have if I hadn't seen your drawings. When I came here, I thought I'd find Wiseman living as Smith, not some guy I never heard of named Leary, living in Wiseman's battered-up body. Tell me how you flipped names and vanished."

"You make it sound like alien possession." Gabriel laughed and gave in. He might as well trust Denver; he was two days late killing him. "Wiseman and I switched names in boot camp. We looked enough alike. He thought it would be fun. I was eighteen and the promise he'd let me drive his classic GTO was enough to sway me. I didn't care if Wiseman wore my uniform and sneaked off the fort. I figured I could just claim he stole it if he got caught.

"Only Wiseman OD'd wearing my uniform and I was pulled out of a sound sleep by some sergeant yelling at me, calling me Wiseman. I was released from the last few days of boot camp and told to plan the funeral since Leary didn't have any kin and I was the only guy who talked to him in camp. After that, it was easy. I shipped out under his name and found there were advantages to being a Wiseman. I got into schools I never would have been considered for because it seemed the guy came from a long line of dead heroes."

"You let Gabe Leary stay dead and buried?"

"Trust me, no one cared or knew. Like Wiseman, I told everyone I had no kin. I just wanted to be a soldier, and the fact that my father couldn't find me to borrow money or make my life miserable in general was fine with me."

Denver nodded. "One question. When you talk to yourself, do you call yourself different names to keep all the yous straight?"

"Shut up." Gabe's head hurt. "Or we'll take a vote and all three take turns killing you."

Denver laughed.

Gabe pulled his Land Rover into the barn he'd long ago converted into a garage and shut off the engine. "When you called around town looking for me last week, I thought the men I told you about from that night in the hospital had tracked me down. But you found me through the novels, something no one else can do."

Denver climbed out and waited until Gabe did the same before saying, "I made no calls about you, Gabe. Not last week and never around here. I followed the trail of G. L. Smith to your office and then waited for you to drop by there. When you did, I followed you home and camped out, waiting to make a move. I knew I'd be dead if I just walked up. I knew you well enough to figure that you had a darn good reason for leaving that hospital as banged up as the doctors said you were. It took me days to figure out the sensors on this farm so I could get close enough to leave you the smiling message."

They walked toward the house, guessing who might have called. When Gabe unlocked the door, Pirate darted out for a quick run.

Both men laughed.

"I guess Pirate thought we were gone a bit too long," Denver said.

Gabe didn't comment. He just listened, then raised his fingers to his mouth to whistle the dog back.

Just as the signal cut the air, a gunshot came through the night in answer.

Like a movie suddenly switched into fast forward, both men moved into action. Denver pulled his Glock from his leg and hit the ground rolling. Gabe flipped off the light and slid into the blackness at the side of the house.

They waited. The night was as silent as death. Somewhere near the road Gabe thought he heard the faint sound of a car starting, but it could have just been passing by.

"Ready?" Gabe whispered, knowing Denver was close.

"Ready."

They didn't close the distance between them but moved parallel with one another across the rocky ground. Denver was silent, but Gabe slipped once as they moved in the direction Pirate ran. He fell to his knee and then slowly stood, ignoring the pain as he moved on into the blackness.

Gabe's logical mind was clicking away facts, calculating the possibilities as he continued. If Pirate had heard the whistle, he would have been back long before now. They'd heard one shot. The dog had to be hit, maybe dead. He and Denver were no more than shadows, but if someone fired again, fire would be returned in a blink.

The night was cold, but Gabe barely noticed. Step by step he crossed the field.

"Found him." Denver's voice was little more than wind.

Gabe closed the distance, seeing the outline of a man kneeling. Once he was within a few feet of them, Gabe widened his stance and faced the road, knowing his role was guard in this mission.

"He's alive," Denver said. "I can't tell where he's hit but I can feel lots of blood. Cover me."

Denver picked up the dog as Gabe walked a few steps behind, his eyes scanning the night.

Nothing moved as they retraced their steps.

Once they were inside, Gabe switched the alarms on, locked the door, and made sure all blinds were closed. Denver moved to the kitchen table and gently laid Pirate down.

"Know any vets?" Denver asked as he began washing off enough blood to find the wound.

Gabe looked down at Pirate. "No. I don't think we could make it to town and find one in time."

"I agree. We do what we can here."

Both men had been trained to react in crisis with

minimum waste of time. Denver took the lead, giving orders and demanding supplies as he put pressure on the hole on Pirate's neck.

For almost an hour they worked, pulling the bullet out, trying to stop the bleeding, and sewing the dog up. Pirate whimpered a few times, but never fought. It was almost midnight when Denver poured hydrogen peroxide over the wound, then sat down.

Gabe covered the dog with a towel, grabbed the whiskey and two glasses, and joined Denver.

"We did the best we could," Denver said. "But I don't know if we did any good. He looks far more dead than alive right now."

Gabe brushed his finger along the dog's nose.

Denver downed two fingers of whiskey and said simply, "Let's list what we know about the situation."

It was as if they were back five years, putting their heads together to figure things out, to plan, to survive.

Gabe went first. "We know it wasn't an accident."

"Agreed. Whoever placed that shot was trained, well trained. You think they were warning you?"

"No, I think they meant to kill Pirate so they could get to me, but I'm paranoid, remember."

Denver shook his head. "If you are, I'm in the boat with you. Someone's after you, Gabe. Maybe they think you're Wiseman or maybe they just hate your novels, but someone is out to get you."

"It might be safer for you to leave."

Denver smiled. "Not a chance. I haven't had this much fun in years."

"So, Lieutenant, what do we do now?"

"We act like normal folks and call in the law."

Gabe wanted to say no, that he'd handle whoever was out there alone on his own, but he knew Denver was right. If someone was watching, it was better if they thought Gabe

ran to the sheriff for protection, otherwise they might figure out that Gabe was getting ready for a battle he always
knew would eventually find him.

Denver pulled out his cell and punched 911. By the time
the deputy responded to the call, Gabe had covered the security panel with a poster and all weapons were out of sight.

Gabe thought the deputy was polite, but not really very
interested in a dog being shot. He said it might have been a
deer hunter's wild shot or kids driving by shooting at fence
posts. He said he'd turn it in.

As the deputy pulled out of the drive, Denver mumbled
to Gabe, "You have a lot of deer hunters who hunt at night?"

"Nope," Gabe answered as he stepped back into the
house. "I've got a bunk in storage we can set up in the back
room. If you're staying, you might as well make yourself
at home."

After they'd hauled the bedding in, Gabe lit the fireplace in the main room while Denver carried Pirate in and
spread the dog out on blankets in front of it.

"The bleeding looks like it may have stopped," Denver
said as he packed a bumper of towels around the dog. "I
don't see any fresh blood on the bandage."

"We'll know by morning." Gabe patted Pirate. "Hang
in there, partner."

"I'll keep the fire going." Denver spread out on a blanket
without even removing his boots.

"Fine." Gabe stood and moved to a ladder in the entry
closet. "I'll take the first watch."

He slowly climbed up to a small square hole in the ceiling of the closet and disappeared into a floored attic. It
was warm, but dusty. He rolled over twice and reached the
small vent window. Flipping the shutter, he looked out over
the silent night and his land. For once he'd left the yard
lights on. He'd see anyone coming within a hundred feet
of the place. Whoever planned to come after him might be

smart enough to make it past the first few rings of security, but he'd see them before they reached the house.

As he watched the night, he thought of Elizabeth sleeping in her office. If she knew all the trouble he was in, she would run as fast as she could. Denver was probably right; if Gabe claimed to be Wiseman, not only did he have two strangers wanting to kill him for what they thought he saw the day of the bomb, but the army was also looking for him. If they found out he'd been only pretending to be Wiseman for ten years, he'd probably go to jail. If they thought he was Wiseman, then they saw him as a deserter. Either way looked like prison time.

Best-case scenario: The deputy was right, it was just kids or a deer hunter not noticing it was three hours after dark. If that was true, Gabe wouldn't go to jail, he'd be carried off for being insane and his friend downstairs would be in the next padded cell.

No matter what, Elizabeth needed to stay away from him. Whether he was in danger or paranoid, she was no longer in his life.

A little after four, Denver yelled up that he'd take watch, and Gabe came out of the attic. He checked Pirate, then fell into bed asleep before he could pull up the covers.

In what seemed like minutes, Denver shook his shoulder. "Wake up, Gabe. There's a hearse coming up the drive."

"I didn't hear the alarm." Gabe was fully awake and reaching for his rifle.

"I shut it off. I don't know who this guy is, but if he's a killer, he's got to be the dumbest one alive. When he saw me at the door, he waved. Looks to me like he's just more company."

Gabe moved to the door with Denver following in his wake. "I don't have company." He glanced at Denver. "You're like the first roach. If I'd stepped on you, no more would have followed." He'd managed to live here for four years without anyone dropping in, and now they were wearing out the road.

Denver laughed. His skin was far too tough to suffer the ping of words. "Maybe the whole world got together and figured you were already dead. They're just sending the undertaker before the stink gets too bad."

Gabe didn't laugh. He felt more dead than alive most days. Until he met Elizabeth, he'd feared he might disappear and no one would notice.

He propped his rifle by the front door and stepped out onto the porch as Tyler Wright pulled up. Denver, despite his jokes, stayed behind, fully armed and ready.

"Morning, Mr. Wright. You lost?"

Tyler Wright climbed out of the long black hearse and walked up to the porch. "No, I'm on my way to Tulsa to pick up someone."

He didn't need to tell Gabe the someone came boxed.

"I just stopped by because Jeremiah Truman called me and said he wants to give his niece Reagan a party Sunday night. Said she's already started inviting. Wanted to include you since you were the one who saved her life, but didn't know how to get in touch with you."

"So you're delivering the message." Gabe tried to smile. Mr. Wright had taken care of pretty much everything when his father died, including bringing along a wheelchair so Gabe could attend the graveside. They could have skipped the service—Gabe, Wright, and Old Man Truman were the only ones watching the casket being lowered into the ground—but Gabe still appreciated the effort.

"I don't . . ."

"It's going to be a real sit-down dinner. First one I ever heard of at the Truman place. Seems Reagan is not only happy to be alive, thanks to you, but she's turned eighteen and you know that's a big birthday."

"I can't . . ." Gabe began to shake his head. "I can't go."

Denver stepped out to help. "He'd love to come, Mr. Wright, but as you see, he's got company." Denver offered his hand. "I'm Denver Sims, an old army buddy of Gabe's. I'm sure you've heard him talk about me."

"No." Wright grinned. "But, to tell the truth, I've rarely heard Gabe talk at all." He pulled out his cell phone. "I'll call Truman. I don't think he'd mind one more guest."

Denver had the nerve to wink at Gabe while Tyler dialed. "While you're asking, suggest that he should invite Liz Matheson since she's Gabe's lawyer, and so she doesn't have to come alone, maybe her sister could come too."

Wright turned away toward his car when he said hello as if worried that the uninvited guest might invite more uninvited guests.

Gabe elbowed Denver hard in the chest. "I don't want to go," he whispered.

"It's food," Denver whispered back. "Real food. You know, that strange stuff you never seem to eat. All you've got in your cabinets are cereal boxes and cans."

"No." He'd survived the meal at Elizabeth's house because she was next to him and Denver drew most of the attention. "I can't go."

"Don't worry," Denver teased. "I'll teach you to eat with a fork before Sunday."

"No. I'm not going. What if trouble comes?"

"If it comes, it'll find us wherever we are. My guess is whoever shot Pirate doesn't want any witnesses around. We're probably safe at Truman's. Maybe I should suggest the old man invite the sheriff and her boyfriend. I kind of liked talking to them."

"Why don't you just plan the whole damn party?" Gabe said between clenched teeth.

"I wouldn't mind. Does this old guy have money for steaks?"

Wright walked back from his car. "I couldn't get Truman,

but I got Reagan. She was all excited at the idea of having more guests. Laughed and said to tell everyone to bring presents."

Gabe was too shocked at the idea of going to an eighteen-year-old's birthday party to answer. He'd never attended any party, or had one.

Tyler Wright waved and climbed back into his car.

Gabe looked at Denver, smiling like some kind of rabid wolf. "I didn't want to go," he started, "and now I have to bring a gift. I have no idea what to give a girl that age."

Denver frowned but seemed to go with his first guess. "Ammo?"

Gabe swung, but Denver was too fast for him.

Chapter 32

FEBRUARY 15, 2008
WRIGHT FUNERAL HOME

Drove the back roads to Tulsa this morning. Thought of you. Thinking you might join me one night for a glass of wine again.

TYLER STARED AT THE SCREEN AND THE WORDS HE'D JUST written. He sounded pitiful. Maybe writing Kate had become a habit. Maybe that's all it was. They'd met once— no, twice. The first time they'd shared dinner at a lonely lodge in Oklahoma. The second time she'd seen him at his worst. In between they'd sent e-mails. Not even romantic notes, just funny little things, things people pass the time talking about.

But once, he remembered in the time between their

meetings, she'd called him *dear one*, like he was someone who mattered to her.

Oh, I almost forgot to tell you. I'm going to Reagan Truman's birthday party Sunday. Do you remember her? She's the girl who fought so hard two years ago to save her uncle's farm from fire. It was in the paper. She's turning eighteen. Wish I had an idea what to buy her. Any suggestions?

Her uncle came by to make sure all the arrangements are made for his funeral. He's a hard old guy, but he loves her dearly. I've seen it before. He knows his time is close. I'll walk him through all I can, then I'll stand next to her and see she gets through the rest.

I've always felt I was helping people, but sometimes I wish it would get easier.

Good night, Kate.

Ty

Tyler read it through before he clicked Send. Tonight's note had been depressing. He'd been in a down mood for days. Maybe it was the weather: cold, windy, threats of snow. Maybe it was watching Mrs. Biggs at the cemetery grieving for a family she'd lost years ago.

He glanced at the flyer he'd picked up at the bookstore. Saturday morning palm reading and coffee.

Why not? He turned off the screen. With no funerals in sight, going to the bookstore tomorrow was as good a way to waste time as any. He went to bed thinking, if he could know one thing about his future, what would it be? After two hours worrying about it, he took a sleeping pill and decided there was nothing he'd want to know ahead of time. If it was something good, it would spoil the surprise. If it was something bad, it would haunt his future.

The next morning he dressed and arrived at exactly nine o'clock thinking there might be a crowd. His was the only car except for the bookstore owner's, which was always in the same spot. So much for a crowd.

He waited in his car with the window down until he saw Martha Q pull up and climb out carrying what looked and smelled like apple turnovers.

Tyler got out to help her with her load, thinking that turnovers would go perfect with coffee and palm reading.

"Morning, Mr. Wright. You come for the palm reading?"

"It sounded interesting. Do you believe in such things?"

"I certainly do. When I was young, a palm reader took one look at my hand and told me I'd meet a handsome man and fall madly in love. It's happened several times."

Tyler smiled. "Maybe there's a stutter in your lifeline."

Martha Q laughed. "You better watch your heart, Mr. Wright, or I may decide you're the next in line."

He knew she was kidding, or at least he hoped she was.

Inside, the bookstore owner, George Hatcher, had set up a circle of eight chairs. He appeared to be expecting a crowd. Tyler recognized Dallas Logan and her daughter Ronelle. They were a pair. Dallas never stopped talking and Ronelle never said a word. Martha Q might have been hated in town years ago for all the wild things she did, but Dallas was generally hated for no particular reason and that seemed far worse. Tyler remembered something his grandfather used to say and thought it would apply to Dallas Logan. She'd complain even if she was hanged with a new rope.

He nodded at both women as he took his seat as far away from them as possible.

A girl from the bank named Mary also came in and sat down. Tyler wouldn't have remembered her name, only she had her nametag pinned to her sweater. She looked nervous, and he almost told her that as far as he knew palm readings were not painful.

Bob McNabb was already in the store looking at the books in the fishing section, but when he heard there was free coffee, he took a seat too and helped himself to a turn-over. Bob's wife was probably at the funeral home working. They were one of the nicest couples in town. Still married after more than forty years.

They all waited.

George went to the windows and turned the sign from CLOSED to OPEN. From his frown everyone knew there was no fortune-teller in sight. Tyler and Bob helped themselves to more coffee while Dallas lectured her grown daughter on not biting her nails. Martha Q told the girl from the bank that her shoes were "to die for," and they began talking about nothing, as women who are complete strangers sometimes do.

About the time Tyler was getting uncomfortable, Bob McNabb leaned over and said. "I like your shoes. Where'd you get them?"

They both burst out laughing, making all the women look at them as if insanity had invaded the bookstore.

A half hour later, the group broke up and wandered out depressed.

On the way back to the funeral home, Tyler smiled. Tonight he'd have something funny to tell Kate. The others in the circle might not see it, but Tyler saw humor in wasting even a small part of your life trying to see your future.

He might even tell her about the laugh he and Bob had over shoes.

Chapter 33

Reagan watched from her bed in the sunny front parlor as three women dusted and polished everything in the house. She knew her uncle had left because he couldn't stand the thought of them touching his stuff, and in truth she felt the same way. The nurse he'd hired insisted he call in help to clean because she feared Reagan would be hobbling around on her crutches trying to get ready for her own party.

Reagan would have too. What had started as an invitation for Brandon to come over had quickly grown to a full party. She guessed if Jeremiah was going to allow one person in for dinner, he thought he might as well invite everyone.

If she could have, she would have felt his forehead for he was certainly acting strange. He'd ordered barbecue to be delivered an hour before the party and asked them to bring along the bakery cake decorated with rainbow icing.

Just before he'd left, he'd ordered her to stay in bed. It was too soon, he claimed, for her to be doing anything but the necessities.

Reagan was about to explode with excitement. She'd invited Brandon and Noah first, then decided she should invite Gabe Leary for saving her life and his lawyer for helping him get out of jail. Then there was Leary's house-guest and Elizabeth's sister who had to come along. Reagan didn't want to leave anyone out so she invited Noah's sister, the sheriff, and Hank because he was her fiancé and Tyler because he was everyone's friend. Uncle Jeremiah said they might as well invite all the Mathesons if three were already coming as well as all the McAllens. So Noah's parents were called, as was Hank's mother, who was told to bring her two aunts who lived with them and little Saralynn.

Fifteen people were coming to dinner. The only salvation seemed to be to take the furniture out of the country kitchen and set up plywood on sawhorses to make a long table that ran from the kitchen counter to the far end, where a TV had been. Reagan knew her uncle would never be able to handle the details, but her nurse turned into a fairy godmother, calling friends to bring over a long tablecloth from the Methodist church and the community china a Bible study class had bought fifty years ago.

At six o'clock, the table was set, the food was on long trays around the counters, and candles glowed in the wide kitchen.

When her phone trilled Reagan answered it on the first ring.

"Hi, Noah," she said, recognizing his number.

"Happy Birthday, Rea," he said. "How you feeling?"

"I'm fine. I've been eighteen long enough to get used to it, but I'll still take the party. I asked for strawberry cake 'cause I know it's your favorite."

"You shouldn't have done that."

She grinned. "You're my best friend, Preacher. I even said to order food for twenty so you wouldn't go away hungry. What time did you think you'll make it in from Dallas?"

There was a silence on the phone, then he said, "I didn't. I'm still here. I got invited to stay with some friends of my dad's for dinner. They got this grand ranch just east of Denton. He and Mom are going to be at your party, but I'm afraid I'm going to have to miss it."

Reagan couldn't speak. She was afraid if she opened her mouth, she'd start crying.

"Don't be mad, Rea. I got you a present. Dad's bringing it tonight. I'll see you at school tomorrow. I just couldn't turn down a chance to see a ranch like I want to have someday. You understand, don't you?"

She knew he was waiting for her to tell him it was all right. They were friends, best buddies. But he didn't understand. This was not just any birthday, this was her eighteenth birthday. This was her first ever real party.

She wasn't old enough, or wise enough, to say anything. She just closed the phone and turned off the ringer.

All at once her world didn't seem so sunny.

Chapter 34

SUNDAY HAD TURNED SUNNY WITH ONLY THE HINT OF chill in the air, but by midafternoon the clouds foretold another storm. For a farmer, it would have been a good day to be outside, brisk air with little wind. Only Gabe had never considered himself a farmer even in his early years when his father tried to make the farm pay and used Gabe every day as free labor. Some men are born to love the land, but not Gabe. The only thing he loved about his land was its isolation from everyone else, and tonight the distance between him and humanity seemed to be corroding away. He was about to attend his second dinner party in a week.

He parked his Land Rover at the edge of where someone

had planted grass in Truman's yard and walked toward a wide porch painted blue against the gray brick of the house. Truman's old home was a huge two-story built with window boxes and gingerbread trim. The walls were brick on the first floor, wood on the second, and river rock along the north wall to hold back wind.

When he'd seen the place four years ago, most of the windows were boarded up and the homestead looked to be on its last leg. Now there was even a brick patio off one side that updated the place at least into the present century.

Denver walked a few feet behind him, carrying their gift for Reagan's birthday. They'd thought long and hard about what to buy her and finally settled on a quality shotgun. With a half load it wouldn't knock her down when she fired it, probably wouldn't kill anything when she did, but the noise would scare the hell out of anything or anyone coming around her place uninvited.

Denver caught up to him and slapped Gabe on the back. "You know, if you keep coming up with friends, we could eat good. I don't want to wear out my welcome, but maybe I should spend all my leave with you. I could always catch a flight to Dallas, rent a car, and drive up. But no more Mustangs in winter. I thought we'd never get that little car out of the mud."

"You didn't have a welcome to wear out." Gabe frowned at his friend as they stepped onto the porch of the Truman place. After four days he was starting to get used to the lieutenant. Denver had a sense of humor about life. Gabe would miss him when he left, but he'd never let him know it.

The old man met them at the door. "Gabriel, about time you boys got here."

Gabe shook hands and introduced Denver while thinking Truman had finally gotten so old that his wrinkles had wrinkles.

As soon as Gabe said "an old army buddy of mine," Truman seemed to warm to the guy.

"Welcome," he said simply, and showed them into what was obviously the dining room of a house. The entire place was sliced into little rooms, most packed with twice the furniture needed. It reminded Gabe of a time when people used to ask each other, *How many rooms you got in this place?*

The dining room didn't look like it had been updated since *Little Women* hit the presses.

The oak dining table that might hold eight thin people around it was set with appetizers of pigs in a blanket with mustard on the side, salsa with chips, and a square of cream cheese with some kind of jelly dripped on top.

"Appetizers," Denver pointed.

"I know," Gabe snapped as he picked up a plate. "They look great." He could figure out that the sausages wrapped in bread were finger foods, and the dip and chips made sense, but he had no idea what to do about the cheese and jelly.

Denver cut his gaze to Gabe as if he were questioning the man's sanity but said only, "Yeah, great."

The chairs had been pushed to the walls, forming two long rows. Aunt Pat and Aunt Fat were already planted on two of the chairs with an empty chair between them for their plates. "Hello, gentlemen," Aunt Pat said as if she were talking to children. "We were told to help ourselves. Reagan made these herself."

At the mention of her name, Reagan appeared on her crutches. Gabe introduced her to Denver, who quickly told her the appetizers were the best he'd ever seen and if everyone else didn't get here fast he planned to eat them all.

Reagan giggled, but her eyes were on Gabe. Somehow by just trying to help her, he'd become her own private guardian angel. He had the feeling he'd always be there for her if he could. She had the kind of eyes that really saw people, not for what they looked like, but for what they were.

"You all right, kid?" he asked, noticing the trails of tear stains washing away the makeup she'd probably been experimenting with.

"I'm okay." She smiled. "How about you? All these people going to bother you?"

She was reading him loud and clear. "Mind if I eat on the porch?"

"I'll make you a plate." She grinned, the light back in her eyes. "Takeout."

No one else had noticed them talking; they were all too busy welcoming the rest of the Matheson tribe. Hank, his mother, Claire, six-year-old Saralynn. Behind them, the sheriff, Alexandra McAllen, walked in with her parents. She moved directly to Hank's side, and her parents hugged his mother the way lifelong friends do.

Suddenly, the room was packed. Gabe greeted everyone with a jerky nod, learning fast that in this group he really didn't have to say anything as long as he smiled. His eyes kept searching the room for Elizabeth, expecting her to be at the end of the parade of people.

"She's coming," Saralynn whispered to him. "She told me to tell you she'd be a little late. Legal business."

Gabe found himself backing out of the crowd a few inches at a time. There didn't seem to be enough air in the room . . . in the house. He was on the porch before he was even aware that he was moving. Too many people talking all at once. He could still hear Denver telling all about Pirate being shot and how after three days he was finally lapping up milk.

Gabe looked back through the window at the group. Denver seemed to be at the center; Claire hung back, dressed tonight in a black pantsuit and a cream-colored scarf covering her long auburn hair. She reminded Gabe of a Georgia O'Keeffe photograph he'd seen in an art gallery once. She seemed to be making a point of ignoring everyone in the room except her daughter.

Smiling to himself, Gabe thought that if he ever had to draw the sketch of an artist, he'd use Claire and her classic looks as his model. Gabe decided if Denver thought she liked him, he must have brain damage. The woman was not only out of his league, she was out of his atmosphere. Denver wasn't bad looking, Gabe guessed. He had enough battle scars and stories to be interesting and a degree in history he'd never use from a college no one ever heard of, but he lacked the polish a girl like Claire would go for.

He moved to one of the chairs at the end of the porch and watched the last glow of sunset while he waited for Liz. If the storm hadn't happened eleven days ago, Reagan wouldn't have been hurt, he wouldn't have gotten tossed in jail and called Liz, and they all wouldn't be having dinner. If nothing had happened, he'd probably be visiting her at her office once a week, answering whatever question she came up with and then kissing her like there was no tomorrow. They wouldn't have spent the night at the bed-and-breakfast holding one another, or cuddled on her mother's couch after a meal with the family. He wouldn't have grown used to the feel of her against him. So used to it that he missed her every hour they weren't together. For Elizabeth this was probably just one of her monthly flings she had with men. If she knew what she meant to him, she'd have a restraining order posted against him.

He wasn't sure he could endure all these people around even with Liz in the room, but he knew he couldn't without her. The thought crossed his mind that he might just leave; Reagan would understand. The kid saw him for what he was. Denver might be mad that he got left behind, but maybe Claire would give him a ride back to Gabe's place. Or, Gabe reasoned, once it was fully dark, he could walk home and leave Denver the Rover.

He watched an old clunker of a Ford rattling down the road toward the house. Jeremiah must have heard it too, because he stepped out the door and watched the boat of a car putter toward them. "Reagan!" he yelled. "That kid you invited is here."

Gabe heard the old man mumbling something about the car needing a death certificate because there was no help for that engine.

Reagan hobbled past her uncle and made it to the edge of the porch before the car pulled to a stop.

Gabe sat still, not wanting to intrude as he watched.

A big kid of about her age climbed out of his car. He had on jeans and a black leather jacket with chains hanging from it that clanged when he walked. Gabe thought if this party had a worst-dressed list, this kid would win first, second, and third place.

"Hi, Bran." Reagan smiled as he neared. "I'm glad you could come."

"Look at you, Rea, you're on your feet, almost."

He patted her awkwardly on the shoulder, telling Gabe that the kid was not her date for the night. Strange that she'd invited him, Gabe thought. The boy looked unkempt, unprepared, unwanted . . . pretty much what Gabe must have looked like at seventeen when he left this town.

The kid must have glanced through the window, because he took a step backward. "Who are all those people?"

"My uncle invited a few more to dinner than I'd planned." She reached for his hand, but Bran was already moving backward.

"Maybe I should come some other time. I don't know about this. I thought it was going to be just me and you and the old man."

Gabe heard the panic in his voice and recognized it. The kid was afraid.

Reagan missed the step when she tried to catch up with him. Gabe and the kid both jumped toward her, but it was Bran who caught her by the shoulders as the crutches clamored on the walk.

"Are you all right?" He sounded near panic.

"I'm fine." She laughed. "I just guessed wrong. I'm still not too sturdy on these things."

Gabe reached them. "Reagan," he snapped. "Are you hurt?"

"No, I'm fine, Gabriel."

Gabe fought the urge to help the girl, knowing there was something else he had to do first. "Who are you?" he said to the kid.

"Brandon Biggs. I was invited." If he hadn't been holding Reagan up, Gabe had no doubt the kid would have puffed up preparing to fight.

"Well, Brandon, do you think you can carry her inside without banging her leg against the door? I'd do it, but I've got a bum leg myself and I'd hate to take a tumble with her."

"Yes, sir," Brandon stuttered. "I can do it."

He carefully lifted Reagan.

She put her arms around his neck and looked back at Gabe. In the last blink of light before night, he saw understanding in her eyes. She knew exactly what he was doing and how dearly his actions would cost him, because he'd have to go back inside with them.

"I'll bring the crutches and hold the door, Bran, but you be careful."

When they were inside, Gabe let everyone know that Brandon had caught Reagan as she took a tumble off the porch. Everyone gathered around, fretting over Reagan and patting Bran on the back. No one seemed to notice his clothes. Aunt Pat insisted he sit down next to Reagan while she made him a plate of appetizers. Hank said they could use a good man like him at the volunteer fire department. He winked when he said that catching women in peril was their favorite duty.

Gabe moved back. It felt good to think of someone besides himself. As they moved to the kitchen to fill their plates, Gabe held the swinging door for all, then stood watching the chaos of people finding chairs and filling plates and passing drinks down the table.

A gentle arm slid around his waist a moment after he smelled Elizabeth near.

"Sorry I'm late," she whispered as she leaned one hip against his leg. "Did you miss me?"

"Yes," he whispered as he let the door swing closed. They were alone in the dining room. She shifted and was suddenly in his arms.

"Aren't you going to kiss me hello?" she asked. "Or do I have to think of a question first?"

He kissed the top of her head. "I'm glad you came. I was about to bolt," he said, moving along her cheek toward her mouth.

"Prove you missed me," she whispered, and in the few minutes before anyone noticed they weren't in the kitchen, he did.

When they joined the others, they found that the only seats left were across the table from one another, but it didn't matter. He noticed that her cheeks were flushed and her lips slightly swollen. They had no chance to talk, but when he rubbed his thumb across his bottom lip, she blushed, and he knew they were both remembering how she'd pulled his lip into her mouth and bitten down gently.

Gabe could have been eating dog food for all the attention he paid. He loved watching the way the stray curls on her forehead sometimes brushed over her eyebrows and how she laughed when her brother teased her. Gabe liked the way she looked at him with those fiery green eyes.

Never had a woman affected him so, and he had a feeling none would ever again.

Chapter 35

TRUMAN FARM

DENVER SIMS SAT AT THE END OF THE TABLE, A ROOM away from Claire and her little girl. He watched her as he talked and laughed with everyone around him. She spoke only to Saralynn and to her aunts on either side of her. Most of the meal he thought she looked bored, as though this were just something she had to endure.

He made up his mind about the time everyone moved to the parlor for cake and the opening of gifts that he wouldn't say a word to her, wouldn't try to get close, and definitely wouldn't touch her. If Claire wanted a repeat of what had happened in the hallway of her family's ranch house, she'd have to come to him.

While Reagan opened her gifts, Denver ate two pieces of cake and tried to act like he cared about the books and necklaces and jewelry boxes she opened. He thought, of course, that the shotgun he and Gabe gave her was the best present, but no one else seemed to think so. Claire even frowned.

Truman got her the strangest gift. An apple tree. He told her it was one of fifty he ordered, and come spring they'd start a new orchard behind the house just for her. By the time she was twenty-five, she'd be making pies from her own apples.

No one else thought the gift was special, but Reagan cried and kissed her uncle's cheek.

When Truman brushed away the kiss, he said, "It's time you put down roots that will last a lifetime, girl." Then as an afterthought, he handed her a piece of paper.

Reagan opened it and looked up at him. He nodded and said, "It's legal. I had Elizabeth make sure today."

Liz smiled.

Everyone else remained silent for a moment before Reagan said without looking at anyone but her uncle. "He deeded the place over to me for my eighteenth birthday. He'll have managing control of it as long as he lives, but it's mine as of today."

No one spoke. They all knew Truman. He hadn't bought a new car in his life. He used and reused everything on his place. He pinched every penny. He loved his land above all else.

And he'd just given it away.

When the realization of what Truman had just done spread across the room, everyone started talking at once. The old man wasn't telling Reagan he loved her and she was family, he was showing her that she was more important than his land. Denver understood because he'd grown up with people who loved their land, but understanding and feeling the same were two different things.

He could never love land more than his freedom. Whenever he went home he always felt like his family was tied to the land. Two of his sisters had never even flown in an airplane. When he offered them free flights, they both said no because they didn't think they could get away.

Denver watched Reagan Truman's face. She loved the land. Her uncle had guessed right. He'd just given her the world.

Denver noticed that Gabe stood silently behind them all, watching. These were the descendants of the three families who had started Harmony. They had roots so deep in this town that no one and nothing would ever blow them down. No matter how long Gabe stayed around or how many dinners he attended, he'd never be a part of them.

And neither will I, Denver realized. Men like Leary and him were drifters. They were the soldiers, the cops, the warriors of this world who fought for and believed in a life like this, but never lived it.

Denver moved through the swinging door to the kitchen, knowing that no one would miss him now. They were talking of the town, their land, their homes.

He wrapped a white butcher's apron around his waist and began picking up dishes. When he was growing up, boys and girls alike were expected to help with cleanup. Sometimes he thought his older sisters kept having babies so they could get out of most of the chores.

He had the table cleared by the time he heard the swinging door creak. When he looked up, he was surprised to see Claire.

For a moment, their eyes met and he knew she hadn't expected to find him in the kitchen.

"All the men went down to see the tractor Truman is restoring," she said with the emotion of a news anchor.

He turned back to the sink. "Where's everyone else?" He really didn't care, but he had to say something or the door might swing closed.

"The McAllens went home. Their son, Noah, called and

decided to drive in late tonight from Dallas, and they were a little worried about him being on the roads. It might freeze after midnight. My great-aunts are showing Reagan how to quilt, since she's going to have to stay off her feet for a while. My mother is looking bored. Saralynn is asleep with her head on Mom's lap. Liz has vanished, which is nothing unusual."

"Oh," he said, without looking at her. "Thanks for the report."

"I left out Tyler Wright, who missed the whole party because he had to make a pickup tonight."

He could sense her coming closer, but he didn't turn around.

When she was three feet behind him, she drew in a long breath and said, "I think I should take this opportunity to tell you that I hate you."

"Oh," he said, as if she were still giving the weather report.

"Yes, but don't take it too personal. Since my husband left me three years ago with no money and a child with thousands of dollars' worth of medical bills, I've pretty much hated all men."

He dried his hands on a dish towel and turned around, leaning against the sink.

He could tell it bothered her that he now faced her. She moved a few inches back and jerked slightly.

"What happened the other night should have never happened. I'm not ready for something like that. I may never be ready. We should both forget it happened because it will never happen again." Every word sounded rehearsed.

He saw her chin lift and a tear threaten to fall. "It's all right," he said softly. "Nothing happened. Nothing's going to happen that you can't handle . . . that you don't want."

She looked at him then, surprised by his words. Then she gave a jerky nod, and a few strands of her hair pulled free of the knot she'd so carefully constructed. "Then it's settled between us."

"It's settled," he echoed, knowing he had no idea what he was talking about. Nothing was settled, and they both knew it.

One tear bubbled over and slid slowly down her cheek.

He tossed the towel on the sink and lifted his hand. "Come here, baby, let me hold you."

She didn't move.

He brushed his fingers along her arm until he reached her hand, then tugged her to him. She was stiff in his arms, but he hugged her. A big bear kind of hug that his sisters told him women want from the cradle to the grave.

"It's all right, Claire," he whispered against her ear. "It's all right."

Slowly she warmed against him, and he felt her silent tears on his shoulder. When she pulled away, he didn't try to hold her.

"Meet me, Claire. Anywhere. Anytime."

She smiled for a blink. "All right, for a few minutes." She straightened, as if what he asked was only a small favor, no more. "Coffee at the Blue Moon."

"I have no idea where the Blue Moon is, but I'll find it. What time?"

"I take Saralynn to school tomorrow morning. I'll meet you there a little after eight."

"I'll be waiting." It took all the self-control he could muster not to kiss her. She was the sexiest woman he'd ever encountered. Beautiful, strong, aloof, vulnerable.

A moment later their time together was over and everyone was leaving the party. There were hugs and promises to do dinner again sometime, but Claire kept her distance and Denver didn't mind. She was a quest, a mountain to be climbed, and he'd take his time. Easy women were rarely worth the effort, but women like Claire might just be worth a lifetime if he thought he could make her happy.

"Ready," Gabe said, pulling him back to reality.

"Let's move." They were out the door and rushing to his

Land Rover. Both had had about all the socializing they could stomach.

Once on the way, Gabe said, "You think Reagan liked our gift?"

Denver laughed. "No."

"You still crazy about Claire?"

Denver shrugged. "Yeah. Why?"

"I could tell at dinner she was really starting to warm up to you." Gabe fought down a laugh. "Well, at least she didn't throw any silverware at you or try to kill you. You do know she paints pictures of men dying horrible deaths, don't you? She's not your type."

"I don't have a type, but if I did, she'd be it. Watch, she'll be crazy about me in no time." He wished he were half as sure as he sounded.

A few minutes later they pulled up to the house. Both men were now on full alert. The laughter of the dinner was forgotten. They were worried about what might be out there in the night, waiting. They went through the house and checked the alarms as if it were a drill they'd done a hundred times.

But all was calm. Pirate even got up and slowly walked to meet them. All seemed normal. Gabe reset the alarm and said, "I talked to Alex before dinner tonight, and she said she read her deputy's report and thinks it's probably kids. This time of year they like to go out shooting at coyotes at night. Some of the ranchers have a real problem with them."

"The coyotes or the kids?" Denver asked.

Gabe smiled. "Both, I guess. Alex said if they were just driving down the road, they might have thought my dog was a coyote. We need to be very careful. I don't mind killing someone coming after me, but I'd hate the thought of hurting one of the locals."

"Yeah, I know what you mean." Denver added, "She say anything else?"

"Just a weird fact one of the deputies noticed. He said until a few months ago, Timber Line Road rarely had a car down it after dark, but lately traffic has picked up."

"More teenagers?"

Gabe shrugged.

"You're thinking it could be whoever is looking for Wiseman, but I don't know. What are the chances, after five years, that the guys who talked about shutting you up for good are still looking?"

"Not much, I guess."

"I've been thinking it's probably about a one percent chance. Every year you don't talk, the odds go way down. They might just figure if Wiseman—you—did see anything wrong that day of the bomb, he would have told someone by now."

"What are you trying to tell me?"

Denver shrugged. "I may be wrong, but maybe it's time you stopped hiding. If they haven't found Wiseman by now, they're never going to find you."

Chapter 36

Brandon Biggs sat next to Reagan watching the others pull away from the farm.

"I had a great time," he said.

"Thanks for coming, but you still didn't get your pie." Reagan realized she hadn't spent much time talking to Bran, but whenever she'd checked on him he seemed to be having a good time. "I still owe you a slice."

He laughed. "I'm going to hold you to it too, Rea. I guess I'd better leave too. You're tired out, and I got work tomorrow."

He stood, the chains on his pants sounding like wind chimes.

Reagan watched her uncle move onto the porch. She wished she could explain that Brandon Biggs was just a friend. Truman acted like he thought the boy might steal her away at any moment.

"Before I forget"—Uncle Jeremiah did his best to look like he had a real reason for stepping onto the porch—"the sheriff asked me tonight if you had any relatives named Biggs."

"No. Just my little brother. He's staying over in Bailee now with some of my mother's relatives." Bran hesitated, then seemed to decide to talk. "My brother, Border, said they weren't too happy to have him, but they'll be better to live with than my stepdad. My mom took off for parts unknown last week. I'm out of that mess, and when I get my own place, maybe he'll come live with me."

"Sounds like a plan." Reagan smiled. She'd known him two years and he'd only mentioned a little brother a few times.

He nodded, as if the idea were just forming in his mind.

"See you, Bran." She expected her uncle to hurry Bran along, but Truman surprised her.

The old man moved forward and offered his hand. "Good night," he started. "If you have the time some weekend, drop by and we'll work on that car of yours."

"Really?" Bran sounded as surprised as she was.

Truman nodded and watched the boy walk away, waving.

When Bran was in his car backing away, Reagan whispered, "That was nice of you to offer your help."

"I watched that boy," Truman said as he helped her with her crutches. "He's rough, scarred by life more than most, I reckon, but he cares about you. I won't always be around to protect you, but I think you could depend on him to knock a few heads together if you needed him."

"He's just a boy I know," she said as she moved inside.

"Maybe to you, but to him you're someone special. Knowing you is going to make him a better man."

"If you think so."

He grinned. "I've lived long enough to know so." Holding the door, he added, "Now come along inside. I'll get us more of that passable cake and we'll plan. Come spring I was thinking we need to make some changes in this place, and I want an outline of every detail that needs doing already in your mind before spring. Then once the weather clears, we can get started."

She wanted to tell him she was tired, but when her uncle wanted to talk nothing got in his way.

Chapter 37

EARLY MONDAY MORNING
FEBRUARY 18, 2008
BLUE MOON DINER

DENVER HAD TROUBLE SLEEPING ALL NIGHT. AT SUNUP HE was still wide awake, his mind filled with thoughts of Claire. She seemed totally different from any woman he'd ever known. An artist. He'd never even met an artist. She must have a great deal of talent if she showed in New York. The article he'd read on the plane said she painted men dying strange and terrible deaths, like every divorced woman wishes her ex would.

What did it matter? Talent was talent, and he could see it in any art. Though Gabe's inked sketches, masterfully done in both fine detail and bold lines, haunted Denver. His was the art of one who'd suffered in battles and lived to draw the rawness of it that few understood.

Denver prided himself on being honest, at least inside. His gut told him it didn't matter what Claire did, he'd still feel an attraction so deep that logic evaporated when she was near.

He believed he could size most women up in five minutes. He usually guessed right about what they wanted, or more accurately, what they wanted to fall for. Some liked romance, compliments, talk of possibilities. Others liked it honest, no strings, no games. He even ran into a woman once in a while who giggled about being drunk after one glass of wine so she could wash away the night at dawn by saying she didn't remember a thing.

But Claire wasn't playing. She didn't even seem to know the game. She was pushing him away and drawing him to her at the same time. For the first time in years he didn't feel like he was standing on solid ground when it came to a woman.

He couldn't wait to see her again.

By seven thirty Monday morning, he had already downed two cups of coffee at the Blue Moon Diner. Everyone in the diner seemed to know each other. He was the only stranger, which suited him fine. For once, he didn't want to talk to anyone but Claire.

The morning crowd had died down by the time she finally came in. She wore a long camel-colored wool coat over a black sweater and pants. A colorful scarf covered her hair, and glasses hid her eyes, but she still took his breath away.

She walked straight to his table and didn't look at him as he stood while she took the seat opposite his chair.

"Morning." He smiled at her dark glasses. "You want to order some breakfast? I could read the menu to you."

"No," she said. "I've already had breakfast."

"Well, how do you like your coffee, or would you rather have tea or juice?" He didn't care what she had. They could gnaw on the table for all he cared.

"Nothing," she said, tugging off her gloves. "I'm fine."

He got the picture. "I see. You're just here to tell me we shouldn't have set up a time and place to meet, right?"

"Right."

He waited. When she didn't say anything else, he guessed what she was probably thinking. "You remembered that you hate me along with all men on the planet and this, like the other night in the hallway, should be filed in the 'never happened' folder I'm supposed to forget."

"Right."

Denver tried not to let his anger show. "Take off the damn glasses, Claire."

She slowly raised her hand and tugged off the glasses. The moment he saw that she'd been crying, all the anger left him. He grabbed the menu and stared at it as if he hadn't memorized the thing in the hour he'd been waiting.

"Want to talk about it?" he said without looking up at her. He had no idea what would make such a beautiful woman cry, but he had a feeling his name would be mentioned somewhere in the explanation.

"No," she answered.

Denver closed his menu and fought down a string of swear words. This was why men climbed on the boat with Columbus. The end of the world looked better than trying to figure out women.

The waitress took the hint when she saw the closed menu and circled by the table with her pad in hand.

"I'll have the two-egg special, scrambled, wheat toast dry, and she'll have the blueberry pancakes with sausage on the side." He glanced up at Claire. She'd shoved her glasses back on. "She'll have orange juice and I'll take another coffee."

When the waitress moved away, Claire said in a calm, dull voice. "I said I didn't want breakfast."

"Fine. I'll eat them both." He waited long enough to take a deep breath and asked, "Now you want to talk?"

"No," she said simply.

She didn't look happy to be with him, but she wasn't getting up and leaving. He saw that as progress. He ate, she watched, until both plates were empty. Then he ordered more coffee and they sat, silent. He'd asked twice. If she wanted to talk, she'd have to start. He wasn't asking again.

She didn't look at him. She played with a pack of sugar, watched the people across the street, straightened the collar of her coat. She didn't talk.

When he paid the bill, she stood and they walked out together without saying a word.

"Which one's your car?" he asked.

She pointed to a black Dodge Caravan.

He took the keys from her hand and said, "Get in."

She didn't say a word as she climbed into the passenger seat. Maybe she'd said all she came to say, but until she walked away they'd play the game out. Denver thought of himself as a pro, an expert at short affairs and one-night stands, but this time, this woman meant more to him than he wanted to admit. He had the feeling this was her first time on the field.

He drove ten miles out of town to where a roadside park leaned out over a small canyon. In the summer it would make a great picnic spot, but now in the dead of winter, it looked stark and abandoned. When the trees were green, the picnic area would have been hidden, almost private, but now occasional traffic blinked by, the aspens serving as open blinds.

He stopped the car and climbed out, walked around to her side, and opened her door.

She didn't move.

He leaned in, unbuckled her seat belt, took her hand, and tugged her out. They walked twenty yards to a picnic table striped with the shadows of branches from a huge willow. The morning was cold, but for a change, the wind barely whispered around them.

At the end of the table, he turned her to face him, gently pulling off her glasses and scarf that had hidden her hair. The long loose strands flowed around her face as he studied her. She didn't look afraid, or angry, or even worried. To his surprise she looked curious.

"You've got the most beautiful eyes." He placed his hands on her waist and pushed her back until the top of her legs bumped against the table. "Among other things." Then, without another word, he kissed her.

After a few seconds, he pulled his mouth away. "I don't care if you hate me. Open your mouth and kiss me back, Claire. I've been thinking about kissing you all night."

To his shock, when he touched her lips again, she opened her mouth and he was lost in the taste of her. After a while, without breaking the kiss, he opened her coat and slid his hands inside. The feel of her body wrapped in cashmere drove him mad. She made no move to pull away as he explored.

Sometime, while he touched her, she wrapped her arms around his neck and leaned back, allowing him more freedom to feel.

He grinned. She might hate his guts, but the woman loved his touch.

She made little sounds of pleasure as his hands cupped her breasts. He gripped her waist and lifted her hips onto the table before pulling her legs apart so he could be closer. They were now equal height and she came to him hungrily.

She liked to kiss deeply and dug her long fingers into his hair as if to hold him closer. Once, when he would have broken the kiss, she held tight. When he finally ended the kiss, he brushed her cheek. "It's all right, baby, I'm not going to let you go. It's all right."

She drew him back to her.

A car passed on the highway twenty yards away and they pulled a few inches apart. Another moment and he might have jerked off her clothes and made love to her atop the picnic table, but reason stopped him as the cold air passed between them.

When the car was out of sight, he kissed her one last time, then stepped back. As she slowed her breath, he lifted her off the table and turned her so that her back was to the road. She didn't move. He almost felt as if she were clay in his hands, just waiting for his touch. He pulled her back against his chest, loving the way she came to him so willingly. "We're not leaving yet, Claire. I've got to touch you one more time. If you've any objection, you'd better say so now."

She didn't make a sound.

He pulled her coat off her shoulders and shoved it down until it hung at her elbows, then began to caress her. "Don't feel the cold, darling, just feel me touching you." His hand moved along her throat, over her shoulder.

She leaned the back of her head on his shoulder and let him stroke her wherever he liked. When he moved his fingers to her waist and slipped his hand beneath her sweater, she drew in a sharp breath. He spread his palm out over her bare skin.

"I love the feel of you," he whispered against her ear, then kissed the soft flesh at her neck.

When she was completely fluid in his arms, he lifted her up and carried her to the car. She rested on his shoulder, crying silently. He opened the car door and lowered her onto her seat. Before he could pull away, she cupped his face and kissed him. Her warm tears brushing across his cold cheek were the most sensual thing he'd ever felt.

They didn't say a word as he drove back and parked in front of the diner. He left the keys in the ignition and the heater running. For a long moment, he watched her leaning back with her eyes closed and a slight smile on her lips as if she were having a dream and he could be no part of it.

"Name the time, Claire. Name the place. I want to see you again."

She didn't answer.

"Then here. Anytime." He pulled his card from his pocket and shoved it into her hand. "That's my cell number. I'll be waiting."

He had no idea if she heard him. A few minutes later when he pulled past her in his own car, she was still sitting in the passenger seat, her eyes closed.

He wondered if she'd meet him again. As he drove away, he realized he was already missing her. He'd never been close to a woman like her. He didn't know how to handle her, what to say, when to push, when to stop, and she gave him no hint or direction.

Denver only knew one thing for certain. For the first time in his life he was falling in love . . . really in love.

Chapter 38

Tyler picked up Mrs. Biggs at nine thirty Monday morning. Martha Q had been taking her to the cemetery, but she complained of a cold when she called asking Tyler to assume the duty.

He didn't mind. He drove over to the cemetery a few times a day, checking on one thing or another. Mrs. Biggs was a quiet woman, but not bad company. She always thanked him for his kindness.

"I'll be back in an hour." He pulled away, leaving her with a blanket for her legs. "Weatherman says there's a cold front coming in today."

"That would be fine," she answered, already lost in the past.

Tyler thought of asking her if she needed another blanket, but he knew she wouldn't answer. This was her time with her ghosts. The only good thing seemed to be that over the weeks she'd shortened her visits to an hour. He didn't know if she was passing through her grieving or if Martha Q's constant advice had gotten to the dear woman.

The thought of Martha Q made him smile. Everyone around town called her Mrs. Anyone. Maybe that was because after all her marriages, no one knew which name she preferred. Tyler remembered seeing her when she was young. She had a beauty about her that even a boy could recognize as something special. She might not have slept with every man in town, but she certainly flirted.

She was a woman who liked to play with people. Say outrageous things to see how they reacted. Ask questions that removed them from their comfort zones. Younger, she'd been dangerous; now she seemed more comical.

She was also unhappy. Probably for the first time in her life she was without a man. She knew she didn't need one, didn't want one, but she couldn't quite figure out what to do without one. Tyler hoped she picked up a hobby before she drove everyone around her crazy.

He frowned, wondering why her manipulation didn't bother him. He usually hated people who tried to talk him into anything from insurance to religion. He disliked people who weren't truthful—even embellishments bothered him—and he doubted any of Martha Q's stories were true.

Tyler grinned as he drove out to the trailer park at the edge of town. Maybe he'd write Kate tonight and ask her what she thought.

When he pulled up to Edith and Lloyd Franklin's mobile home, he reconsidered what he was about to do. Over the years, he'd almost become friends with Edith. She served him breakfast a few times a week at the diner. Like everyone who ate there, he guessed there was trouble between her and her husband. Lloyd had been a big high school fullback when Tyler was in school. Edith was six or seven years younger, but Lloyd started dating her about her freshman year. He was long out of school, but she seemed mature for her age. They married long before she graduated high school. Tyler remembered hearing Lloyd brag that he was going to keep his little woman barefoot and pregnant. He'd said he wanted her young enough to raise her up right to be a good wife to him and a mother to all his kids.

Only they'd been married almost twenty years with no children except the three premature babies Tyler had helped her bury alone because Lloyd was too drunk with grief, she claimed.

Not long after the third baby didn't survive, Tyler started seeing bruises on Edith. He liked to stay out of people's lives except when called in, but he'd finally got up the nerve to tell the sheriff his fears.

Dan Reeves, the sheriff then, had told Tyler he wasn't the first to notice. He said he'd been by to talk to her, but she wouldn't press charges. She claimed she was just accident prone and bruised easily. Sheriff Reeves might have been in his sixties, but he was a bull of a man. He went out and had a little talk with Lloyd and the accidents Edith seemed to be having on a regular basis stopped, or at least they had until six months ago when Lloyd lost his job.

Tyler wasn't like Dan Reeves. He'd never threatened anyone in his life. So he thought up another plan. Maybe if he offered Lloyd work, at least until he got a regular job, it would help.

With determination, he got out of his car and walked up the steps to the Franklins' front door. Little Lady put her paws on the window and watched from the backseat. For once she didn't look like she wanted to come with him.

Lloyd answered on the third knock. "Tyler Wright," he said. "I remember you. You were a few years behind me in school. Didn't go out for football, did you? I seem to remember you played in the band." He laughed as if he'd told himself a joke no one else would understand.

"Drums," Tyler said, surprised Lloyd remembered him. Even in a town as small as Harmony, it was unlikely their paths would cross often. "Lloyd, how are you?"

"I'm doing just fine. Thanks for stopping by to ask." Lloyd laughed, knowing this was not a social call. "My wife forget to pay you for the last burial?"

Tyler knew Edith had paid him out of her tip money because the envelope had mostly one-dollar bills in it. "No," he said, "I just came by to ask you a favor. The guy who handles my backhoe at the cemetery is down with his back. Doctor in Lubbock says he may have to have surgery. I was wondering if you'd like the job. It'd only be temporary, and I'd understand if you quit when you got a full-time job."

Lloyd looked like Tyler might be trying to trick him. "Why would you be offering me a job? I barely remember you."

Tyler had already prepared a lie for this question. "I didn't expect you to remember me. I was just a sophomore the year you were a senior and took us to state finals. You were a hero to the team."

Lloyd's yellow smile crossed his face. "That's right. I could fly that year."

Tyler knew the rest of the football story. He lost his scholarship before Halloween his freshman year in college for fighting in the locker room. Some said he would have been gone in a few months anyway because Lloyd never considered going to class a priority. "You were fun to watch. We almost won that year. After you left we were three and eight my junior year and four and seven my senior year. Nothing to brag about those years."

Lloyd nodded, taking all the credit. "Look, pal," he said in a friendlier tone than before. "I'd like to help you out, but I got this project with my cousin going that might pay off big."

Tyler tried to act like he was disappointed. "I understand." Maybe Lloyd did have some other work. Maybe his and Edith's hard times were over. "Thanks for listening."

Lloyd closed the screen door. "Anytime."

Tyler backed down the steps and climbed into his car. He still had forty-five minutes before he needed to pick up Mrs. Biggs. He wanted to drive a few miles farther down the road, past the Truman place and the Matheson ranch.

He'd heard that two hundred years ago there had been a Spanish hacienda near the river. The men had come up from Mexico long before the fort line formed to protect settlers and set up a ranch. Legend was, the Mexicans had made a treaty with the Apache and Comanche in the area. They were allowed to live in peace and raise sheep for the price of a dozen head a year. If the rumors were true, maybe he could walk the river's edge and see some sign of where the stucco buildings would have been. If the wagon ruts still existed at the Washington-on-the-Brazos where men hid out in 1835 to write the Texas constitution, maybe there would be some signs leading from the river to what had once been a small ranch.

For Tyler, this exploring was high adventure.

Ten miles past the Matheson place, he turned off on a dirt road and found a spot where he could drive to within a couple hundred yards of the river. Tyler didn't get out of his car. Clouds had gathered above, making the day seem colder with the sun blocked. He needed to get back to Mrs. Biggs. Tomorrow he'd try his luck again. The trail had waited two hundred years. It would wait a little longer.

He drove back thinking what a find it would be if there was still part of the foundation or better yet, one side of a wall.

When he picked up Mrs. Biggs, she seemed ready. He drove her back to the bed-and-breakfast, then went home to his quarters over the funeral home. He thought of his place as an apartment, built by his grandfather, but in truth his living quarters held five bedrooms, three baths, a kitchen with an elevator for bringing up supplies, a dining room to seat a dozen, and a game room he'd converted into a TV room. More than three thousand square feet for one person.

Tyler went upstairs, changed his sweater for a suit jacket, and went back downstairs to his office to catch up on paperwork and wait until five before e-mailing Kate. There were no funerals today, no one lying in state, and no calls, but he would be ready if someone walked in. He believed in being dressed and ready to work all day. When the day ended at five, he relaxed, sometimes had a glass of milk, and put back on his sweater. Then, every night, he opened his e-mail.

He was like an alcoholic who didn't think he was a drunk because he only drank in the evening. He might have been e-mailing the same person for two years without an answer, but he wasn't obsessed unless he e-mailed early.

Evening, Kate, hope the weather's better where you are. I wonder if all people feel as lost on Mondays as I do. It's the only day of the week I don't usually have a plan for. I just have to wait and see what happens. I don't have any family to have dinner with, which from what I see of some families that could be a blessing. I've never liked football so the game on Monday never interests me, but I'll check the scores at news time because in Texas, if you don't follow football you're considered a talking form of plant life. Even the vegetarians will eat you alive.

He laughed at his own joke and signed off.

Chapter 39

WEDNESDAY EVENING
FEBRUARY 20, 2008
LEARY FARM

GABE WALKED HIS LAND AT SUNSET. THE COLD WIND BLEW hard from the north, whispering another round of snow, but he barely noticed. He needed to think. For four years he'd held himself away from people. He'd made a life alone and he was comfortable. Maybe not happy, but comfortable. He had his work and Pirate to keep him company. Happiness wasn't something he thought much about.

Denver, on one of his general rants, had told him to think about what he wanted. Gabe had never done that. It seemed he'd lived his whole life reacting to what he didn't want to happen. He didn't want his father to beat him. He didn't want to starve on the streets. He didn't want to die.

Pulling his hood up against the wind, Gabe tried to think

of one thing he did want. His feet turned toward town, but ten yards later he shifted direction and headed toward the barn and his Land Rover. He wanted to see Elizabeth, and it would take too long to walk. Maybe he'd just stand outside her office or maybe he'd tap on the door and offer to answer a question. He didn't care. He just had to see her.

Reason told him he could also drop by the sheriff's office and see if there had been any more Smith break-ins. Alex had shared two meals with him last week; surely she'd talk to him. He couldn't remember if Elizabeth had mentioned that his pen name was Smith, but he'd tell Alex that fact. He wasn't ashamed of his writing; he just liked to keep everything in its place. His life—correction: his lives—had always been in compartments. Here, in Harmony, he was Gabe Leary. In his work he was G. L. Smith. In his nightmare he was still Wiseman, running with a lie, fighting to stay alive.

Winter seemed like a recurring cough this year, blowing in snow and frost every few days, but tonight Gabe could feel the temperature plummeting. If he didn't take this chance to see Elizabeth, it might be a few days before he could get into town if snow started to pile up.

His uninvited houseguest, Denver Sims, had left before supper, saying he wanted to go into town for a while. He lived his life around strangers and didn't handle the silence of Gabe's house well. Gabe gave him directions to the little mall and knew he was there by now downing fast food.

In the morning he'd complain about the few thousand calories he'd downed wrapped in fat. He'd put on his running shoes and head for the pavement of the main road. An hour later he'd return exhausted and starving for a hamburger before he went through the machines in the basement. Denver was on a vicious cycle interrupted only occasionally by a salad.

They still maintained a security watch, but both finally

agreed that the shot that almost killed the dog had probably been just what the sheriff said it was. Kids driving by looking for coyotes.

Gabe parked his Land Rover in the back parking lot beside Elizabeth's sports car and bound up the steps. He didn't even bother to check his mail before he tapped on her door.

No answer.

He tapped again. It couldn't be much after seven. Where could she be on an icy Wednesday night? The few minutes they'd shared Sunday night behind the swinging door seemed a lifetime ago. He'd wanted a real kiss, but she'd been giggly, complaining that her family was only a door away. Finally, they'd struck a bargain. One kiss, then they'd join the others. At the time he thought there would be another time alone before the night ended, but the party was over without them even hugging.

Reason told him if her car was parked, she couldn't be far away. He checked the used bookstore downstairs. A dozen ladies were circled around knitting. They clutched their yarn to their chests and looked up at him as if he might be an armed robber when he stormed in.

The bookstore owner stood from behind the counter and pointed with his open book. "We're closed unless you've come to knit."

Gabe backed out without a word.

He climbed into his car, circled around to the town square, and began driving slowly around it, glancing in the few stores still open. Most were empty except for employees.

At the second corner he glanced left and saw the light of the Blue Moon Diner. The sound of country-western music from the bar across the street drifted in even with the windows of his car closed. He had a feeling she'd be one place or the other.

He parked in an empty spot near the diner and tried the bar first. The only people sitting around looked like the leftovers from the original *Dating Game*. Most were drinking alone, waiting for closing time, when they'd all turn pretty and hook up.

Gabe decided he'd go back to the knitters before he stayed here. Outside he took a deep breath of fresh air and headed across the street.

When he walked into the Blue Moon, he was surprised to see Reagan sitting at the counter, her crutches beside her.

"What are you doing here?" he asked as he shoved his hood off.

"I could say I came to make sure you had takeout, but look at you. You walked in the front door. I'm proud of you." She lifted her arms, and he had no choice but to lean down and let her hug him. The kid reminded him of a puppy he'd let in from the cold, and now she thought they were best friends.

Gabe wanted to tell her that he wasn't the hugging kind, but he couldn't hurt her feelings.

She started to get up. "The place is closed, but I haven't emptied the coffeepot yet."

"Don't tell me you're working here?"

Reagan laughed. "No. Today was my at-home nurse's last day. She brought me in a few hours ago for a checkup. Uncle Jeremiah was supposed to pick me up at the hospital, but he doesn't seem to have any telling-time brain cells left. Next I guess it will be the days of the week or month then finally night and day. When he was late I called to remind him of the time and asked Mary to bring me by here so I could see how Edith's doing."

"She been sick?" Gabe moved behind the counter and poured his own cup of coffee.

Reagan looked at him. Ancient eyes, he thought, a hundred lifetimes old. She might be eighteen in years here, but she saw more than most people five times her age. "She's heartsick," the girl began. She didn't have to say more. Gabe knew what she meant.

"Where is she?"

"A few minutes after I got dropped off, she got a call from her husband. *He* was at the hospital. His brother found him on the floor of their trailer throwing up and flopping like a 'dock fish.' His words, not mine." Reagan giggled. "I can kind of picture it in my head, though."

Gabe fought down a grin.

"Anyway," Reagan continued, "the brother brought him in. Doctors pumped his stomach and told him he had food poisoning. Edith told me, as she packed up her things, that he was so weak she could barely hear him when he called."

Gabe looked up from stealing two cookies out of the display case. "Good," he said slowly, knowing Reagan was following his thoughts. Weak men don't beat their wives. "Any chance Lloyd might die?"

"No. The hospital is releasing him as soon as Edith gets there." She looked down at her cast covered in purple and pink writing, then met his eyes again. "Something's wrong with Lloyd. Something's mixed up in his head. It scares me a little sometimes. I told Edith she should leave him, but I think she's afraid of what he'd do. I even said she could come out to the farm and stay with Uncle Jeremiah and me, but she didn't look like she believed me." Reagan twisted her hands.

"What else is bothering you, Reagan?" He took the stool beside her and gave her his full attention.

"Maybe it's nothing, but Lloyd comes in here some- times when I'm covering for Edith, like he doesn't know she's home sick. When I tell him, he doesn't seem in any hurry to leave. He kind of hangs around like he's flirting or something. He orders things that aren't on the menu and makes jokes about how I should leave him a tip." She twisted her fingers together. "Gabe, I try to be nice to him, but he's old, and creepy and dumb and doesn't bathe regularly. I don't even want to look at him, much less talk to him. Last time he stopped by he laughed and said as soon as I was eighteen he'd take me across the street dancing." She made a face as if she'd tasted something rotten. "The way he said it . . . it was like he thought we were friends."

Gabe figured the guy was close to being in his midforties, which made him a pervert to be trying to flirt with Reagan. "Does he make you feel uncomfortable with how he talks to you?"

"Major." She laughed. "Like maybe-I-should-bring-that-birthday-present-you-and-Denver-gave-me-to-work uncomfortable."

"Are you going to work Edith's shift again?"

She shrugged. "Probably. She needs a night off and I think she picks Wednesday because it's the slowest night. Fewer tips. When I get this cast off in another month or so, I'll cover for her again, but I'm thinking of telling her to keep her creepy husband home."

"How about I come in for coffee and stay awhile?"

"Great. He usually leaves if there is anyone else around." Reagan smiled. "I'm probably overreacting, but if you could drop by it would mean a lot. Brandon Biggs will probably stop by too. When he does, he'll stay until closing if I ask him."

"Do you trust that kid?"

Reagan laughed. "Sure. I've already beat him up once. He's half afraid of me."

"As long as you're not here alone. Don't worry about Lloyd. He probably still sees himself as the big football star who almost took Harmony to state." Gabe saw her relax and wondered how long she'd been waiting to tell someone her feelings about the guy. He changed the subject. "By the way, I know a Mrs. Biggs who works over at the B&B. Any chance this friend Brandon is related to her?"

"No, you're the second person who's mentioned it, but Brandon said he only has a little brother. His mother has married a half dozen times since Brandon's father died ten years ago. He says she's going to have to start using the phone book to find a name she hasn't married."

"If this Mrs. Biggs over at Winter's Inn were related to him, he'd claim her. She's a nice lady."

A pickup pulled up and left its lights shining on bright. "That's my uncle," she said standing. "Would you lock up?"

"Sure," Gabe said, thinking he knew where Cass kept an extra kitchen key out back over the yard light. Once in a while, just out of boredom, he'd slipped in and sat in the dark watching the town from the windows of the diner.

She tugged on a coat that swallowed her in puffiness. "And turn off the coffeepot and the lights."

"I'll take care of it." She was trying to mother him now, and they both knew it.

With her crutches under her arms, she faced him. "Gabe, I know you're a lot older than me and I don't want you to think it's a boy-girl thing, but I think you should know something. I love you. I think maybe you're my guardian angel."

He almost choked on his cookie.

She laughed. "You and me don't have much family around this place, where everyone else has relatives packed by the dozens. So from now on, I've decided you're part of my family. . . ." She hesitated, looking very young. "If it's all right with you?"

"It's all right with me," he managed. No one in his life had ever said those words to him, and he had a feeling no one had ever said them to her.

She hobbled to the door before he found his voice. "Hey, kid," he managed. "I love you too."

She grinned. "I know." She smiled. "Thanks for saying it, though. Oh, I almost forgot. If you're looking for Liz, she's at Martha Q's place. She was in here buying a pie when I came in. I heard her tell Edith that if she saw you tonight to tell you where she was."

"How'd you know I was looking for her?"

Reagan shrugged. "I'm an adult now. I guess I got woman's intuition. Besides, I watch people and you make her blush just by looking at her."

"I'm not the type of man she needs." He said his thoughts.

"Maybe not"—Reagan opened the door—"but she might be the kind of woman you need."

She was out the door before he could think of anything to say.

Truman had climbed out of his pickup and was waiting for her. He helped her in with great care.

Gabe finished his coffee, rinsed the pot, and turned out the lights. He left two dollars on the counter and locked the door as he walked out. He really wanted to see Elizabeth, but he wasn't sure he could take much of Martha Q. The woman had seen him naked, and now her eyebrows wiggled up and down every time she looked in his direction. Since she was old enough to be his mother, he wasn't sure if she was flirting or stroking out.

Gabe left his car in front of the diner and walked the dried-up creek bed to the bed-and-breakfast. He let himself in the back door. He didn't plan on walking into another knitting party.

In the dark dining room, he heard women's voices and was glad he'd followed his instincts. The parlor was full.

Martha Q, who always talked like half the people in the room were hard of hearing, was leading a meeting of a half dozen women. "Now, Dallas," she said to a woman frowning. "It's really very simple. We're forming the Follow Your Dreams Club. One of my dreams is to help others this year, and I'm starting with this group whether you like it or not. We'll all meet once a week and think of things that make us happy and dreams we all have. We'll do fun things and we'll eat foods that make us smile. So get with the program and smile."

"I don't have any dreams beyond staying alive." Dallas continued to frown. "And I *am* happy. I don't know where you got the idea I'm not. If someone suggested to you that I don't have dreams or I'm not downright brimming with joy, just give me their name and I'll go pound a little happiness into their skull."

Martha Q hit the woman on the top of her arm, making the bottom of both their underarms jiggle from shoulder to wrist. "You are *not* happy. You haven't been happy since your husband died, leaving you with no one to torture, and your misery disease is catching. Look at your daughter. She hasn't said a kind word to anyone in years. If she didn't have that job at the post office, she'd just sit in your living room by the window and we'd have to water her once a week."

Dallas blustered, "You think you're the town saint come to save us. Half the women in town still hate you for what they think you did with their husbands, brothers, and fathers. You haven't had a thought about anyone else but yourself in forty years. You're such a clown that if your husband hadn't left you money for this place you'd be wearing a red nose and blowing up balloons on street corners so you could twist them into weenie dogs to make money."

Gabe swore he heard Liz giggle. He knew she must be in the room even if he couldn't see her. He wasn't about to break up the happy meeting.

Dallas turned her wrath on his cute little lawyer. "Why is she here? To make us all feel bad? She's smart, and downright adorable." Dallas poked her daughter in the side with an elbow. "Take a few lessons, Ronelle. I told you to go to college. Even if you'd taken a few correspondence courses, you'd have moved up the ladder a bit. You don't have the family money of a Matheson, but you can still get a few pointers. Half the men in town would marry Liz tomorrow if she gave them a smile."

Martha Q pointed one manicured finger. "She's here

because she's my lawyer and I asked her. You don't know, Dallas, how unhappy Liz is. You just don't know. The dating pool's so low in this town she's having to go out with men she springs from jail. I know that for a fact."

"Like I believe that," Dallas snapped. "Give me one real reason to have her here."

Liz stood and tried to join in. "Because I brought the pie, and everyone knows pie makes you happy. In fact, while you ladies are ironing out the rules to this club, I'll go slice it up." She ran from the room like a rabbit at a pit bull convention.

Gabe snagged her as she hit the kitchen door and pushed her inside, laughing. "Hello, trouble," he whispered. "Causing problems again, I see."

She wrapped her arms around him and touched her nose to his. "I hoped you'd come. Save me, Gabriel. I've tumbled into the Bitches and Broomstick Inn. Martha Q meant well. She invited all the women she thought needed help. The fact that they don't seem to want it never crossed her mind."

"I don't care about them. What makes *you* happy?" he whispered.

"Having you hold me," she answered, combing back his hair with her fingers. "When I'm with you there's no pressure to be anyone but just me. So tell me, are you only seeing me because I bailed you out of jail?"

"You didn't bail me out. I was never charged, remember? And we're not dating. Near as I can tell we've never had a date."

"I know. I like it that way. From my experience, dating is overrated."

He kissed her lightly. "Any chance you'll leave this party and run away with me?"

She pushed him away. "Give me ten minutes. I'll make up some excuse and meet you back at the office. Right now I have to serve pie before a fight breaks out. From what I've learned tonight, Martha Q and Dallas were once friends. Probably the only friend either of them ever had."

"I can see why. Did Martha Q sleep with her husband?"

Elizabeth raised her eyes to heaven and shook her head. "If you remembered Dallas's man, you'd never ask that question."

Gabe helped her cut the pie into six slices and place it on plates. She delivered it along with hot tea for everyone. When she returned for her slice and tea, he'd vanished along with the last of the pie.

She found him ten minutes later waiting outside her office door.

"How'd you get away?" he asked as he stroked his hand along her back while she unlocked the door.

She looked at him, her eyes full of laughter. "I acted like I got a call, stepped out in the hallway so they could still hear, and said, 'Of course, Sheriff, I'll be right there. No, Sheriff, I won't tell anyone.' Then I grabbed my purse and said I had to leave. No one asked me a single question."

They didn't turn the lights on as they crossed to the couch. The curtains were open. Frost in the air made the streetlights look like fuzzy stars. As they wrapped themselves in each other, he kissed her hello and then they did something they'd never done.

They talked.

A FEW MILES AWAY AT THE MALL, DENVER DOWNED HIS second plate of fried bread balls covered in powdered sugar. The food court was small, but it was busy tonight. Every predriving teen seemed to be there along with a dozen mall walkers in jogging suits. Denver didn't see a single person carrying a shopping bag. In a strange way, it reminded him of the airport shopping where hundreds of people wander around stores, but no one buys.

He wasn't paying as much attention to the people as

usual. His mind was full of Claire. Three days and no call. He hadn't expected her to phone Monday after they parted, or really Tuesday. It would take time to set something up. She had her art and her little girl. But today, Wednesday, he'd been sure she would call to at least make plans. They needed a night, or maybe a weekend together. Once they were too exhausted to do anything but talk, maybe he would learn enough about her to know if this feeling he had was really love.

This had to be the strangest almost-affair he'd ever been involved in. His usual mode of operation was to be friendly, pay a few compliments, let the woman know he was interested, then wait for her to make a move. The minute she did, he knew where the relationship was heading. Bed. It might take a half hour or a week, but he'd be waking up with her beside him.

Claire was different. He wasn't sure she even liked him. She liked his touch, but if he asked her how she felt about him, she'd be as likely to say *Drop dead* as to whisper an endearment. She hadn't given him her number. If she didn't call, he'd have little chance of running into her. He couldn't see himself hanging out at the school waiting for her to drop her daughter off, and as far as he knew she never left the house otherwise.

Two women dressed as red bowling balls stood in front of his table.

"Look, Pat, it's Gabe's guest, Denver Sims."

Aunt Fat just giggled. She had that kind of delightful laugh that made anyone who heard it smile.

Denver stood and almost cracked his lip smiling. "Evening, ladies. Great running into you two. Is the rest of the family here?"

"No, just us. Hank drove us in so we could go to our Walk a Hundred Miles class, and Claire is picking us up."

"How's the walking doing?"

"Great. We're at the six-mile point and it's still February."

"Sit down and share my donut holes." Denver had no plans of leaving the ladies' side until they were picked up. "Can I get you a drink?"

Aunt Pat looked at Aunt Fat. "We've made it around three times. That's almost a half mile. We have to pace ourselves."

Aunt Fat nodded.

Denver ordered their drinks and another order of fried bread with powdered sugar and then tried to keep up with the conversation while his mind ticked off the minutes until Claire was due to pick them up. He even insisted on walking them outside, where they said she'd be waiting.

Her Dodge Caravan was there. Parked close to the door in a red zone, he noticed. Wouldn't want the walkers to have to walk all the way to the parking lot, he thought.

After he helped them into the van, he circled to Claire's window. While the aunts chattered and thanked him, he whispered to Claire. "Where? When?"

She didn't look at him. She simply whispered back, "I can't. I'm working."

He smiled at the aunts and waved, but to Claire he added, "I'll wait." His fingers brushed the side of her arm lightly.

She rolled her window up and drove away without looking directly at him. Every action was that of a stranger, not the woman who'd cried in his arms as tenderly as a child and kissed him with a passion that made his blood boil.

He went in search of something stronger than cocoa to drink. He found it at Buffalo's Bar, and sometime after midnight when he stumbled out far too drunk to drive, he found Gabe's car parked across the street in front of the diner, the door unlocked.

Gabe and Elizabeth talked until the evening aged and holding one another replaced all other communications. Neither seemed to want to hurry what was developing between them. He wished he could tell her he was new at this game and maybe she'd explain to him why, after talking about all her wild times, she just wanted to be held. He knew she was attracted to him; the way she kissed couldn't have been faked. He was attracted to her also, but for now, this was enough, maybe even more than he had a right to ask for. Somehow he knew that what they shared meant more to her than anything had in a long while.

When he kissed her one last time and walked back to his car, it had started snowing but thoughts of her kept him warm.

The moment he opened his car door, reality slammed back. Gabe had his Glock out and his elbow locked ready to fire before he realized the growl he'd heard was a snore and the animal in his backseat was Denver.

Gabe hit his friend hard in the back of his head. "I almost shot you . . . again."

Denver leaned forward and swore. "Go ahead. I feel like I've been double-dipped in death already." With that, he threw up in the Rover.

The car wash was frozen, so Gabe drove home with the windows down. Denver swore several times that his ears were freezing off. Gabe half wished he'd circled by and traded for Denver's little rented Mustang, but he didn't want to drive the car on these roads. The last thing either of them wanted was to be stuck in a ditch tonight.

Denver was sober enough to clean up his own mess by the time they made it back to the farmhouse. The water hose was frozen, so he had to haul water from the house.

When he came back in, empty bucket and sponge in hand, he stopped in front of Gabe. "Say something. Don't just look at me." His words were still slurred.

"All right. Don't throw up in my car again."

Denver walked off into the kitchen talking to himself, saying all the names he thought Gabe should call him.

Gabe turned back to his drawings and began to work. He smiled. He didn't care about what Denver had done. Life was good right now. Maybe he should join Martha Q's Happy Club.

Chapter 40

Tyler sat down at his desk. It was almost midnight and this was the first chance he'd had to write his e-mail.

Sorry I'm so late tonight, Kate. The weather's turning ugly even as I type. Forecasting another three inches by morning. If there's wind that means we'll be dealing with three-foot drifts at the cemetery, and I have two funerals complete with gravesides tomorrow. The only good news I see is Mrs. Biggs won't be out in it. She's agreed to stay here at the home tomorrow and help Stella McNabb out with all the viewings. Not only two funerals tomorrow, but I've a body to get ready. The family hasn't decided on a time for the funeral but

I don't do them on Sunday, so if they can't be ready by
Saturday, the earliest will be Monday.

You remember Hank, the fire chief here? He put an
announcement on the front page of the paper asking
everyone to check on their neighbors. Four days below
freezing might leave some folks in trouble.

This winter seems colder than most for me. Maybe
I'm just missing you.

I'm longing for a pretty day. I've got two sites I'd
like to investigate where an old settlement might have
been. If I can find an earlier ranch in the area, years
before Harmon Ely's trading post, I'll change the writ-
ten history of Harmony. I'm guessing sheep herders
came around 1830, forty years before Harmony. I have
no idea what wiped them out long before the cattle
drives started passing through here, but if I can find
their settlement, I might find a clue.

Stay warm,
Ty

He clicked Send, realizing he was rattling on about
something no one in the world cared about but him. Even
if he did find something, it would end up no more than
a paragraph in a history book. His e-mail to Kate would
probably put her to sleep, if she read it.

Tyler closed his laptop, telling himself that if he just
knew she was out there reading her e-mail, that would be
enough for him. If she'd just answer once.

When they'd first started, everything had been light
and casual. No personal questions. He'd been careful not
to say anything about his work. He'd learned the hard way
from a half dozen blind dates that telling a woman you're a
funeral director eliminates the second date.

But over the months, as the notes got more and more
personal, he realized they were both hiding. Lying simply by omitting facts. When chance finally brought them

face to face, she'd seen him at his worst. He'd thought she'd forgive and meet him as they'd planned at the same place where they'd first met more than two years ago.

But she hadn't shown up. He'd learned all about her, but he hadn't been brave enough to go find her. If she'd wanted to meet him, nothing would have stopped her.

If she wanted to answer his e-mail, she would. Until then, he'd keep writing because it was all he had left of a woman he'd met on a rainy night once and thought there was a chance for love.

He stood and walked out of his study and along the hallway to the stairs leading up to his apartment. Little Lady followed, offering Tyler little comfort while he was lost in his memories. He wasn't strong enough to give up on the dream or weak enough to let it die. Until his e-mails came back, he'd write every night and hope.

Chapter 41

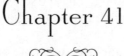

HANK MATHESON FELT LIKE HIS BONES WERE FROZEN. He'd been out in the storm since before dawn. By nine he'd pulled Tyler's Cadillac loaded down with grieving family and a dozen other cars attending the funeral out of the ditch.

After noon, people might wise up enough to stay off the streets, but right now everyone seemed to want to get out and test the ice. The snowstorm coming off the Rockies had been predicted for days, but no one paid any attention to it but him.

His own mother had insisted on flying to Dallas yesterday to attend an art show featuring some of her pots. She'd taken Saralynn out of school to go with her, since Claire promised she'd attend also. But Claire backed out, claiming far too much work to do. To keep from disappointing Saralynn, who'd told everyone since she got her first set of paints at Christmas that she planned to be an artist like her mother and grandmother, Claire and his mother agreed to hire a nurse to go along. The nurse was just out of school and excited to fly on a chartered plane and stay overnight at a grand hotel.

Only the one-night trip was now stretching into two, and it might go four or five before Harmony's best pilot could get his little plane up. Joyce refused to fly commercial, partly because she hated being around so many strangers and partly because the hassle of it was hard on Saralynn. Hank called them twice a day. Saralynn and the nurse were having a ball ordering room service and movies. His mother was among her kind and seemed to be enjoying long meals with friends in the business.

Hank took a few minutes and checked in on the aunts and Claire at the ranch. The aunts were fine. Claire was painting madly, as she often did. With none of the Matheson women needing him, Hank decided to stay at the station. The bad news: a bunk for a bed. The good news: He was across the street from the sheriff's office. He and Alex would manage to eat every meal together no matter how long the day.

When he stepped into the station, he smiled at the warmth and frowned at someone sitting in his office. The last thing he needed was company dropping by for a visit.

"May I—" he started as the man turned his head toward Hank. It was the kid from Reagan's party. Brandon was his name, Hank thought. "Biggs, right?"

"You said drop by if I wanted to help." Brandon smiled. "My work let us all off today and I figured since I already got my layers on, I might come offer."

Hank smiled. "Help I can use." He shook hands with the boy, a blink away from being a man. "Willie," he yelled as the youngest fireman passed his office door. "You heading out?"

"I'm on my way. Dispatch e-mailed me a list of calls from people stuck somewhere. I figured I'd head out east, working them one at a time."

"You want a rider?"

"Does he come with a shovel?" Willie asked. "I could move twice as fast if I had some help."

Hank handed Brandon the shovel he'd been using. "He does."

Brandon hesitated. "You mean that's all there is to it? I don't have to pass a test or climb a burning building? I just walk in and I'm a fireman?"

"You're a helper," Hank said. "Step one. But if you work today, we'll teach you what you need to know."

Brandon looked so excited Hank wouldn't have been surprised if the kid hugged him. "Willie, do all you can and keep in touch. I want you both back here by one. Martha Q from the Winter's Inn is bringing a hot meal."

"We'll be back on time." Willie motioned for Brandon to follow him.

Hank looked at the kid. "You'll be helping a great many people today and you'll be exhausted before dark, but you'll know you did some good and that's what it's all about."

"Thanks." Brandon disappeared out the door.

Hank filled a coffee cup and headed toward his quarters, just beyond his office, wondering if the boy would still be thanking him tomorrow morning when he had every muscle hurting.

Sitting on his bunk, Hank pulled off the first of three layers. The other volunteers who managed to make it to the station were gone in the trucks helping with a ten-car pileup east of town near the interstate ramp. As soon as he thawed and ate a bite, he'd climb back into his huge Ram and join them.

The door opened and closed with a bang. He heard Alex swearing at the weather before she appeared, all red nosed and smiling.

"Will this day never end? Got time for a late breakfast? Cass is keeping the diner open."

Hank shook his head as he moved toward her. "How about we skip food? I'm the only one home here and I have to man the phones until someone gets back, but we could relax for a few minutes."

Alex giggled. "No way. I'm starving."

"Martha Q is bringing over lunch in a few hours. We could eat after we relax."

She winked. "Not now. I'm not taking off all these clothes for anything that doesn't last half the night. How about coming across the street to me when things settle down tonight?"

Hank frowned. "I'm not doing it in one of the cells again. I know we're alone, but I can't get over the feeling we're in a prison movie. I want to take off all our clothes and roll up in each other and a few hundred blankets until we see the first sign of spring."

"Me too," she whispered, kissing him lightly.

He grabbed her and drew her as close as four layers of clothes would allow. "I need you so much, Alexandra. Marry me. We could run away."

"I'm planning on it," she said, kissing him again. "I started thinking about places to run to, then I decided that if you're with me it really won't matter where we go."

He couldn't believe it. She sounded like she was almost saying yes to a plan . . . to a date. "You serious?"

She pulled a flyer from her pocket. "There's a ship that leaves Galveston every week. As soon as this snow is over, I say we run away to the beach."

He kissed her, not completely convinced either of them would really be able to get away, but she'd made an effort and for now that was enough.

A pager buzzed.

SOMEWHERE ALONG THE WAY

He pulled away. "Mine or yours?"

They both fumbled in pockets for their phones. A moment later, a second pager echoed the first.

"Must be something important," Alex said, all business now.

"It's been something important since five this morning," he added as he pulled his phone out from the pocket of his coat. "Hello!" he yelled.

He listened for a minute and said, "She's with me. We're on our way. Notify the hospital."

Alex stood frozen, waiting as he closed the phone and stepped back into his boots. "A 911 call came in to dispatch. Reagan Truman. She thinks Jeremiah is having a heart attack."

"The ambulance?"

"Both are transporting people from the pileup and won't be available for at least thirty minutes. We can get to the Truman place and be on our way back to town by then."

They were running moments later when they hit the door. His Dodge Ram wasn't the perfect vehicle to transport in, but it was the best they had. The Ram would eat up the snow on back roads faster than the police cruisers. He kept medical equipment in the lockbox in the bed, and it was big enough to lay a man on the backseat.

Hank drove. Alex got on the phone with Reagan. He could hear the girl's panic as Alex talked to her calmly, pausing between each comment. "Where is he? Good, if he's on the floor we don't have to worry about him passing out and falling. Is he awake? Can he talk to you? Good. First, Reagan, I need you to calm down. Is there oxygen in the house? That's okay, we'll bring it in when we get there. Cover him, elevate his head, and try to get him to relax. Panic will only make it worse. Have you got an aspirin you could give him? Good, do that, we're almost there." She held the phone away for a moment, but didn't say anything to Hank. They both knew what was at stake. Alex waited, then said, "Now, Reagan, we're close. Get your coat on, and his if you can. Collect as many blankets as you can. Unlock the front door, we're turning off the county road. I can see the house."

Alex closed the phone, unbuckled her seatbelt, and grabbed two of the aid bags in the backseat.

Hank slid up to the house, bumping the steps before he stopped. They were both out of the cab and running.

Reagan met them at the door.

They followed the drills they'd both been taught. Within five minutes, Jeremiah was surrounded by blankets in the backseat of Hank's truck. Reagan knelt next to him, tears streaming down her face.

The drive to the hospital was measured in heartbeats.

Alex made sure a crew was waiting at the emergency door. In what seemed the time it took to blink, Jeremiah was rushed away and the three of them stood alone at the entrance.

The snow fell silently just beyond the wall of windows. Wind blew in each time the doors opened, but they didn't notice. Reagan asked no more questions. Alex offered no more advice. They just waited.

Chapter 42

Denver pounded on the door where he knew Claire had been holed up for days. No one answered at the ranch house, so he pounded again. He'd stay here until he froze, but someone would have to eventually answer the door.

He heard them talking, trying to guess who would come to the front door during a snowstorm, before he confronted Claire's two great-aunts. They were bundled in layers of flannel and fluff, Aunt Pat in pink, Aunt Fat in purple. As always, they looked adorable.

"Oh, look, Pat, it's Gabriel's friend, Denver Sims." Aunt Fat held the door wide. "Come on in, Mr. Sims. We were just about to have our morning tea. We usually have it an hour or so earlier, but sister wanted to make scones to go with it and with no one else to eat with, we decided to set our own schedule this morning. Tea after ten. Lunch after our naps."

Denver walked in, stomping his boots on the entry rug.

"How did you get here in this blizzard?" Pat asked as she motioned for him to leave his boots on the rug.

"I borrowed my friend's Land Rover," he said as he followed the silent order. "I was driving him crazy. He said if I didn't come over here now, in a few more hours I might not be able to until the storm blew over and I couldn't wait that long. Is Claire here?"

Both aunts stared at him as if they needed time to have their hearing catch up with his fast speech.

Aunt Pat recovered first. "She's painting and can't be disturbed, but we'd love you to have tea with us."

Aunt Fat just nodded as if she needed an interpreter.

Denver could imagine them seventy years ago at Halloween going from house to house with Pat leading the charge, doing all the talking and Fat simply holding out the bag.

Denver fought the urge to storm past them and climb the two flights of stairs to where he'd heard someone say Claire had her studio. He'd gone mad waiting for her to call. Gabe had tossed him the keys and almost kicked him out.

Denver wasn't going home until he saw her, even if he had to have tea first.

The aunts drew him back down the hallway he remembered so well to their quarters. They chatted as he drank tea, telling him all about the days when they were young and once dated twin brothers.

"Pat always swore they kept switching on us," Aunt Fat said. "She claimed one kissed better than the other."

"Now, Fat, you know it's true."

Denver couldn't think of anything to say, but it didn't seem necessary. They told him all about Joyce and

Saralynn's adventures in Dallas and how Hank and Liz were both staying in town.

"The house is just far too quiet." Aunt Fat patted him on the knee. "We're glad you came by."

After twenty minutes, Denver stood, thanked them for the tea, and said he had to leave. He mumbled something about just dropping by to see if they were okay, even though Leary's place on Timber Line Road was nowhere near their ranch.

When they started to walk him to the door, he stopped them with gentle hugs. "I'll show myself out. You two need to get back to your quilting. One of these days I may be begging for one of those quilts. If you ask me, they're as much art as anything anyone else in this house does."

Both aunts giggled and waved him good-bye.

Denver was careful to close both hallway doors to the rest of the house, then climbed the stairs silently and tapped lightly on Claire's studio door.

She answered after a long minute. Her beautiful hair was tied up on top of her head in a haphazard knot. Her shirt was spotted with dark paint and the pants she wore were skintight with thick socks pulled over them past her knees.

He thought she looked sexy as hell.

Before he could say a word, she blocked the entrance and snapped, "What are you doing here?"

Denver told himself he hadn't hoped that she'd be glad to see him. She never was, but still her words stung. No woman who'd kissed him like she had in the hallway downstairs and again at the roadside park could be anything but crazy about him. Maybe she needed to work on her verbal communication skills, but her nonverbal skills were coming through loud and clear.

"You didn't call." He pulled her to him with a quick jerk and leaned down to kiss her. "I decided to surprise you."

She shoved away, reaching for the door. "I'm working, Denver. You'll have to go."

He smiled. "Well, at least you know my name. I was beginning to wonder."

"Go away," she said slowly.

"Not before we talk," he said, shoving the door open and stepping inside before she could stop him. He'd made up his mind on the way over that he wouldn't leave until she set a time to meet him. He would wait a week, a month if he had to, but he would see her, preferably somewhere alone.

The high-ceilinged room was warm, with wide shutterless windows that made him feel like he was on a grand stage. Painting supplies were on every surface, and the smell of turpentine and oils filled the air. Pencil drawings carpeted the room around a window box. Half-empty cups were scattered everywhere. This was where she lived and worked. This was her sanctuary.

"Get out," she ordered. "Get out right now. I told you I'm working."

When he turned toward her, thinking she'd forgive him once he was holding her, he saw a huge canvas four feet high and maybe eight feet wide covered in a black cloth. Sketches were everywhere around it: taped to the wall, on the table beside the canvas, and even scattered on the floor below. Drawings of winter trees, and whirling snow, and *him*.

He ripped the covering off, knowing that this work had to relate to him . . . to them. Her scream echoed through his brain, but nothing registered but the painting before him.

Denver stood frozen as he stared. She'd painted the roadside park they'd stopped at. He could see the hazy outline of the canyon in the background and the road running at the bottom. The picnic table pushed beneath a willow was the same, but the rest of the picture was wrong. Very wrong.

A man's body lay frozen on the ground, his face turned to the shadows. One bare man's foot, gray and lifeless, rested in the center of the table.

He glanced down at the gold tag in the corner of the painting: *Barefoot Picnic by Claire Matheson.*

"Is this some kind of joke?" he asked, already knowing it wasn't. The memory of how her work had been described came to mind. Haunting, cruel, vengeful.

"No, Denver, it's what I do." Claire's voice was calm, cold, dead as the man in her work.

He moved to the next draped painting and pulled off the cover. A man, relaxed in death, was hanging by a noose between two pictures in a long hallway. The tag read, *Latest Acquisition.*

"Are there any more?" he asked. He wasn't sure he could take it if there were. Both works showed the face only in shadow, but the body build, the hair, even the color of clothes was his.

"No. I'm finished. Two was all I planned to do."

"And we're finished, right?"

"Right." She moved away from him. Folded her arms as if blocking him from her thoughts. She looked out at the storm as though simply waiting for him to leave.

"You were just using me." He felt like the biggest fool in the world. Of course she was using him, that's why they never talked. She didn't want a lover, or even a friend, she wanted a victim for her latest work. "Admit it, Claire. I'm just someone who came along and was convenient to use for a model."

"I let you touch me," she said as if in defense. "I let you play it out any way you wanted. I would have let you go further in the paying of my dues, but you stopped both times. In the end I knew you wanted more than I have to give, but what you gave me will go down as some of my best work."

For years he'd been just playing at loving, figuring it

was just a game and everyone knew the rules. All the one-night stands, the affairs that were counted in lost week-ends, the quick encounters never meant to mean anything, came back to him. Mocking him.

Finally, he'd met a woman he thought knew nothing about the game, and she'd played him completely. He'd thought she'd been on the way to real love for him, and all he'd been to her was something to be used.

Anger finally boiled over in Denver, and he swung around toward her, fighting down a yell that would shake the house.

She covered her head and ducked, curling into a ball at his feet.

Denver stared at her. "You think I'm going to hit you, don't you?"

She lowered one arm enough to look at him.

"You don't know me at all, Claire. For once in my life I wasn't playing and I wasn't just touching you. Idiot that I am, I thought I was loving you." He turned and stormed out of the attic and down the flights of stairs. He was in the Land Rover before he drew in a breath. She'd not only murdered him on canvas, she'd left him dead inside for real. He'd finally let himself believe in a tiny hope that he might have a real life. A life he shared with someone. She'd shattered that possibility and left him hollow.

He drove slowly back to Gabe's farm without bother-ing to turn on the heater. He felt like he was frozen from the inside out. Somewhere in the silent white of the storm, his hurt had turned to anger, not toward Claire, but toward himself.

Chapter 43

MARTHA Q WATCHED AS TWO YOUNG MEN STORMED INTO the fire station. They were laughing and joking around as if the snow shovels were swords, reminding her of two mighty crusaders returning from battle. For a moment she just watched, waiting for them to see her.

"I thought we'd never get that last car out." One shook off snow like a dog does water.

"Me either. I considered telling the guy I'd pay his parking ticket if he wanted to just leave it on the median until spring." The second one tugged off his heavy coat and hung it on a peg. "Thanks for coming along, Bran. I'd still be out there if you hadn't."

Both stopped as they saw Martha Q.

When neither spoke, she smiled and announced, "I cooked lunch for an army and no one came. I hope you boys are hungry."

The first one, maybe two years older than his buddy, laughed. "You bet, lady. We're starving." He began removing the first layer of thick winter clothes. "Thank you for coming. I'm Willie Davis. Everyone's probably like us, running late, but they'll all be hungry when they make it in."

Brandon took his lead from Willie. "I'm Brandon Biggs. This is my first day as a volunteer. It sure does smell good."

Both were down to sweaters and stocking feet by now. Martha Q moved aside and called, "Well, come and get it. Me and Mrs. Biggs have been cooking all morning."

Brandon glanced in Mrs. Biggs's direction, shrugged, and kept pulling off his outer layer of clothes.

The boys washed up and sat down as two more teams of volunteer firemen came in. Suddenly, the place was loud with laughter and stories.

Martha Q served, talking to the men as if she'd known every one of them since birth, but she kept her eye on Mrs. Biggs. The quiet lady hadn't taken her eyes off Brandon Biggs since he'd said his name.

Finally, when the men were all packing food in as fast as possible, Martha Q had her chance. "Brandon, you kin to any Biggses from Harmony?"

He shook his head. "I don't think so. None that would claim me, anyway. I don't know much about my dad. Never even heard Mom say where he was from. My mom said he didn't have any family. He was never around us much either. We heard he died years ago."

Martha Q shrugged as she passed the bread around. "I thought you might be related to Mrs. Biggs here."

Brandon looked sad as he faced the thin woman near the stove. "I'm sorry, ma'am. My brother and I are the last of our line. Like I said, my dad died and he didn't have any kin left."

The woman nodded her understanding. "I know how you feel."

Martha Q wasn't ready to let hope die. "What was your daddy's name, Brandon? Maybe he's a relative Mrs. Biggs forgot."

"My mother rarely talked about him except to say he showed up about as often as a bad cold, but I remember her calling him Andy."

Mrs. Biggs straightened. "Brice Andrew Biggs."

"Yeah," Brandon said. "That's what's on my birth certificate. Did you know him?"

Everyone had stopped talking and was listening to the conversation. They all looked at Mrs. Biggs.

The thin woman raised her head and said simply, "He was my son. My only child."

Then, before anyone could move, she crumbled to the floor.

All the men except Brandon scrambled to help the old lady. They lifted her up as she came to, helped her into a chair, got her water, and asked her questions about how she felt.

"I'm fine," she whispered.

Finally, Martha Q ordered them all back in their seats so the poor woman could get enough air around her to breathe. While the men went back to their meals, Brandon stood and walked over to Mrs. Biggs.

He got down on one knee and looked at her carefully as if trying to see the truth in her eyes. "Lady," he said in a whisper, "are you trying to tell me you are my grandmother? My father's mother?"

Mrs. Biggs touched his cheek lightly. "You look a little like Andy did when he was your age. That was about the time my husband died and he said he never wanted to speak to me again. He was so angry. He blamed me for his dad's death. I moved away, always planning to come back when he cooled down, but the time never seemed right. The few times I tried calling, he never answered. I'm so sorry."

"Don't be sorry for me." Brandon shook his head. "I barely remember my old man. He was a drunk with a temper. He never took any time to care about me. My one goal in life is to grow up to be better than him."

One of the men answered the phone while Brandon stared at the old lady.

Martha Q could see the hurt in both their eyes. As she always did, she stepped in without being invited. "Brandon, maybe you could come to breakfast at the inn tomorrow morning. The two of you could talk."

"I guess I could do that," Brandon said. "But, lady, I got to tell you straight out. I never had much luck with relatives, and I'm not looking to add one."

"I understand," Mrs. Biggs whispered. "Just breakfast."

A moment later, the man on the phone yelled, "Hank's on the line. He says Old Man Truman had a heart attack. They're taking him into surgery right now. He'll keep us informed."

Bob McNabb, the oldest of the volunteers, came farther into the kitchen. "Hank would want us to keep going. With half the men still at the pileup on the interstate, the rest of us have to take the calls. I'll man the phone and keep in contact with you all. We've got to do our job now or people might die."

Brandon stood. "I need to get to Reagan. We're friends."

McNabb shook his head. "You'd only be helping her wait. The old man could be in surgery for hours. We need you here. I'll phone you the minute I hear something and Willie will drive you out to the hospital. Fair enough?"

Brandon hesitated, then nodded. "You're right. Rea would probably want me to help out here. She thinks this whole town belongs to her personally." As the others headed toward their coats, Brandon added to Mrs. Biggs, "Thanks for the meal. We could talk later. I'd like to know what my dad was like. I never heard one good thing from my mom."

"I'd like that too." She touched his cheek again with the palm of her hand.

Brandon ran to join the others, and for the first time Martha Q saw Mrs. Biggs smile.

Martha started banging around the room, knowing that if she stopped to think about what just happened she'd probably cry. "Come on, Mrs. Biggs, let's get this place cleaned up so we can get home and make these boys some cookies."

Mrs. Biggs nodded.

Chapter 44

GABE LEARY WATCHED HIS FRIEND COME INTO THE HOUSE, knowing that he was back far too soon for it to have gone well. Denver went straight to the cabinet, where he stocked a few bottles of whiskey, and poured himself a drink.

Gabe went back to work, ignoring him for a half hour, then said, "Want to talk about it?"

"No."

"Fine. I've got to pack up some pages and get them in the mail." Gabe had to think of something to do. Even risking his life on icy roads sounded better than sitting around watching his buddy get drunk.

Denver didn't look like he was listening. He was too busy pouring himself another drink.

"Want to ride along into town with me? That way if I get stuck, I'll have someone to push."

"Sure. Why not, better than staying here alone."

Denver finally looked up. His eyes were already blood-shot. Another hour and his army buddy would be spread out on the floor too drunk to make it to bed.

Gabe reached for his coat. "How bad were the roads?"

"I didn't notice," Denver answered.

"Great," Gabe said, thinking he hadn't really meant it when he and Elizabeth joked about Claire killing Denver. Apparently, she had.

Five minutes and another drink later, they headed into town. Gabe didn't break the silence. With the snow, he felt like the whole world was silent. They didn't see another car on the road.

Denver sat in the Land Rover while Gabe went into the post office. He usually made his trips at night and used the drop box. Interacting with people was not his strong point.

The man behind the counter looked at the envelope being express mailed. "So, any chance you are G. L. Smith, I mean the G. L. Smith, the writer? I've seen these envelopes before, but they're usually dropped in the box."

"No, I just post his mail." Gabe didn't want to talk, but he was trapped.

"Oh, I figured that. You don't look much like a writer. I'd guess you're a farmer." The man smiled, showing a mouth in great need of dental work. "I'm right ninety-nine percent of the time, you know, on guessing people. I can tell an accountant from a bank teller and a librarian from a science teacher, and that's not easy."

"That's me, the farmer. You're right, you're very good at guessing," Gabe said, hating the words. "I have a farm a few miles away."

"Wouldn't want to tell me where Smith lives?"

"Not a chance."

The postmaster finished with all the stamps and Gabe paid with cash.

Gabe didn't ask until he had his change in hand, "You know of a G. L. Smith, do you?"

The man nodded. "My grandson reads all his work. Says he's a master. Me, I prefer my novels without pictures, but I got to tell you, my grandson wasn't reading until he found them graphic novels. I bought him a few comics; now he's reading every time I see him. If I ever meet the man, I'm going to ask if my grandson could just say hello. A guy like that has no idea what he means to readers. He may only be saving the world in print, but he's giving people hours of adventure right in the comfort of their home."

"Thanks." Gabe backed away. "I'll tell Smith if I see him."

"You do that." The man smiled. "You tell him I'd really like to meet him too."

Gabe walked out smiling, until he saw Denver sitting in the front seat looking like he was plotting his own death. When he climbed in, Gabe said, "I saw the lights on when we passed the Blue Moon Diner. Wanna stop in for some fried food?"

Denver looked up. "You'd actually go into a place to eat? Not takeout or drive-through, but a real sit-down meal?"

"Sure, anything to cheer you up."

Denver nodded. "I'll buy." He thought for a moment. "You're right. It might be the only thing that would help."

"I was hoping you'd pay." Gabe pulled away from the post office and headed down the street, wondering how it was possible that he'd picked the worst weather he'd seen in two years to go out to eat. If the fried food didn't kill him, the icy roads would.

He was surprised how many people were in the diner. They looked to be mostly the unlucky people who had to work even when the weather was bad. He and Denver took the empty table next to a group that all wore scrubs.

Denver was busy ordering the left side of the menu while Gabe tried to find one meal that wouldn't clog his arteries.

After Denver gave his order, he excused himself, leaving Gabe still trying to decide.

"Want me to just make you something, Gabe?" Edith's low voice asked. "I'm surprised to see you in here."

Gabe looked up. Edith Franklin smiled down at him. He didn't know if it was because he'd never visited with her in the daylight, or if he just took a minute to really look, but this time he saw the years of pain reflected in her eyes. There were scars on her arms: one that looked like a burn, one a cut that had been stitched up haphazardly. When she raised her hand to brush her hair back behind her ear, he saw bruises on her arm. Defensive wounds, he thought.

"How are you?" he said with no hint that he was asking a casual question.

"I'm fine," she lied. "Had a problem getting here today. My car wouldn't start and Lloyd fell on the steps when he got out to take me in his van."

Gabe didn't know how to make light conversation. "How many times did he hit you?"

She let out a breath and stared at the gray day already darkening into night. "Only twice, but it was my fault. I poured hot water on the porch ice, thinking I'd make it better, but it's so cold outside the water froze before it could melt down to the wood."

Gabe calmed his anger. "It wasn't your fault, Edith."

Edith smiled. "Lloyd got the brunt of this battle. When he swung the third time, he slipped and hurt his back. He's over in the emergency room right now hoping they'll give him some painkillers. The half bottle of whiskey he drank only took the edge off, he said. Hospital workers at the next table say with all the fender benders around town, he may have a four-hour wait. I told him when he dropped me off that I'm leaving him. That kid, Reagan Truman, helped me see the light."

Gabe had thought of telling her to leave Lloyd. He'd been bad news since the day they married, but Gabe wasn't in the habit of telling people how to run their lives. He couldn't even run his own, but he wasn't surprised Reagan had stepped up to help.

While Edith waited for him to decide, she added, more to herself than Gabe, "You know, funny thing is I don't remember a time when I wasn't married to him. It'll take some getting used to, but I've made up my mind. I'm just waiting around for the new girl to get here, then Cass said I could take his truck and go pick up my things."

Gabe nodded at Edith, silently wishing her well, then ordered a bowl of soup just as Denver returned from the restroom.

"You okay?" Gabe asked as soon as he saw Denver's pale face.

"Yeah, I threw up the whiskey. Now I feel like I'd have to die and come back as a frog to feel better."

Claire had clobbered Denver almost as badly as Lloyd had beaten up Edith, but his scars didn't show. Gabe decided he should go back to life as a hermit. The only person he'd really miss if he moved to the middle of the desert would be Elizabeth.

"I should have never gone over to the Matheson Ranch." Denver settled into the second verse of his sad song. "Having her never call would have been better than knowing that she used me. I thought she really cared for me deep down and was just acting like she didn't. Now I know she hated me deep down and was just acting like she liked me. And that woman's acting like she liked me would never win an Oscar. For a quarter I'd go back out there and tell her what she can do with . . ."

Gabe had to stop the rant. "Was Elizabeth at the ranch?" he asked the minute Denver breathed.

Denver looked at him as if he'd interrupted a bar fight going on in his mind. He glared at nothing, then said,

"Why don't you call her Liz? Everyone else does. She even said she likes it, but you have to call her Elizabeth. Half the time I don't know who you're talking about."

Gabe saw that he'd just detoured the anger, not cooled it. "I was just wondering if she was there," he said slowly, knowing his friend was looking for a fight. "I call her Elizabeth because I like to take my time saying her name. Sorry if it confuses you. By the way, how'd you get out of college with all those defective brain cells?"

Denver rolled his eyes but seemed to realize what he'd been doing. "Okay. No, she wasn't there. The aunts said she's staying in town."

Gabe closed his eyes. If he went out the back door and ran a hundred yards along the gully, he could be at the back stairs to her office without having to fight the roads. He could see her. Just for a minute. That's all he needed. He wasn't sure why, but he knew he needed to hold her more than he needed food.

"I'll be back in ten minutes," he said as he stood and tossed his keys on the table. "You'll still be on the three appetizers you ordered when I get back."

Denver watched as Gabe stood. "Don't bring her back. I'm not fit company."

"You're telling me." Gabe started toward the back. "Don't worry. If I'm not back soon, I'll call you."

"If you take more than an hour, I'll be across the street wasting my time drinking again."

"Fair enough." A moment later Gabe heard the cook yell at him as the back door slammed.

He crossed the gully and was at Elizabeth's office before he had a chance to feel the cold. Her light was on.

He climbed the stairs but heard her voice a second before he knocked.

"I understand," she yelled. "I could come over. I know, but my car could make it. Don't worry, Hank, I'll get there."

Silence.

Gabe guessed she'd been talking on the phone. He hesitated, afraid he'd be intruding.

Just as he was about to turn around, Elizabeth opened the door.

"Gabe," she whispered, and a moment later was in his arms.

He hugged her tightly, asking, "What is it? What's wrong?"

"Jeremiah Truman had a heart attack. Hank took him to the hospital and they operated a few hours ago. The doctor says he's got the old guy stable, but it doesn't look good."

Gabe stared down at her, loving the way she cared about people. "Where's Reagan?"

"She's at the hospital alone. That's why Hank called. He and Alex have been with her, but they were pulled away to a bad wreck. He said she's there alone now. He's afraid the old man will die and she won't have someone to lean on." A tear rolled over Elizabeth's cheek. "There's no one to call. Reagan has no other family."

"She has us," he whispered. "I'll drive. You call Hank and tell him we're on our way."

They ran down icy stairs and climbed into Elizabeth's tiny car. Gabe gunned the engine as he adjusted the seat to accommodate his long legs. "I agree with Hank," he yelled at Liz. "You shouldn't be driving this thing in weather like this. I've seen go-carts that look like they'd get more traction."

She stuck her tongue out at him, and Gabe almost ran off the road wishing he could kiss her.

It took twenty minutes to get the two miles to the hospital. The place was packed with people. Gabe decided half the town must have been playing bumper cars and the other half, over sixty mostly, had tried ice skating without skates. What made it worse, every injured person had a half dozen family members circled around them.

As they moved through the crowd looking for Reagan, Gabe glanced around trying to see a man who looked like

Edith's husband. He remembered someone saying Lloyd was big, but nothing more. Funny thing, men who beat their wives don't always look the part.

He wasn't sure what he'd do if he saw Lloyd. Maybe walk up and give him a little taste of what he liked to hand out. Not that it mattered any longer. By the time Lloyd worked his way through this mess and made it back to his trailer, Edith would be gone for good.

While they waited for a nurse to look up what room Truman had been taken to, Gabe leaned over to Elizabeth and whispered, "Do you know what Lloyd Franklin looks like?"

"Of course," she answered. "Dumb, potbellied, and dead if his wife had her way."

"I thought he was the one beating on her?"

"He is, but I think she's plotting. And if she kills him, I've already decided I'll take the case. Why are you looking for him?"

Gabe smiled. "Edith said he had an accident on the ice. Said he's here trying to get painkillers. He claimed he hurt his back." Gabe hesitated and added, "She also said she told him she was leaving him for good. She said he was so drunk, he didn't even try to argue. He just stared at her and laughed."

"Did she have anything to do with him being hurt in the first place?"

"Not that I know of," Gabe said finding it hard to believe that kindhearted Edith would ever try to kill someone, but everyone has a breaking point, he guessed, and she did smooth out the porch with hot water.

"Miss Matheson." A nurse caught their attention. "Mr. Truman was moved to ICU." She pointed with her pen.

"Thanks," Elizabeth said, and started rushing down the hallway.

"You know that nurse?" Gabe asked.

"At some point, if you live here long enough, you know everyone, or more precisely, everyone knows you."

The intensive care unit was closed, with posted visiting hours for fifteen minutes every two hours. Liz crossed the hall. The small waiting room that served both the operating room and ICU was empty.

They traded guesses as to where Reagan might be, but everywhere they looked was a waste of time. With a hospital this size it would be hard to disappear. The cafeteria, a room surrounded by vending machines, had only eight tables. There were four bathrooms on each of the two floors, three waiting rooms total, an emergency room, four small operating rooms, and a birthing room.

After twenty minutes, Liz tried her brother's cell. He said he'd left Reagan in the ICU waiting area. The girl had told him she planned to sleep there. A nurse had even brought her a blanket. Unless she was in with Truman, she should be where he'd left her.

While Hank tried Reagan's cell, Gabe asked one of the passing nurses if Reagan was in with her uncle.

She shook her head and said simply, "Not allowed."

Elizabeth's phone rang. She answered, listened for a few seconds, then shook her head. "It's Hank. Reagan isn't answering her cell. He said he knows she has it, he watched her switch it to vibrate."

Liz closed her phone. "Hank sounded worried. Reagan's protective of the old man. She wouldn't just leave. Not on crutches. Not without a car. Hank says he's calling Alex. Something has to be wrong. She couldn't have just disappeared."

Gabe felt the same way. He stepped back into the ICU waiting room as if he'd missed something. As he lifted the hospital blanket left on a chair, Reagan's red cell phone tumbled to the floor. Now he knew something was wrong. She wouldn't have left it. Reagan was in trouble. He could feel it inside. "Can you call the Blue Moon and see if Denver can report here as soon as possible? He's got my Land Rover."

"Sure, but I don't have to call the café, I've got his cell number. Claire gave me his card the other day." She dug in her purse. "She told me to give the card back to him. Do you think he'll be of some help?"

"I don't know. I just sense something's wrong and I need him here." Gabe didn't want to tell her his fear, but the pieces were beginning to fit together and he prayed the picture emerging wouldn't come into focus. If it did, he might need Denver to cover his back. Reagan wouldn't, couldn't, walk away from her uncle. Not without her cell. Not willingly.

Gabe spoke slowly so he wouldn't frighten Elizabeth. "Check all the women's rooms, every stall. I'll check the men's, then we'll go to hospital security. She's got to be here somewhere. She couldn't have left the hospital without someone seeing her."

They moved fast, checking every room that wasn't locked. In his mind he kept guessing. Maybe she'd found a place to sleep, or cry . . . no, she wouldn't leave Truman, not when he was dying. Maybe friends talked her into going somewhere to eat . . . not likely. She had no car and little chance of walking away on crutches. She had to be in the hospital. She had to be!

When he and Elizabeth reached the emergency entrance, the two security guards joined them. Dividing the room, they began asking everyone if they'd seen a girl with a walking cast pass by. Most were too concerned with their own problems. At the check-in desk, they finally got lucky. One of the nurses had noticed Reagan leaving.

Gabe shot questions in rapid fire. "Did she say where she was going? Did she seem distressed? Was she alone?"

The nurse shook her head until she heard the last question. "I saw her hobbling out behind a big guy," the nurse said. "She yelled something at him, but he didn't stop. Maybe he didn't hear her, or maybe he was just in a hurry. I didn't get a good look at the man, but when the girl went through the door, she hit her cast on the facing but she didn't slow down."

"Did she come back inside?"

The nurse shook her head. "I got busy. I'm sorry. I couldn't say."

Gabe looked up and saw Sheriff Alex McAllen running toward them. She motioned them into the first empty office. Elizabeth filled her in while Gabe asked the guards questions. No, there were no cameras. No, they didn't keep a guard outside. No, neither of them were stationed in the emergency room. One had gone upstairs to have supper and the other one had been asked by a nurse if he'd talk to a family who were making too much noise.

Gabe fought down his anger. The two men were not security, they were doormen. He glanced up. Alex stared right at him, and he had a feeling she was thinking the same thing.

"Liz," Alex began, "while Gabe and I step outside to look for any sign of Reagan, can you stay here with Truman? Call my cell if there's any change in him. We need to get Reagan back by his side before he wakes."

"I'll take care of it," Liz said. "Just find the girl."

As Gabe and Alex moved to the front door, the sheriff asked the security men to run another check of the building, and then, as they took off down the first hall, she whispered to Gabe, "You know what we might have here?"

"I do," he said. "Reagan didn't just step outside. Not on crutches. Not alone."

"I agree." Alex was all business. "Can you help me with this? I may need backup."

Gabe glanced out the glass door and saw Denver pulling up. Before the engine of the Rover died, he was out and running toward them. "You've got two of us and we're both armed."

She smiled. "I had a feeling you would be."

Chapter 45

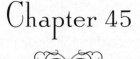

FRIDAY NIGHT
FEBRUARY 22, 2008
TIMBER LINE ROAD

REAGAN TRIED TO BRACE HERSELF IN THE BACK OF A
cluttered, dirty van. She wanted to scream her head off,
but she doubted that would do any good.

She'd been an idiot to try to stop Lloyd. Edith must have
told him she was leaving him. No telling how long he'd
been at the hospital stewing over their fight when he passed
the ICU waiting room and noticed Reagan alone.

The horrible man had yelled at her, told Reagan it was
all her fault. If she'd minded her own business his wife
would never think of leaving him. Reagan smelled whiskey
on his breath and guessed he was high on pills as well. His
world seemed to be falling apart, and she was the closest
person to blame.

Reagan had tried to explain. Tried to calm him down. Then, suddenly, Lloyd bolted, saying simply that he'd stop Edith.

Reagan followed, planning to at least slow him down to give Edith time to get her things out. But he wouldn't turn around, wouldn't listen, and she couldn't catch him on her crutches.

Halfway to his parked van, Reagan grabbed Lloyd Franklin's arm, making one last effort. A second later, she realized her mistake. In only a few steps she'd gone from being surrounded by people to being alone with a man who blamed her for all his trouble.

He turned on her and shoved her hard against a snow-covered car.

"Wait," she said, holding up her hands. "I can explain."

"I don't have time to wait." He grabbed her coat and pulled her up. "How about you come along with me and talk my wife out of leaving me the same way you talked her into it."

He collected her crutches and dragged her to the back of his van. "I've been thinking about how you could help me out in another way, and now's as good a time as any to begin the negotiations. I'm feeling like I haven't got much to lose, so I might as well run full out."

She kicked and screamed, but he was like a man possessed. He slammed her cast hard against the bumper as he fought to hold on to her and open the two doors in the back of his lawn equipment van.

"You're nothing but trouble, girl," he said as he shoved her inside. "It's time someone taught you a lesson!"

Pain shot up her leg, and for a moment Reagan couldn't draw a breath. The break was too new to take a blow. She gulped for air as tears streamed down her face. She wiggled atop dirty tools and pieces of sprinklers as her crutches clattered in on top of her.

"Stop," she yelled. "Let me—"

She didn't get any more out before he slapped her hard across the face, busting her lip. "There's no need to start hollering," he said almost calmly. "It won't do any good. I'm about to offer you a business plan that you won't be able to refuse, but first we need to get somewhere that we can talk."

Reagan stopped screaming as she tasted blood, then balled up all her energy and kicked him hard in the stomach with her good leg. The effort caused her more pain than it did him.

He staggered a step back, straightened, grabbed her arm and pulled her a few inches closer, then hit her again with his fist.

Her shoulder took most of the blow.

"Quiet," he said, raising his hand for another blow if he heard a sound. Bruising her arm with his grip, he added low and sharp, "The next one will be harder. I learned a long time ago some folks don't listen unless you get their attention first."

She'd stopped screaming, shocked and frightened by the wild look in his eyes. Even out of shape, he was a big man who could do a great deal of damage with his beefy fists.

He let her arm go and smiled as if he'd simply settled a problem.

Raising herself with her arms, she tried to back away from him and move farther into the van.

"Good." He nodded. "I'm glad you've decided to be sensible about this."

He slammed the back of the van doors and ran around to the front, climbed in, and gunned the engine.

Reagan tried to scramble over pieces of machinery and long pipes, but her broken leg made it impossible to reach the door. She could hear him yelling from the front. Something about how she thought she was too good to go have a drink with him. How she never liked him so she poisoned his wife. Edith would have never talked of leaving him. Somehow, in Lloyd's mind this was all Reagan's fault.

Reagan leaned back and tried to think. Her head hurt, her leg throbbed, and she thought her foot was bleeding where pieces of her cast had been shattered. She wouldn't have believed the day could get any worse. Her uncle might be dying. She needed to be with him. Yet, somehow, she'd let an idiot kidnap her. Suddenly she was far more angry than frightened.

"I can't help you!" she screamed at him. "Edith isn't leaving you because of something I said."

"I'm not so sure about that, but you can help me. I've been thinking. You got land and those that got land got money. Maybe if you loaned me some money, Edith would think twice about leaving."

"My uncle just had a heart attack. He won't give you money even if he was able. Take me back right now."

Lloyd laughed and turned a corner, sending Reagan rolling across the back, along with tools and pipes. "I don't need your uncle, girl. Edith told me you own the land; I heard he gave it to you for your birthday." He pulled a bottle from beneath his seat and took a drink. "Now, you can give a little over to me."

"I'll never do that." She said the words, but he didn't stop talking long enough to listen. Lloyd Franklin was piecing together a plan in his mind. A plan to keep his wife and solve his money troubles.

"I don't see why you wouldn't want to help us out. My brother and I talked about it the other night at the bar. He said since you're so close to Edith, you might want to float a loan. I don't plan on hurting you, kid, but it's not right for someone so young to have all that land. You didn't do nothing to earn it."

"I won't give you any money *or* land." Reagan had no idea who his brother was, but the gene pool was definitely polluted. "Let me out of here. I want nothing to do with you."

Lloyd slid over icy roads again, sending her rolling. "That's what Edith used to say when she was fifteen and going out with me, but I talked her into it. The day she turned sixteen, we ran off. She was like you. She didn't have any folks to speak of. Her mom didn't like the idea, but she had her own problems.

"When we were first married, Edith thought I was perfect, but bad luck and people turned her against me. You're not much older than she was. I'll talk you into seeing things my way, and Edith will see the light once I got money."

"My uncle will shoot you." Reagan thought of adding that he'd be shooting at a dead body because she planned to murder Lloyd first. The instincts that had kept her alive all those years without anyone to help her came back to her now. She couldn't get too upset, she couldn't let the pain show, she had to be ready to act. One thing she'd learned was that there would be a moment when the tables could turn and when they did, she'd act.

The loneliness she'd hated now circled her like a shield, reminding her she could survive. "Take me back!" she yelled. "I'm not going to give you a dime of money or a handful of land."

"You will," he protested. "You'll give me plenty."

Lloyd pulled out his cell and punched a number. After a short wait, he yelled, "Donnie, I got the Truman girl in my van, and all I got to do is talk her into giving me a little of what she got for her birthday." He hesitated a few seconds and added, "Calm down. Stop yelling at me. This is going to be easy. The hardest part is over. She came running out following me, so I just picked her up. Nobody even saw me. Not a soul, I swear." He glanced back at her lying on the floor of the van. "She's all quiet. I don't think she'll give me much trouble at all. I'll be there in a few minutes and you'll see."

The van hit a sheet of ice and spun around. Reagan rolled into as tight a ball as she could and held on to the inside of the van.

When he finally stopped in the middle of the street, he

turned back to her. "Look what you made me do, girl. I dropped my phone."

Reagan raised her head a few inches and glared at him. "I didn't do anything," she said as she felt the phone against her side.

Lloyd rummaged on the floorboard around his feet, then straightened and swore as someone honked at him to move.

"Don't you say another word," he said in a low voice. "Or I swear I'll dump you out right here. I could do it too. I could toss your body somewhere no one in the state would ever look. Edith told me you looked like a runaway when you came to town two years ago looking for your uncle. I figure if you disappeared they'd all just think you ran away again."

Reagan didn't move until he'd turned back and started driving again. Her fingers brushed over the clutter around her until they came to rest on a hammer. Carefully, she shoved it beneath her body so it wouldn't shuffle away. Then she palmed the phone.

Lloyd Franklin might think she was easy to kidnap, but he was about to learn that she would not go easily. Sixteen years of being tossed around from foster homes to orphanages had taught her how to survive.

She punched 911, then slid the phone between her arm and body. When the tiny light disappeared, she punched redial. She might not be able to talk, but she would let someone know she was in trouble.

Chapter 46

SHERIFF ALEX MCALLEN EXPLAINED THE FACTS TO HANK on her radio while Gabe and Denver searched for clues in the hospital parking lot.

Hank took the news without emotion. "Do you need me?" he asked in a tired voice that silently whispered that he'd come if she said yes. "We're dealing with several injuries out here on the interstate, but if you need me, I'll be there."

Alex hated to pull him away. "Reagan wasn't in the hospital. We found plaster from her cast in the parking lot. There was no mistaking all the purple writing. The bastard must have slammed her leg against something hard enough to break part of her cast off."

Alex couldn't bring herself to say the words to get Hank to come to her. Reagan needed Hank's help, but not her. Alex was the sheriff; she shouldn't need anyone.

"Do you need me?" Hank asked again, his voice the only calm in the mist of the snowstorm.

"No," she finally said. "Gabe Leary and Denver Sims are here."

"Good," Hank said. "We've got a hell of mess here and it's getting darker. I'll be there as soon as I can. Keep in touch."

Alex closed the phone. For once she had no backup. She was on her own. The memory of her brother crossed her mind. Five years ago he'd been alone when he'd been out on routine patrol. He'd stopped a car on a lonely road and been shot. Alex couldn't help but wonder if he'd hesitated when real trouble arrived. And would she?

"We don't know it was her blood in the snow," Denver commented as if trying to make Alex look less worried.

Alex pulled her thoughts back as he continued, "It could be Lloyd's blood or someone else who came in hurt, but from the signs, there was definitely a struggle in the parking lot. My guess is she fought getting in the car."

"Van," Gabe corrected from five feet away. "He drives an old van. Edith said she was having car trouble, remember. He had to take her to work."

"Get the guards to rope off the area," Denver yelled. "I don't know what is going on, but right now we're treating it like a crime scene. Tell one of those security guards to keep people away."

He stepped to the back of the Rover. A moment later he reappeared, strapping on what looked like a military tool belt. "I can track the van on foot in this storm probably as fast as you could in a car and far more accurately. I'll stay in touch." He nodded toward Gabe. "When I make visual contact I'll call you and wait for you to move in and pick me up."

"But it's snowing, it's freezing." Alex couldn't believe he was heading out into the storm. "You can't run for miles in this mess."

Denver smiled. "I can and I have."

Gabe watched Alex take a few steps to her cruiser, then turn and ask, "Who are you guys?" She glared at them both.

"We were Special Forces five years ago. Trained to search and destroy the enemy in any terrain," Gabe said as Denver moved away, waving his flashlight over tracks.

"I'd call for backup," she commented as she climbed into her cruiser, "but they're all busy right now."

Gabe moved to her side of the car. "I'm with you," he said. "The lieutenant and I were once the best at what we did. For Reagan's sake, I hope we remember more than we forgot."

"Can you . . ."

"Yes," he answered as if it were the answer to anything she was about to ask.

"Do you know where Lloyd lives?"

She nodded. "The trailer park just outside of town on Lone Oak Road. Third trailer on the left. You think we should start there first?"

"Catching her alone at the hospital was an opportunity, not a planned abduction. He's probably been planning something in his mind for a while, maybe even collecting supplies. My guess is Edith's announcement tonight fired his plan into action. Now he'll have to go home to pick up tape, ropes, whatever he needs to hold her."

"Unless they were stored in the van."

Gabe watched as Denver reached the end of the parking lot and began to jog. "I've never worked a kidnapping like this," he admitted to Alex, "but I've trained for it. I don't know what he wants her for. If it's money, she'll be all right as long as he thinks the plan is working. If it's rape, she's got a good chance of surviving it unless she fights, but then he might dump her somewhere and with a broken leg she'd freeze." He hesitated. "If I know Reagan, she'll fight, and if she fights . . ."

When he couldn't finish, Alex added, "We may be guessing the worst cases, but no matter why he took her, we have to get to her fast." Alex's laugh held no humor. "Time is our biggest obstacle here. The more time he has her, the greater the chance that she'll be hurt."

"I know," Gabe said as Alex's radio came to life. He heard all he needed to hear. The dispatcher had no surprises. Reagan was not in the hospital, and security had found two people who ID'd Lloyd Franklin leaving just before a girl with a cast on her leg.

Gabe ran to the Rover and climbed in. By the time Alex had backed out of her parking slot, he'd pulled up to her window.

"I'll follow Denver. If we're lucky, we'll all meet up at the trailer park." He was gone before she could answer.

She drove carefully toward the edge of town. Snow was now falling over ice, making every turn dangerous. The town looked so beautiful, so peaceful. How could a kidnapping have happened in her town?

Alex fought panic. She reached to call Hank, then stopped. He had his hands full on the highway. It would take him thirty minutes to get to her even if he did try to come. Reagan's life might be at risk, but so were the lives on the highway.

She called dispatch and gave a string of orders as she crawled along the road toward the edge of town.

Finally, she pulled off into the trailer park and waited, lights off.

Five, ten, fifteen minutes. Not one car passed.

Alex called dispatch. No word from anyone. Jess said the only thing coming in was a 911 call from a cell phone, but no one answered when he picked up. He couldn't get a location, but he was having the number traced.

Gabe pulled up behind her and motioned for her to climb into his Rover, then parked across the road from the dark Franklin home.

"Where's Denver?" Alex asked.

"The van tracks circled around town a few times and disappeared. I picked Denver up and we came here. Lloyd may be driving around making sure he's not followed or waiting until he thinks he's safe."

Alex looked in the backseat. "So if you picked him up, where is your friend?"

"I let him off when I pulled up behind you. He's already watching the back of the trailer. We'll give him a few minutes to move in close, then we'll go pay a call."

"I'm glad you're here," Alex said honestly. She was in over her head.

Gabe whispered, almost as if he didn't want to say the words out loud. "I've been asking myself why he'd take her. I don't think he plans to kill her. He probably thinks he's just going to frighten her a little. Who knows, the guy may even think they're on a date."

"You're kidding."

"No, I think, in his mind, he thinks he can charm her like he did Edith twenty years ago. Or he may try bullying her."

"So," Alex guessed, "you think he's tired of Edith and wants a younger wife?"

"Maybe. Reagan told me about him acting friendly when he came in the Blue Moon, trying to flirt with her. Maybe he thinks that now she's eighteen he can't be accused of kidnapping if she says she went along with him willingly. He pretty much got Edith to believe anything, maybe he figures his charms will work with Reagan."

"He'd have to be pretty sick to believe that."

"Exactly," Gabe said.

Alex stared at the Franklin trailer. "Edith was a frightened child; maybe she figured Lloyd was as good as she could get. Maybe she loved him, I don't know." Alex put her hand on the door handle. "All I know for sure is that Reagan isn't Edith. She didn't leave the hospital willingly."

"I know," Gabe said. "And if she didn't, you can bet she won't go along with anything Lloyd has in mind."

"You think he might kill her if he doesn't get his way." Alex stepped out of the Rover.

"He's desperate. I'm not sure what he'll do."

They pulled their weapons and held them at their sides as they moved in on the home. The place was dark and silent. The falling snow left a soft blanket on the drive and road beyond. No one had turned into the drive in a while. Wherever Lloyd had taken Reagan, it wasn't here.

Gabe whistled softly and Denver answered back. He knocked, then waited. "No one is here," he whispered, and motioned for her to go over to the trailer across the drive. Lights were on there, and the windows faced the Franklin trailer.

Alex left Gabe looking around the yard and crossed to the next home. She asked the neighbor to call in if he saw any movement of any kind at Lloyd's trailer. The man said he'd be happy to do whatever he could to put Franklin's ass in jail for anything. "I'll turn off my light and post myself, with phone in hand, by the window. If a rabbit hops on his land, I'll let you know."

Alex walked back to her car and called dispatch to pull in anyone not working a bad wreck. "Get in touch with Hank and have him call anyone with a four-wheel drive that he trusts. They'll need manpower to handle this. I'll meet them at the fire station as soon as I can."

Gabe moved to the other side of her car and nodded as he listened.

"I'll call the highway patrol. They'll block any roads that haven't already been closed because of the storm. We might get lucky if he tries to take her out of the county. Very few people will be out tonight."

"You know, if you pull in men, untrained men, they'll be more in the way than help."

Alex didn't argue. "I don't know what else to do."

Denver appeared beside Gabe. "He's got a handgun. I saw the half-burned box in the trash."

Denver stared at her a moment and said simply, "Alex, if you'll pick up Edith and take her in, maybe she'll know something. Gabe and I will meet you at the fire station as soon as we can."

"Where are you going?" she asked.

"It's a long shot, but I want to check out the address on the box the gun came in." Using his flashlight, he read off the numbers and road.

Alex didn't have to check her computer; she knew the address, she'd worked a few calls there. "That's Lloyd's little brother's place. You want me to go with you?"

"No," Denver said, already moving with Gabe toward the Rover. "If it's a dead end, maybe you'll have other leads after you talk to Edith."

They pulled away without saying another word.

Alex forced herself to drive slowly even though her heart was pounding about a thousand beats a minute.

She called dispatch and asked them to check on Truman. No change. He had not come out of recovery from heart surgery. If he did come to before they found Reagan, the news would probably kill him.

Alex fought down panic. She felt like her world was falling apart. She'd always been in control at her job. Always been able to handle whatever came her way. Prided herself in playing every hand by the book.

Only tonight, she wasn't sure. The minutes were ticking by and they were no closer to finding Reagan. The storm had closed in around them. There was no way help could get to her anytime soon.

"Sheriff? You still there?" Jess's voice cracked over the radio.

"I'm here," Alex answered.

"That 911 call that keeps coming in . . . it's from Lloyd Franklin's cell phone."

Alex smiled. Reagan. It had to be the girl calling in. Somehow she had managed to get his phone. That had to be the only reason. Lloyd would never make the call. "I'll be there as fast as I can." Alex whispered, "Hang on, Reagan."

Chapter 47

SOMEWHERE IN HARMONY

REAGAN WAITED FOR JUST THE RIGHT MOMENT. LLOYD had stopped the van on a dark street she didn't recognize. She could hear him banging on a door ten feet away. The thought of running crossed her mind, but with her leg in a cast she'd have no chance of standing, much less escaping him.

The wind howled like a wild animal coming for her. Even if she could get out of the van and get away from Lloyd, being outside in the wind and blowing snow would probably freeze her before she could find help.

Someone finally answered the door, but Reagan harbored little hope they would help her. She could make out two men arguing, but she couldn't understand what they were saying.

The van's back doors opened and two huge shadows stood in front of her. Lloyd and a younger, smaller lookalike.

"See, Donnie," Lloyd bragged as if showing off the catch of the day, "she's not even yelling or crying. She just came out of the hospital. I told her to come along. It was like she knew about what you and I talked about. She's saying now that she won't give us money, but she'll change her mind."

"Yeah"—Donnie shook his head—"I can tell she came willingly. How come she's got blood all over her chin? It's dripping down like a leaky faucet."

Lloyd reached in and jerked her toward him so suddenly Reagan didn't have time to bolt.

She lost her grip on the hammer beneath her body as he pulled her halfway out. "Help me carry her in. It's too cold to talk out here."

Her broken leg hit the ground, shattering off another piece of her cast.

Reagan fought as Donnie grabbed her legs and Lloyd seized her hands. They half carried, half dragged her across the snow.

She tried to see where she was. They had to still be in Harmony, but she couldn't see a streetlight, much less the lights of another house. Then she heard a flapping sound of old boards rattling in the wind and knew. Back behind the abandoned railroad station was a storage building that had been left to rot for years. So much of the original brick had fallen away or been stolen that only thin wood framed the walls in places. Noah had taken her there once to listen. He said the building sounded like it was shivering in the wind.

Beyond the shivering building stood a row of little houses that had been used for migrant labor in the forties. Someone had made an attempt to fix them up as cheap rentals maybe twenty years ago, but now they looked as bad as they probably had sixty years ago. Only one seemed to be occupied.

The one she was being carried into.

When they got inside, Donnie dropped her legs and went after tape while Lloyd still held her hands high in one of his big fists.

She opened her mouth, and he raised his free hand and doubled it into a weapon. She got the message and remained silent.

Donnie brought the tape, then whined as Lloyd wrapped it around her wrists. "I didn't think you'd really do it, Lloyd. I thought you were just kidding. You know, talking about making fast money like it was a game we were playing in the bar." He shook his head as he looked Reagan up and down. "We could go to jail for this. This ain't right."

"Shut up." Lloyd finished binding her hands in front of her and shoved her hard. "The brat asked for it. She's been telling my Edith to leave me. Once she gives us the money, I'm going to get her to take back all she said to Edith as well."

Reagan tumbled onto the floor without a sound. She could hear it in Lloyd's voice now. Like a child who knew he'd made a big mistake and wasn't willing to admit it. He wasn't backing down. He planned to storm ahead.

Donnie stared down at her. "Look, Lloyd, she can't even walk and she doesn't look to be more than a girl. She's bleeding all over and it looks like you hurt her foot bad. I've heard what they do in prison to guys who hurt children."

"I didn't hurt her. She slipped on the ice."

"You busted her lip and I'll bet there are bruises all over her from rolling around in the back of that junk van."

Lloyd grabbed her hair and jerked her head up so he could see her face. His wide thumb moved over her chin, then he wiped her blood on his trousers. "I don't remember doing that, but if I did, she asked for it."

Donnie swore.

Lloyd shoved his brother so hard the younger Franklin almost tumbled off his feet.

"She don't look any the worse for her trip," Lloyd insisted. "And it's good she's got the bad leg. She can't run out on us while we're trying to talk to her. All we have to do is keep her here for a few hours until she starts thinking about making a deal. She may be all mad right now, but give her a little time and she'll calm down."

Reagan stared at Donnie. He had the dull look about him of a person who'd sold his soul to drugs. If they kept her here a hundred years she wouldn't make a deal with him or Lloyd. From the way he jerked when Lloyd moved suddenly, she guessed Donnie had probably been Lloyd's first punching bag.

"Tell your brother to let me go," Reagan tried. "If you don't, you'll both go to prison for life."

Lloyd glared at her. "Don't listen to her. She could bring us enough money to live in style. When we was talking I was thinking about asking her for a loan, but now I've decided maybe we should just get her to give us what we need to live awhile. Way I see it, she owes me for the trouble she's caused."

Donnie shook his head. "No. I want no part of this, Lloyd. It's not right. Get her out of here. I don't want the police coming here, thinking I had any part of this mess you got yourself into. You're not thinking right."

"Me? You're the one who said she'd be the easiest girl to lean on for a little money." When Donnie didn't agree, Lloyd looked like he might hit his brother, but to Reagan's surprise, he didn't. "I can't just take her back."

"We were drunk when we thought of this plan, Lloyd. She's not going to cooperate. It don't work like that."

Reagan watched Donnie. He was afraid of his brother, but he wasn't a fool. He saw a glimpse of the trouble they were in. She found it hard to believe, but this brain-fried little brother was the smarter of the two.

"We could give it a try."

"It won't work." Donnie shook his head.

"What am I supposed to do with her? I can't get her out of town; what roads that are still open will be slick. I barely made it here. Another hour or so, there won't be anything moving in this town."

"I don't care what you do with her. Toss her in the snow. She just needs to be gone." Donnie paced, trying to think. "We've got to get somewhere where people see us so we'll have an alibi. That's it. We'll go over to Buffalo's and have a beer. He never closes and if he does, we'll wake him up and demand a drink. Since he sleeps upstairs, he probably won't mind. Then, when folks realize she's missing we can act as surprised as everyone. Maybe even help with the search."

Lloyd slowly nodded, as though what he'd done had finally sunk in. "You're right. I know a place where I can leave her where nobody will look for her till spring."

"Don't kill her," Donnie said. "Promise me you won't kill her. I think that could go really bad for you if you do."

"I won't." Frustration boiled in him. "I'll just leave her tied up. If she freezes, that's not my problem, right? I'll go back tomorrow. If she's still alive, she'll probably trade keeping quiet for being untied. I might even claim I found her and saved her. That way I could be a hero like that Gabriel guy who found her when she broke her leg. The whole town's talking about what a great guy he is."

Donnie frowned at him. "You've been fired from every job you ever had, Lloyd, for acting when you should have been thinking, but this is by far the dumbest thing you ever did."

"Take me back," Reagan demanded as if she had a right to be part of their conversation. "Drop me off at the hospital entrance. I'll say I fell. I won't tell anyone."

Annoyed as though this were somehow her fault, Lloyd slugged her so hard she tumbled backward and hit the corner of a wooden box. She saw stars, as if someone had fired off fireworks in her head.

"Never trust a woman," he said as he wound the tape around her mouth and head. "All they ever do is lie." He bound her good leg to the one in a cast.

When she tried to struggle, he slapped the side of her head once. "Be still, girl. You've caused enough trouble tonight." Just for good measure, he slapped her again, taking all his anger out on her.

Reagan's head spun and the room went dark. She felt them gripping her, lifting her without care and carrying her back to the van. She didn't fight, she just let the blackness melt over her.

When she woke, she was alone in the silence of what smelled like a shed. Through dirty windows, she could see the back of a big two-story house. It was only fifty feet away, but it might as well have been a million miles because she was tied against a pole almost as big around as her waist. The wide industrial tape crossed over her chest and around the pole. Her arms were bound to the elbows.

Most of her body was covered with rags and dead leaves in a halfhearted effort to bury her. When she wiggled, the trash tumbled away from her face and shoulders.

She twisted her finger and found the phone still tucked in her sleeve. It wasn't easy to pull past the elastic of her cuff, but she finally held the phone, Lloyd's lost phone, in her hand. Guessing at the numbers, she dialed 911 but couldn't lean forward enough or raise her arms to quite reach her ear.

"County sheriff's office."

"Help," she cried, but the word couldn't get out past the tape. "Help."

She heard the click of the call being disconnected.

A light blinked, then went out in one of the windows of the house and she was alone in the darkness.

Totally alone.

Chapter 48

LATE FRIDAY NIGHT
FEBRUARY 22, 2008
HARMONY FIRE STATION

ALEX MET WITH THE FEW MEN WHO COULD MAKE IT IN TO
the fire station, wishing they were her deputies, but happy
that some would come out on a night like this. Three fire
volunteers; one retired deputy; her brother, Noah, who was
always thinking about volunteering, but never seemed to
have the time; and Bob McNabb, a nice man in his sixties
who helped out whenever he could. None could handle
Lloyd Franklin if they ran into him. Not much of a force,
but all she had.

Brandon Biggs, the kid who came to Reagan's party,
rushed in late just as she began to explain what she feared
might be happening. Bran didn't have a four-wheel drive,
but he wanted to help. He was rough around the edges and

looked like walking trouble, but now and then Alex saw what Reagan must see in him. Potential.

She set the ground rules. *No one drives out without chains on their tires.* That left out Bran, the retired deputy, and one of the firemen. *No one staying out too long.* With a forecast in single digits, the windchill factor would be below zero. *No one carries a gun unless he's also carrying a badge.* That left Alex and Denver as the only two armed. She didn't ask if Gabe had his gun with him. She didn't want to know.

Denver and Gabe took the time to talk to each man, then divided them into three groups. Each team would have cells and radios with them at all times. The plan was simple. Drive every street, every alley they could get down, every parking lot until someone spotted the van. Edith had told Alex that Lloyd didn't have many friends to go to if he was in trouble, but he might try a few of the houses he mowed lawns for in the summer.

Denver stood before the search party, a map of Harmony in his hand. "So far we've found two crime scenes where Reagan has been. First the hospital where she was abducted, then a house on the west side of town where we believe she was taken for a short time. We found crumblings from her cast and drops of blood in both the driveway and the house, but no one was home to question."

The retired deputy asked how they got in the house without a search warrant.

Denver explained that the door was open when he walked up. "It looked like they left in a hurry and must have forgot to close the door."

Alex had a feeling no one in the room, except Noah, believed him.

"The weather may be keeping him in town," Denver explained. "We don't have much time to find him. If you spot anything, call in. The radios will broadcast to everyone on the team. Punch one and the cell will ring here. Do

not go near him. We have reason to believe he's armed."
Denver looked straight at Noah and Brandon. "Do you two
understand?"

"Loud and clear," Brandon said. "How about we get
going? The sooner we get on the road, the sooner we find
Reagan."

For once, Noah agreed. The two boys might not like
each other, but right now they had a common enemy.

Denver passed out slices of the map. "One man drive,
the other mark off streets. Look for a garage or barn or
anything big enough to hide a van. Both watch for tracks.
Not much is out there but him and us, so we've got a good
chance of crossing his path. Fresh tracks could be a lead."

As the men moved out, Tyler Wright walked in and
headed straight to Alex. The little dog he claimed wasn't
his followed right on his heels. "Hank called me, Sheriff.
He said you might could use my help. I guess he figured
since the funeral home was so close, I was one of the few
in town who could get here."

Alex smiled. Hank was taking care of her the best he
could. "Thanks, Mr. Wright," she said, calling him what
everyone in town did even though she considered him a
friend. "If you could help Bob McNabb man the phones,
that would be great. Our teams will be calling in and you
need to keep one line clear for dispatch."

Bob was lining up cells, radios, and phones with paper
in front of each.

Alex pointed. "Log in all calls, which phone, which
man. If anyone doesn't call in or answer when called, it
could mean they are in trouble."

"Got it." Tyler set his laptop down at the end of the table.
"If you give me five minutes, I'll have a spreadsheet set up
that will make keeping up with this easier."

Alex pulled on her gloves. "You got everything you
need?"

Tyler nodded. "I've been here enough trying to teach

Hank to program that I know where everything is." A sadness washed over his face. "Except our Reagan," he said. "I
don't like the idea of her being out in this storm."

"We'll find her." Alex almost ran out the door. She
wanted to check with dispatch across the street and then
begin her search. She would be going alone. Her section of
the map was the two blocks around the downtown square.

While Denver and Gabe had checked out Lloyd's brother's house, Alex had talked with Edith, his wife, and found
out little. Lloyd wasn't answering his cell phone, which
didn't surprise her; he could never keep up with the thing.

Edith said she was staying at the diner all night. If Cass
closed, she planned to sleep in one of the booths. Cass was
in the back if Lloyd came in before they closed. Edith said
she'd told Lloyd before she came to work that she was leaving him, but he didn't believe her. He never did.

Alex checked her watch. Lloyd usually picked up his
wife after midnight on Friday. Cass liked to catch the bar
crowd as long as he could.

Alex would take an hour to work her piece of the map,
circling by the diner now and then to make sure he hadn't
shown up. If she had to, she planned to be waiting for Lloyd
at the diner when he came to pick Edith up. If he came.

When she walked into her office, Jess yelled, "That
caller's doing it again. Calling in, not saying anything and
then hanging up."

"I'll take it this time." Alex sat down and waited. Ten
minutes. Twenty. Time she could spend searching, but
something held her in place. No more than a gut feeling
that somehow this silent caller was the answer, the clue
she'd been waiting for.

Thirty minutes. The storm rattled the windows as if
reminding her it was waiting outside. Forty minutes. The
teams were reporting in at fifteen-minute intervals and
Tyler was calling in dispatch as soon as all had checked in.
Fifty minutes.

One hour. She could have walked the entire downtown area by now, but she had to trust her instinct.

Finally, the call came in.

"Hello, 911 emergency," Alex said.

No answer.

Alex gripped the phone so hard she was surprised it didn't shatter in her fingers. "Reagan," she shouted. "If it's you, make a sound."

Nothing.

Just as she opened her mouth to yell the demand again, the phone clicked as if someone had punched a number.

"If it's you, do that again."

The phone chimed once. Alex couldn't breathe. Somehow Reagan couldn't talk, but she was on the other end.

"One for yes. Two for no," she said. "Are you hurt?"

One chime.

"Do you know where you are?"

One, then another chime. No.

"Are you in town?

One beep.

"Are you inside a van?"

Two beeps.

"Are you inside someone's house?"

Nothing. Alex fought down panic. She had to ask yes or no questions. If Reagan didn't know, she might not answer. Or, she might be in too much danger to answer.

Alex tried again. "Are you inside?"

One beep.

"Are you alone?"

One beep.

Jess had moved behind her, following along with speakers on. "She's inside, but not in a house, Sheriff."

"Are you in a barn?" Alex yelled.

Two beeps.

"A car?"

Two beeps.

"A business?"

Two beeps.

"A shed?"

One beep. Alex breathed and jotted down for Jess to notify the others that they were looking for a shed.

While Jess called, Alex continued to play the game with Reagan. She wanted to ask where the girl was hurt and who had kidnapped her and why, but none of those mattered. All that mattered right now was finding her. Alex began naming things that Reagan might be able to see.

After a dozen tries, she wrote down *two-story house* and passed it to Jess so he could relay.

"That eliminates most of the town," he said as he dialed. "The historical district and over by the golf course are about all we got in the way of second stories."

"We've got teams moving toward you," Alex yelled to Reagan, guessing the phone was not close to her ear. "Are you still alone?"

One beep.

"Is he coming back?"

No answer. She didn't know.

"Are you warm?"

Two beeps. No. She was probably freezing.

"Are you tied up?"

One beep.

"Is there any light around you?"

Two beeps. Wherever she was, she was in the dark. Alone, cold, and frightened.

The courthouse clock began chiming the midnight hour.

"Can you hear the clock?" Alex closed her eyes and waited, counting the chimes in her mind.

One beep.

Alex was on her feet running. "Call the others. Tell them all that she's close to downtown. She has to be in the historical district. If she can't see streetlights, she'll be in the back behind a two-story house."

"Got it!" Jess yelled.

Alex was already heading down the steps. The fastest way to the back of the historical district was along the creek bed. She pulled the hood of her coat low and turned into the darkness.

It was dangerous tromping through snow on uneven ground, but Alex knew every minute counted.

Chapter 49

EARLY SATURDAY
FEBRUARY 23, 2008
STREETS OF HARMONY

GABE ANSWERED THE PHONE WHEN TYLER CALLED TO tell them the news about how Alex had talked to Reagan and she was somewhere near downtown.

"Tell me all you know, fast," he said to Tyler as Denver drove the Rover toward the center of town. "We're coming in from the south."

Tyler's voice sounded nervous, but determined. "Do you know the creek path through town?"

"Of course."

"In the historical district a lot of those old houses have sheds out back. If you go under at the bridge on Elm and Third on foot, you can walk the creek faster than driving down the road and crossing behind every house."

Gabe agreed. "I know the creek. We'll cross down to it at Elm. I can find my way in the dark."

He hung up and grabbed one of the extra crutches they'd picked up at the hospital. "Turn left in two blocks," Gabe told Denver. "You'll see a bridge crossing the road. We can cut down to the creek there."

"I have no idea what you are planning," Denver said. "But I'm with you."

A few minutes later they stepped out in the snow. Gabe hated a cane, but this was no time to think about himself. He could move faster with the crutch, plus test for solid ground.

Neither said a word as they moved away from the street-lights and into the creek bed. The air was still, with only the swishing sound of their boots eating up the snow. The ugly bed looked like a wonderland in the snow with icy branches swaying above, but the men saw none of the beauty.

Gabe knew the twists and turns of the creek. With the help of the crutch, he ran. He stopped at each house and shone his light as Denver climbed the five-foot bank and searched shed after shed.

A few times Gabe swore he heard locks being snapped and wood splintering, but time after time Denver returned. "Nothing," he'd say and Gabe would continue the march.

Gabe's cell rang while Denver was up top at the fifth house. "Yes," he whispered.

Tyler's voice came loud and clear. "Noah and Brandon found the van parked behind the used bookstore off the square. You know, the building where Liz Matheson has her office. Blood inside. No one around."

For a heartbeat Gabe thought he'd explode. The lot behind the bookstore was Elizabeth's lot. Then he remembered leaving her at the hospital. She was safe, and when he got back to her he planned on telling her just how much she meant to him.

"Nothing," Denver said as he slid down the snow to the creek bed. "Let's keep moving."

A few houses later Gabe saw the beam of a light coming toward him. He clicked off his light and waited, signaling Denver to do the same.

The beam came closer, waving wildly from side to side.

The two men stood as shadows among the roots of the trees. Friend or enemy, it made more sense to wait.

"It's the sheriff," Denver whispered, flipping on his light when she was thirty feet away.

For a second, Gabe saw Alex reach for her weapon, then she watched them step out into her beam. "Any luck?" she said, knowing the answer.

They moved to the first of only three houses left. The snow had finally slowed to a soupy fog in the air. Gabe saw the little garden shed in the Winter's Inn backyard before the others did. He knew the moment he saw it, just like he knew the moment he'd seen the driver's eyes before the bomb hit five years ago, that they were in deep trouble.

"That's it." He pointed.

Denver scrambled up the embankment and moved silently toward the shed.

Alex was on her radio. "Tell Reagan to do anything she can to make a noise. Tell her we're close, very close."

Alex climbed up using crude steps Gabe remembered Martha Q saying her yard man had dug out for her.

The pieces were falling together. He followed as fast as he could.

Ten feet from the shed, he heard a tapping sound. One-two-three. They all moved in. Gabe smiled as he heard Denver say his thoughts. "One-two-three, come get me."

Reagan was sending an SOS and didn't even know it.

Denver reached her first. His light flashed across a pile of leaves and trash, and curly red hair.

He knelt and began gently digging her out of all the trash, careful not to touch her any more than he had to.

Reagan's big eyes looked up at him, then over his shoulder as Alex and Gabe entered. Panic and fear filled her gaze.

Alex set her light down and pulled the tape from Reagan's mouth. "You're all right, now. We've got you." Then both she and Reagan were crying so hard they could barely talk.

Gabe stood guard at the entrance. All was silent in the yard, but he'd be ready if Lloyd picked this moment to return.

While he waited, he hit redial on the cell Alex had insisted he carry. As soon as Tyler answered, he said, "We got her. Winter's Inn."

Denver gave him a thumbs-up sign as he pulled the last of the tape away.

Gabe moved to the back door and banged. Lights came on. While he waited, Tyler shouted into the phone. "Is she hurt?"

"Yes," Gabe answered, "but real glad to see us. We'll know more when we get her inside in the light."

Tyler paused for a few seconds, then said, "Noah is two miles away. They are on their way in case she needs to be transported to the hospital."

Gabe remembered the blood at both crime scenes. "Yes, she'll need transport."

Mrs. Biggs turned on the light, peeked out at Gabe, then opened the door a few inches.

"I'll explain later, Mrs. Biggs. We need to get Reagan in the house. She's been hurt."

There was no hesitation. Mrs. Biggs cleared the way. Gabe held the door and Denver carried Reagan inside.

They moved to the kitchen and placed her on the tiny table. Mrs. Biggs ran for blankets. Alex grabbed towels and washed away blood. Reagan's lip had stopped bleeding, but the front of her jacket was bloody.

When Denver touched her bleeding foot covered in dirt, Reagan jerked it away.

"I need to take a look at it, honey," Denver tried again, obviously not comfortable.

"No," she said.

"We need to . . ."

Reagan looked up at Gabe.

He sat in the chair and lifted what was left of her cast onto his knee. "Will you let me see it? I promise I won't hurt you any more than I have to, but this looks like it's still bleeding."

Reagan nodded.

Slowly, carefully, Gabe washed the blood and mud away. The cut across the inside of her arch was deep and in need of stitches, but not life threatening. He wrapped it as tight as he could, worrying more about infection than blood loss.

Martha Q finally showed up. She'd taken the time to slap on makeup and comb her hair before attending the emergency.

By the time the boys arrived a few minutes later, they had Reagan's foot taped and had wrapped her in blankets. Noah and Brandon stormed in the front door, almost knocking Martha Q down when she answered.

Gabe felt like a traffic cop. Everyone was talking at once. But when Reagan said Lloyd and his brother were at Buffalo's drinking, Gabe met Denver's stare. Both men nodded at once. They knew where they'd be going next.

"Get her to the hospital," Alex said to Noah and Brandon. "I'll go after Lloyd." She looked at her little brother. "You. Be careful."

"I will," Noah said. "I could say the same for you. I'm facing the ice, you're facing the Franklin boys alone. Maybe you should wait for backup?"

"We'll be with her," Gabe said simply.

Denver nodded. "You boys can get Reagan back to the hospital safely." He kissed the top of Reagan's head. "We'll back up the sheriff."

Gabe leaned down to Reagan. "We'll be there as soon as Lloyd's locked up."

Reagan shoved tears aside. "I knew you'd come for me. You're my guardian angel."

Brandon leaned down and lifted her up as carefully as he could, blankets and all. Without a word the boys carried her out the door.

Martha Q hadn't said much, but as Alex, Denver, and Gabe turned to leave by the back door, she spoke. "You're all welcome back here when all this is settled. I'll have food and coffee waiting." She wanted to help, but was totally unaware that no one was thinking of snacks with the crisis.

Gabe managed to tell her thank you as he moved toward the back. Just as he stepped outside, Martha Q leaned forward and kissed him on the cheek. "You're a grand man, Gabriel Leary, a grand man."

Gabe heard Denver, ahead of him in the dark, laughing.

Once they were back in the creek bed, they moved fast and silently through the heart of Harmony to the back of the Blue Moon, then across the street to the bar. It was long after closing time, but Alex didn't seem surprised to find the door was still unlocked.

A few feet inside the cave of a bar, Alex stopped them. "You two are for backup only. I'm not here to cause a scene. I just want to arrest them."

"Got it," Denver said too quickly.

Gabe could read his friend's mind. They weren't trained to baby bad guys. "We play it by your rules." Gabe nodded once to Denver and they moved silently inside.

Chapter 50

SATURDAY, 1:00 A.M.
FEBRUARY 23, 2008
HARMONY HOSPITAL

ON THE WAY TO THE HOSPITAL, REAGAN HAD TO SIT IN
Brandon's lap, her bloody foot between Noah and the steering wheel as they drove through the streets. Now that she was warm and safe, the throbbing in her leg didn't matter. In fact, if Bran would stop patting her on the head, she might doze off.

"You're safe now, Rea. You're safe. No one is going to hurt you. You're safe," Bran kept repeating as he patted.

"Stop saying that, Bran. She knows she's safe. We're here, aren't we?" Noah glared at Brandon so hard, Reagan was surprised by the anger she saw. Streetlights made his face seem to blink like an old black-and-white movie.

"Don't tell me what to do," Brandon yelled. "If it wasn't for me we'd be stuck in the ditch you drove us right into a half hour ago."

"Me? I might have been driving, but you were the one who yelled, 'Turn.' Next time you might think about giving me a direction. I'm not a mind reader, you know."

"No, you're not. You got to have a mind first. You've landed on your head one too many times in that rodeo dirt, Preacher. You drive about like you ride. Every eight seconds or so you're plowing into the dirt."

"Well, at least I'm not the stop sign at road construction. How's that working out for you? Job has a lot of turns to it. Stop. Go. Stop. Go."

"I'm getting paid!" Brandon shouted. "Unlike you. You're hauling shit on your daddy's ranch and not making a dime."

Reagan burst out laughing. She hurt all over. She'd just been frightened almost out of her mind and frozen, but the sound of her two best friends yelling at each other was music to her ears.

The two guys stopped and stared, but she couldn't stop laughing.

Finally, Brandon sounded worried as he whispered, "You think she cracked up, Preacher?"

Noah shook his head. "I don't know, maybe you're right. We'd better get her to the hospital fast."

The sound of them panicking made her laugh harder. She didn't calm until Brandon carried her into the emergency room. "Take me to see my uncle first," she said, suddenly sobering.

The emergency room was quiet. A tired nurse met them halfway across the waiting room. "Tyler Wright called and said you two would be bringing her in. She can see her uncle later. Right now we need to check her wounds."

"No," Reagan said. "I'll see him first."

The nurse looked like she might argue.

Noah stepped between the nurse and Reagan. "She's got to see him first. One look and then we'll bring her back down here. A marshal told us she had a field dressing on her foot that would last a while."

While Noah talked, Brandon was already moving, following Reagan's directions. When he broke from the nurse, Noah had to run to catch up.

The nurse watched the three of them storm toward the ICU. A minute ago they'd been children. Tonight, they were adults.

A doctor met them when they reached the ICU doors. "He's still resting," the doctor said as he directed them down another hallway where the walls were glass. "Don't try to wake him."

Reagan nodded.

Brandon carried her in and she looked at the frail old man who'd claimed her as family when no one else would.

Liz Matheson was asleep in the chair next to him.

"He's resting easy," the doctor whispered, "but he's not out of danger. Miss Matheson insisted on staying with him. When I told her to wait in the waiting room, she threatened to sue me."

Reagan laid her fingers on top of Jeremiah's veined hand. Just to feel its warmth was enough. He was alive. Her worst fear hadn't happened. He wouldn't have to die alone. Whether he lived a few hours or a few more years, she planned to be by his side. They were family, if not by blood, then in spirit, and Trumans didn't die easily.

"Did you have a fall, miss?" the doctor asked.

"Yes," she said simply as she nodded for Brandon to carry her away. "I tripped and fell into hell, but my friends came after me."

They went back down to emergency and Reagan didn't say a word as they took her to have X-rays. It took over an hour to reset the leg. Her foot had eight stitches and bruises were coming to the surface all over her body, but she didn't care. She'd learned something tonight that she knew she would carry with her the rest of her life.

She had friends close as family. Friends who would come out in a snowstorm to find her.

Chapter 51

SATURDAY, 1:10 A.M.
FEBRUARY 23, 2008
BUFFALO'S BAR AND GRILL

GABE TOOK THE DOOR GUARD WHILE THE OTHER TWO stepped into Buffalo's Bar. If Lloyd ran, he wouldn't make it past this point.

The place looked like it was closed except for two men near the back so drunk they were half lying on the table. The bartender, or probably owner, was working at his computer at the corner of the bar. He was a bear of a man who had hands so beefy Gabe was surprised he could fit them to a keyboard.

The owner/bartender looked up when he saw the sheriff and raised one eyebrow.

"I'm not serving anything but coffee," he yelled at the

sheriff. "They bought their bottle before closing and I fig-ured they were safer drinking here than on the road."

Alex waved him away. "We're here to take them some-where warm to sleep it off."

The bartender nodded and motioned them on. He disap-peared into the back a moment later, wanting no part of what he knew was about to happen.

Denver moved in a circle, coming up behind the two Franklin boys while Alex walked right up to the table and widened her stance.

Lloyd looked up and seemed to be trying to get his eyes to adjust enough to recognize the sheriff coming toward him. Gabe saw him jerk the moment he figured her out.

"Hi, Sheriff," he said loudly, as though the bar were still full of people. "Good to see you. What's been happening tonight?" He poked his brother, but Donnie seemed to be out cold. "We've been sitting in here all evening drinking and waiting for my wife to get off work."

"It's late" Alex said calmly. "Time for you boys to call it a night. How about you come with me over to the station? I'd like to have a little talk with you over coffee. I've even called a car for you."

"No, I don't think so." Lloyd tried to stand, but his alibi seemed to be making the room spin. "I think I'll just go home."

Alex smiled. "You're both going with me."

Even drunk, he bulled up and would have stomped the ground if he'd thought it might frighten her. "I'm not going with—"

Denver stepped in and ended the debate. He jerked one arm behind Lloyd and shoved the man's face into the spilt beer on the table. "The sheriff asked you to come along."

Lloyd struggled and Denver twisted his arm higher. When he yelled and stopped fighting, Alex slipped the cuffs on.

"Those are too tight!" he yelled, finally waking his brother. "You can't treat me like this."

"I didn't bring the key." Alex pointed for Donnie to head to the door. He didn't hesitate. He raised his hands in surrender and walked right over to Gabe.

"I have my rights!" Lloyd shouted. "You can't just walk in and arrest innocent people. Don't you have to tell me what you think I did? Don't you have to read me my rights?"

"I don't even want to talk to you." Alex shoved him toward the door. "If you keep talking, we'll be walking the block to the jail." She watched as Denver patted Lloyd down and removed the gun at the back of his belt. "Ready, Marshal?" she asked.

"Ready, Sheriff."

"I don't have my coat," Lloyd complained. "I can't go outside without my coat. It's freezing out there."

Denver shoved him from behind. "We can't find it. Keep moving. It's stopped snowing anyway. Way I see it, we're in a heat wave right now."

They marched the Franklin brothers out and put them in the deputy's cruiser. "We got here as fast as we could, Sheriff," one of the deputies said, "but I see you have it all wrapped up for us."

"I had help," she answered.

Gabe heard one of the two deputies reading the Franklin boys their rights as they drove away.

Alex turned to Gabe and Denver. "Thank you," she said simply. "If there is anything I can ever do. . . ."

Denver held up his hand. "One favor. Drive us to Gabe's Rover. I've been down in the creek bed enough for a lifetime. We need to check on Reagan, and my friend left his girl at the hospital. Soon as we know she's fine, I'm heading for the nearest shower."

"You got it."

They didn't talk much on the way to pick up Gabe's car, except about the weather. The storm was over and the sun would melt away the snow on the streets in a few days. Gabe thought of the times he'd been in battles and how peaceful the world seemed afterward. Harmony had never seemed as peaceful as it did right now.

They said good-bye to Alex and headed toward the emergency room.

"Lieutenant," Gabe began once they were alone. "I remembered something about that day I got hit by the bomb five years ago. I remember the last thing I saw."

"Yeah, what?"

"I think I know who set it up or at least who was in on it. I remember seeing the driver's eyes. There was no surprise at the attack. He knew what was going down. I'd stake my life on it."

Denver shook his head. "Not knowing may be the one thing keeping you alive, Wiseman."

Gabe stared at Denver. A part of each of them would always be back in the war zone. No matter how long they lived, Denver would always be his lieutenant and he'd always be Wiseman. The bond between them would never break. In a strange way it seemed stronger than blood.

"We'll talk about it later," Denver said, pointing with a nod of his head toward Brandon and Noah sitting outside the emergency waiting room. "One thing at a time."

It was obvious from their body language that the two eighteen-year-olds weren't speaking to each other. But, Gabe thought, they weren't yelling either, so he saw that as progress. "Where's Reagan?"

"She's in the waiting room by ICU," Noah said. "The doc made her leave while they're examining the old man."

"How's her uncle?"

Brandon shrugged. "He's probably a hundred years old and he's had a heart attack, how do you think he is?"

Gabe had to hold Denver back. The lieutenant hated a smart mouth. "Wait a minute, if she's upstairs why are you two down here?"

Brandon pouted. "Take a wild guess how many women are in that little waiting room with her."

"Why don't you just tell me?"

Noah did the countdown. "Liz, she's been here all night. She called her great-aunts. It seems one of them used to date Jeremiah and got so upset that he might be dying before they made up that she made Claire, the crazy artist, drive her over. The other old aunt came along to chaperone the two former lovers, I guess, which wouldn't have been so bad, but Martha Q and Brandon's grandmother showed up with muffins because they baked them and no one came over to eat them. It's a regular gray-hair convention."

"She's not my grandmother," Brandon added.

Noah fired up. "Like I told you before, Bran, just because you don't recognize her doesn't mean she's not. If she's your father's mother, she's your grandmother. There's no *maybe* about it."

Gabe saw that the two were a hair away from a fight. The fact that neither had probably had any sleep in over twenty-four hours didn't help, or that they'd been worried about Reagan. If he thought about it, he'd guess both were in love with the kid. If she didn't pick between them, the two could be fighting over her for years.

"Any chance Granny brought coffee?"

"No," Noah said. "And the machine only takes one-dollar bills."

Gabe pulled out a half dozen ones he always carried. "Noah, mind getting us all a cup? I really need to talk to Liz."

"Yeah, Preacher, go get us all some coffee."

Denver reached past Gabe and pulled Brandon, all two hundred pounds of him, out of the chair. "How about you help him?" Denver asked, his teeth clenched together.

Brandon was smart enough not to argue. He almost ran to catch up to Noah.

Gabe heard him whisper, "I don't know about this

fireman gig. One minute you're the hero and the next you're the mule."

"Tell me about it," Noah answered. "I not only get ordered around by Hank at the station, my sister comes over and yells at me just to make sure I'm listening to him."

Gabe turned to Denver. "You think they'll make it back with four cups of coffee?"

"It's a long shot."

They moved to the ICU room and looked in. Brandon was right, it did look like a convention.

Denver pushed Gabe forward as he whispered, "Did you ever notice, when there are five women together three of them are talking? How does that compute?"

Aunt Pat was crying; her sister was trying to console her. Martha Q was generally running down the male side of the human race, and Claire was staring out the window, looking bored as always. Mrs. Biggs circled the room, asking everyone if they wanted a muffin.

"I'm not going in there," Denver said as he took a seat in the hallway.

"Chicken." Gabe laughed, and stepped into the waiting room.

Only Mrs. Biggs paid him any attention. She offered him a muffin and asked if he'd seen Brandon.

"He'll be here in a minute." He tried to ignore her worried look. "Have any idea where Elizabeth is?"

"She was with Reagan. The doctor decided to check Reagan in a room down the hall. I think he knew the girl wouldn't go home, and now at least she can rest between visits. Liz said that as soon as she got the girl tucked in, she planned to run back to her place and pick up a few clothes for Reagan. She didn't want Jeremiah seeing his niece with blood all over her clothes."

"How's the old man doing?"

"He's slipping." Mrs. Biggs shook her head. "I've been with two husbands when they died. There are signs most folks don't notice. Signs that tell someone watching that the person is passing. Funny, most folks don't die all at once; they slip away a little at a time."

Gabe didn't comment. Most of the people he'd seen who'd died did it all at once. He thought of telling her it must be a great luxury to get to pass a little at a time, but in truth he doubted dying that way was any easier.

Brandon walked into the room and handed Gabe his coffee, then offered his cup to Mrs. Biggs.

She shook her head. "Can we talk?" she whispered. "Just for a minute."

Brandon looked like he was trapped. "All right. Let's talk."

Gabe watched as they moved to the hallway and sat a few chairs away from Denver. He couldn't hear what they were saying, but Brandon finally lifted his hand and put it over hers. Mrs. Biggs looked like she was silently crying. After a while, she wiped her eyes on a napkin and smiled. They were a mismatched pair, but they seemed to be forming the beginnings of a family.

For years Gabe felt like he'd been closing himself off to any relationships. The mailman wouldn't even know his name if it wasn't written on the box. It was time; he could feel the shell around him cracking. Time for him to join the human race.

The one person he needed to talk to was Elizabeth, and she seemed to have vanished. After he checked everywhere they'd let him enter, Gabe walked over and sat down next to Denver.

"Why don't we head home and get some sleep?" Denver complained.

Gabe grinned. "Food, then sleep."

"I've already had a half dozen muffins. Mrs. Biggs should have never set the basket beside me. I'm not a person who can be trusted to guard sweets."

Gabe laughed. "The diner should be open by now. How about I buy you the left side of the menu?"

"Fair enough."

As they stood, Claire stepped in front of them. "Mind if I join you?" she asked, as casually as if she talked to them on a regular basis.

Gabe wanted to yell *No*, but to his surprise, Denver said, "Sure, come along. You know the diner. I believe you've been there before to not eat."

Gabe tried to think of some reason, any reason to get out of going with the two of them, but short of faking his own death, he couldn't come up with anything.

Claire followed them to the diner. When they walked in, Denver took one side of the booth and Claire took the other. Gabe said he needed to wash his hands and realized neither one of them noticed him talking or cared if he self-combusted on the spot. If he dropped dead over the table, they'd probably have breakfast on top of him.

Walking out of the diner, he headed toward the square and Elizabeth's office. When he glanced back, they were glaring at each other.

INSIDE THE DINER, DENVER FELT AN ICE STORM WORSE than he'd lived through the night before. He had no idea why Claire had come along, but he wasn't ruling out the idea that she'd done so just to torture him. Or maybe all the women he'd spent a few nights with and left got together and wished her on him, thinking Claire rated up there somewhere in the "worse than death" category. Hell, he thought, for all he knew he'd done something terrible in a former life and this was his punishment, to fall for a woman who not only broke his heart, but painted it for the world to see.

A sixteen-year-old waitress, obviously in her first day on the job, dropped by to try to take their order. While she chewed her gum at light speed, she admitted that she might not get it right, and would that be okay. Apparently she wasn't willing to take the order unless some leeway was allowed.

Denver shrugged and ordered two breakfasts, thinking he might have a third for dessert. Claire ordered coffee.

After the girl left, he watched Claire. She didn't look at him for a few minutes and when she did, he saw the tears floating, threatening to fall.

Denver shook his head. "You know, I think I hate you. No woman's hurt me in a long time like you did. Funny thing is, even though I know you'll probably poke my eyes out, I can't stop looking at you."

When she didn't talk, Denver waved his hand. "Oh, you don't have to say you're sorry. I know you did it all for your art. I was just someone you needed to use as the bowl of fruit for your study. You don't have to say you didn't mean to destroy me."

The waitress delivered their drinks.

He had to lighten the mood before he started yelling at Claire. Forcing himself to face the waitress, he asked, "Where's Edith this morning?"

The waitress shrugged. "She left a note saying she was taking the first bus out of here this morning. I have no idea where she is by now, but she's definitely not in Texas."

"Thanks." Denver decided not to ask any more questions. She'd already given him more information than he wanted to know.

The waitress took the hint and moved away.

Claire played with the tiny cream cups and didn't look like she was following the conversation.

Denver waited. When she didn't say anything, he tried again. "Maybe you've been hurt by some guy and just figured you'd go around killing us all one at a time." He meant to tell her off, he really did, but honesty stopped him. "You fooled me, Claire. I fell for you hard. I didn't go further, because I didn't want a onetime fling with you. For the first time in a long time, I wanted something that might last longer than breakfast."

They sat in silence for a while. The waitress delivered his food, but he didn't eat.

"As it turned out," he said, "we didn't even make it to breakfast."

She finally met his stare. There she was, the most beautiful woman he'd ever known. That unbelievable mixture of sophistication and vulnerability. She was the kind of woman he would have spent a lifetime trying to figure out. The kind he could wrap a life around.

For once, he had nothing else to say. He had no idea why she'd wanted to come to breakfast with him. Maybe just to get another few minutes of torture in.

She stared down at her fork for a few minutes, then picked it up and ate a bite of his scrambled eggs.

He just watched her.

When she took her third bite without looking at him, he said, "Those are my eggs."

"I know." She picked up a piece of toast. "I thought you'd share."

He shoved the plate on her side of the table. "You're not going to apologize, are you?" Frowning at her, he continued, "And you're not going to promise never to do that to me again."

"No." She cut a slice of his steak.

"And I may see myself on some other canvas someday, facing another horrible death."

She added ketchup to his hash browns. "It's a possibility."

"I don't like ketchup on my hash browns."

She smiled up at him. "My hash browns."

"You're not giving them back?"

"Not a chance." She smiled at him, her knife pointed at his chest. "If we're to have breakfast together, you need to order another meal."

Denver grinned. "Lady, you're a heartache waiting to happen." He pulled the pancakes he'd ordered to his side of the table before she cut into them and added, "You're not getting any of my pancakes."

She smiled. "We'll see about that tomorrow."

Chapter 52

SATURDAY, 10:00 A.M.
FEBRUARY 23, 2008
WRIGHT FUNERAL HOME

TYLER WRIGHT SLEPT SIX HOURS IN THE SILENCE OF HIS rooms over the funeral home before Little Lady woke him up wanting out. He pulled on his jogging suit and took her out the back door. The air had climbed above freezing and the sun was shining on a snow that made the whole world look newborn.

He checked his watch. Ten o'clock. He never slept until ten. But then he'd never manned the phones at the fire station. Surprisingly, he'd loved it. He felt like he was in the center of the action. Talking to the dispatcher, the sheriff, the men on patrol. When they'd finally found Reagan, Tyler shouted like he hadn't yelled since his band won first in region.

Little Lady picked her favorite spot under the eaves of the house, where the snow was only dusting the ground. Tyler waited patiently.

"You know, Little Lady," he said to the border collie, "you could come here to live if you like. After all, you never chew on anything or make a mess. You can reach the elevator buttons, and the families who come seem to love you." He'd noticed it almost every time. A few people walk right past dogs, but most stop to visit. Little Lady seemed to know who needed her. She'd sit by their chair as if holding their hand through the process, and they'd reach down to pet her whenever they needed an ounce of comfort mixed in with their ton of pain.

One man asked how Tyler got the dog, and when he told the widower, the man said, "She must have lost her owner because I can tell she knows how I feel right now."

When he came back a week later to pick up the ashes of his wife, he asked if he could sit on the porch with Little Lady awhile.

The collie tugged on her leash, and Tyler started back inside. When he passed his office, Tyler realized that in his haste to get to the station last night, he hadn't turned off his computer.

He started the coffee and then sat down, planning to read the headlines before climbing the stairs and getting dressed for the day.

An hour later, he was still staring at the screen.

He'd been writing his nightly note to Kate when Hank called and told him about Reagan. Tyler had jotted down, *Have to run. Emergency. Reagan Truman in danger.* Then he'd clicked Send, planning to return in an hour and jot another note. But the night had been long and it was so late he'd gone straight to bed.

Now, a message waited for him.

Ty, are you all right? Is Reagan safe? I saw you folks had quite a storm.

She'd answered him. After two years, Major Katherine Cummings had finally answered him.

He made his fingers move across the keyboard. *Reagan has minor cuts and bruises, but she's safe. Sorry I didn't get back to you. It was late when I got back.*

He wanted to ask a million questions. The most important . . . why she'd waited so long to contact him.

Instead, he let his heart guide him. He typed: *I've missed you, Kate.*

He clicked Send. Finally got up and poured himself a cup of coffee and sat back down as his computer dinged.

The message read, *How about you tell me all about it a week from Monday. Order me red wine.*

He typed *Quartz Mountain Lodge* and clicked Send.

The message came back. *I remember.*

Tyler sat back in his chair. It no longer mattered where she'd been for two years. He'd ask no questions.

For now, it was enough that his hazel-eyed friend was back.

Chapter 53

LIZ RUMMAGED THROUGH THE CLOSET IN HER OFFICE FOR something that looked like an eighteen-year-old would wear. She felt like she'd been run over by the snowplow. She'd spent the night worrying about Gabe and Reagan and Jeremiah. She'd called Jess so many times he threatened to get a restraining order against her phone. Then, to top it all off, her big sister shows up at the hospital this morning looking great and reminding her of how wrinkled and terrible she looked.

This was not a good day. She wanted to go back to college, where all she had to do was study and think about who to date. Trying to run an office and manage family was stressful on a good day, but last night was crazy.

She had learned something, though. Her family was much more than just the people she was related to in this town. "This is an impossible place to be self-centered in," she complained aloud. "Before I know it I'll have to give up thinking about myself all the time and start worrying about everyone else. It's downright depressing."

Someone knocked on her door.

"I'm closed!" she yelled. The last thing she wanted to deal with was the young couple wanting to rewrite their will to include the goldfish they just bought. Or the bookstore man downstairs wanting to sue the palm reader for false advertising.

The pounding came again. "Elizabeth." Gabe sounded angry. "Answer this door."

Liz waddled through the clothes on the floor of her closet and answered the door. She'd planned to tell him to come back after she'd had a shower and put on makeup and had caffeine, and decided to join the human race.

But when she saw him, all muddy and unshaven, and adorable, she was in his arms before either of them could say a word.

He lifted her up in a hug and walked a few steps into the office before he kissed her. And when he kissed her, all Liz thought about was herself. She felt wonderful. She loved the way he kissed her. She loved the way he touched her.

When he finally came up for air, he whispered, "I missed you so much."

She laughed. "You just saw me last night."

"No." He rubbed his face into her hair. "It was a lifetime ago." He gripped her shoulders and held her away from him a few inches. "I've something to say, and I want you to listen."

"Could we have breakfast first? I'm starving."

"No, if I don't say this now, I may never get it out."

"All right. Let me have it, but if you're breaking up with

me I think I should remind you that we've never really had a date. I seem to be an expert on breaking up. You are right about one thing—the morning is the best time, except of course it ruins your whole day, but it beats the night. Breakups at night are terrible. You end up crying all night and look like death warmed over in the morning."

"Elizabeth."

"Yes?"

"Stop talking."

She pouted. Gabe never wanted to talk. How could he hate doing one of her favorite things in the world? She was about to ask when he spoke.

"I think I'm in love with you," he said. "No. That's not right. I'm sorry. I *know* I'm in love with you."

"The like-maybe-we-should-start-dating kind of 'I'm in love with you' or the let's-not-see-other-people kind of 'I'm in love with you'?" She couldn't bring herself to mention the third kind. The let's-get-married kind.

He looked as if he might shake her to see if she'd stop rattling on, but then he simply leaned toward her and kissed the top of her head. "The I-want-to-be-with-you kind of 'I'm in love with you.' I know we need to spend some time together before you make up your mind about me, but I've already made up my mind about you. I don't want to live without you. Not today or tomorrow or the rest of my life."

"Well, I'm not running off to get married like Hank and Alex did a few minutes ago." She slapped her mouth. "I promised I wouldn't tell. After last night, they both decided they needed each other and what house they lived in wasn't important as long as they were together. They just called me and said if anyone was looking for them, they'd fallen off the face of the earth and wouldn't be back for a while."

Gabe laughed. "Back to you and me, Liz. Are you saying you don't want to marry me or you don't want to run away?"

"I'm saying it's time I stopped talking and started showing you how I feel about you." She pulled his mouth to hers
and melted against him. For once, she'd shut *him* up with
a kiss.

They were lost in one another when Denver tapped on
the door. "I don't understand it. You don't even talk and
every woman in this town hugs on you. I, on the other
hand, am a teddy bear and get paintings of me dying."

Gabe hugged Elizabeth close and smiled at his friend.
They were exhausted and muddy, but all seemed right with
the world somehow. "How did breakfast go?"

"I'm not sure. We agreed to have breakfast again tomorrow to discuss my meeting her in Dallas for the opening of
her next show."

Gabe kissed Elizabeth one last time, then groaned as he
pulled away. "We're heading home to clean up. I'll meet
you back at the hospital later."

"What time?"

"It doesn't matter," he said, meeting her gaze. "I'll be
waiting for you."

"Fair enough." She pulled him back to her.

Their kiss lasted so long, Denver got bored and went
downstairs.

On the way home, Denver was silent for a while, then
finally said, "I've got a confession to make and I might as
well do it when we're both too tired to fight."

Gabe didn't say a word.

"I didn't just come here to look up an old friend. I stayed
in the army after you disappeared five years ago. They
called me in to find you when you vanished from the hospital. I guess they knew no one else would have a chance
at tracking you."

Gabe fought the urge to reach for his gun. He'd trusted
Denver, believed every word. Now, the man was admitting
he'd lied.

"I investigated the bombing and knew you must have

had your reasons for disappearing. The bombing hadn't been random. The army knew it too. They put you on medical leave, then we went after the men hunting you." Denver hesitated. "We found them. They confessed that the bombing was set up to kill everyone in the convoy. If we hadn't caught them, eventually they would have found you. You were right to set up security."

Gabe had almost convinced himself that he'd been paranoid. He gripped the steering wheel and waited for the rest.

Denver finally said, "You're safe, Gabe. Whether you remember or not, you're safe. You have been for over a year."

"Then why are you here? To bring me back?"

"No. The army gave up looking for you. Me, I finally left the service and took an air marshal job, but I could never forget about you. When I traveled, I was always searching. The part about seeing your work in a graphic novel was true. I did find you by luck. The minute I read your stories, I knew it was you. You're writing our life, our skills, our way of thinking back then."

"So what do you want?" Gabe tried to see his friend around the lie between them.

"I want to tell you the army will straighten your past out if you want to go back, but I'll not tell them. You've got years of pay coming, an honorable discharge, and their understanding as to why you ran."

"What about the name? They think I'm Wiseman."

"I don't know about that. You might want to get yourself a good lawyer." Denver laughed. "One you can stop kissing long enough to tell her your whole life story."

Gabe realized he didn't need the cover of Wiseman anymore. He was Gabe Leary. He had friends. He was respected. He had a kid who thought he was her guardian angel, a sheriff who trusted and relied on him, a lawyer who'd figure out one day that the kind of *I love you* he had for her was a forever kind. "I don't want to go back. I want to stay right here. Let Wiseman vanish."

Denver seemed to understand. "Fair enough, but I'm still glad I kept searching for you. Friends, the kind who will cover your back, are hard to find."

They turned onto the road to his house. A dozen cars were scattered like toys across his land and around his house.

Gabe frowned. "Did you turn on the alarm when we left?"

"No. Look at all these cars. What's going on?"

Both men did what they did best; they observed details. Local and out-of-state tags. Old cars, sports cars, junkers, all with stickers of teams and bands on the back windows. The kind of cars high school kids drive.

Gabe wove past them to his front door. As he climbed out, teenagers began to crawl out of every car.

"What's going on?" he asked Denver.

"I have no idea. Teenagers. I've heard they travel in packs and eat everything in sight."

"But what are they doing here?" Gabe frowned.

One boy got within twenty feet of Gabe and yelled, "It's him. It's him. Everyone, it's G. L."

Gabe froze. The kid had one of the first comic books he'd written in his hand.

Denver saw it too and laughed. "They're fans, Gabriel. Your fans."

Another boy moved closer, a novel in his hand. "My grandfather at the post office said you looked like a farmer. Great disguise. I've been on the Internet for weeks figuring you out. G. L. Smith. Gabriel Leary. Right here in Harmony."

Gabe frowned at Denver. "So, it takes an expert to find me."

Denver shrugged. "A highly trained expert or apparently a kid with Internet skills."

Others were moving toward Gabe. All smiling. All with books in their hands.

"I drove from Dallas," one shouted. "Will you sign my book?"

"I came from Oklahoma City," another said. "I love your work." He pointed at Denver. "Look guys, that man looks just like the lieutenant in *Soldier Force, Fight for the Planet*. I'd recognize him anywhere even without the scar parting his hair."

Gabe and Denver backed up until they hit the door.

"Great." Denver swore. "I might as well give up working and start modeling for artists. Apparently I'm a pinup in two art forms."

"Shut up and tell me what to do," Gabe said.

Denver grinned. "How many bullets you got?"

"Get serious. I need help."

Denver opened the door so suddenly, Gabe almost fell in. "All right, kids," he yelled. "I'm going to give you a once-in-a-lifetime tour of G. L.'s workplace, but don't touch anything. He'll even sign your books provided you promise one thing. Tell no one where he lives."

They all promised.

"Fat chance," Gabe said as he moved backward into his house.

An hour later he'd signed all the books and the kids were gone. Gabe turned on the alarm system so he'd know if any teenagers decided to come calling, took a shower, and had two cans of soup cooking when Denver, clean and wet headed, walked into the kitchen.

"What you going to do G. L.?"

"Move to a desert island?" he said.

"No, I mean about this place?"

"I don't know. There's a few places down in the canyon where I could build and no one could find me without a map."

"How about selling this old trap to me? I'm thinking I could use a reason to drop by this way from time to time."

Gabe shook his head. "No. This is home. I think I'll

stay." He'd come a long way in less than two months and learned one thing. This was where he wanted to be.

He was home and he was no longer alone. Harmony was where he wanted to stay.

Denver grinned. "Then sell me the front half of your land. You can build you and Liz a place down in the canyon. I could keep the kids off the land." Raising his hands, he added, "No weapons, just signs, I promise."

Gabe offered his hand. "It's a deal. Welcome home, Lieutenant."

Denver took his hand, and they both knew they'd finally found where they belonged.